DREW CULLINGHAM

ALBION

The Beginning of the End

MONK3YS INK

First published by Monk3ys Ink 2023

Copyright © 2023 by Drew Cullingham

This novel is entirely a work of fiction. The names, characters and incidents portrayed in it are the work of the author's imagination. Any resemblance to actual persons, living or dead, events or localities is entirely coincidental.

Drew Cullingham asserts the moral right to be identified as the author of this work.

First edition

ISBN: 978-1-7395763-0-1

This book was professionally typeset on Reedsy.
Find out more at reedsy.com

To Victoria and Indiana

'Perhaps in time the so-called Dark Ages will be thought of as including our own.'

GEORG C. LICHTENBERG

Contents

VI MEMENTO MORI

VII CARPE DIEM

VIII VAE VICTIS

Preface

After centuries of occupation and integration, the last of the legions of Rome finally withdrew from the island of Britannia in 410 AD.

Within a generation, Roman culture had all but disappeared from the island. The remaining population fragmented into tribalism, leaving the Britons vulnerable to invasion.

It is now 447 AD.

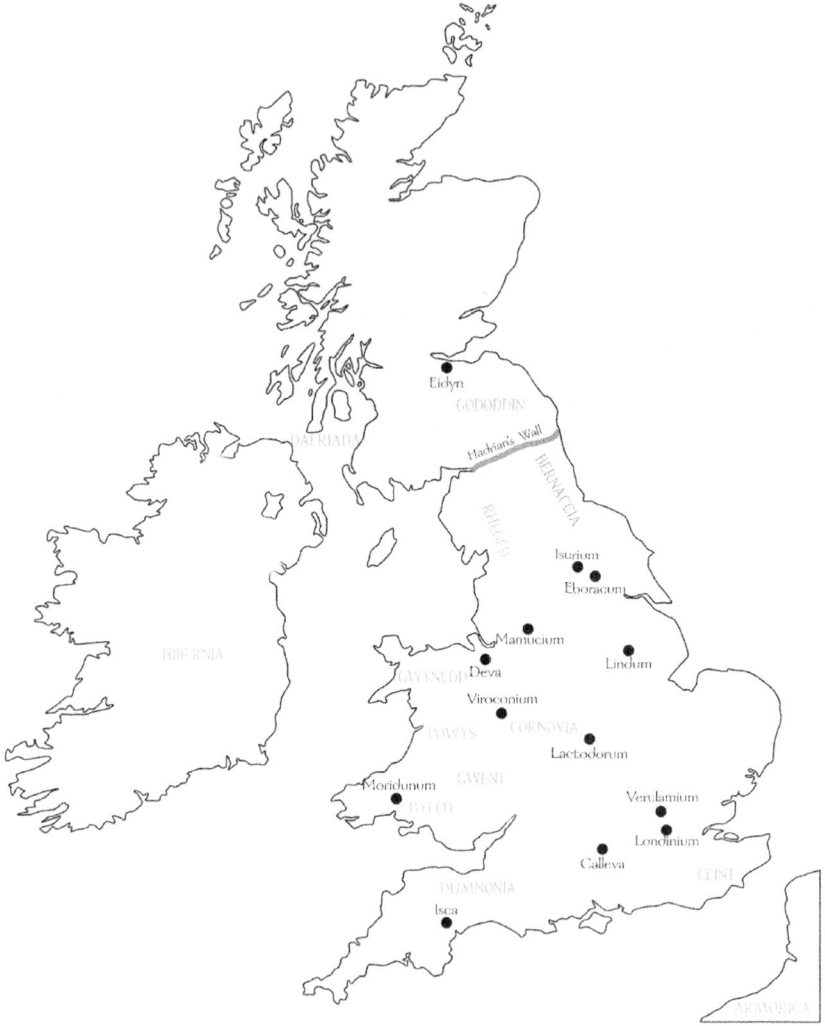

Eidyn

GODODDIN

DALRIADA

Hadrian's Wall

BRYNAICH

HIRNAICCIA

RHEGED

Isurium

Eboracum

HIBERNIA

Mamucium

Deva

Lindum

GWYNEDD

Viroconium

POWYS

CORNOVIA

Lactodorum

Moridunum

DYFED

GWENT

Verulamium

Londinium

Calleva

CEINT

DUMNONIA

Isca

ARMORICA

I

URSA MAJORIS

'I dare do all that may become a man;
Who dares do more is none.'

('Macbeth', William Shakespeare)

The Painted Ones

The bear was hungry. With autumn draping the canopy of the great forest in a honeyed yellow, she instinctively felt this year was colder than the previous one, and knew winter would be cruel. It would soon be time to hibernate, and she needed to feed well to see it through. To give her unborn cub every chance of survival.

* * *

Emrys hung back. Letting Tugen get ahead made the chase more satisfying. He waited until his friend had concealed himself by the trees up ahead before quickening his pace slightly, treading as best he could between the fallen leaves and relying on his hearing to track his quarry.

When Tugen disappeared and the forest fell silent, Emrys knew to expect an ambush. He was a whisker older than Tugen and, having not long turned thirteen, knew that the wooden training sword he clutched would soon give way to metal. If needed.

He slowed to a walk, listening intently and scanning the trees. The dappled sun tumbled through the autumn foliage in flashes. And he thought of Rozena.

Rozena was a year or more older than him and, even though his concept of manhood was largely confined to thoughts of combat rather than forging any kind of relationship with a girl, her changing body had not gone unnoticed by him. It was the source of great curiosity, more keenly felt because he knew Tugen had noticed as well.

Tugen had bragged that he had kissed her in the summer and, while Rozena had dismissed the allegation with a smile and reddening cheek, Emrys believed him. The bitter disappointment that it had not been him was a feeling unlike any other he had ever felt, and his games with Tugen had since taken on a more aggressive tone.

Rozena. *Surely she could not like Tugen above him?* She had commented on the colour of his eyes a few weeks earlier, when the sun was setting, and had marvelled at how they appeared as, in her words, 'two suns'. Even though they'd known each other all their lives, and she'd seen his amber-coloured eyes thousands of times, he hadn't thought much of it at the time. In fact, he hadn't given it any thought at all until Tugen told him he'd kissed her.

Tugen's war cry, beginning barely a heartbeat before he appeared from behind an oak tree with his sword already in full swing, snapped Emrys from his daze. Emrys lifted his own weapon instinctively, and the solid wooden clunk as the swords met coincided perfectly with the crescendo of Tugen's roar.

The boys fought. Tugen was probably stronger, and Emrys the more agile of the two. They fought with undiluted enthusiasm, both secure in the belief that, apart from the odd scuffed knuckle, neither was likely to be seriously hurt. It was more slash and parry than the finesse of the thrust, both revelling in the clash of wood on wood. Advantage passed freely between them, although Tugen had pushed the fight back towards the edge of a bracken-covered slope that tumbled down towards a small stream.

Perhaps sensing this advantage, Tugen grinned and his guard dropped for a second. Emrys found the gap, catching Tugen across his knuckles. Tugen yelped in pain and dropped his sword. Lifting his hurt hand to his mouth, he glared at his friend angrily. Emrys looked back at him, lowering his own sword in a conciliatory gesture, as both paused to catch their breaths.

Behind his grazed knuckles, Tugen's face opened into a grin. He roared and hurled himself wantonly at Emrys, sending them both to the ground.

They grappled for superiority. Tugen's bulk and strength helped him. He pushed his hand under Emrys' chin and held him against the soft earth, laughing, his other hand pinning Emrys' sword arm down.

But Emrys was not about to yield. He twisted his legs, wrapping them around his opponent's, and sent them both down the slope. As they rolled over each other, and then independently, Emrys kept hold of his sword. When they came to an ungainly halt in the gulley, he leapt to his feet, levelling it at the recovering Tugen, a triumphant smile on his face. Tugen's resentment only lasted a second. He grinned as he accepted the outstretched arm of his friend, and allowed Emrys to hoist him to his feet.

Tugen's eyes suddenly opened in horror. Emrys spun himself around just in time to see a great brown bear rising to its hind legs just yards away from them, its mouth stretched wide in a horrible guttural roar. Emrys was tall enough for his age, but the bear still towered over him.

'Get up a tree!' He shouted at Tugen, who backed away hesitantly. 'Now!'

The bear crashed forward into the trickle of a stream, water splashing around it as it barrelled towards them. Emrys raised his pitiful weapon and started swinging it wildly, shouting at the oncoming animal, the blunt wooden blade carving ineffectual arcs in the diminishing space between them. In his peripheral vision, as he backed away from the attack, he saw Tugen scampering up a sturdy-looking tree.

'Run, Emrys,' Tugen yelled. 'Just run!'

Emrys' show of defiance did at least give the bear reason to slow. It pulled up just short of him, eyeing the training sword cautiously for a moment. And then it decided on its own superiority, and lunged forward towards Emrys, a great paw easily swatting the weapon from his hands. Emrys reeled from the contact and staggered backwards, struggling to keep his footing. As the bear's other paw descended towards him, he instinctively jerked his head back. And promptly lost his balance.

It was only his fall that saved him from certain death in that instant. The enormous claws failed to fully find their target as he dropped to the earth at the bear's feet, although one of them still raked his left cheek, opening the skin just beneath his eye. Crashing into the fallen leaves, his vision reddened as blood flowed over his eye. The bear's breath was hot above him as it rose tall again with a triumphant roar. Emrys tried to scuttle back away from the beast before it went for the kill, but he knew he couldn't possibly escape.

The sound he thought was the last he would ever hear changed. The rattling, guttural undertone that had shaken his bones gave way suddenly to a higher pitch, a cry. A cry of pain. The bear moved as well. It twisted its body awkwardly, turning to look back upstream, and Emrys saw the javelin jutting out of its flank, the dark fur already wetting with blood. Emrys seized his opportunity and crawled quickly along the earth to hide behind the tree Tugen had climbed.

Looking back, he watched the bear swatting at the spear that punctured its side, knocking it free. Beyond the bear, he saw a dozen Kaldi warriors. He knew they were Kaldi because their exposed skin, where the blood of some fight hadn't darkened it, was patterned in blue woad designs. He watched as they fanned out, preparing to surround the hungry bear.

Emrys looked up the tree to Tugen, who had clearly seen them as well, and began inching around the trunk to a branch that afforded him some cover. A bear was one thing, but they had both heard the stories. The Kaldi were not their friends. Emrys hadn't heard of them venturing as far south as Bernaccia.

The bear bellowed and made a run towards the warriors. Perhaps it was charging, but Emrys imagined even the bear would not want to take on so many aggressors. Despite the blood on his cheek, he hoped the beast could find a gap in the closing circle. But it wasn't to be. Several javelins flew at the bear, and the Kaldi soon had it surrounded. Spears and swords pierced its dark fur as it turned and twisted, not knowing where best to direct its own attack. Emrys closed his eyes.

When he opened them, he was looking at a pair of feet. Bound in hide and twine that wound its way over the shins, they belonged to a Kaldi warrioress. Her painted blue face looked down at him. Emrys didn't move. *What point was there?* He stared back at her. Her features were sharp and lean, yet amid the fearsome artwork that covered her face, her dark eyes were soft. When she put a finger to her lips, he just nodded blankly. Incredulous.

Emrys watched her as she stooped down slowly and lifted her javelin from the ground, giving him half a smile and a subtle nod. He watched her as she walked towards her kin. He watched as she joined the circle around the bear. The bear that was now just a dark unmoving hulk on the forest floor.

* * *

Emrys felt troubled. They were nearly home. Having slipped away unseen by the rest of the Kaldi, they had made straight for the village, stopping only briefly by a brook so that Emrys could wash the blood from his cut cheek.

'You'll have a great scar,' Tugen had remarked to him as he handed him a strip of cloth torn from his tunic, 'and an even better story to tell.' Tugen had promised that one day he would save Emrys' life, as he felt Emrys had saved his.

Emrys grimaced as he felt the still weeping wound. He didn't want a scar. Or a story. The gnawing doubt in his belly intensified as they emerged from the forest at the top of the hill overlooking their village. And all his unrealised fears became horrifically real as the pair stopped at the treeline and looked down at their homes, seeing them and all the others in the village aflame, belching black columns of smoke into the now leaden autumn sky.

The Wolf in the Fog

There was an acrid taste to the fog. A slight smell of eggs gone bad. If you'd been twenty feet from the column of men that either rode or walked across the Dumnonian moorland that morning, mused Vitalinus, you probably wouldn't have seen them. The slow rhythmic clop of horses and the occasional metallic clunk or thump of a wooden cartwheel on a concealed granite crag were all that gave them away. The few among them that talked did so in hushed voices, and a feeling of wariness and suspicion hung over them as thick as the fog.

Selwyn, charged with the command of Vitalinus' men, stretched over his saddle, and squinted into the murk. 'I preferred the road,' he remarked glibly.

Much of the journey from Viroconium had been aided by mile upon mile of reasonably intact Roman road, but they had left that behind now.

'As did I, Selwyn,' Vitalinus muttered drily, 'but the road goes only where the Romans wanted to go. The men do not complain, do they?'

'No, sire, not yet. Your father would say that where a road doesn't go, isn't worth going to,' Selwyn said in an attempt at levity.

Vitalinus didn't even offer a smile in reply. 'My father is an old fool who still believes the Romans will return,' he said, and Selwyn fell quiet. Vitalinus softened. 'You can agree silently. I won't think it treason.'

He noticed a slight smile flicker across Selwyn's face. Then, some distance off, he thought he heard the howl of a wolf.

* * *

Jac didn't mind bringing up the rear. There was a certain level of responsibility, he assumed, to such a task. Even being asked to come on this mission of mercy and potential peril was all the acknowledgement he needed to know that he was finally a man. He still reached instinctively for the pommel of his sword when he heard the howl. It came from behind them. As if they were being stalked. He shivered.

'Just a wolf.' Zeki, the tall, lean Ethiope beside him, smirked confidently. 'Maybe a pack. They will not trouble us.'

The lumbering bulk of a man in front of them shook with laughter.

'What are you laughing at, Saxon?' Jac asked nervously.

The bulk, Osric, turned his head to the young Briton. 'Perhaps it is Fenris, free at last. If so, we are all fucked.' He narrowed his eyes. 'And I am a Jute, not a Saxon.'

'Who's Fenris?'

'He is a great giant wolf. Son of the god, Floki.' Osric dropped a step and fell in beside Jac and Zeki. 'And if he has broken free of his restraints, then the world will soon end. With this stinking dragon's breath around us, I'd say there's a pretty good chance of it!'

As if to punctuate his harbinger words, another howl filled the air, seeming to come from all around them. Jac kept his hand on the top of his sword, suddenly unsure about the honour of being in the rear-guard. 'It's as well I don't believe in your gods!'

'*You* don't need to,' grinned Osric.

* * *

A flurry of hooves brought Vortimer past the flank of the column and alongside Vitalinus.

'What news?'

'The men are anxious, Father. They talk of magic and evil.'

'Little wonder.' Vitalinus looked sidelong at his son. 'The weather is bad, and the wolves are hungry. Nothing a decent pair of boots and a sharp blade won't see to.'

9

Vortimer frowned. 'They say the air even smells wicked. It does have an odour, don't you think?'

'And what would you have me do, son?' Vitalinus asked.

Vortimer's reply didn't come. In place of his opening mouth came another howl, this time from in front of them. And this howl was different, as much human as hound. Vitalinus nodded to Selwyn to call the men to halt. Silence spread back through the ranks as all feet, men and mount, came to a standstill.

Silence.

Selwyn gestured to the men behind him. Two riders stealthily rode forwards, flanking the front three men. They were Nobatian, from the upper regions of the Nile, dark-skinned and incomparably lethal as mounted archers. Using only their thighs to manoeuvre their horses, they nocked arrows dipped in poisonous black tar, looped metal thumb rings around the bowstrings, and drew them back in readiness.

Silence.

The fog swirled in front of them, some indistinct darkness inside it appearing to grow and move. A figure. A man, perhaps. Not a wolf. The Nobatians pointed the blackened arrowheads in its direction. Vortimer's horse whinnied lightly, its hooves tapping at the hard earth below. Vitalinus took a breath, and drew a few inches of his Roman sword, a long-bladed *spatha*.

'Are you friend or foe?'

The shadow in the mist stopped moving, although the white skeins still writhed around the shape.

'You would be wise to answer.' Vitalinus audibly eased another couple of inches of steel from his scabbard.

'Well, well,' a thin voice said from out of the gloom. 'Nobatians in Dumnonia. This may well be a first.'

A tall, slender man materialised, a dark cowled cloak hanging from his narrow shoulders. He dragged the hood back from his face, revealing long grey hair and a beard. The man eyed the archers with amusement.

'Friend.' He smiled with little evidence of caution other than his stillness.

'I am a friend. And you are Vitalinus, king of the Cornovii.' He bowed his head in deference, and it was far from clear whether he was sincere or mocking.

'I am Vitalinus, but I am no king. That privilege yet belongs to my father.'

The grey man made as if to step closer to continue the conversation more privately, but glanced at the two bowmen, now at full draw. Vitalinus shot a glance at Selwyn, who motioned to the men to stand down. The two bows creaked menacingly as the strings were gently relaxed, a quiet reminder in the dullness of the fog that they could be tensed even more quickly if required.

'Perhaps so,' continued the man, 'yet such a man as you will surely be more than your father. So much more.'

Vitalinus shifted in his saddle. Something about this strange man had his palms moistening with warm anticipation. This was no chance meeting; of that, he was certain. Though not given to superstition, he felt a crackling electricity surging through him. A sense that this was a moment of importance.

'Who are you, old man?' he demanded with as much clarity as he could muster. 'And who has your oath?'

'No man,' the stranger brazenly answered. 'I am Ossian. I merely offer counsel to those who would listen.'

Vitalinus wanted to listen. He quickly dismounted, surprising Selwyn and Vortimer beside him. Vortimer looked like he was about to say something but thought better of it, and instead watched his father with a protective caution. Selwyn blurted out, 'my Lord' instinctively, only to be silenced by a wave of his master's hand.

'And have you counsel for me, Ossian?' Vitalinus asked.

Ossian smiled, his face slightly downward so that his heavy brow shadowed his eyes, making it impossible to gauge his true meaning. Then he looked up. Straight into Vitalinus' eyes.

'You need not fear the wolf,' he spoke, 'only he who brings the bear.' Ossian lowered his head again.

'And what is that supposed to mean?' Vitalinus was not a patient man.

Oblique talk always raised his heckles. But Ossian just smirked and backed away a step, the fog welcoming him again as it squirmed around his limbs.

'Wait!' demanded Vitalinus.

'Are you lost?'

'No. Maybe.'

'You left the Fosse Way. That was the right thing to do. Leave the Roman path behind you.' And with that, Ossian nimbly spun on his feet and slipped back into obscurity, suddenly nothing more than an indistinct darkness in the white again. Fading.

Vitalinus' knee-jerk reaction was to give pursuit. He ignored the cries of his son and Selwyn, who swung down from his horse, and he too disappeared into the murk. Quickly, all he could hear was the heavy fall of his own feet. The odd glimpse of some shadow ahead of him tempted him forward.

'Come back,' he shouted into the shifting mist; a mist that choked his voice and silenced it before the words had fully left his mouth. 'I want to know more.'

Was that a howl again? A wolf? But he didn't need to fear the wolf. His feet gave way under him, good balance alone stopping him from falling. There was granite shale on the ground, slippery with the moisture from the air. A bank reared beside him, and he steadied himself, letting his fingertips graze it as he blindly followed a path. The shadow flitted ahead of him, taunting him.

'Stop. I command you.' His voice fell flat, muffled. Certainly not commanding. He reached out for the shadow, lunging forward, and this time could not catch himself. His feet slipped from under him, and he tumbled to the ground. Only it wasn't the ground. A gap appeared in the fog, a breeze hitting his face as he fell, and beneath him was air. Air and, a long way down, the angry white of the sea, foaming at the base of a cliff. In the heartbeat it took him to register what he could now see, he also realised that his own momentum was his undoing, and nothing could stop him from plummeting to his death.

He screamed.

But his foot caught on something. *No, not something. Someone.* Selwyn was there, his other hand reaching for his master and pulling him back from the precipice.

And Ossian was gone.

* * *

Erbin leant out over the wooden tops of the hill-fort's wall. He liked to idle at least part of his day up on the narrow rampart that extended either side of the top of the fort's gate. He knew full well that he would one day take his father's place, ruling Dumnonia, and he wanted to get used to both the isolation that height afforded him and the view. His mother had been dead for several years now, and his father had said scant kind words to him since. Few words of any description, really. That was fine with him. He understood that his father had a difficult job, especially with the new threat of raiders along the coastline.

Despite the pair of sentries stifling boredom a few yards from him on the rampart, Erbin was the first to spot the men approaching the fort. While a guard called out, Erbin was already shinning his way down the rickety ladder and into the muddy courtyard. He heard the formal response announcing the heir to the kingdom of Cornovia, and scampered towards and through the slowly opening gates, despite the unconvincing protest of a gatekeeper.

'Welcome. I am Erbin, son of Custennin,' he greeted the man called Vitalinus. 'One day, I will rule this land. As far as the eye can see!'

Vitalinus smiled down at him from his horse. 'And you are every inch a prince, young Erbin. Well met.'

Erbin beamed as he led the men through the gates.

His father had emerged from within and waited on a stone dais raised out of the grime of the courtyard. His frown was enough to chasten Erbin.

'Come here, boy.'

And Erbin obeyed.

'How many times must I tell you not to meddle in the affairs of men?'

Erbin looked at the ground. 'Sorry, Father.'

'Get inside. Go on.'

Heading inside, Erbin heard his father address Vitalinus, apologising for his son and calling him 'simple'. And the last he heard was Vitalinus saying, 'he caused no offence.'

Erbin decided then that he liked this Vitalinus.

* * *

Vitalinus didn't like Custennin. The Dumnonians were a famously proud people, happy to isolate themselves from the rest of the Britons and wary of outsiders. He wasn't sure how shrewd his father had been when he sent him on this mission, but there was certainly an advantage to be gained from it. If he had to insinuate some kind of mutual respect to get what he wanted, then so be it. The meeting with Ossian still vexed him. The man was clearly a druid, a follower of the old order. His words, even to the most sceptical of Britons, were as good as prophecy. *If only they weren't so cryptic.*

Vitalinus dismounted and took a step forward. 'King Custennin.' He bowed his head, hiding the insincerity in his eyes.

'I don't call myself king,' the older man muttered gruffly. 'We have no need of fancy titles here.'

'I am Vitalinus, son of Lucius Vitalis of Cornovia. My father sends his good wishes.' Despite the parochial reception, Vitalinus spoke formally. He knew his father didn't much like Custennin, and it was easy to see why.

Custennin made no immediate response and instead had a good look around the assembled men and peered up and down at Vitalinus.

'You carry a spatha. A Roman sword to go with your Roman name.' He sneered, not even trying to hide his contempt. 'And doubtless Roman blood as well.'

'I am Cornovian.' Vitalinus bristled, but kept his tone reverential. 'A Briton like yourself. May I introduce my son, Vortimer?'

Vortimer nodded respectfully, but Custennin still leered at Vitalinus.

'A better name. So, you are here to support to our fight against the barbarian raiders?'

'That was my father's instruction.'

'How is he, your father?' Custennin had a wry smile on his face, likely aware that there was little love lost between them.

'Stubborn as the day is long,' replied Vitalinus, patiently playing the game. 'He was well when I left him.'

'You have Nubians in your ranks,' the Dumnonian stated, a distinct look of disapproval on his face.

'They are Nobatian, the finest bowmen and riders I command.' Vitalinus glanced over his shoulder at the two brothers, Shabaka, and Tsekani. They sat in their saddles proudly, unbothered by the frosty welcome.

'It's not exactly an army, but it will do,' grumbled Custennin. 'However, you can take the Nobatians back with you. Unlike the Romans, I prefer to know the kind of men I command.'

Vitalinus grimaced slightly, then nodded to the men nearest to the cart they had brought all the way from Viroconium. The men peeled back the hides covering the wagon, revealing the dull glint of steel.

'I bring arms, Custennin, not men. These weapons are yours. The men are mine.'

Custennin stepped into the mud, treading the driest path he could past Vitalinus to the side of the cache of arms. He looked at them for a moment before raising his voice.

'You came all this way to bring me a box of blades?' He walked back towards Vitalinus, facing up to him. 'I asked for aid. For men. Not metal and wood!'

Vitalinus held his ground. He had every physical advantage over this man, and enough men to take the fort easily, now that they were inside it, but that was not why he was here.

'Surely you have men,' he posited gently. 'They just need to learn to fight.'

'My men are farmers. Fishermen! And now savages plunder our shores,' Custennin raged. 'My people will die as fast with sword in hand as without. You insult me. Your father insults me.' He spat in the mud at Vitalinus' feet.

Vortimer's hand instinctively moved to hover above the hilt of his sword. Custennin's eyes flashed towards him angrily.

'And your son thinks he might cut me down where I stand? What strange aid you bring!'

Vitalinus glowered at his son, who quickly relaxed his sword arm.

'I do not mean to offend,' Vitalinus said calmly. 'Perhaps we could teach your men to better bear arms? I am sure we can be of some assistance before we journey back.'

Custennin levelled his gaze at Vitalinus, irritated at the lack of proportionate reaction to his ire. 'Perhaps,' he muttered. 'Then again, perhaps you could start by kissing my—'

'Father!' A female voice cut the old man off. A girl, almost a woman, stood in the entrance to the hall, hands on hips and a scowl on her face. She stepped brazenly into the muck and marched towards the men. 'Father, these men are our guests. They have doubtless been in the saddle, or worse—on foot—for many long days.' She frowned at her father, before smiling at Vitalinus and then at Vortimer, who smiled back at her quizzically. 'Father?' She returned her expectant attention to Custennin. The old man softened and looked at her for a moment. He turned back to Vitalinus.

'My apologies,' he mumbled through a forced smile. 'I appear to have lost any sense of good hospitality I once had. It is as well Lamorna keeps me straight. You are my guests. Vitalinus, you and your son will dine with us. And your men and animals must rest.'

Vitalinus nodded slowly. He held out his hand. Custennin looked at it for a moment before offering his own.

'Perhaps some drink will loosen our stiff efforts at diplomacy,' the Dumnonian suggested. He turned and took his daughter's arm in his before heading towards the hall.

Vortimer, who had watched Lamorna all the way back inside, turned eventually to his father. 'Was that all part of the plan?'

Vitalinus smirked.

* * *

Thank the gods—our gods—for the brightly burning braziers, thought Jac as he filled his cup from the barrel of mead. Summer was well and truly gone and the nights were even colder here than they had been on the walls of the fort that crowned The Wrekin, the huge hill that shaded Viroconium. He sat next to the burly Osric, who drank as enthusiastically as he fought. The big Jute lifted a horn to his lips and poured the warm liquid down his throat and over his beard.

'I tell you,' Osric rumbled in his thick accent, 'it was dragon's breath. It reeked of it. This is a strange part of your land.'

Jac snickered. He liked Osric. The Jute made everything more bearable. Though he didn't think he'd mention the pang of desire he'd felt when he saw Lamorna through the ranks and imagined for a moment that one of her smiles had been directed at him. He'd known a few women back home, but there was something about this one. Something about the way she had stamped out the rising hostility as if it were nothing more than a few embers in the kitchen hearth after a night of carousing. *No, he wouldn't mention that.* Osric would dine out on it for weeks.

'Nubian! Hey!' Osric boomed through the flickering tongues of flame. Shabaka looked up. 'What do you say?'

'To dragons?' Shabaka's accent was just as unfamiliar, clipped and musical.

'Yes!'

'I have seen none on this island.' The Nobatian smiled.

'On this island?' Osric pressed.

Shabaka stood up from beside Tsekani and walked around the brazier. 'Or any island,' he admitted.

'But there are such things?' the Jute asked.

'You see my armour?' Shabaka ran his hands down his breastplate, a tight mesh of sharp triangular scales.

'Yes! Is it dragon?'

'Crocodile,' Shabaka announced mysteriously, as if he expected anyone

17

to know what that meant. 'Where I am from, we have what you may call dragons. This was my father's armour. He killed the beast that wore this hide.'

'I knew it!' Osric clapped his hands together excitedly.

'The crocodile does not breathe fire. Nor fly. Yet it has many teeth like daggers and will drag a man to his death at the bottom of a river.'

Osric leant closer, a grin on his face. He loved a story. The other men nearby had stopped their own conversations to listen.

'Once, my father saw one of these terrible beasts crash into a boat, sending everyone in it into the dark water. The water boiled red with blood, teeth, and tail. My father, a great warrior, leapt into the water from the shore and swam, with only a small knife between his teeth.' Shabaka paused, looking around him at the faces watching him, all red and orange and dancing shadows. 'For an age, he went beneath the blood and the screams and fought the monster, gutting its soft belly with his blade. And now I am wearing it.' He ran his hands proudly over his armour.

'And you saw this?' Osric's normally booming voice was finally hushed.

'No. I was born here. I have never seen such things.'

Osric looked at the Nobatian for a moment, as if he might feel cheated, but then roared with sudden laughter before demanding everyone had another drink. And another story.

Jac's mind wandered. Someone began a story that they promised would send chills down the spines of every man there, but Jac was again thinking of Lamorna. Her hair must reach her waist, he thought, although he pictured it as he had seen it, blowing freely around her soft face.

Selwyn walked past slowly. Jac called out to him. He asked him what he thought was going on inside.

'Much the same as here, I imagine,' Selwyn muttered stoically, 'but warmer.'

'You think we're safe?'

'Safe?'

'It wasn't the kindest of welcomes,' Jac offered.

'It never is,' sighed Selwyn. 'That's why we are forty men armed to the teeth. That makes me feel safe.'

Jac shivered.

* * *

It was warmer inside. Vortimer listened to his father and Custennin talking over the table, while wondering if he'd have been happier outside trading stories with the men. Erbin visibly hung on every word Vitalinus uttered, obviously excited by the influx of new people to his small life, while his sister was more interested in Vortimer, looking at him coyly in between dutifully attending to her father. Vortimer tried not to let on that he had noticed.

'Usk is all but abandoned now,' Custennin explained to Vitalinus. 'When the legion left, they were the last to go.'

'But why? Surely such a fortress offers more safety for your people.'

Custennin's face creased into a derisory frown. 'We were never as enamoured with the Romans as your people were.'

'I don't want the Romans here either,' Vitalinus retorted.

'No?'

'No. Doesn't mean we can't learn from them. We just need to be able to defend ourselves.'

Custennin bit down into a shank of meat, the grease slickly coating his thin beard in the firelight. Vortimer glanced at Lamorna, half hoping to catch her eye, but she had her head down in quiet reflection.

'How many men do you have? Fighting men.' The word 'fighting' came with an inadvertent glob of fat from Custennin's open mouth. Vortimer leant back and took a drink.

'Never enough. The Picts are venturing further south than before.'

Vortimer glanced at his father, who met his eyes for a moment as if to encourage him to pay closer attention.

'Picts!' Custennin spat again. 'You even talk like a Roman. I gather they call themselves Kaldi.' He laughed.

'Quite so,' Vitalinus replied quietly. 'And they are merciless.'

19

'As are the Scotti, or the Hibernians, or the Dalriadans, or whoever the fuck is attacking me. I need men, Vitalinus. I need them now!'

Custennin's outburst caused Lamorna to look up, and this time Vortimer caught her eye. He smiled at her, as if to offer her some comfort from the red-faced beast of a father that sat beside her spitting his dinner over the table. She flushed and looked down a little, then up again with a smile and a light in her eye.

Custennin noticed. He swallowed hard, gulping down whatever unchewed food was in his mouth, and jabbed his short eating knife towards his daughter.

'Lamorna, the men need to talk. Take your brother and ready yourselves for bed. Go!'

Lamorna leapt to her feet obediently, her hand already held out towards her brother, who was less keen to comply.

'But I am nearly a man!' Erbin blurted out.

'Nearly isn't enough, boy. Now do as I say!'

'Father?' Lamorna spoke quietly.

'Later!'

Lamorna took Erbin's hand and pulled him, huffing, from the table. Custennin watched them go, then motioned to a hooded figure that stood in the shadows. The figure slunk forward into the light, pulling back the hood.

'Ossian. Come.'

Vitalinus started. Vortimer snapped his head round to look beyond his father at the mysterious man they had encountered in the fog.

'Ossian is my advisor,' Custennin introduced him. 'Ossian, this is Vitalinus and his son, Vortimer.'

Ossian looked intently at the two Cornovians, not allowing any glimmer of recognition to register on his face. 'I have heard much about you.'

'I am afraid I cannot say the same of you,' Vitalinus announced drily.

'You hail from the great town of Viroconium, one of the few Roman settlements that is yet to be abandoned.'

'And nor will it be. It serves our purpose well since the Romans left.

Have you been there, Ossian?' Vitalinus pronounced the druid's name slowly, and it fell like a hiss from his lips, sounding to Vortimer like an accusation. A suspicion of subterfuge.

'Many years ago.' The druid smiled back. 'And a fine place it is. The Wrekin casts a long shadow.'

'Longer than this one, for sure,' Custennin chimed in.

Ossian levelled his gaze at Vitalinus. 'Even the lowest hill can conceal the sun if the hour is late enough.'

His father and the druid were talking in code. A code that Vortimer had no clue how to decipher.

'Come now,' laughed Custennin, perhaps also feeling a little excluded, 'we'll be comparing cocks soon. I am already humbled enough to have asked for aid. And speaking of which—'

Vitalinus looked a moment longer back at Ossian, then turned back to Custennin, his face serious. 'May we speak alone?' he asked.

* * *

Custennin sloshed ale into two cups before offering one to Vitalinus.

'All but a handful?' he asked.

Vitalinus took the drink and held it in front of him. He had Custennin exactly where he wanted him now. 'Your need is greater,' he smiled, and took a long draught. He had, in private, acquiesced to the demand for men as well as arms.

'And your conditions?'

Vitalinus wiped his beard with his sleeve. He looked around Custennin's private chambers, draped in animal furs and hides. A generous fire crackled in the middle of the room, smoke billowing up into the cloudless Dumnonian night above.

'I want you to give me your proxy at the council when I need it.'

'Fine. I rarely attend anyway. You can have it.'

'I am grateful.' He was. This corner of the land was isolated and mostly well protected, despite the apparent threat of raiders. The support would help him sway the opinions of the other chieftains and self-proclaimed kings.

'I don't know why you made the pretence of offering me just a wagonload of weapons.' Custennin was in a much-improved mood.

'That was my father's wish, not mine,' Vitalinus lied. His father had grumbled and moaned at the request for aid and called Custennin 'a belligerent and cantankerous old shit who's probably fucking his own daughter'. Vitalinus could already vouch for the first part of that assertion and had strong suspicions as to the second part. No, it had been Vitalinus who had conceived the whole idea of honouring the request. And how he would do it.

'And what else do you want?' Custennin, however curmudgeonly, was still shrewd; cunning enough to see that Vitalinus had his eyes on more.

Vitalinus had another long drink. 'My son, Vortimer, will remain with the men I leave here.' He paused, searching for a reaction, but Custennin waited. 'And he shall be wed to Lamorna.'

And there was the reaction, possibly confirming his father's second accusation. Custennin twitched and looked away quickly, as if pierced in the heart.

'It is a good match, Custennin.' Vitalinus twisted the knife. 'It binds our people together.' He knew Custennin would struggle to find a reason to refuse.

'And Erbin?' The old man muttered.

'He is still your rightful heir.'

'As he must remain.'

'You have my word.'

Custennin looked up finally, a diplomatic smile fastened to his face. 'As you have mine. But, like I said, you can take the Nubians and that Saxon I saw lurking in your ranks. You can keep your Roman ways.'

Vitalinus knew he had Custennin where he wanted him. He allowed him the foolish discriminatory outburst. He wasn't about to trade the Nobatians or the Jute for anything, anyway. Instead, he just held out his arm for Custennin to take and sealed the agreement.

'I shall go and inform my son,' he smiled.

'And we shall prepare for the wedding. The sooner the better.'

Vitalinus nodded and took his leave. Once out of sight, he was rewarded with the sound of a cup being hurled across the room.

* * *

Ossian slid from the shadows and took Vitalinus' place in Custennin's chambers.

'You heard it all?' Custennin was seething. All pretence dropped.

Ossian nodded. Indeed, he had smiled to himself at the caged battle of wits that he had witnessed. Vitalinus had a clear advantage, for sure, and was by far the quicker of the two men, but even Custennin had showed great self-control.

'And what do you make of it?'

'He gives thirty strong men, weapons, and a union between your peoples. And all for your support in matters you don't even care about.' Ossian stated the facts only.

Custennin snorted. 'He wants power.'

'He will probably get it.' There was no point lying. Vitalinus was destined for some kind of greatness.

'He means to breed us out! And when his kingdom is five times what it is now, and he is on his deathbed—'

'Then a son born to Lamorna will stand to rule it all.'

Ossian had heard the rumours. Not that he needed to rely on rumours for his intelligence. He could smell the old man on Lamorna. He had watched her change from the sweet and pretty child who played with her brother to a withdrawn girl who shrunk from all men, and finally to the precocious young woman who was probably the only person, aside from him, who could stop Custennin with a word. With a tone.

Custennin contemplated the druid's carefully chosen words, a slow grin finding his face. 'Yes, yes. He will, won't he?' The penny had dropped. 'You have knowledge of poisons, Ossian?'

'Naturally.'

The smile turned crueller.

'No Cornovian half-breed is ever going to rule in Dumnonia. Inform Lamorna that I want to see her immediately.'

The druid bowed his head in obedience. All the pieces were now in play.

The Roman Road

The road was arrow straight, as far as Emrys could tell. Hanging swollen above them, the moon beamed its cool light over the flattening landscape, and the cobbles below his feet glistened with the evening's dew fall. The heavy clouds that had smothered the land earlier in the day had dispersed and now stars pricked the inky sky in clusters of tiny lights that promised comfort. But today his life had changed. Forever.

When he and Tugen had run down the hill towards the plumes of black smoke that rose over the homes of their families, there had been minor consideration of potential danger. When they had got closer, they could make out the orange tongues of the fires that raged in every building and hear the crackling racket of the thatch as the blaze consumed all.

They had slowed to a walk.

Not out of caution.

Emrys had seen the first body. A twisted, blackened caricature of a human lying mid-crawl a few yards from the entrance to a house, the hot air above it still rippling from the fire that had eaten its fill and moved on. Another, less burnt but no more recognisable, had sat grotesquely lifelike against a fence post, blood-soaked hands still clutching an opened abdomen. A woman whose hair was matted where it wasn't burnt had lain sprawled face down in a puddle, its inky waters spread with another darkness. Blood. The crops in the field had been smouldering, pockets of fire still charring the life out of the vegetation that had been due for harvest any day now.

Tears had come. He hadn't cried or sobbed. Tears had just rolled down Emrys' blanched cheeks. Tugen had been the same. But angrier. The bigger boy had wanted to investigate a house, his parent's house, and had pulled his arm away from Emrys' cautionary grip. The heat had been stifling. Tugen hadn't been able to make it past the threshold for the heat and the smoke, but still he had tried another dwelling. And another.

Emrys had walked into the field, among the devastated crop, and had sat on a woodpile the blaze had spared. How cruel, he had thought as he watched his friend amidst the stinking black fog, that the only thing unburned was the firewood.

And that's where, numbly reflecting on his own loss, he had found Rozena, sooted cheeks lined with her own tear tracks, mewing and clutching her knees to her chest. When she squeezed him hard, arms tight around his neck, he had seen behind her the body of her father. And next to him the unmistakable woad-stained flesh of a Kaldi warrior, a short sword jutting defiantly skyward from his bloodied chest.

'I hid,' Rozena had sobbed into his hair. 'That's all I could do.'

'You're alive. You did well.'

Tugen had appeared at that point and taken Emrys' place. As he had spun Rozena around in a warm embrace, Emrys' eyes had met Rozena's properly for the first time. Even in all this devastation, there was something in them that had said, 'it's going to be all right.'

They had resolved to travel south to Dere Street, and on to the town of Eborakon. Emrys had wrapped his slim fingers around the hilt of the sword that had finished off the Kaldi and drawn it with a wet suck from the blue chest.

Walking beside Rozena on the Roman road, Emrys rested the palm of his hand on the rounded pommel of the sword. He had held it up earlier, testing the balance. It was significantly heavier than the wooden training sword he was used to, but he would get the hang of it. Tugen had picked up the Kaldi javelin and now led the way, clutching it tightly in his fist.

'We should stop for the night,' Rozena announced.

So they did.

* * *

A while later, he huddled with Rozena next to a fire. They had gathered some loose cobbles from the road and set them in a small circle around the burning twigs. Tugen stood a little way off, claiming he was taking watch, although Emrys knew him well enough to know that he just didn't want to talk.

'Come on, Tugen,' he eventually spoke up, 'we must keep warm. Even you!'

Tugen kicked at the ground, sending a flurry of dirt toward the fire. Rozena glanced at Emrys, concerned.

'We're going the wrong way.' They were the first words Tugen had spoken since they had left the village.

'No, no, we're not,' Emrys argued softly. 'We just need to follow the road.'

'What if I don't want to?'

'Tugen, we agreed,' Rozena sided with Emrys.

'*You* agreed.' Tugen's face was dour, set with determination.

'Well, I—' Rozena began.

'We're cowards.'

Emrys pulled away from Rozena, not wanting to antagonise the situation by isolating Tugen physically as well as in terms of opinion. He instantly felt colder, less comforted, and wanted to calm Tugen quickly so he could return to Rozena's touch.

'We're alive,' he said, with his arms outstretched.

'Yes,' Tugen admitted bitterly. 'I know.'

'We're alive because Rozena hid. Because you hid. Because—'

'Because that blue bitch didn't kill you,' Tugen cut him off angrily. 'Why, Emrys? Why did she spare you?'

Emrys had no answer. He shrugged, looking at his feet inadequately.

Tugen wiped a tear from his cheek. 'They're all dead,' he choked on his words. 'And we should be too.'

'There's a reason we're not,' Rozena smiled warmly up at Tugen.

'Oh, and what reason is that? Oh yeah, you don't have a clue, do you?'

Tugen sobbed, turning away again. 'I want to go back.'

'Why?'

Tugen stood still, his back to them, and Emrys knew he was hiding tears. He stood up and approached his friend.

'You can't avenge them. Not yet.' He reached out and hesitantly rested his hand on Tugen's shoulder. It was shrugged off.

'I'm going to.'

'Yes, you will. But not right now.' Emrys stepped around Tugen and looked him in the face, saw his wet, angry eyes.

'And I'll ask her, before I kill her, why she spared you.' Tugen ground his teeth.

'At least come with us to Eborakon first,' Emrys pleaded. 'For Rozena?'

Tugen's eyes, proudly brimming with fresh tears, finally fixed on Emrys. He gave the slightest nod.

* * *

Rozena opened her eyes. Emrys was there. She had fallen asleep facing him and was happy to see that he hadn't rolled over in the night. She lay there for a while, looking at his face in the cool light before the sun came up, quietly wanting him to open those golden eyes of his and smile at her. The cut on his cheek had dried, and his shallow breath misted in the morning air, obscuring his face for a moment before dispersing. Rozena shivered, then closed her eyes again, as if doing so would warm her a little.

The quietest of noises woke her. She didn't know how long she had slept again. She wasn't even aware she had fallen asleep. But she opened her eyes in a start and saw Tugen bent over Emrys. His hand was on the hilt of the sword Emrys had liberated from the dead man, and he was pulling gently. He stopped when he saw Rozena was looking at him.

She didn't move, just stared at him, into his still-burning eyes. Anger and hatred filled them, and she understood it. She had watched her own father fight and fall. He had died saving her, and she had hidden herself away behind the logs. Tugen hadn't been there. He hadn't had a say in the raid.

28

Doubtless, he would have perished as well, like the rest of them. Part of her wanted Tugen to feed the beast inside him that demanded vengeance. Until she reminded herself that he was still a boy.

She glared back at him imploringly, then glanced at his hand and shook her head. And he nodded and let the sword lie. He stood tall and took a silent step backwards and away from Emrys' sleeping form, then bent and picked up the javelin, nodded at her again and turned on his heels and walked away. North.

When Emrys had woken an hour later, he was less understanding.

'We should go after him,' he blurted out in irritation as he scattered the few glowing embers of the fire with his feet.

'No. He has his own path. We have ours. I want to go to Eborakon.'

'He'll be killed.'

'Or not. We don't know.'

Emrys stopped and looked at Rozena. She knew she was right. As likely as it was that he would be killed, there was every chance he wouldn't, and there was no point in always assuming the worst.

'You let him walk away,' Emrys accused her.

She giggled. 'How was I going to stop him?'

'You could have woken me!'

Rozena shrugged. Sure, she could have, but what would that have achieved? They'd have argued, possibly fought. Tugen was so close to becoming a man, and if this is what he needed to do to get there, then so be it. Although she wondered how different it would have been if Emrys, not Tugen, had insisted on leaving.

Emrys picked up his sword. 'He should at least have taken this. I would have.'

Rozena smiled at him sweetly. She liked Emrys. She felt safer around him than anywhere else. He was a boy still as well, but despite Tugen's clumsy kiss and pawing hands, it was Emrys that made her heart beat a little faster. Not that she'd ever tell him that.

'Come on.' She slapped his arm. 'I'm starving.' She set off walking, her feet finding the reassuring hardness of the Roman stones.

And Emrys followed.

Hubris

The cool fresh water sloshed over the brim of the pail as Petroc pulled it free from the well and set it on the stone wall. A thin mist clung to the moors inland, but already the first warm light in the East promised a clearer day than the one before. He picked up the bucket and turned towards the villa. His mother had used to fetch the water in the mornings before his father passed away, but as well as taking it upon himself to be the man of the house, he also liked to make her life easier. He was sixteen now and proudly shouldered any additional responsibilities where possible. They could barely manage the upkeep of the house, however, and help was increasingly hard to find.

Some of the sun's rays were already falling on the patchy thatch that had been used to replace broken roof tiles. Petroc spotted a fresh gap that would need fixing and resolved to take care of it after they had eaten.

Still untouched by the dawn light, the sea was a dull grey. The dark shape of a boat skulked close to the shore. Built around a natural cove with a shingle beach, the village was a collection of just half a dozen houses. There were usually a few boats in the cove later in the day, after the men had returned, so it was a little odd to see just one. Didn't the fishermen usually set out earlier than this? He pondered. But although he enjoyed the fresh fish that the men in the village brought up to the villa every few days, he admitted to himself that he was no expert in the trade. One man had drunk too much the night before. It wasn't unknown, especially the day after a good catch.

The sunlight stretched down the hill towards the village and it was then that a bright glint caught his eye. He stopped walking, creasing his brow as he peered down the slope. He thought he could make out a few shadowy shapes between the houses. And then he heard the scream. Part of one, at any rate. Just as it reached its crescendo, it stopped abruptly. And Petroc realised what was happening. The dawn sun flashed again on what he knew could only be blades. Raiders.

He didn't wait to see them better. He dropped the pail and raced to the villa, all but careening into his mother in the doorway.

'Petroc!' she scolded him. 'Be careful.'

'They're here!'

His mother, needing no clarification, blanched. Her eyes flashed with fear, and she pulled him inside.

Petroc tore into his father's room from the vestibule. He had barely been in there since his father died, and the trappings of his office now lay filmed in dust. Petroc flung the heavy wooden lid from a chest in the corner, revealing a tunic of scale armour and a scabbarded spatha. He grabbed the mail and began pulling it on.

'You can't fight them, Petroc!' His mother stood in the doorway. 'We need to run.'

He tightened the straps on the mail. His hands were shaking a little, but he controlled them well.

'Please,' his mother begged.

Petroc bent over and picked up the sword. He dropped the scabbard back in the box, clenched his hands around the hilt, and took a deep breath.

'Mother, run away,' he said as calmly as he could. 'Now.'

She stood there for a moment, looking at him. No words came, and her panic faded for a moment, replaced by what appeared to be a look of pride. She nodded and backed out of the room.

He followed her to the door and watched as she took off toward the moors. Then he turned his attention to the unwelcome visitors that, by the sounds of it, were slaughtering everyone in the village. He set off at a jog down the hill, uttering an oath to his dead father that he would die with honour, sword in hand. A man.

The foremost raider was also the biggest. They had already plundered the handful of houses by the sea, and were doubtless set on what was probably the real prize: the villa on top of the cliff. His home. Petroc felt a surge of anger. Fuelled by this fury, his jog turned into a run, and he just had time to see the confident grin on the big man's face as he brought his father's sword flashing down towards it.

His opponent swayed effortlessly out of the reach of the blade and leant forward to deliver a fist to Petroc's chin, stopping him in full run and knocking him ignominiously to the ground. His sword fell from his grasp and clattered to the rocky path. Dazed, he twisted his neck to look for it, knowing he had little or no time to defend himself from the inevitable further attack. He reached for it, his fingertips just about scraping the pommel, but time had already run out. A heavy foot stamped down on his wrist, pinning his arm to the ground.

'It's a fine sword, boy,' the russet-bearded man grinned down at him, 'but it'll do you no use.' And a fist descended on Petroc's face. The world crashed in on him, darkness folding rapidly over his swimming vision. The blurred redness of his vanquisher receded as the blackness crowded in. 'Bind him as well.' The voice was far away. 'He's coming with us.'

When Petroc came to, he vomited down himself immediately. The world was rolling. His hands were tightly lashed together and a girl from the village was crushed up against him. She was whimpering. His eyes adjusted and he could make out his home ablaze on the cliff top far away, twenty men pulling at oars in front of him, and the sea all around.

* * *

Custennin snored. His bare chest, daubed with tufts of wiry hair, rose with each noisy intake of breath. Lamorna looked at him coldly. He had been more insistent the night before, urgently emptying himself into her as she focussed on the dancing flames of the fire. And then he'd just flopped down and gone straight to sleep. She had preferred that. The strange moments of tenderness he usually forced upon her afterwards made her stomach churn. She knew well enough that, in the cold light of day, he still recognised her as his daughter. But night and drink resurrected her mother's likeness instead. Several times he had held her close and called her by her mother's name and sobbed into her long hair. Her mother's hair. In those moments, she pitied him. Now, in the morning, she despised him.

Lamorna quietly slipped out from under the blanket and pulled on a thick woollen dress, picked up her shoes and left the room. She could put her shoes on outside. She didn't want to be there when he woke up.

In the courtyard, some of Vitalinus' men were already awake. A few fires crackled in the crisp morning air below the bubbling of blackened metal pots. A young man rubbed his hands together vigorously and blew into his palms. Lamorna skirted around the wall, not interested in talking to anyone. Another man, older, was pressed up against the fence, pissing.

'Here love, hold this for me?' he guffawed, his hot breath mingling with the rising cloud of steam in front of him.

She ignored him and walked a wide arc behind him, her pace quickening until she reached the ladder. She climbed up to the rampart. Erbin was there, as usual. She suffered at the hands of her father, but so did he in other ways. The ramparts were a good place to go to get away from prying eyes and the derisory whispers that spread behind their backs.

'Morning, Sister.' Erbin affected an air of formality, his hands clasped together behind his back. He had a somewhat different interpretation of reality to most people and seemed to think he was on sentry duty. 'Did you sleep well?'

'Yes, thank you.' Lamorna felt herself redden a little. Erbin had never mentioned how their father terrorised her, but she didn't doubt that he was aware of it, although it was likely he didn't comprehend the actual mechanics.

'We have another visitor.'

She followed his finger and saw the solitary figure of a woman half-running and half-stumbling up the hill towards the gates.

* * *

Vitalinus sat beside Custennin. The Dumnonian had oddly requested his presence receiving the woman who had fled the raiders. It was an opportunity to see Custennin's leadership in action.

'My boy, Petroc, took up arms.' Joceline sobbed before them, and Vitalinus was quick to assure her that his death would be avenged.

'How old is Petroc?' Custennin asked her quietly.

'Sixteen.'

'You husband—Calpurnius—he was a Decurion, was he not?' It was an odd question. Custennin was publicly indifferent to Roman practice, so it was unlikely he held this out-dated administrative office in any great regard. Vitalinus glanced wryly at Vortimer, who stood to his side.

'He was.' Joceline seemed equally confused by the question. 'When such positions mattered.'

Custennin nodded, and Vitalinus realised he was just affecting sageness. As surely as he was affecting compassion as well. He was playing at being the benevolent leader.

'And the village?' Custennin asked as he tugged at the end of his beard.

'They had to come through it to get to the villa.'

It was unlikely there were any survivors.

'You will remain as my guest,' Custennin proclaimed magnanimously. The cracks in his performance hopefully were not obvious to the poor woman who had lost her son. 'We shall send riders to your home to assess the situation.'

Joceline nodded and looked at Vitalinus, as if expecting something more.

'Vortimer,' Vitalinus addressed his son. 'Take a few men and see what you can find.' He wanted to rile his host a little, so added, 'with your permission, Custennin.'

'As you wish,' came the frosty reply, and Vortimer took his leave.

'My lady,' Vitalinus smiled at Joceline, 'your son sounds like a very brave and honourable young man.'

'My daughter, Lamorna, will see to your needs.' Custennin clearly wanted the last word.

Afterwards, when they were alone, Custennin made his true feelings more apparent. He was on his feet, pacing.

'While we sleep!' He ranted. 'That's when they come. We eat, we drink, we make promise of marriage, of alliance. You come here pledging aid.' He flashed an angry look at Vitalinus, who refused to rise to the bait. 'And while we sleep, those bastards come and rape my lands, steal my gold, my people. Yes, they take slaves. Her son won't be dead. He's sixteen, ripe as a slave. Better for him if they had killed him, probably. And your forty useless fucking men sit in my home, eating my food, laughing the night away. Forty blades that could have been put to good bloody use.'

'And if we had been a day later arriving?' Vitalinus poked the bear.

'What?'

'Don't vent your anger at me or my men, Custennin. It is you that fail your people, not me.'

'How dare you!' Custennin was almost frothing at the mouth.

'And that is why I am here,' Vitalinus said quietly.

'You are here purely for my support in the council. You don't care about these people,' spat Custennin.

'A Decurion's son?' Vitalinus continued to provoke. 'You've made your thoughts on Roman stock very plain until now!'

'Calpurnius is gone. The boy is a Briton. His mother is a Briton. They are my people.'

'And as Britons, they are my people too,' Vitalinus retorted with sincerity. Custennin recognised it.

'So do something! Do something or I will make sure I go to every council meeting with the sole intention of speaking out against you. And there will be no marriage. Now kindly leave me to my thoughts.' He slumped down in his chair.

* * *

The fisherman's wife had been cut from navel to chest and lay crumpled in the doorway to her cottage. A shirtless man, probably her husband, was splayed in the mud not far away, his hand inches from a crude wooden club that clearly hadn't been enough to prevent him too from having a sword shoved through his gut. When Jac had finished throwing up, Vortimer put his hand on the young lad's shoulder, for all the comfort it could offer.

It had been a brief ride from the hill fort, but there hadn't been much in the way of conversation. There would be even less on the way back, after they had buried the dead. Vortimer instead had given some thought to the proposal his father had told him about. So, he was to be married to Lamorna. He couldn't decide how he felt. She was pretty enough and looked strong. She certainly had a way with her cantankerous father. It was more the prospect of having to remain here, in Dumnonia, that troubled Vortimer. It was a long way from the place he knew as home. The land was beautiful, but stark. Life would be harder here, less comfortable, even with the prospect of a new bride to warm the nights. He didn't know what his father's plan was, but he knew that there would be one. The man left little to chance. As the eldest, Vortimer thought he would have been better placed at his father's side, learning from him, and preparing— eventually—to succeed him.

Vortimer looked towards the beach. There were definite signs that not everyone was dead. Furrows in the shingle indicated that at least two people, perhaps three, had been dragged down the beach to waiting boats.

'Where did they take them?' Jac, recovered, had come to the same conclusion.

'Hibernia, I suppose,' Vortimer muttered. He didn't really know the difference between them and the Scotti or the Dalriadans that he had heard mentioned. Jac was a good lad, bright and keen to make a good impression, and he was clearly embarrassed at how he'd reacted to seeing death first hand. 'Don't worry, Jac,' Vortimer reassured him, 'you handled it better than most.'

They and the other men set about burying the dead left behind by the Hibernians. As best they could, they buried husbands and wives together, and the couple of children that had been brutally slain in their mothers' arms, they also laid with their families. Jac had turned away and cried at that sight, and nobody there could blame him.

The sun was blood red, low over the quiet sea, by the time they mounted up to return to the fort.

* * *

Vitalinus had prepared for further attack. The raiders had a pattern. They would likely make landfall again before taking their laden boats back across the sea to Hibernia. He had tasked small units of men with cliff-top watches, and with building warning beacons that could be lit if they saw boats. The rest of the men were primed to ride at a moment's notice.

'Might I have a word?'

Vitalinus hadn't heard the druid enter. He looked up from his thoughts. 'Now that we have been formally introduced,' he said with a wry smile. 'I didn't take you for a man that waited for permission. Speak, then.'

'You believe in Albion.' A statement rather than a question. The druid sat down opposite him. 'You wear the trappings of Rome, but Rome is long gone. You are not your father, and you believe in greatness outside of the Empire. Outside of Rome. You believe that Albion, the nation of Britons, can become,' he affected a pause, 'as it was.'

Vitalinus drank in the words. *Was it that obvious?* He did believe that the ways of the Romans, all his forefathers had known for centuries, could equip a man of vision such as him to unite the shattered nation they had left behind them. Albion was the stuff of legend, little more than an idea, a shadow of a memory that still flitted behind the eyes of those whose bloodlines tied them to this island, to a time before the Romans had carved it up and built villas and roads and walls. *Even then*, he thought, *there hadn't really been unity.* That was a dream. People had always fought, and if there weren't Romans to fight, or invaders from over the sea, then people would just fight each other. It was only now, learning from their absconded masters, that Britons could, perhaps, come together as one.

'Maybe I do,' he admitted quietly.

'Do you believe a man can betray another, but still hold loyalty close to heart?' Ossian pressed cryptically. 'Loyalty to a belief. A creed that goes beyond men.'

'I'm not sure I know what you mean.'

'There is something I must tell you.' The druid leant closer. 'For the sake of Albion.'

* * *

An ominous red ribbon hung a little above the horizon. Jac pulled his cloak tight around him. It would be light soon. But for now, it was just bloody freezing. He'd slept a little, exhausted from the physical and emotional exertion of burying those poor people. But even then, he had seen them again in his dreams, dead eyes opening grotesquely and mouths spewing the sticky blackness of old blood. They had voicelessly begged for vengeance, broken hands pulling at his legs as he tried to run away. He looked bitterly at the stack of wood next to him, a lightless cold hulk of potential heat that was primed to burn quickly when needed. Now would be a pretty good time, he thought. Only it wasn't there to keep him warm. Or Zeki. The Ethiope shivered beside him. Nearby, the horses grazed at the short grass on the cliff top, unbothered by the chill.

'The sun will be up to warm us soon.' Zeki's teeth clattered as he spoke. He got to his feet to get his blood moving and jumped up and down. That seemed like a good idea, so Jac hauled himself up, his limbs stiff. A little light had spread across the coast below them. Jac frowned as he looked off the edge of the headland. On the grey water below, there were a couple of darker shapes, moving with the waves. Zeki ceased stamping his foot and clapping his hands and stood beside Jac. He pointed at the shapes. They could only be boats. Hibernian currachs.

Jac took a few steps forward and crouched down, wary of the cliff edge. Sure enough, on the beach below them, several dark figures were mobilising, splashing towards the waiting boats.

'They were here all along!' Jac whispered triumphantly. 'Should we light the beacon?'

'They might see it,' Zeki cautioned.

'Let's see which way they are going. Their boats are still no match for a fast horse.'

* * *

Erbin raced into his father's chamber.

'A rider approaches,' he blurted out excitedly. He had just come from the ramparts and a conversation with Vitalinus, who had been awake for hours. Vitalinus had addressed him with a smile and called him 'young prince' and told him that his father was 'too important' to risk in battle. And the rider had appeared with news of the raiders, and Erbin had wasted no time running to give his report. 'There's going to be a battle, isn't there?'

'I certainly hope so,' Custennin smiled grimly.

Erbin repeated what Vitalinus had said and wondered why his father angered. He was still pondering why he was too important to risk, yet Vitalinus, a great man, was going to lead his men into the thick of the fight.

'You're a foolish, naïve boy, Erbin,' his father chided him.

'I'm not. I'm nearly a man.' Erbin had already asked to be among the warriors sent to intercept the raiders, but his father had denied him. He was sure he could hold a sword as well as some of the men, but perhaps because he was destined to rule, he was too important as well.

'As you keep saying,' Custennin muttered, irritated, and threw open an immense chest. His armour and weapons lay there neatly. Erbin couldn't remember seeing them before. He certainly hadn't seen his father use them.

'Are you going to fight?' he asked in breathless anticipation.

'Yes,' came the gruff response. 'Now run and tell the Cornovian that Custennin is no coward.'

And Erbin ran off and did just that before scrambling up the ladder to the ramparts to watch the men leave. They waited for his father a while, and when Custennin appeared, Erbin thought he saw Vitalinus share a smile with Vortimer. They must be happy to have him ride beside them, he thought.

'You know where they are, then?' Custennin pulled himself onto a waiting horse.

'I had watchers on the cliffs all night. It turns out they made camp on a beach near here. And we have a good idea where they're headed next.'

'What are we waiting for, then?' Custennin spurred his horse forwards and out of the open gate. Erbin was impressed. Though he struggled with the disdain his father showed him, he supposed it couldn't be easy being a leader of men and having a 'simple' son to deal with every day. Erbin desperately wanted to show his father that he was learning, and that he could fight and lead and make wise decisions. He liked Vitalinus because he was kind to him. And while he didn't particularly like his father, he respected him. And his chest puffed up with pride as he watched him lead the column of Cornovians out to battle.

Forbidden Fruit

They had been walking for at least a couple of hours without talking. Rozena's stomach grumbled angrily. She sneaked a surreptitious glance at Emrys, but he didn't seem to have heard. His eyes were locked forward on the Roman road that stretched out in front of them, his fingertips idly tracing the hardened skin along the cut on his cheek. She hadn't considered what that must have felt like until now. Facing a bear with nothing but a stick. It must have been terrifying.

If he had offered little conversation about his encounter with the bear, he had said even less about his friend leaving them. She hoped he didn't really blame her, hoped that his silence wasn't some bitter reproach for her not waking him. Then again, she mused, if it was, then it wasn't working. She felt no guilt at all. Tugen may not be old enough to take on a Kaldi war band, but he was certainly old enough to have made his own mind up. She pushed her chin forward and looked, as he did, straight ahead.

Several plumes of pale smoke were visible on the horizon ahead of them. They didn't look like the dark belching columns that spelled destruction.

'It's Eborakon,' Emrys announced. 'Look, they're making our breakfast.'

'It's still miles away.' While she had for a moment smiled at the prospect of a fire that for once offered welcome, warmth and sustenance rather than death and destruction, it had to be said that they were unlikely to reach the source of the smoke until well after lunchtime, let alone breakfast. She huffed, and her foot found an uneven stone in the road.

Emrys was quick to help her up, one hand taking hers and the other steadying her under her arm. She rose to meet him. To look into those yellowed eyes. She caught her breath as he looked back at her.

'I'm OK,' she whispered. And she realised she wasn't just talking about the fall. She let her eyes tell him she was coping. She had lost her parents, same as him. Tugen was gone. It was just her and him. And that was perfect. Her eyes filled, somewhat muddling the message, and he pulled her closer and hugged her. Her stomach growled again, and he laughed.

'You need food. I know I do.'

She pulled away from him, nodding with a grin. She wiped her moist eyes; glad the silence was over.

Some distance ahead of them, a line of trees extended away to the side of the road, likely along a track. At the end, she could just make out the warm colour of a tiled roof.

'Come on.' Emrys took her arm gently.

* * *

Where they came from, trees just grew. Nobody planted them. Emrys hadn't seen a Roman villa before, but he knew that's what he was looking at. The strange avenue of trees shading the long dirt track had built his anticipation. And when the stone and terracotta building had come into sight, he had glanced excitedly at Rozena. He could tell that they weren't seeing it at its best. It was clearly abandoned. Several roof tiles lay broken on the ground, and creeping plants spidered the crumbling walls, pushing the stones slowly apart. And still, this vast edifice was a sight to behold. How many rooms did it have, he wondered, and how many fires did it need to keep it warm in the winter?

They trod quietly as they pushed their way through the pendant curtains of a willow and into a paved square surrounded by colonnades. Broken bits of wood that had once been chairs, maybe a table, littered the stone flags. Emrys tried to imagine how it had looked before. They stood there, in the middle of the square, and Emrys became conscious of how quiet it was. Rozena's breathing next to him betrayed her apprehension. She gripped his arm as she, too, looked around in awe.

A sudden crash caused Rozena to squeal. Emrys snapped his head around toward the noise and saw the shattered evidence of a roof slate on the stone beside them. He looked up and saw, on the damaged roof, a large black bird. Its dark eye stared back at him as its beak opened with a guttural caw. Emrys realised his heart was beating faster. He put his hand on Rozena's and turned to give her a comforting smile.

'Is it a bad omen?'

'I don't think so,' he replied honestly. His knowledge of the gods was scant, but he didn't recall any of the fireside tales his parents had occasionally regaled him with involving sinister birds foretelling disaster. At any rate, he mused, that horse had already bolted. 'Come on.' He motioned towards an archway.

He peered into the gloomy interior, his hand resting on the cool stone. Silence had reclaimed the villa. He led the way, Rozena holding his hand as she padded cautiously behind him. A corridor, occasionally speckled by bits of sunlight that found its way through cracks, eventually opened into a large room. More sun poked through holes in the roof here and illuminated a sunken floor. Emrys frowned. His father had traded with merchants in Eborakon and had told him stories about rooms like this. Baths, he called them. Magnificent rooms with floors that fell away like this, and water up to the brim. Men had talked about politics there and agreed on trades, none of which Emrys understood. He had found it hard enough to imagine a room full of water. But here there was no water. The smooth tiles of the side of the 'bath' dropped precipitously down to another floor several feet down. A floor, where visible, that was made of tiny, tessellated tiles that formed pictures. Emrys could make out men with swords, a few large animals, and familiar looking colonnades. The rest of the pictures were obscured by animal hides and furs that lay on the mosaic flooring and crept up and over a ramshackle timber structure leaning against the side of the bath. A tarnished pot hung above a smouldering fire.

While Emrys eyed these signs of apparent occupation with caution, Rozena lowered herself nimbly over the edge, fingertips white against the brim of the bath for a moment before she dropped onto the coloured floor. Emrys' stomach flipped, his instincts telling him this was a bad idea.

'Wait!'

Rozena turned to him with a grin on her face. A grin that disappeared almost immediately. She called his name, eyes flashing beyond him and towards the entrance to the room. He spun around. A huge bare-chested man loomed over him, standing in the doorway, holding a vicious curved blade like nothing Emrys had seen before.

'Get out! Get out now!' the man roared threateningly. Everything about him was flexed and tight. The muscles in his arms rippled with tension, and the steel glare of his eyes would have been enough to put many men to flight. And yet there he stood, as if reluctant to advance. Emrys, as much confused as scared, took a step back. 'I mean it. Get out. I've never killed a child before, but I will if I must.' And he took a slightly hesitant step forward, as if Emrys posed a threat to him as well.

'We're just hungry,' Emrys tried his luck. 'Please, can we share your food?'

'There's nothing here for you,' the man growled. 'Now go, quickly!'

Rozena's hands gripped the side of the bath hurriedly, and she pulled herself clumsily upwards, her eyes wildly looking for another way out of the room.

'Come on, Emrys,' she pleaded.

Emrys barely heard her. His blood was drumming in his ears. His hand, slick with sweat, reached for the hilt of his sword. And where other men may have laughed at the gesture, the man in front of him instead frowned remorsefully.

'Listen to your girlfriend, boy,' he said through gritted teeth. 'Go back to Eboracum.' And he came half a step closer, raising his sword. Emrys, his hand still on his own weapon, shuffled backwards uncertainly. And suddenly there was nothing beneath his feet. His left heel sank into thin air and took him with it, and his world upended. His pounding heart throbbed in his chest as he dropped his sword and grappled for something, anything, to grab onto. But there was nothing. And when his back smashed levelly onto the mosaic floor below, all he could hear was a faraway scream. Rozena.

And his head snapped back and thudded against the stones.

And blackness.

Blood and Sand

Lorcan tugged at his beard. The dawn light gave it an almost vermilion hue, as if stained by the blood of all his enemies. And there had been plenty. He stood with one foot up on the side of the currach as it rounded a headland and grinned at the sight of a small settlement nestled among a fold of rising land above the cove. He didn't expect much in the way of treasure here, but another pair or two of hands that could work the land back home would make the so-far profitable journey all the richer.

'Easy pickings, lads.' He turned to look at the others who rowed behind him. As one, they expertly slipped their oars into the glassy water. The blades then rose clear again in perfect unison, diamond droplets chiming back onto the slick surface.

The two currachs slowed as they neared the beach, and the Hibernians jumped into the shallows and pulled the prows of the boats up onto the wet sand. Only a couple of them remained in one boat to mind the prisoners. Lorcan slipped his left arm into the straps of his round shield and flexed his fingers around a long-handled axe. He turned to his men and grinned, and the thirty men strode up the beach.

Something wasn't right. Lorcan stopped, and the men all stopped with him. He looked up at the houses. Quiet. He looked along the length of the beach. Cliffs walled the thin crescent of sand in at both ends. Lorcan noticed that the cliff at one end had a darkness at its heart. An opening. A sea-cave. Quiet as well. He frowned and took a couple more steps forward, towards the base of the shallow slope. He stopped again and fell to his haunches. There were small round indentations in the moist sand.

'Horses.' He poked a flat part of the sand with the shaft of his axe and watched as the hole slowly self-levelled. 'Recent too.' He looked up at the houses again, just in time to see the whistling shadow of an arrow. The missile found a target. It sunk itself into the sword-arm of one of his men. He called for shields, and the warriors raised their wooden bosses skyward and fanned out into a line behind them. A second arrow thudded into Lorcan's shield.

The man next to him, Finn, pulled the first arrow from the flesh of his upper arm. Its barbed tip tore at the sinew as it came free, and Lorcan saw that, in with the blood, a black tar-like substance glistened on the head. Finn shrugged at his leader and grinned unconvincingly. Lorcan looked over the rim of his shield and saw their attackers. Only a dozen men, mostly on foot. Two strange dark-skinned men flanked them on horseback, controlling their steeds with just their thighs as they pulled back bow strings. Two more arrows zipped down the slope towards the Hibernians and found shields. They were accurate. Frighteningly so since they were riding at full pelt.

'Hold,' commanded Lorcan. 'They have the hill, but we have the numbers.' He could feel his men tighten in anticipation. Often there was little if any resistance to these raids, but if called upon to fight, his men were more than capable. More than a few of them would even relish the prospect.

* * *

Vortimer had his sights on the man in front. His father had often told him that the quickest way to kill a snake was to take its head off. And if Vortimer was leading this charge, it was up to him to stare the snake in the eyes. And kill it. Without mercy. Unless Osric got there first!

The Jute positively lived to kill. He wore the same grin with sword in hand as he wore with cup in hand, and likely wench as well. Vortimer paced himself next to the big man and broke into a run when he did, knowing that his pace would take him face to face with the red-haired raider first. According to plan, Shabaka and Tsekani were riding wide of the rest of them, already making obvious moves to flank the line of little round shields that waited at the bottom of the hill. There was no need to conceal that tactic. Hopefully, it would scare a portion of the raiders and give the Britons an advantage in morale as well as terrain.

And in a heartbeat, they were upon them. Vortimer brought his sword down on the lead Hibernian's shield. The impact nearly shook the blade from his grasp, but he held on and sized up against the man. Beside him, he saw Osric's great broadsword crash into another shield, shattering it and probably the man's arm as well. Vortimer ducked his opponent's axe, feeling the wind from it as it passed inches above his head. Arrows found true paths into the melee and felled a couple of the raiders.

The first seconds of the fight saw the Hibernians pushed back into the wet sand, but they weren't looking like they were going to flee. They were still nearly thirty men against a dozen. It didn't take long for them to rally and hit back hard. Vortimer kept his eyes on the man he intended to kill, his sword finding a rhythm against axe and shield, but finding no opening. He lost sense of who was fighting beside him, but still his peripheral vision told him that the fight was balancing out now. A Briton beside him made a misstep and folded over a long blade that pushed through his stomach and out of his back. Another over-swung his weapon and was rewarded with a crushing blow that shattered his skull instantly. The red-haired man lowered his shield and grinned at him. *Grinned!*

And then, from the beach behind the Hibernians, came the clamour of hooves and war cries. Vortimer saw, over the shoulder of his opponent, the rest of the Britons being led by his father across the sand. And it was Vortimer's turn to smile. He took his opportunity and lunged forwards with his sword, a move that if ill-timed could prove fatal to himself. But his enemy had been distracted, rightly so, by the new wave of attackers, and his frantic parry came too late. Vortimer's blade, caught only at the last moment by the axe, found flesh. It sliced into the raider's thigh. The man roared like a bear and rounded quickly on Vortimer, his axe carving the air between them. Vortimer was ready, his sword up in defence, but the power of the blow pushed him back on his feet, almost sending him to the sand.

Vortimer steadied himself, aware that he had perhaps overreached, suddenly afraid that he wouldn't be ready for the next blow. But it didn't come.

'Back,' the red beard yelled. 'Back to the boats!'

* * *

The spear flew from Vitalinus' hand. It found an easy target. Vitalinus didn't much care that the man it hit never saw it coming. He saw his son, deep in the melee, and was proud to see that he had picked out the leader to fight. The man was a clear foot taller than his son, and broader too, but Vortimer had held his own. The Hibernians were being called to retreat already.

The mounted men were quick to crowd the retreating raiders, swords swinging down at them. Even Custennin was making a decent effort, though Vitalinus noticed his blade consistently failed to land anywhere that mattered. He sneered and coldly cut another pirate from shoulder to sternum, tightening his legs on his horse's sides as he tugged the blade free again.

'Away!' came the cry from the flame-haired leader. 'Flee!' And Vitalinus watched him push his way through the ranks toward the boats. Custennin, mounted, blocked his path, and swung his sword clumsily, but the man ducked it and in one smooth motion reached out to grab the Dumnonian's foot, tipping him deftly from his mount before charging on towards escape. Custennin crumpled onto the wet beach.

Vitalinus dismounted and crossed the distance between him and Custennin in a matter of seconds. He looked around briefly, content that the few Hibernians that weren't fleeing already were now outnumbered and falling fast. There were several Britons dead on the beach as well, but Vitalinus was intent on Custennin. He scabbarded his sword before he reached him and leant over him with his left arm outstretched. Custennin, winded and pained from his fall, clasped his forearm and offered a weak smile. Vitalinus hoisted him to his feet, pulling him towards him. And he kept pulling him. Onto the narrow dagger that he had drawn. The slim blade slid easily into Custennin's stomach and up into his chest cavity, pushing blood from his surprised mouth.

'You would poison my son?' Vitalinus whispered in the dying man's ear before pulling back a little to see the look on his face. Through the pain and the shock, Vitalinus thought he could see what he wanted to see.

'Ossian.' The blood bubbled from Custennin's lips. There it was. The realisation that he had been betrayed.

Vitalinus gave him a grim smile. 'Dumnonia is mine now.' He pushed the knife a little deeper, a little more upwards, then let Custennin drop.

* * *

There was nothing wrong with Ossian's eyesight. He was older than most, but still blessed with a keenness of vision that defied his age. Even from his cliff-top viewpoint, he might not have been able to see the knife in Vitalinus' hand, but he saw Custennin fall and knew he wouldn't get up again. So Vitalinus had done what had to be done.

Ossian watched the battle as it came to its inevitable conclusion. He saw the surviving Hibernians splash through the surf and clamber aboard the two currachs. A couple more fell to the Nobatian arrows in the foam. Their numbers were depleted, but they still made a good fist of rowing away. Whether they would manage the crossing of the sea, he wasn't so sure. Vitalinus, with Vortimer beside him, watched them go. And Custennin, in a heap nearby, was presumably staining the sand with his blood.

* * *

His father looked stronger in death than he ever had in life. Perhaps it was because he was lying down. Like a board. His legs straight and together, arms neatly by his side and chin almost defiant the way it jutted upwards amidst the swaying shadows cast by the candles that burned in a neat circle around him. The thin beard had been combed and lay in greying skeins over his still chest. A wooden bowl rested there too, partially laden with a few trinkets of jewellery, shining stones, and fruit. Apparently, these were gifts for him to take with him to the next world. Erbin wasn't sure he understood how either fruit or valuables would be of any use to a dead man. However, he conceded to himself; he didn't really understand what the next world was or how it worked. All he knew was that it was supposedly better to go there fighting than not. And he'd been told that his father had died in battle. So that was good.

He reached out and touched his father's head with the tips of his fingers. The candles were warm to be around, but the face of the man who had berated him daily was now cool to the touch. And even the cosy light of the flames was not enough to hide the greyness of the skin. He pulled his hand back when he heard footfalls behind him. It was Vitalinus. And Ossian.

'Did you know he would die?' Erbin asked. There was something frighteningly confident about Vitalinus. Erbin had liked him before, and maybe still did, but seeing him with the old man in tow was ominous.

'No.' Vitalinus moved towards him. 'He fought bravely for his people.'

'Did he?' Erbin doubted the truth in that. He had never seen his father fight in any sense, let alone bravely.

'They are your people now.'

Erbin puffed up his chest. They were. That was true. He needed to act like a leader. Vitalinus rested a hand on his shoulder, and Erbin shrugged it off coldly.

'Thank you for helping Dumnonia.'

'Ossian is here to help your father on his journey.'

The druid slithered into the room. *A snake among the shadows*, Erbin sneered to himself. He'd never liked the old man. And suddenly all he wanted was to be lost on the moors for the day, away from everyone. He wanted to be free to shout where none could hear him, and cry. *Yes, he might cry*. He felt it welling inside him, growing like a dark stain. *And then?*

Then he would be ready to lead his people.

Ossian knelt beside the body and began whispering into its dead ear, but Erbin didn't care. He pushed past Vitalinus and away.

* * *

Of the two life-changing events facing Lamorna, she was less happy about impending marriage than she was about her father's burial. The relief that had flooded over her when she heard her father had been killed had made her hide her face for fear of someone seeing a smile that, though outwardly imperceptible, seemed to light her up inside. From her first flush of womanhood, that man had no longer seen her as his daughter, but as his dead wife. Her mother. And every day he had held her tighter. She had fallen further away from any kind of love for the man she once called 'Father'.

And it wasn't that she didn't like Vortimer. He was handsome, with a more ready smile than his father. Even before the news that they were to be matched, she had stolen looks at him, relished the irritation that had caused in her father, and could have screamed with joy when her father told her of the deal he had made with Vitalinus. She had looked down at her feet, concentrating on keeping them still when she just wanted to watch them kick up and dance. She had hoped that being paired with Vortimer would free her, but Custennin being dead was better still. Her only reservation about the whole affair was that she knew well how Erbin would take to his succession. Her poor brother would truly believe that he, the male heir, would rule Dumnonia. But it would be Vortimer, left behind in command of the garrison, who would lead. And she would be there beside him.

She scaled Erbin's favourite ladder to the ramparts, having seen Vortimer climb up a little before. And there he was. And beyond the walls of the fort, several men strained to line a freshly dug pit with great flags of granite. Her father's burial chamber.

'Be careful, my lady.' He extended a hand. 'It is a long enough fall, and the walkway is a little slippery today.'

'You forget, I grew up here.' She tried to place her tone somewhere between coldness and coyness. 'Perhaps it is you who should take care.' She had already decided that she was going to assert herself to Vortimer. If she was to be with him for the rest of her days, she would not allow herself to be walked and talked over. He would love her for who she was, not who he wanted her to be.

'I am sorry.' He smiled at her kindly. 'And I am sorry about your father, too.'

Lamorna stood close to him, pretending interest in the preparation of her father's grave.

'He died in battle,' she muttered. 'What other honour does he need?'

Vortimer nodded quietly.

'I am not sad.' She reached out slowly and slipped her fingers into his hand. 'I understand I was promised to you.'

'We should bury your father first.' Vortimer shuffled awkwardly.

'I will see to it that Erbin follows your counsel to the letter,' she suddenly blurted out. She wasn't sure what he wanted to hear. Perhaps he was not taken with her. Perhaps he considered her a child. 'I will be a good wife. I know how.' She left the idea hanging there. She knew what men wanted and doubted Vortimer was any different. He needed to know that she was not a little girl.

'My Lady—' Vortimer began but was silenced by the long note of a horn. And four men bore Custennin out of the gate and towards the icy embrace of the granite slabs. 'We should go down.' Vortimer tried to leave, but she held his hand tighter.

'I want to watch from here. Stay with me.' She heard the quiver in her voice. She cursed it inwardly, begged it to be quiet. Nothing in her should be sad at the sight of her father's body about to be buried forever. And yet, now, seeing the shrouded corpse suddenly hurt her. It was as if, from beyond the warmth of life, her horrible father had just reached his icy fingers into her chest and clenched a fist around her childish heart. Her legs went wobbly, and it was all she could do to remain standing.

* * *

There was no fog this time. No wolves howled. The moors were bathed in sunlight, their autumn colours stretching out on all sides like a tapestry. True to the late Custennin's request, Vitalinus had decided that he would retain the services of the Nobatians and the Jute. Besides them, a few Britons returned home with him. And Selwyn rode beside him.

His farewell to Vortimer had been brief and formal. He had confidence his son would do as he should, and Dumnonia would only benefit from his guidance. The Hibernians would present something of a challenge, but he had good men at his command and a strong young bride to continue the bloodline. Vitalinus thought of his own wife. He hadn't seen her in some time and suddenly yearned for their reunion.

Ahead, on a ridge, he could see the silhouette of a man on horseback, unmoving as they approached.

'Wait here,' he told Selwyn.

He spurred his horse forward alone and approached the rider confidently. Even before he could make out a single feature, he knew who it was that waited for him. As he reached the summit, he could see beyond the ridge. And as Dumnonia fell away behind him, in front the Fosse Way forged a straight line across the levelling landscape.

'So, will you serve me now?' He asked Ossian.

The druid gave him a crooked smile. 'I will serve Albion.'

'That's good enough for me.'

Mosaic

His mind swam back from dreams of painted blue women and bears and spears and blood and fire. The fire consumed everything in its path, levelling roundhouses and crops, its flickering tendrils snaking around the limbs of screaming men and women who quickly blackened and petrified into shadowy statues that crumbled into dust as the blaze tore on. And there was Rozena, sooted in the flames, crying but unburnt. He reached out for her, becoming transfixed by the white heart of the inferno, caught in its deadly gaze as it intensified.

He opened his eyes a crack. A dusty beam of sunlight fell onto his face. His head hurt. He reached up and found it bound in cloth. His cheek burnt. Touching it, his fingers came away dirtied by some dark salve that now caked his wound. He remembered the bear again, as much from his dreams as anything, and suddenly everything came back to him. Rozena. His eyes flashed open, and he lifted his head from the soft furs to look around him. That really hurt. He couldn't help but groan in pain.

'Mother!' A girl's face peered at him; eyes wide.

'Ah, you're awake.' Another voice. He forced his eyes to focus. A woman looked at him too. He glanced around him. He was still in the bath, surrounded by pelt and fur and wooden beam, and the woman and child, and a fire. Something bubbled in a pot over the fire, and it smelled good. Emrys was hungry. He tried to lift himself up on his elbows.

'Careful,' the woman cautioned. 'You hurt your head when you fell. And I've put something on that nasty cut to help it heal. It's going to leave quite the scar.'

Emrys opened his mouth to say something, though he hadn't really decided what. He wanted to ask where Rozena was. And to ask for some food. But his mouth was dry, and whatever words he might have got out became caught in his throat. The woman shuffled towards him and held a cup to his mouth. Cold water trickled between his lips and made his head spin. He coughed.

'I'm Krestell,' the woman smiled down at him, 'and this is my daughter Carina. The man who tried to kill you is my husband, Viction.' She giggled, as if it had all been some silly prank.

'Emrys.' It was all he could manage to say.

'I know.' She took the cup from him. 'Your friend told us.'

Rozena. Thank the gods.

'She also told us you didn't come from Eboracum, which is just as well.' She used the Roman name for Eborakon, which Emrys supposed made sense, given where he found himself.

'Why?' he croaked.

'The plague is there. That's why Viction was so worried.' She chose her word carefully. 'But you are safe here.'

Emrys wanted to see Rozena. It appeared she was probably perfectly safe, but where was she? And where was this Viction?

'And where is here?' he asked, almost out of politeness.

'Well, this room used to be a bath.' Krestell looked around her with an odd sense of pride. Emrys couldn't help but think he'd rather have seen it as a bath than what it now was. 'But *here* here is the old ludus. Viction's father used to be the Doctore.'

Emrys didn't know what a ludus was. Or a Doctore. And he must have frowned because the grimy faced Carina was quick to explain.

'He taught gladiators, and he was a great fighter. Like my father.'

Gladiators. He had heard that word before. The Romans used to have slaves fight, often to the death, for their own entertainment. He sickened to imagine it, and even despite the friendly faces in front of him, he suddenly felt a surge of irrational panic. He looked around himself better at his surroundings, searching for his sword. There it was, leaning against the wall of the bath.

'Emrys!'

Rozena.

She dropped easily onto the mosaic floor beside him and threw her arms around him.

'Owwww!' he cried out, but his heart filled with relief and happiness.

'This place is amazing!' She beamed at him when she pulled away. Beyond her, in the doorway, Viction smiled too.

The Forgotten Legion

The rain fell on Tugen's face like shards of glass. Freezing. He pulled his jerkin tighter with one hand, the other in an icy grip around the shaft of his stolen Kaldi javelin. He had made it this far.

Two days before he had passed through his home. Rain had dampened the flames there too, but the bodies still lay strewn in the mud among the charred timbers of the houses that had once echoed with the laughter of children. He wasn't sure laughter would ever come easily again. Childhood was a blurred memory now. He'd never lift a wooden sword again or run through the woods with unbridled joy. He'd probably never see Emrys again. Or Rozena. But they had each other. He felt a blackness in his heart now, a void that needed to be filled. And fill it he would, with blood and vengeance.

He blinked through the deluge, the rain running in icy rivulets down his face, and saw the wall. The base of it was littered with dislodged stone and broken timbers, but it was still something of a barrier to the northern lands. A wall alone was never going to stop the Kaldi venturing south, and the legions of Rome that had garrisoned its length were all gone now. Tugen looked left. The wall stretched away from him, disappearing into the mist and the rain. He looked right. There, at the limits of his vision, he saw the square turrets of a fort.

He kept the wall to his side as he approached, finding an open gate to a courtyard. There wasn't meant to be anything to defend against this side of the wall, he supposed, despite knowing well that the Kaldi had already ventured much further south. A pelt canopy hung above the open yard, a notional defence against the elements, and still the ground was muddy underfoot. Tugen nearly lost his footing in the mire once or twice as he walked towards the wooden great hall that presided over the square.

He hadn't seen a soul since he had snuck away from Emrys and Rozena on Dere Street. And this place was as deserted as anywhere he'd been since. He paused at the sturdy door to the hall, trying to hear over the thrashing of the rain, his hand raised in readiness to knock. For all he knew the Kaldi could be using this fort as a temporary shelter, and his desperate desire for revenge could come to a sudden end.

Suddenly, there were several voices behind him, whooping and calling, and he spun around. This time, he could not prevent himself from losing his balance. He fell back clumsily into the mud, feeling a fresh curtain of rain lash across his upturned face. Hooves churned the surrounding morass, and he held a protective hand up to his face. A dozen or more men towered over him on their horses, dressed in Roman-styled armour. One of them swung heavily down from his mount, landing shin deep in muck, and glowered down at Tugen. His face was dark, as dark as the mud.

'Where have you come from, boy?' the Ethiope demanded. 'And answer fast.'

'Bernaccia.' Tugen hid his fear.

'Why?'

'I want revenge on the Kaldi,' Tugen said. He suddenly felt quite small. He was a boy, not yet a man, no matter how many times he told himself otherwise. Looking around at the other men, he noticed that most of them were also dark-skinned. He had never seen the like. 'I can fight,' he said. And they laughed. All but the man in front of him, the leader. He looked down at Tugen with a stern but unthreatening face and held up his hand to silence his men.

'You want to kill Picts, eh, boy?'

Tugen nodded, suddenly wishing he was back on Dere Street or in some warm, dry house in Eborakon with Emrys and Rozena. The man's face opened into a broad smile, and he held out a hand to help Tugen up.

'Then you've come to the right fucking place, right, men?'

And Tugen rose to his feet to the cheering of a dozen Ethiopes, his momentary fears allayed. This was a new beginning. This was how he would become a man, how he would fight the painted people. And the big African, who later introduced himself as Kiros, pushed open the door to the great hall, and the orange of firelight instantly warmed the hard contours of his face. Tugen peered inside as the men filed in and saw women and a few children sitting in circles around small fires, all looking back at him. He felt Kiros' hand on his shoulder.

'Welcome to Hadrian's Hell.'

II

MALEDICTUM

'Adieu, farewell, earth's bliss;
This world uncertain is;
Fond are life's lustful joys;
Death proves them all but toys;
None from his darts can fly;
I am sick, I must die.'

(Thomas Nashe)

Ludus

Viction had seen the plague before. When he was a boy. He had been twelve when the legions had packed up and left Eboracum, and disease had ripped through the city a year before that, claiming his mother amongst its victims. He hadn't been allowed to see her from the moment she had showed signs of the illness. His father had cloistered him away with some of the gladiators in the ludus–strong men who simply refused to be sick–and tended to his wife. When she died, the soldiers came. That's what their duty was reduced to. Disposing of the corpses. And Viction had watched them carry her, wrapped in a shroud, from the place he had known as home. It was dawn; he remembered. Her arm had fallen loose from the pale fabric, blackened dead flesh that appeared like a piece of burnt meat in the pale light before the sun came up.

The ludus moved from the city after that, but the legions were already heading for the boats. Rome was under attack, they said, and Britannia was to be left to its own devices. Viction's father found himself in the empty ludus. His Dominus had offered to take him back to Rome, but there was nothing there for him. He elected to remain. And in the absence of gladiators or slaves of any kind, he had trained Viction. There was always a need for prowess in combat, for tactical and physical and mental strength, whether in the arena or on some battlefield. Viction had been an excellent student, devouring every piece of wisdom his father had to offer, pushing himself to the extremes of fitness and mastering every kind of weapon he could, driven by anger. He was angry at being abandoned.

By Rome. And by his mother.

The sun's first rays caught the thin cord of the snare, and it glistened. He saw it from several paces away, and he knew by the angle of the reflection that he had caught something. It was a rabbit, a young buck, still warm. It would feed them all at a push. The newcomers needed a good meal.

He had snuck out while they all slept, huddled together in the empty bath. There was a chill in the air, and his breath had clouded in front of him as he went about his rounds. The ground would go hard soon, and food would become harder to come by. He cut the rabbit free from the snare and stuffed it into the sack that hung on his belt before kneeling and carefully setting the trap again. At least while vegetables still grew in the small plot near the ludus, the rabbits would come.

* * *

The weapons were laid out in front of him. Viction told him their names. There was a huge, forked spear called a fascina, a coarse net that was weighted with lead balls called an iaculum, spears and javelins, shields and daggers. They all had names. And there were swords; the long-bladed spatha, and the sleek curved sica that Viction had carried when Emrys first saw him. There were the wooden training swords as well, but Emrys wasn't interested in them.

'This is a pilum.' Viction held up a long spear. 'It needs a good throwing arm. The lancea is a better start.' He indicated a smaller weapon, a bit like the javelin Tugen had taken from the dead Kaldi warrior.

Emrys picked up a broad dagger, a pugio apparently, and ran his fingers over the cold steel. Was Tugen even still alive? He wondered how his village would have fared had Viction been there to defend it. The man was old, sure, but his torso still rippled, and his arms bulged with muscles Emrys had never seen before. His mind drifted as he recalled the charred corpses of his friends and family, and the pugio bit into his thumb, drawing blood.

'Careful!' Viction snatched the dagger away from him. Emrys lifted his thumb to his mouth, tasting the bud of dark red that blossomed there. It was metallic, but sweet as well. 'You think I don't keep these blades sharp? I could take a man's heart out through his scale mail with this.' He wiped the dark stain from the steel with a rag, more concerned with the dagger than he was with Emrys' thumb.

'Why are you so afraid of this plague?' Emrys asked, pulling his thumb free from his lips with a smack.

'Why do you think?' Viction grumbled back at him. 'Though I suppose you've never heard of anything like it?'

Emrys shook his head.

'I've only known it once before. It's an enemy you can't see. That's the worst of it. You can't fight it or kill it. And it doesn't care who you are. If you get it, you're fucked.' He went on to tell Emrys about how on the coast they had piled bodies onto boats and cast them out to sea, unable to bury any more. And the bodies had washed up on the beaches, bloated, black and stinking. And great pyres had been built, and the stench had been unbearable. People back then had believed in a single god, but they had also believed in demons.

'What's a demon?' Emrys asked.

'I don't know,' Viction said, 'but it might have just been an angry god. I don't understand these things. People said they saw the demon in their dreams, and the next day they were sick. And once you're sick—' Viction paused, looking away, pained.

'Well, I'm glad we came here before we went to Eborakon.' Emrys looked at his thumb. The bead of blood was smaller now, and the sting had gone. 'Can you teach me how to fight?'

Viction smiled. 'That I can do,' he said.

* * *

Rozena watched Emrys sparring with Viction. She had smirked to herself when he'd sulked about having to use the wooden training swords, knowing how he treasured the blade that he had pulled almost ceremoniously from the dead Kaldi. He was an impatient learner, prone to becoming easily frustrated at his own failures. At one point, he threw what he referred to as a 'silly stick' into the dust and turned his back on Viction. The old man gave him a well-deserved rap on the rump with his own stick and cajoled him into resuming the lesson. It didn't seem that difficult, wielding a stick.

Carina had come and sat next to Rozena, where she sat against the trunk of a gnarled old tree that hadn't grown very high.

'It's an olive tree,' Carina told her, and then smiled. 'It's nice to have a friend.' Rozena got the distinct impression that Carina didn't really know anyone her own age, that she'd lived her life among these crumbling walls with their seasoned creepers that were slowly pulling the villa apart at its seams. She felt sorry for her, and smiled back, happy to make a new friend herself, and then felt a pang in her heart when she saw how Carina watched Emrys.

Carina was pretty; prettier than her. She could admit that, if only to herself. They were the same age, give or take, but Carina was showing more of her imminent womanhood. Rozena looked at her mouth, her lips parted and stuck in a smile as she watched Emrys being schooled by her father.

'He's doing well,' Carina said, turning to Rozena gleefully. Rozena nodded hurriedly, hoping Carina hadn't noticed how she'd been looking at her rather than the fight. 'I think he'll make a fine warrior.'

'He fought a bear.' Rozena instantly regretted bragging to her new friend, especially since she quickly realised that it could only fuel her regard for him.

'Really?' Carina's eyes widened. 'I've never even seen a bear.'

'Nor have I.' Rozena hoped that would be the end of the matter.

'What happened?'

'I don't really know. I wasn't there. And he hasn't told me much about it. But the scar on his cheek—'

'I'll have to ask him.'

Rozena grimaced. And at that point Emrys bound over towards them, grinning. His eyes gleamed golden and looked at Rozena. Not Carina.

'Did you see? I found the gap.'

Rozena nodded, smiling back at him. She had no idea what he was talking about, only that he was talking to her. Just to her. Beside her, Carina clapped her hands together and gave a little squeal, enough to tempt a glance from Emrys.

Earlier in the day, after Viction had triumphantly dropped the dead rabbit at Krestell's feet, Rozena and Carina went to gather vegetables for the pot. Rozena had been happy with that, being already a little squeamish at the thought of Krestell's sharp little knife opening the unfortunate animal's pelt and spilling its innards. They went out behind the villa into the dappled shade and a plot of land where Krestell had planted all manner of foods. Rozena knew by sight the turnips and the cabbages and even the onions, but Carina showed her leeks, shallots, radishes and celery, and other plants she didn't even know existed.

'I've never seen so many different things you can eat.'

'We have fruit trees as well,' Carina promised her, then showed her the figs, the mulberries, the damsons, and the plums. 'And grapes. We make our own wine. I've had some, watered down.' They picked a plum each and Rozena bit down into its soft flesh and didn't think she'd eaten anything so delicious in all her life.

The wall of the villa, lined with climbing plants that spread like green veins over its mottled surface, provided a shadier spot for a few smaller plants. Carina pointed out the parsley, the borage, chervil, mint, thyme, rosemary, and sage. She dug up a white bulbous thing she called garlic and cut several leaves from the plants she had just pointed out, even though Rozena had already forgotten most of their names. Half listening, she was wondering why she was on her knees among the plants while Emrys was learning to fight. Hadn't it been a woman that had felled the bear and spared him? She wanted to know why the Kaldi were so different that their women fought alongside the men. More than that, she wanted to be next to Emrys, sword in hand, and ready to kill or be killed. Not brushing the dirt from roots.

All they gathered had gone into Krestell's pot. Rozena had been happy to see the rabbit all but submerged in its bubbling stock already, furless, and barely recognisable. Krestell added a handful of fresh leaves, and cut in the turnip, radish, leeks, and the rest.

While the stew simmered for the afternoon, Rozena had slipped away to see what Emrys was doing, and found him with a wooden sword in hand, desperate to learn. He was so serious. So earnest. She knew him well enough though to know that he could soften at a moment's notice, and she loved that sudden smile of his that came from nowhere and the way he gave a little squeeze with his arms when he hugged her like it was their little secret and theirs alone.

And then Carina smiled at him. Her hands were clasped together, and her lips were still parted. An annoying curl of hair fell across her eye, and she swatted it away. She was pretty, sure, but it was Rozena that Emrys smiled at. For now.

'Let's eat,' Krestell called as she emerged from the villa, and Viction put the swords back in the rack and grinned at his wife.

'Rabbit stew,' he beamed.

Emrys held out a hand to Rozena and pulled her gently to her feet with that grin of his, warming her instantly.

'I'm glad we're here and not in Eborakon,' he whispered.

And she remembered the columns of smoke. They burn the bodies. That's what Krestell had told her. They can't bury them all. They pile them up and set fire to them. And she thought of her father, spared the Kaldi fire and certainly free from plague.

But dead all the same.

Pestilence

Viroconium was one of the few towns in the land that was still occupied. It clung to what little Imperial ethos had trickled down the generation since the Romans had gone. That was largely down to Vitalinus' father, Lucius Vitalis. He saw himself as a kind of caretaker overseeing this little pocket of Rome until, as he believed, the legions would return and bring back with them all the civilisation that had deserted with them; the baths, the forum, the markets, the trade, the coins. Coins were nothing now. Vitalinus had seen them, holes bored through the precious metal, hanging on cords around the necks of people who had no concept of their previous value. They were now little more than tarnished trinkets.

Lucius was already old and had given Vitalinus the charge of the soldiers. He had, despite derision from his father, taken no time in building a hill fort on The Wrekin. It was arrogant of the Romans not to take advantage of such an obvious strategic position. They had barracked their legions on the flat land, and the town had grown up around them. And yet this unnaturally steep hill towered over them. He didn't have the numbers the Romans had, but still had several hundred reasonably trained fighting men that would follow his every command. With the Romans gone, and threat from the north and the west, it made perfect sense to him that an almost impenetrable fortress would not only be a formidable deterrent to would-be raiders but also, in the worst case, a perfect fall-back position.

The Wrekin was always a welcome sight when, like now, he returned home. Rounding its broad circumference, he got his first sight of

Viroconium. The fields leading to it were given to farmland, and much of the crop had already been harvested, but there was a conspicuous absence of people.

'Where is everyone?' He asked Selwyn, who rode beside him. He was rewarded with a frown and a shrug, so looked to his other side, to Ossian. The druid shifted in his saddle, scowling back at him. There was an unnerving quiet in the air that nobody wanted to break by talking. Vitalinus looked behind him at the few men that accompanied him, but they were tired from the journey and offered nothing in return. They were probably keen to get up the hill to their billets and a well-deserved rest, but for now would escort him to his family home in the town.

Nearer the town gate, a woman's crying hung on the wind, but little else. A weary sentry saw them coming from a distance away and opened the gate, standing back, grey-faced and downcast, as Vitalinus led his men into the town.

'You there,' Vitalinus called out to him. 'What ails the town?' Something wasn't right. It didn't take a druid to see that. The guard looked at him, a fear behind his eyes clouding his duty.

'Pestilence, King Vitalinus,' he muttered. 'Pestilence is among us.'

'Selwyn.' Vitalinus stopped suddenly, and they all stopped with him. 'Take the men back to the fort immediately and await my command. Ossian, will you stay with me?'

The sentry shrunk back, ashen. Selwyn spurred his horse around with a nod to his master and led the others away from the town. Two things bothered Vitalinus. The first was obvious to anyone. Pestilence. Some disease had Viroconium in its grip. But second, the sentry had called him 'King.'

* * *

Lucius had died only a few days after sending his son to Dumnonia. It wasn't the plague. That came later. He was old, and Sevira wasn't one bit surprised when he didn't shuffle into the garden one morning as he usually did, grumbling about who knows what. He had gone to sleep the night before, and mercifully slipped away in his bed. *If only we could all be that fortunate*, she had thought.

She stood at the foot of his bed, looking at him for a while. He was grey and cold. He had never liked her, and she hadn't much cared for him. She didn't suppose her husband would mourn him for long, either. Vitalinus had little in common with his father and was far too focussed on his own rise to power to see this as anything other than a step forward.

Pasha slid into the bedchamber beside her and took her hand, jolting her from her daydreams. Sevira looked at her daughter and smiled thinly.

'Come,' she whispered. 'I don't want Catigern to see his grandfather here. Not like this.' Her youngest boy was nearly a man at thirteen years old. But he was a sensitive one and would take the news better from his mother than by seeing with his own eyes.

Only a day after Lucius had been laid to rest, the first signs of the plague appeared. It fell to Sevira, as wife of the heir apparent, to offer what leadership she could. One of the merchants came begging her to issue a decree closing the market. Apparently, some trader fresh from Londinium had fallen ill in a local tavern after vomiting blood onto the whore he'd taken a shine to after a particularly lucrative day. The poor woman had emptied the bar with her screams and grisly visage, while her unfortunate client lay unconscious in her bed. There he lay, never to reawaken. And there they found him, bare chested, on sheets drenched in blood and sweat and pus, with oozing dark sores under his arms, his breathing shallow for a while before it stopped altogether. His face was still contorted in a horrible grimace, the very picture of agony. The merchant had not been shy with the details.

Within a few days, half the traders, the patrons of the tavern, their families, and their friends and friends' families were burning with fever, arid throats rasping with unquenchable thirst and their faces and bodies mottled and slick with sweat. Sevira ordered the market to close. And the tavern. And the shops. The streets were emptied and quiet, but for the wailing of those whose loved ones were succumbing to the illness. Sevira gathered Pasha and Catigern to her side and bolted her doors and begged whatever gods would listen to see that her husband be detained longer in Dumnonia than she feared he might be.

He wasn't.

* * *

It was practically a palace. Ossian wasn't sure what claim Lucius had felt he had to assume leadership of the region, but he had certainly picked out the finest of Roman buildings to govern from. Lucius was dead. That much both he and surely Vitalinus had guessed. They hadn't spoken as they'd led their horses through the empty streets and into the courtyard. No servants had greeted them. A fine-looking woman in a white gown had run barefoot into the dusty quad. Her hair was long but pulled back from her face, a single streak of grey running down one side of her head and falling with the darker hair down her back.

'Sevira.' Vitalinus dropped his rein and quickened his pace towards her. She wrapped her arms around his neck and squeezed. They embraced for several seconds before Vitalinus pulled away and mumbled an introduction. 'This is Ossian. Ossian, this is my wife, Sevira.'

The druid tethered both horses to a post and nodded his head respectfully.

'There is much to tell you.' Sevira still clung to her husband's hands with both of hers, arms outstretched between them.

'Father?'

'He died in his sleep. Before—'

'Before the plague.'

'You reign here now.'

Ossian knew Vitalinus was intent on power. He wouldn't have followed him back here if he hadn't thought him ambitious enough to lead his people to a better future, but he was a little surprised at the coolness with which his new master accepted not only his untimely rise but also the calamity that faced the town. A great shadow hung over Viroconium, and Ossian wasn't sure anyone there knew quite how devastating that shadow might become.

'Come, you must both be hungry.' Sevira looked at Ossian for the first time, a thin smile of welcome, cordial for now, flashing across her face.

'I, for one, am starving,' agreed Ossian.

'Father!' A tall and handsome boy emerged from the house. Ossian thought that a year or two ago, this boy might have run into his father's arms with the untainted enthusiasm of youth. Now, on the cusp of manhood, his greeting was measured, even cautious.

'Catigern. Have you grown?' Vitalinus patronised him.

'Hardly.'

Vitalinus looked beyond his son, into the shadows of the palace interior. 'Pasha?'

'She's around somewhere,' Sevira offered.

'Then let's eat. I will require your counsel, Ossian.' Vitalinus took his wife's hand and headed inside.

'Who are you?' the boy asked.

'My name is Ossian.'

'Do you know magic?'

'Magic is just a word we give to things we don't understand,' Ossian told him, briefly taken aback by the directness of the question.

'But you do understand, don't you?'

'Some things.'

Catigern nodded thoughtfully before following his parents inside, and the quad fell quiet again. Ossian looked at the horses pulling hay from a trough, their dark eyes regarding him back. It might be that his understanding of things was going to be roundly tested in the coming weeks.

From without the walls, another wail floated up into the still air. Another husband or father or brother had fallen to the disease, and there was every chance that whoever felt this loss so deeply and vocally would soon join their loved one in the next world. Ossian briefly pondered that he might have fared better remaining in Dumnonia but pushed the thought from his mind. Any great change, any great decision, was bound to be met with challenge. His loyalty was to building Albion, and if this was how the foundation stones were to be lain, upon the ashes and bones of plague pits, amid the wails of the Britons who would survive, then let it be so.

* * *

For a moment, just after his climax, with arms rigid on either side of his wife and his cock still inside her, Vitalinus revelled in his new power. 'King,' the sentry had called him. Sevira had clearly already spoken to the people and told them how he was to be addressed. His father hadn't taken the title, convinced as he was that such a word would not sit well with the Romans when they returned. But they weren't coming back. And if they did, let them deal with a king rather than some scraping magistrate. Let them make humble requests rather than arrogant demands.

He pulled himself free and stood up. While Sevira covered her own nudity, he still basked in his own manliness and poured himself a cup of wine. And why shouldn't he? He was king now. King of a land beset by plague, perhaps, but he had to start somewhere. He had brilliantly deposed Custennin and secured the unknowing support of all Dumnonia, and the other regions would fall either that way or another. He was confident already in the support of Dunvallo in Bernaccia. Triffyn in Dyfed was loyal, and Cunedda in the north would be persuaded, especially if the old bastard Ceneu fell into line. If now wasn't the time to stand, wine in hand, with cock jutting out at right angles to his body, then when was? He cut a fig in two and shoved half into his mouth, looking over at his wife.

'You should have seen his face. He thought he had the better of me.'

'And he may have done, if this new druid friend of yours hadn't had a hand in it.'

'That just made it easier.' Vitalinus took a long draught of wine and set about pouring another. 'How could anyone serve such a man?'

'A deluded fool that confused his daughter with his dead wife?' Sevira teased her husband.

'A sack of shit that didn't have any idea how to rule his people. He would have sat up there in his bed, Lamorna cowering at his feet, while his people were slaughtered and enslaved.' Vitalinus felt the flush of the wine now. He leant heavily on the table. He was tired.

'Come to bed,' Sevira asked quietly. 'You've had a long day, and there is much to do tomorrow.'

'The wife wants more,' Vitalinus slurred impishly. 'How is it, being queen?'

'It sits well,' Sevira smirked, pulling the furs down a little to show the flushed curve of her breasts. Vitalinus felt his cock surge again, pointing the way back to bed.

And then Catigern burst into the chamber.

'Mother,' he called out with a quivering voice.

Vitalinus turned on him angrily. 'What is this?' he demanded, not even trying to hide himself.

'It's Pasha,' his son told him, looking at the floor.

Vitalinus glanced at Sevira. She was already half out of bed, pulling a gown towards her.

'What of her?'

'She is not well,' the boy admitted.

And Sevira let out a single dry sob as she flew from the room.

Consummation

Vortimer had been with other women. Only a couple, and they had been of lower birth, happy to satisfy his needs. But he could have had plenty more, perhaps even chosen a wife. His father had never been keen on the idea, and now he knew why. He had waited until he could use his son as a pawn in his own hunt for power. It was to be expected and, to be fair, the match was not an unpleasant one. Lamorna was, despite her youth, as feisty as many women ten years her senior, and more than agreeable to the eye. There were prettier women in Viroconium, but Vortimer wasn't that interested in aesthetics. A marriage should be more about companionship. If he wanted beauty, it was usually there for the taking.

Their wedding had been a muted affair. The usual binding ceremony had been little more than a formality, and their actual union was celebrated by a feast that was more for the entertainment of others than anything profound between man and wife. He had looked into her eyes as their hands were gently ribboned together and felt as if he had seen inside her. Her eyes betrayed her as warm and caring, devoted even, yet also introspectively thoughtful and self-aware. But without conceit. He didn't see anything there that suggested underhandedness. She would be vocal; of that, he had no doubt. She had already practically admitted to being happy at the death of her father and felt no shame in the sentiment. But there was no malice. She looked back at him in silent commitment, content with her side of the bargain, and smiled. And in that smile, he saw a shadow, a flicker of something that haunted her. For a moment, he wondered if it was more than a reflection of what had been. He felt, inexplicably, that it was a portent of things to come. And so, he resolved to love her.

Unlike many other men might have, he didn't force himself upon her brutishly that night, fuelled by wine and ale and desire. She had chattered and giggled with him as they feasted, and in bed had curled into him like a child and appeared desirous of nothing more than warmth and closeness. He lay awake listening to her soft breathing, gazing at a strand of hair that lay across her chest, rising and falling in the moonlight.

Little changed for a dozen days. Vortimer had wondered if perhaps he should be more forceful. After all, his father was probably expecting some kind of continuation of the bloodline, and that didn't come about from watching someone sleep. So, he wooed her a little, told her she was beautiful, even caught that lock of hair one evening when they were talking and rubbed it between his finger and thumb while smiling dumbly at her. She just leant forward and kissed him softly on the lips, then giggled. Perhaps she was just too young.

In the days he was busy with bolstering the defences of Dumnonia. He had taken his father's lead and set up a network of beacon fires on suitable headlands and clifftops. Any Hibernian incursion on the coast was quickly announced to a waiting cohort of fighting men. Twice they had already repelled the raiders, and with only a couple of casualties.

One evening, after leading a defensive strike himself, he reclined on the furs in Custennin's old chamber, nursing a slight wound to his abdomen. He had been slow in his riposte, and a thrusting sword had glanced off his side. It was nothing that a wash and a clean cloth wouldn't hide, but still he felt angry at his own failing.

'Be still.' Lamorna wound a length of material around his side and stomach. He looked at her, frustrated.

'I don't know what happened,' he growled. 'I saw it coming. I was just slow.'

'You were scratched. And how many Hibernians lie dead on the beach?'

'A dozen or more.'

'And how many Dumnonians didn't die because of you?'

Vortimer grunted. Something else was bothering him. That treacherous lock of hair, with that perfect curl in it, falling over her face, over her breasts. He looked past the hair, at her curves.

'Is there wine?' He knew full well there was. And Lamorna looked at him. She looked into him. And she smiled.

'You don't need wine,' she murmured, standing up straight. She wriggled out of her dress and was naked. 'I am yours, you know. You can have me whenever you want.'

Given the past two weeks, he wasn't sure if she really meant it. But the invitation seemed genuine in the moment. He raised his hands and held her breasts, his thumbs moving across both proud nipples. He had the sense that finally it was her that wanted him, which was fine because he wanted her too. Twisting his body, he moved to pull her down beside him so he could mount her, but pain shot through his side. She just smiled and, with a slight shake of the head, straddled him in a single smooth motion.

'And you are mine,' she whispered as she freed his manhood. He looked up at her, surprised, his head suddenly fogged by desire. 'Shall we consummate this marriage, Lord Vortimer?'

And she lowered herself onto him.

* * *

The frost lay heavy in the morning. Autumn was on the turn. Lamorna, as so many times before, had crept from the bed in her father's old chamber and wrapped herself warmly and sought the grey light of day. Only this time, she was happy. Vortimer was a good man, and she was a good wife. He had only taken what she had given. That, she resolved, was how it was going to be.

She climbed the ladder to the ramparts. The rungs were white with frost and hurt her fingers a little, but she didn't mind. A couple of fires smouldered in the courtyard below, with a few of the men huddled in their makeshift shelters, slumbering still. The rampart planks were slippery, so she steadied herself with a hand on the beams that topped the wooden walls. The sun wasn't visible yet, but a weak glow defined the crags of the moors to the east. To her right, a solitary figure stood in gloomy silhouette.

It wasn't Erbin. She always half expected to see him up here, though his morning visits had fallen off since their father had died. She supposed he no longer needed the escape this spot offered in quite the same way. Perhaps she didn't either, but waking naked beside Vortimer had forced the habit in her.

'Hello,' she called, her breath fogging. The figure half turned towards her. It was Joceline. Her head was wrapped in the blanket that she had pinned tight around her. She nodded in reply, and Lamorna trod carefully towards her.

'Do you think the raids will stop now?' Joceline said quietly.

'I don't know.' Lamorna stood next to her, looking at what little of her face she could see in profile. Her eyes, puffy and red, looked out over the frosty landscape. 'Maybe. I wouldn't want to row across the sea at this time of year.'

'That's what I thought.' Joceline choked on her words.

Lamorna knew the story. She had heard it all from Vortimer. The Hibernians had taken this woman's only son. She had feared him dead, but his body had not been found, and everyone knew slaves were as valuable, if not more so, than any riches that could be plundered.

'What do you suppose they do with their slaves?'

Lamorna studied Joceline. She was a striking woman, with sharp cheekbones and piercing grey eyes that, in this light, were impossibly pale. 'I don't know,' Lamorna offered, 'but if they don't kill them, I suppose they are more valuable alive, uninjured.'

'Yes, I suppose you're right. Why would they hurt him if they need him to work the fields or build boats?' Joceline turned away again.

Lamorna lifted an arm and reached around Joceline, pulling her closer.

'He was meant for better things,' Joceline said quietly.

'Then I'm sure that's what he will do.'

A footfall on the ramparts alerted Lamorna to Erbin's presence. It couldn't be anyone else, and she didn't really care what had driven him to seek solace up here, but he wasn't welcome this morning. She turned her head and scowled at him, mouthing at him to leave them alone. He just looked back at her, his idiot eyes wide with the usual half measure of understanding, before doing as he was told.

'Thank you.' Joceline relaxed, tilting her head towards Lamorna's shoulder. 'You're very kind.'

The first shimmer of redness in the east kissed the cold stones of the tor in the distance as the sun began to claw its way up into the sky, and Lamorna felt a warmth inside.

It was a new day.

* * *

If Jac had been disappointed at not being in the first fight with the Hibernians, when Custennin fell, his fortune had certainly changed since. He'd barely known the dizzying fury and fatigue of battle before he'd come to Dumnonia, and for a while it felt like he was to be denied that experience. He'd helped bury the dead, and frozen his balls off on a clifftop, spotted the enemy and near killed his horse riding back to the fort to carry the news. And he'd been told to stay put, presumably on account of having kept watch all night. And Custennin had been slain, and everything had changed.

He felt he'd bonded with Lord Vortimer, as he now was, that day among the dead fishermen and their wives, when the stench of death had proved too much for him. Maybe he had. The next time the Hibernians came, he had been among the garrison, primed with sword already in hand and ready to ride out in the dawn light.

He'd near shit himself when he found himself in the fray, his ears ringing with the clash of steel. The sound and smell of men fighting for their lives caused his heart to jump in his chest like a caged bear, and he'd gripped the hilt of his sword tighter than he knew he should. *Relax*, a voice had told him. Vortimer stood beside him, legs firmly planted, and sword raised. Jac saw the calmness in his new master and, despite every sensible fibre in his body screaming at him that there was nothing relaxing about the twenty burly red-faced warriors bearing down on them, he shut out every noise and every smell. His grip loosened and his feet, which moments before had felt like they were bound in lead boots, felt spry and airy.

He didn't really remember the details of that first fight, although snapshots of it played in slow motion in his head. An axe blade flew at him, inches from his face as he effortlessly swayed out of its path. His sword sliced a man's arm from his body. A spray of hot blood hit his face. A shield slammed into his shoulder, sending him to the sand. And he was up again, like a cat, lashing out with deadly accuracy. Four Hibernians had fallen to his blade during that first battle.

Vortimer had been impressed by his performance. The second battle was similar. Three more dead Hibernians, and nothing more than a round purpling bruise on his upper arm, where a now dead man's wayward attack had hit him with the pommel of his sword rather than the edge. All Jac's youthful dreams of being a force to be reckoned with in battle were coming to pass. So Vortimer had singled him out.

'You're handy with a blade,' he told him. 'And you're no fool, either. My father told me that everything a man can become is there in his eyes, if you look for it. You're wasted out on the beacons, Jac. I want you to take charge of the garrison. You answer only to me now.'

Most of the men, the Cornovian men at least, were happy with the decision. And the Cornovian men now easily formed the majority, at least at the fort. Jac discovered he was well liked amongst them. And why shouldn't he be? He felt a little embarrassed at being rewarded in such a way after only a couple of battles, but the more seasoned warriors just smiled and told him that being in charge wasn't all it was cracked up to be, anyway.

The imminent arrival of winter meant that fewer raids were expected for a while. Jac's newfound responsibility, a reward that had made him quietly swell with pride to begin with, soon became a less exciting prospect. He diligently hunkered down with the men of the garrison and maintained a careful command of the guards at the gates. The only actual difference was that he had to report directly to Vortimer rather than indulge in wine and storytelling and song like the other men.

It did, however, give a man of intelligence like him a bit more insight into the lives of Vortimer, Lamorna, and Erbin. He began to understand the mechanics of power. Erbin was notionally his father's heir; that much was public knowledge. But everyone knew the boy was, to be kind, a dreamer. He was a simpleton. He disappeared on a whim for hours on end, only to return with blustering ideas of what they should do to bolster the defences or notions cobbled together from fragments of conversations he had clearly heard from Vortimer. It was Vortimer who commanded in Dumnonia now. His father had left him there with that intent, and nothing Erbin could do or say would change the practical effect of that.

But Lamorna, she was different. She carried herself with a quiet confidence that Jac imagined could influence even Vortimer. She was young, younger than Jac, but more than a match for her new husband. He wondered when Erbin would realise that his sister, not him, perhaps not even Vortimer, ruled Dumnonia.

'You've been staring at them for ages,' a voice beside him piped up. Maddock, a gruff old warrior, grinned at him knowingly. 'No good will come of it, but it's nothing a good tug won't cure.'

Lamorna was standing above them on the ramparts, her arm around Joceline. All Jac could see of her was her hair, gloriously unruly, draped down her back and all the way to her waist. He was staring, waiting for a glimpse of her face. Waiting, perhaps, for her to see him too.

The Cold Ground

The birds were deafening. And it wasn't just the harsh caws of the corvids, but the full mellifluous cantata of blackbirds and thrushes and who knew what else, chaotically punctuated by the frantic clicking of starlings. Ossian's head spun as he rested in the walled gardens of Vitalinus' villa. A little sunlight glimmered through the foliage atop the walls, but he didn't see it. He sat on his haunches with his head in his hands. He hadn't slept.

Vitalinus had come to him the night before, with Sevira's voice echoing behind him, begging for his help. Pasha had fallen victim to the plague.

'If anyone can help her, you can.'

Ossian had never seen this illness before, though he had heard of it. Older, wiser men than he had told him about a previous outbreak, but he had been young then and less inclined to take note of what was not right in front of his eyes. Yet, a lifetime of devotion to the gods and careful study of botany and the medicinal properties of nature's generous gifts perhaps made him the best qualified to lend aid to his master's daughter.

Before Vitalinus had burst into his chamber, he was already considering the possibility that town life was not for him. The obvious affliction suffered by this town was colouring his opinion, but he wondered if a man such as he was really meant for a life among so many people. Even if they weren't dying in their droves.

The smell. Gods, the smell. Fortunately for him, he had in a pouch at his side a ready mix of herbs, powders and ointments for all occasions. Among them was a small sprig of meadowsweet. He had cupped it in his hands and held it to his nose as he rode through the stinking streets.

They came to Pasha's bedside, and there was already a stench in the room. She was clearly burning up. The heady smell of sweat and disease already hung in the air, even though her symptoms were not yet advanced. Ossian pinched the bouquet in his pocket and rubbed some of the sweet smell on his septum.

'It is the same as they have out there, isn't it?' Sevira sat holding her sleeping daughter's hand in hers.

'More than likely,' Ossian admitted.

Vitalinus hung nervously over his shoulder. 'Save her. Please.'

Ossian shuffled closer, trying to hide his own anxiousness.

'You should keep away from her,' he advised. 'And wash your hands immediately.'

'Why?'

'It is a sickness. It passes from person to person. As easily as a greeting.'

Sevira reluctantly let go of Pasha's hand, and backed, crying, into the corner.

'Please,' Ossian said quietly, 'leave us. There is nothing you can do here but, with your permission, I must examine her.'

'No,' Vitalinus barked.

'Let him do what he must.'

Ossian smiled reassuringly to Sevira, who then took her husband's reluctant hand and led him away.

He had tended to the sick before and knew how to relieve a fever, knew how to bleed, how to make salves that would turn bad flesh good again, and how to set a bone in a splint and make a limb almost useable again. He hadn't even met Pasha before now; he realised as he studied her pale sweat-drenched face and wondered how she talked and smiled and laughed. She had her mother's looks, a swathe of almost black hair matted to her forehead, and thick dark eyebrows that arched regally over her now closed eyes.

He remembered the teachings of his mentor, and thought to open her shirt, lifting her leaden arm from the bed. She murmured in her sleep. Sickness had an odour, he thought, trying to focus instead on the meadowsweet as he looked at her underarms. His mentor had told him that black lesions appeared there when the sickness had its victim in thrall. There were none. Not yet, at any rate. Just matted dark hair and more stench. He pulled her shirt closed again and resolved to work on the fever.

Those infernal birds, with their unrelenting joy and unbridled musicality. He lifted his head and looked at his palms. His hands were shaking. He spent hours beside Pasha, trying everything he knew to ease the fire that burned her from within. And for now, he had done all he could. She needed to rest, and so did he.

But those birds! Louder and more raucous than he'd ever heard. And it wasn't like he was used to the usual clamour of town life. He imagined their songs would be easily muted by the incessant chatter of merchants and shopkeepers, of people going about their business, even at this time of day. But there was none of that now. Viroconium was quiet. Families were cooped up together in their own houses, too terrified to venture out. Or too sick. The silence of fear would have been deafening if it weren't for the birds.

* * *

The Wrekin was a happier place to be. The fort stood high on the great hill, affording Selwyn a good view, on a clear day, of the gridded streets and byways of Viroconium. He'd barely taken his morning meal when a cry came from the guards that Vitalinus was at the gate. Even at the best of times, a visit from Vitalinus rarely entailed frivolity. But now, with news of the plague the only thing on anyone's lips, such an appearance was unlikely to be anything other than grim.

'Call the men together,' Vitalinus instructed as he strode, ashen faced, into the hall. And Selwyn had given the order.

The men congregated in the courtyard with just a ripple of disgruntlement. Vitalinus waited for their murmurs to stop. He eyed every man there, as if measuring their worth.

'Good to see you, Osric,' he singled out the Jute. That wasn't altogether surprising, as Osric had made his prowess in battle well known in Dumnonia. 'And you, Shabaka.' The Nobatian puffed his slender chest up at the mention, and beside him, Tsekani was happy just to share in his brother's recognition.

Selwyn watched Vitalinus from the corner of his eye, a little perturbed by a tone he had never heard from him before.

'You are probably all aware that Viroconium is under attack.' The slower of the men issued an audible intake of breath, as if being told they needed to take up arms. 'The plague is upon us,' Vitalinus continued, 'and make no mistake, this is an enemy, and we must fight. But you cannot combat it with your swords and your axes. What I need from you is something else.'

Selwyn stood motionless as he listened to Vitalinus diligently ask his fighting men to assume the grave duty (his poor choice of words!) of carefully disposing of the town's dead. The druid had told him that the sickness passed from person to person and the bodies of those already claimed needed to be taken from the town and buried immediately. And when the winter made the ground too hard, the dead would need to be burnt.

Osric puffed up his chest and Selwyn smiled inwardly, realising quickly that Vitalinus had singled him out for better reason than a mere recognition of his fighting abilities.

'Osric, I know you are scared,' Vitalinus said. 'We all are.'

'No. I'm not.' The Jute's chest sank again.

'We need to save our town. Our people. And who have I called on, relied on, time and time again to do this? You.'

Osric nodded. 'You can count on us,' he called out, and an unconvincing muttering of agreement bubbled around the ranks. Vitalinus held up his hand in sombre gratitude and turned to Selwyn.

'I must ask you to organise the men as you see fit, Selwyn.' He murmured. 'My daughter is stricken as well. I must be near her.'

'Pasha?'

'Yes.'

Not Pasha, please, not Pasha. Selwyn swallowed hard, offering his master a supportive smile, but his mind went to her. He hadn't seen her since they had returned from Dumnonia.

'Selwyn?' Vitalinus interrupted his thoughts.

'I shall see to it, my lord.'

Not Pasha. Please. Not Pasha. Selwyn saw her in his mind's eye, smiling up at him. Father will never know, she had promised. Father will never know.

* * *

Somewhere a wolf howled. A long, mournful cry that rose from something guttural into a plaintive glissando, then a pure note that hung in the darkness like a widow's wail. Pasha shivered uncontrollably. Her eyes felt plastered shut, lids heavy with some sticky substance, and the note, the howl, hung around her with a watery echo. That was it. She was under water. Dark, dark water. She wanted to cry out for help but was afraid the inky lake that must lie above her would rush in and fill her with its blackness. Where was everybody? Safe and dry on land, she hoped. They didn't need to be down here with her, in the cold and the dark. But no, it wasn't cold. It was unbearably hot now, and she could suddenly hear the furious bubbling of the water. She was being boiled alive, surely. Where was Selwyn? He promised he'd return. And her father? He surely would. He always did. His shadowed eyes came to her through the gloom, full of disapproval, and went again. He didn't love her. He didn't want to rescue her from this. Mother. *Where are you?* Pasha wanted to say, but still the liquid surrounded her. And Catigern, dear sweet brother, please don't come for me. Stay away. This place is horrible. Selwyn. Please. And she opened her mouth to call to him, but no water charged in. Just hot dry air, burning her throat as she choked on his name. And there was the howl again, closer, angry now, and behind it a low hard growl. And another. A whole pack of wolves surrounded her. She could feel their hot breath on her, the humid smacking of their slavering maws dripping onto her face.

She twisted her neck, trying to find a piece of cool air, a place away from the invisible teeth that promised only to tear the flesh from her cheeks. As her nose filled with the odour of rotten flesh that hung like bloody ribbons from the monstrous jaws that surrounded her, she scrunched her eyes even more tightly closed.

And she tried to scream, but her mouth just filled with sand.

* * *

She was getting worse. Vitalinus stood, backed into the corner of the room, listening to his daughter murmuring deliriously about wolves, about water. Her dry mouth clicked and smacked, and Ossian squeezed some cold water from a cloth onto her cracked lips.

'I don't need to be afraid of wolves,' Vitalinus muttered, almost to himself. 'That's what you told me.'

'Don't heed what the sickness makes her speak.'

'Is she going to die?' Vitalinus had ridden out of the town that morning, where pits filled with corpses lined the route to The Wrekin. Great pyres stood waiting for the next arrivals, as the frost hadn't lifted from the day before. He could not bear to think of his Pasha consumed by their flames. And it would break Sevira.

Ossian backed slowly away from the bed. He turned to Vitalinus with a face like stone and said nothing. Earlier he had showed Vitalinus the horrid black pustules under her arms.

'She is,' Vitalinus whispered. 'I know it.'

'She may.' Ossian's face cracked into an unconvincing smile of encouragement, and Vitalinus felt the floor give way beneath him. He slid down the wall weakly.

'It's my doing.'

'No. It is not.'

'Ossian, I slaughtered Custennin in cold blood. On a battlefield, yes, but we were supposed to be fighting together. And I gutted him like a fish on the beach and left him there for the gulls.'

'He was going to murder your son. You did what any father would do.'

Vitalinus looked at the druid. His words made sense. They always did, but then again it was Ossian's words that had led him to this, to all of this. It was Ossian that had told him of Custennin's plan. What if no such plan ever existed?

'If she dies—' Vitalinus let the threat hang in the air.

'Do not cling to your father's god,' Ossian spoke quickly. 'There is not one, there are many. And they are among us. They do not hold you responsible for your actions, nor punish your deeds. If you feel you did wrong, then it is your guilt that haunts you and nothing more. You are not to blame for Pasha being sick. And if she dies—'

'If she dies,' Vitalinus echoed in interruption. 'If she dies, you will quickly join her.'

The Stag in the Snow

The bow string hurt Tugen's fingers. He had been holding it for an age, one eye on Kiros' raised hand. The animal in front of him would feed them for weeks if he could fell it. A great stag, head bowed among the thin lichen that barely protruded from the first dusting of the winter's snow, stood fortuitously upwind of the silent hunting party.

Tugen had been given the honour of drawing first on the beast. It was the first time he had been allowed to join a hunting party, but clearly his weeks of weapons training with Kiros had paid dividends. Here he was with the opportunity to provide for those that had taken him in, sheltered him from the rain, and offered him a new family. They had given him the chance to prepare himself for his only actual goal in life now. Revenge.

The Kaldi raids, Kiros had told him, would ease off now that the season had changed. Nobody wanted to spend unnecessary energy in the harsh cold of the north, and if everyone had food in their bellies and wood for their fires, hostilities could cease. There had been a few skirmishes before the wind changed, but while Kiros had gone out with his men, Tugen had remained with the women and children within the walls of the fort. Seething, he had paced among the fires, startling the younger children with his frustrated mutterings.

The stag lifted his head a little, jaws still moving, but ears twitching. Kiros' eyes flashed next to Tugen, telling him to hold a second longer. The animal appeared to look directly at them, its antlers growing like trees from its head. For a moment, Tugen felt bad that the poor beast would have to die. He was beautiful, serene, a true king among the animals. A light wind whistled among the branches and a flurry of powdery snow drifted down over the animal's back. And Kiros' hand came down.

Tugen's arrow clattered into the trees just wide of the stag and that was all the warning it needed. It threw back its noble head and straightened its front legs, for a moment unsure in which direction escape lay, then spun away from the hunters. Tugen's heart sank. He had failed. Now they would all have to endure the cold that already permeated their bones for a while longer until new game could be found.

A second arrow flew past Tugen's ear, piercing the fleeing stag straight through its neck, and Kiros took off running towards the animal with his dagger out. His son, Negasi, only a few years older than Tugen, followed at a pace. He held a strung bow in his hand. Tugen, flushed with sudden anger at being shown up, ran as well.

The stag thrashed around on the freezing ground, spatters of blood peppering the snow with dark spots as it tried to regain its feet.

'Mind the hooves,' Kiros barked at his son, who was dangerously close to the twitching legs. Kiros, instead, was close to the animal's head, hands poised to grab its antlers. Tugen stood transfixed for a moment. The stag's dark eyes rolled back in its head and flecks of bloody foam flew from its open mouth, accompanying the hideous pained brays that erupted from its throat.

'Here, Tugen, bring your knife.' Kiros held onto an antler. 'We must end his misery.'

Tugen pulled his own dagger and took a step closer. This was not how he had imagined a hunt to be. The stag barked desperately and threw its head to the side, freeing itself from Kiros' grip, and then snapped its head back again, the sharp point of an antler sliding easily through the palm of one of the Ethiope's hands. Kiros roared in pain and pulled his injured hand free.

'Negasi!'

If the stag managed to get to his feet, any of them could suffer far worse than a hurt hand. Negasi plunged his dagger into the thick fur of the animal's flank, and it dropped back to the ground again with a cry. Kiros made no mistake this time. He gripped the antlers with both hands and looked at Tugen with urgency.

'Do it now.'

In that moment, Tugen wanted nothing more than to see the stag get up and run away. But he was to be a man, and that was not how men thought. He gripped his dagger and brought it to the beast's neck. He closed his eyes as the blade bit and felt the warm blood gush across his hand. And guilt, too, washed over him.

Tugen lagged behind the others as they made their way back to the fort. A couple of the men had strung the stag upside-down from two poles. Kiros, his injured hand now bound in blood-stained cloth as a stark reminder of Tugen's failure, had put his good hand on Tugen's shoulder in an attempt to comfort him.

'Nobody gets a kill on their first hunt, boy,' he had softly said, and Tugen hadn't entirely believed him. He wouldn't be surprised if Negasi had been an exception to that rule.

'I won't miss again,' he muttered, and let the rest of the party move forward ahead of him. He knew he was being hard on himself, but he didn't care. These Ethiopes and their families bore the hereditary toughness of a Roman legion. Fighting and hunting in the freezing north came as second nature to them, even if their ancestors would have probably taken some time to adapt to the weather here.

Only days before, Kiros had held court around the large fire in the centre of the hall, telling stories of the past. Everyone else had doubtless heard them before, so Tugen knew they were meant for his ears.

'There were five hundred of us here once,' he had beamed proudly, 'a small legion, by Roman standards, but a legion no less.' He went on to tell how this legion of black-skinned warriors had been mustered in the dusty heat of Mauretania and battle hardened in Germania, before being sent to repair and garrison the wall.

'Why send them all this way?' Tugen asked. 'Wasn't this the frontier?'

'It was. It still is. And it's brutal, boy. You think the Romans wanted their own kind to stand on this wall and face the spears and stones of the Picts?

'Are *we* a legion?' Tugen asked.

'No, boy. None of us owe anything to Rome any more.'

'So why do you remain?'

'We've known nothing else. When Rome pulled its men away from here, a few of them elected to stay behind. Those that had married and had families, like my father.'

Kiros' father had been a centurion with the legion and had fallen in love with a local girl. She had borne him Kiros, and he had asked to stay with his family when the others left. He was the last of the conscripted soldiers to have died here, three decades later, leaving Kiros in charge of this ragged garrison armed with rusting Roman swords and armour.

Tugen knew little of the Romans. He had once been to Eborakon with his father, or Eboracum as they had called it, and had marvelled at the buildings and streets and the rich colours of the varied spices in the markets. No man or woman there was as dark in the face as Kiros or his people. He would have imagined, with the little knowledge he had, that the Romans would have kept them as slaves rather than reward them with command of a century. He asked Kiros about this.

'It is true that to the Romans, the colour black is an omen of death. But show them a black man who can write and read Latin as well as they, and fight even better, and they will make him a centurion.'

'Write and read?' Tugen frowned.

'The written word. Kamali will teach you.' Kamali was Kiros' wife. Her skin was lighter than his, but her hair reminded Tugen of the jet he had seen on the market of Eborakon. Its blackness gleamed sometimes with an almost deep blue sheen.

'So will I,' offered their daughter, Zala, who had the same hair but lighter skin and beguilingly green eyes. She was a similar age to Tugen, perhaps a year older, and always smiled at him.

'I would like that.' Tugen nodded earnestly to the womenfolk. And Zala giggled.

* * *

Tugen looked up from his trudging feet. The others were no longer in sight. He stopped, listening, but no sound of them carried to him either. He had got used to being alone in the days it had taken him to walk to the wall from Dere Street, where he had last seen Rozena and Emrys, and it didn't bother him much anymore. The brook to his right would break free from the trees eventually and the fort would be there, within an easy walk. He sat for a moment against the broad trunk of a tree and pulled his knife from his boot.

The blade was still wet with the stag's blood. That bothered him. He shimmied down the bank to the trickling water and plunged the steel into the freezing stream, scrubbing at it with his stiff fingers. It reminded him of Emrys washing his bloodied cheek after the bear had come at them. Tugen had promised to save his friend's life that day, and still hoped that one day he would. That day had set his whole life on a different path. And for now, he was intent on proving his worth as a man so that he could kill the Kaldi who had left him an orphan with no home.

A terrible squeal shattered the quiet winter afternoon, and a great crashing sound came from close behind him. Still squatting beside the water, he spun on his heels and fell backwards, barely in time to see an enormous boar rushing headlong towards him. He didn't know what had spooked it, only that he was in its path. In a heartbeat he took in its dark eyes and vicious tusks and just about had time to wonder to himself if Kiros would ever find him out here, gored and bloodless in the ice and snow. And then the boar was upon him.

It sent him crashing back into the water when it hit him and thrashed around, tusks sawing the air in front of his face. Tugen's heart pounded harder. Was this how it would end? Stuck by a pig in the forest. And he thought of Zala. He wanted her to teach him to read. He wanted to see her smile again. Who cared if he wasn't man enough to take down a stag? Maybe he would never be strong or brave enough to avenge his family's deaths. He wondered if he could choose–if it were to be his last sight in this life–between seeing the look of surprise on that blue woman's face when he gutted her, or the bewitching emerald of Zala's eyes when she smiled at him.

The boar's thrashing slowed suddenly, and then it just stopped. Tugen froze, still pinned by its weight in the stream, and listened. The forest had fallen quiet again, and the boar was motionless. He pushed up, and the beast rolled sluggishly from him with a wet sound, freeing his arm. And it was then that he realised he still held his dagger. It was red again, with fresh blood.

It wasn't a bear or a stag, but a boar was formidable prey. He knew that much. And by the gods of the forest and the stream, he would carry the dead animal back to Kiros and lay it at his feet in triumph.

And he would be a man.

Woman at Arms

There was something unavoidably special about him, thought Carina. He carried himself a certain way, with a calmness. A smoothness almost. His every move was liquid, like a river. *That was it. He was like a river.* Not a wide, impassive, meandering one that emptied silently into the sea, nor the crashing white water of rapids that bubbled dangerously over jagged rocks. He was something in between, still carving a path through rocky terrain, but not necessarily a waterway that you would be too scared to wade into, or even to swim in, perhaps. Though she feared, and hoped, that there would be a testing current, a cooler and darker water beneath the surface, that flowed a little faster and threatened to carry the careless away.

And his eyes. Carina had never seen gold in her sheltered life, but there were yellowy renditions of it among the mosaics in the bath, and elsewhere in the ludus. His eyes outshone all of them. They reminded her of the yellow crown in a flame, or the tessellated manes of the lions depicted in the arena. They looked more at Rozena, but that could all change.

'Come for a walk,' she had asked him, though left little in her tone to offer him an alternative. The morning was chilly, so they had both wrapped themselves in furs and taken to the avenue of trees. She liked the fact that it was a straight line, and she wondered when they would have cause to turn, to see the dark marks their feet had left in the thick frost that still whited the ground, and walk the same line back to the villa.

'I like your scar,' she told him, trying to comment on anything other than his eyes.

'I'd sooner not have it.'

'I heard it was a bear that did it.' She chose not to reveal that it was Rozena who had told her, even though there could be no other source of that information. She hoped his thoughts didn't turn to her.

'It was,' he nodded. 'A great big one.' He couldn't resist lifting a finger to his cheek and tracing the outline of the wound.

'I would have been too scared to move.'

'I think I was.'

She almost wanted him to brag a little, to relate triumphantly how he had fought the beast and lived to tell the tale.

'I don't think it wanted to eat me or anything,' he said thoughtfully. 'I suppose we had just disturbed it.'

'And then the Picts killed it?'

He nodded in reply.

'Why didn't they kill you?'

'I don't know. Most of them didn't see me. Just one, a woman.'

'A woman?'

Emrys stopped walking, and looked at Carina, his eyes maybe a little moist. 'I don't think they're all that different from us,' he mumbled.

'How can you say that? They are savages!' Carina felt a surge of anger, almost on his behalf. They had killed his family and burned his home, after all.

'They can't live just to fight and kill. They must want other things. Something has made them the way they are. I don't know.' He looked down. It appeared he'd given the matter a lot of thought.

'Is it true they fight naked?'

'No.' He smiled slightly. 'Not the ones I saw. Nor do I believe they eat babies or sacrifice their own children.'

'But they do slaughter entire villages?'

His yellow eyes flickered then with the first flames of a fire and there it was, the undercurrent she had hoped flowed through him. And she nervously bit back her next question, a flush spreading to her cheeks. He looked away, and she held her breath for a moment.

'We should head back,' he stated simply.

And she just nodded and wanted to take his hand, but didn't.

* * *

Rozena didn't want to feel jealous. But it rankled her so much to see Emrys walking alongside Carina, even more so since she and Carina were friends now. She had only known the girl a short time, but they had come to a quick understanding. Rozena was happy to learn about the plants that grew in the garden Carina and her mother tended so carefully. And she enjoyed regaling Carina with tales of her own upbringing, which admittedly often included accounts of Emrys.

But she had known Emrys for as long as she could remember. She had played with him and Tugen since they first learned to run, and with the other, now dead, children of the village. Children. There was a strange word. Even now, safe from the ravages of the Kaldi, and with a friend her own age close at hand, she felt that childhood was a thing of the past. But she didn't really know what it meant to be an adult. She supposed these strange feelings, the odd possessiveness over Emrys and the bitter resentment of Carina every time she looked at him, were just what it meant to be an adult. And that made her sad. She closed her eyes for a moment, picturing her home, imagined running and laughing among the crops with Emrys and Tugen, and a single tear squeezed from her eye and rolled down her cheek.

'I thought I'd find you here,' she said to Emrys later when she came across him, quite deliberately, practising his swordsmanship alone on the sand. She knew well that he now came here every dusk.

'Rozena.' Emrys smiled as he looked up at her, and she was glad that it was just the two of them again.

'I want you to teach me.'

'Teach you?'

'To fight. If the Kaldi woman can do it, then so can I. I don't care who says I can't.' Rozena picked up a practice sword and waved it around, just as she had seen Emrys do.

Emrys looked at her quizzically and scowled. He surely knew her well enough to know that she was serious, and that argument was futile. He shrugged. 'Fine. I'll teach you what I know,' he said with an eventual smile.

He taught her the basics first, without even a weapon in hand, and she was patient. It was mostly balance; he explained. Good footwork and learning to transfer your weight quickly and without falling over. She picked up the wooden sword again.

'Come on, boy,' she teased, 'show me how to use this.'

And he did. Slowly at first. He showed her how to parry and slash and thrust, and how to move her feet as she did so. Her opponent's feet might tell her where the next move would come from, he explained. He had listened well to Viction, and she realised she was enjoying herself immensely.

'Don't watch my feet, though.' He laughed as he slipped the wooden sword through her open guard and prodded her gently with the tip.

'Ow!'

'And don't watch my sword, either. Let your instincts lead you. If you are watching my feet or my blade to see where my attack will come from, it's already too late.'

'Well, what am I supposed to look at?' She lowered her sword, confused.

'My face. My eyes. Maybe you'll see what I'm planning to do before I do it.'

She looked at his amber eyes and grinned back at him. She nodded and attacked a little harder, meeting his sword with more confidence and surprising skill. It really wasn't that hard.

'Let's use real swords,' she dared him.

'I don't think so.'

'Oh, come on. Just those little ones. I'm sure I can manage.'

'No, Rozena.'

She flashed her eyes at him and darted over to pick up a short sword from the rack of weapons. It felt good in her hand. She picked up a second and held it out to him, hilt first. 'I want to hear the sound they make.' She looked at him imploringly.

'Half speed,' he muttered in defeat. And she grinned at him.

They danced around each other on the sand, the shrill clang of their blades ringing out among the colonnades as they mock fought.

'Do you like Carina?' The question was meant to be innocent, but as soon as the words left her mouth, she heard her own insecurities in them.

'Yes. As do you,' he replied without guile. 'You spend hours with her.'

'I do, and I do like her.' Her arm was beginning to tire, and her sword dropped a little. Emrys slowed and dropped back, letting her rest.

'She's pretty too.'

Rozena stared at him in disbelief. He was smirking, like he wanted to hurt her with that apparently casual observation. He must have seen the shock on her face because, lowering his sword, he just laughed.

'Emrys! I hate you,' she squealed, and slashed at him suddenly with her sword. He swayed out of its path easily and took a step or two backwards in surprise.

'Whoa, Rozena!' He lifted his sword only to raise a barrier between himself and her blade, which she swung in a second angry pass at him. And his feet found a discarded practice weapon in the sand and his ankle gave. Her sword glanced off his and the tip sliced into his forearm. He dropped his weapon and tumbled back onto the sand.

'What are you doing?' He shouted at her. 'Stop!'

She let her own sword fall to the sand and her hands sprung up to cover her open mouth. 'Oh, Emrys, I'm sorry. I'm so sorry.'

Rozena looked down at her beloved Emrys, blood coursing from his arm, and wanted to go to him and hold him.

But she ran.

* * *

Krestell dressed his wound. It was little more than a scratch, but had been close to being much worse. Emrys was still seething, furious at Rozena, but also at himself. He had no idea why he had taunted her about Carina, who sat and watched her mother tend to him, other than to determine if she felt the way he did. It had always been Rozena. Even before he had heard the older lads talk about breasts and hair and the comfort that women could offer, he had always felt connected to her. Manhood was just around the corner, his father had told him, and he would start to look at girls differently. And he had. But only Rozena.

Until now.

'Thank you,' he whispered politely to Krestell, who nodded at him seriously.

'Viction wants to talk to you,' she told him, and he looked down, embarrassed.

He found Viction on the sand, standing close to a few specks of blood that were still just visible in the failing evening light.

'It wasn't often in my life I had two women fight over me, as I'd say is what's really going on here,' he said without looking up, 'so I don't know how much advice I can give on that matter.'

'I'm sorry, Viction,' began Emrys. 'It was foolish of us. Of me.'

'It was. And I don't suppose, among all the things you taught her, you mentioned the rule about respecting the sand?'

Emrys shook his head. He was still wondering what Viction's first comment meant. And then it came to him. Rozena was jealous, not because she thought he found Carina prettier than her, and not because she wanted something that Carina had, but because she wanted him to find her, and only her, pretty. And for the first time, he saw something in Rozena that was not perfect, that he didn't like. He preferred the Rozena that didn't care, that laughed with confidence. And Carina? Was she blameless in this?

'They both like me?' he asked, barely even addressing Viction so much as wondering out loud.

'You're smart out here, boy. I'll give you that. You learn faster than most men with a sword in hand. And for your age, well, I've never seen the like. But you don't know women at all, do you?'

Emrys began to wonder if it was him, and neither Rozena nor Carina, that was at fault.

And later, when he finally found Rozena, sitting against the frigid wall of the villa looking up at the stars, and sat with her for a while, and hugged her, he knew something between them had changed.

The Look of Death

They hadn't buried anyone in days. The ground was just too hard. Selwyn stood as far from the pyres as he could, an already sooted rag covering half of his face, but the miasma of burning bodies was still too much to bear. Nobody would question the tears on his cheeks given the horrid smoke that the fires belched out. Who would question them anyway? Quarter of the good people of Viroconium now either lay in deep pits under the frozen soil or were ash on the wind, their voyages to the next world hastened by the hungry flames that burned day and night outside the town's walls.

He had lost forty men at least from the fort on The Wrekin. Given the grim work the garrison had been assigned, he reflected, that number could yet be far greater. Still, what he wouldn't do for the men he had been forced to abandon in Dumnonia. He watched as his men loaded more bodies from a wagon onto a newly built pyre that would become yet another fearsome beacon in the falling night. And his heart went to Pasha. For all he knew, since he could not look at every corpse that was carted from the gates to this place, she had already been consigned to the fires. And that thought ripped him in two.

He hadn't seen Vitalinus in three full days. He hadn't reported to him. *What was there to say?* As long as the dead kept coming, he had nothing new to tell him and there were no new orders that could supersede the current one. Selwyn had seen plenty of bodies in his time. He'd killed his fair share in battle. But nothing he had seen could compare to this. Old, young, women, children—the disease did not discriminate. They all ended up looking pretty much the same; limbs blackened with infection, their bodies covered in weeping sores and their bloated and grotesque faces wearing expressions of now muted agony, as if death had stolen them away mid-scream. He didn't want to see Pasha that way. He'd rather hear about her passing later and remember her as she had come to him the night before he had left for Dumnonia, all secret smiles and eyes and bewitchment.

'Wagon's clear.' A voice broke his thoughts. Osric, usually seen with cup in hand and smile on face, looked at him dourly. Even the rambunctious Jute had been muted by the day-to-day hideousness of life, his usual buoyant walk reduced to a dreary trudge.

Selwyn nodded at him and called the men to muster. They would sleep well tonight, if sleep would let them, no matter how spartan the billeting in the fort. No lack of comfort could curtail sleep amid this exhaustion. Selwyn had barely dirtied his hands since lunchtime, for once sitting back and allowing himself the privilege of command rather than leading from the front, but he felt like he could sleep for a week. He could only imagine how some of the men felt and, since tomorrow was unlikely to be any easier, he hoped that their dreams would stay quiet long enough to allow them to rest.

Gods, the dreams that came to him. Vivid, violent, epic visions of battle, love, and terror that left him barely less tired when he awoke than he had felt before he went to bed. One night he had slain more men while he slept than he thought possible in a lifetime and, wading free from the blood, had escaped the slaughter to a life with Pasha. She had borne him three children, and he had farmed the land. And years later, in the dead of night, faceless men had come and burned them all to the ground and left him with only cinders and the echoes of his screaming family as they perished.

And he woke before dawn, drenched in sweat, and cried for an hour, barely believing that he had not aged.

* * *

A robin settled on a branch in the garden near Sevira. She hadn't moved in some time. When she had first sat down, the sun had been behind her, throwing her long and quickly static shadow onto the ground and wall beyond. It had slowly risen and moved around to her side and now shone dappled light through the frosted cobwebs of a leafless tree and onto the side of her face. Only her eyes moved to register the bird. Its dusky red chest puffed up and it let out a sweet trill that gave her little pleasure.

'Mother?' Catigern sat nearby. He had done for nearly as long as she had been there and had respectfully remained as still and quiet as her. She answered him with her eyes, her head cocked a little to one side, like the robin's. 'Mother, you ought to eat.'

The robin fluttered its dainty wings and darted off to some other perch. Sevira sighed gently. Catigern had been close to her night and day since Pasha had fallen ill. Ossian, with Vitalinus' decree, had forbidden anyone from seeing Pasha, and while it hurt Sevira deep in her heart not to look upon her daughter or tend to her in her hour of greatest need, she knew it was for the best. For her, and for Catigern. Vitalinus seemed resigned to the inevitability of Pasha's death and, if he was right, was adamant that Catigern should remain as far away from risk as possible.

'Perhaps you should have taken him to Dumnonia as well.' Sevira had chided him. She hadn't ever agreed with the plan to leave Vortimer there, and she missed him horribly.

'Why chastise me for advancing our cause, my love?' Vitalinus had riposted, before spitting predictably bitter words back at her. 'Besides, I have heard no word of pestilence there. He is safe. So yes, perhaps I should have taken Catigern with me too. And you. And Pasha.'

For a moment, grief had almost overcome him. Whatever sadness he felt inside was all too often masked by an ugly anger that boiled over, spilling into everything around him. And, as usual, instead of facing the anger and the sadness head on as he would any enemy in battle, he had flown from the villa and ridden his horse across the fields. Only the gods knew where.

Sevira loved Vitalinus dearly. If he sometimes directed his ire in her direction, so be it. She was his wife. If anyone was going to hear the words that he could not speak in public, it would be her. She believed not only in the resurgence of a greater nation of their people—in Albion—but also absolutely in him as its architect. If she bore any grievance, it was only that, while her husband was indefatigably driven in his cause, he was sometimes absent and remiss as a father to their children. But that too was probably unavoidable, she mused, telling herself that she only felt it more keenly now because of the extreme circumstances that surrounded them all.

She looked up at Catigern. He was such a good boy. And he was going to be a powerful man, already broad in the back and as handsome a youth as she had seen in Viroconium. She smiled at him thinly, her red-rimmed eyes misted with tears that no longer fell but just veiled her vision in a continual blur of sadness.

'Are *you* hungry, Catigern?'

He nodded.

'Perhaps we could have some damsons.'

He rose to his feet with a willing grin and set about finding her the few fruits that remained on the tree, even after the frosts. The soft flesh melted in her mouth, moistening the tight dryness in her throat.

'Good?'

'Very.' She gazed at him, glad that he was confident enough in himself to look right back into her eyes. She hoped he would not see all that was in there, all the pain and dread, but had no energy left to hide anything. Looking into his pale eyes, she saw that he understood.

'We're all fighters,' he whispered, his hand reaching out to rest on her arm. 'We get it from you.'

She almost laughed.

* * *

Vitalinus watched his horse drinking from the icy river. Despite the chill to the air, the sun shone brightly, and a couple of trout that were basking in the shallow clear water flicked their tails and weathered the gentle ripples a safe distance from the thirsty tongue.

He began making plans in his head, muttering to himself. Word had reached him that plague also beset the communities in and around what remained of Londinium and had reached north from there to Eboracum as well. The fort on The Wrekin had suffered its share of casualties, and he worried about the number of men he would have left to fight when it had all blown over. He wondered if it had extended its deadly grip to the lands of the Kaldi and the Dalriadans. Grimly, he hoped so.

Ossian had sworn to him that this was not some personal punishment, but Vitalinus felt quite certain that if Pasha died—when, more like—his world would crumble around him, unless he started building right now. He would reach out to those already loyal to him, those who believed in him and in Albion, and he would gather his forces together. With any luck, the plague would take a few of the naysayers. That would make everything much simpler.

He found Sevira in bed when he returned, a little before sundown. The glow from the pyres had been a sombre welcome home, and his mood was little improved from when he had seen her last.

'What news?' He demanded gruffly.

'None.' Sevira's eyes were heavy; dark circles hung beneath them. 'Your druid is attentive still, so your daughter yet lives.'

Vitalinus bristled. Sevira was as loyal a wife as any man could hope to find, but she wasn't one to censor her private words to him. She was his confidante in most things, and his biggest supporter, perhaps as driven in the cause as he, but sometimes he had the distinct feeling that she endured him personally.

'Our daughter,' she muttered apologetically. 'Don't scowl at me. I haven't got an ounce of energy to waste on sparring with you.'

Vitalinus felt disarmed. He slumped to the side of the bed and let his head fall into his hands. Ossian was more than capable of lying. What good would it do the druid to tell him that Custennin's murder was the very act that upset the natural order of things, that all this death and destruction really was nature's harsh judgment on that vile act?

'It's all my fault.' The grief surged upwards through him like a hot spring.

Tears welled up in his tired eyes and a sob wracked his body. He felt Sevira behind him, arms snaking through his, hands pressed against his chest, her hot breath in his ear.

'Not everything is down to you, my love. Come to bed.' She pulled him back onto the soft furs. 'You should sleep.'

He buried his face in her, letting her fingers knot his hair and pull him closer. And then the anger surged in him. *Was this the behaviour of a man who would rule Albion?* He pulled away and slid from the bed, looking back at her with red and accusatory eyes, as if she had weakened him with her femininity.

'Everything *is* down to me,' he sniped. 'Every fucking thing. Vortimer is alive because of me, and he rules now in Dumnonia. And when this shit is done with, I will build Albion from the ashes and lay waste to our enemies.'

'We only have one enemy now.' Sevira crawled over the bed towards him, pleadingly, refusing to be quieted, 'and that enemy is destroying us.' She burst into tears.

'I will not have it,' shouted Vitalinus. 'I will not have it.'

He turned towards the wall with the intent of seeing what damage his fist could do to the stones, but halted at the sight of Ossian in the doorway.

'The fever has relaxed.'

Vitalinus lowered his hand, staring at the druid. Days and nights he had left him to tend to his daughter, not knowing or understanding what magic or medicine he wielded.

'She will live.'

Vitalinus stood rock still for a moment, then darted forward and gathered the older man up in his arms and squeezed his thin frame.

'She will live?'

Sevira's arms found him, and he gave her his as well. Ossian, clearly exhausted, nodded. And crumpled to the floor. Vitalinus stepped back, fearing the worst.

'Put him in our bed.' Sevira pulled at his arm. 'He will sleep for a day and a night, I'm sure. He has given his all.'

So Vitalinus laid the gaunt druid on the furs and stepped back and into his wife's embrace.

'She will live,' she whispered through happy tears.

'She will live.'

Crannog

She found herself remembering the amber-eyed boy in the woods, his face bloodied by the bear. The bear would be asleep in some cosy den now, had it lived. Instead, its hide now weighed heavy on her shoulders. *But what had happened to the boy?*

The night was clear, and Derelei had left the crannog and walked across the icy wooden causeway and stood now on the shore of the loch, her head filled with the raucous tales of blood and rampage that filled the roundhouse. The farms and wooden houses along the shoreline sat mostly empty under the moonlight, most of the community having gathered to share ale and story and song on the island their ancestors had built. Beyond, the inky flat water of the loch reflected the night sky up at her, and the ring of steep-sided snow-covered hills dipped down into the starry depths. She bent and picked up a flat stone and turned it over in her hand.

The crannog sat on the northern end of the loch, close to the source, a rushing river that emptied into the narrow lake after a tumultuous descent from a spring in the mountains. She had gone there once, curious to see where it all began. She had followed the river uphill, against its current, and clambered up rocky cliffs beside the cascades that fell from them, climbing above the clouds and into the gleaming sunlight. The river shrunk to a trickle there, finding its way between and through the rocks, until it was little more than a cup sized hollow that bubbled its glittering water over a rocky ledge. She had held her water-skin under that first spout, stemming the river's flow for as long as it took to fill it, and then held it to her lips. She could imagine nothing purer.

She lobbed the flat stone in a gentle arc over the loch and heard it drop with a satisfying plop into the still water. Laughter from the crannog floated out across the rippling stars and hills, and she pulled the fur tighter around herself. She didn't really feel like going back inside, but her uncle would doubtless miss her in between accounts of his battle prowess.

'Where you been?' the hulking idiot, Irb, said when she showed her face again. He was pressed up against the wall near the entrance, near the shrivelled yellow flowers of the drying woad that hung from the beams. There would be no more sorties south until the slow melt of the winter's snow began, and by then the leaves of the woad would be more than ready to be ground to powder and paste to decorate their faces.

'Like it's any of your concern.' She muttered past him, trying to see whose turn it was to tell a story.

It was Drust, puffed up and red-faced with ale, surrounded by his admirers. He was old now, but still the younger women—more than capable warriors themselves—sat at his feet. Modwen was there, with her copper hair. And Darlagh. Though everyone knew Darlagh was carrying on in supposed secrecy with the sullen young druid, Cailtram, who rarely left the chieftain's side.

'I was just asking,' continued Irb.

'Well, don't.'

'Leave it, Irb.' A familiar voice spoke up. 'She doesn't answer to you or anyone.' Wroid stared the slightly bigger man down and gave her a wink.

She liked Wroid. Probably not as much as he liked her, but he was a fine man. It was always good, when contending with the likes of Irb, to have a man around who could not only offer a physical challenge but also knew how to smile. Irb was earnest in his moronic pursuit of her, as if he thought she would find his surly manliness in any way impressive. She didn't doubt that even she could better him in single combat. She may be a willow to his oak, but she was fast and lethal. He was just a shambling bear of a man, whose obvious attacks were easily avoided if you didn't get cornered. She'd learned that once to her cost. Once. Wroid had turned up then too. And he'd got his reward that night, and maybe he would again.

She smiled at him with just a hint of promise.

Drust finished his tale and announced loudly to all his people that he needed to relieve himself. He pushed through the crowd, laughing off the adulation, barely staggering under the deluge of hands that clapped him heartily on the back as he passed.

'There you are.' He looked at Derelei. 'Come, I would speak with you.'

'Aye, Uncle.' She followed him back out into the night.

She stood apart from him on the causeway, as his piss clattered steaming into the loch.

'You're one of our finest warriors, Derelei,' he began. 'I don't need to tell you that. It's in the blood.' He turned his head to her, grinning. 'I have an idea I thought I'd share with you.'

Derelei welcomed the winter snow. Her appetite for the raids had waned over the last year. It had only been her third year of bearing arms, but already she felt that there was something pointless about it all. It was as though they were righting the wrongs visited upon their ancestors rather than seeking to improve themselves. Sure, they could use better farmland and milder winters and, if the tales were true, they had once enjoyed both; further south. Before the Romans came. But their way had become merciless, and more often than not, a macho game of carving notches into the shafts of their spears for every life they stripped from people who probably weren't even that different from them. This new way was largely the doing of Drust.

'I want to see if our long boats can get out to sea. Imagine how much further south we can strike if we don't need to contend with that stupid wall and the vagrants that blindly defend it.' Drust, finished with the loch, turned to face her, his expression serious.

'How far south do you want to go?'

'As far as the boats will take us,' Drust grinned again.

'It sounds like you've already decided this,' Derelei offered meekly. Drust was the only man that truly intimidated her, if only in blood. She had so many things she wanted to say to him, but the words stuck in her chest.

'I have,' he chortled. 'I just wanted to share my clever idea with you.' He pulled her towards him roughly and kissed her forehead and walked back into the crannog.

III

PARA BELLUM

'dum vernat sanguis, dum rugis integer annus,
outere, ne quid cras libet ab ore dies'

'While spring is in your blood, while your age is free of wrinkle,
Use it—just in case tomorrow takes the youth from your face.'

(Sextus Propertius)

The Groans

I t was the perfume that finally convinced her it was over. Winter had slowed the disease, but the stench of death had lingered in the thin air for weeks even after the last pyre had burnt to ash. Ash that had become lost in the snow. And when the snow melted and the green shoots cautiously pushed their way up from the dead earth, and the pastel pink blossoms emerged from their buds, she felt relief that the air was clean again. The trees in the villa's garden were especially fragrant, and Pasha smiled properly for the first time in months.

Much of her affliction was little more than a blur to her. Ossian had told her, when she was aware enough to comprehend his words, that he had feared she would set the villa on fire, so hot was her skin to the touch. He was joking—probably out of relief that her fever had abated a little then—but at the time she had taken him at his word. And when she had drifted back to sleep, she had dreamt the walls and ceiling were ablaze, huge flames licking up and over her and roaring like some enraged beast. Dreams were all she could remember from that time. Often they were full of violent, blurry-faced men with dark holes where their mouths should be; holes that emitted strange gargling noises. And more than a few times she had dreamt of her father, always red-faced and shouting.

She found him pacing in the garden, muttering to himself, and felt saddened that he did not revel in the beauty of new birth as she did.

'Father,' she called out softly to him, and he looked up with a spectre of a smile.

'Pasha, how are you?'

'I am well. Perhaps better than you.' She took his hands in hers and looked up into his furrowed face. 'You mustn't fret so.'

'Mustn't I?' He rose to the challenge. 'We have lost so much.'

'You have not lost me.'

He looked at her, and the creases in his brow softened. He nodded and gave her hands a little squeeze. 'And that is the best hope I have,' he muttered, almost grimly.

'Best hope for what?' Pasha withdrew her hands. There was something so impersonal about that remark, even though she could see that he loved her. He looked away, hiding his face from her.

'Dear sweet daughter, I was so sure I'd lost you. You can't imagine my joy that you are still here.'

She knew full well what his ambitions were. Her mother had more than hinted at them, and Selwyn had shared what he knew when he shared her bed. Her father wanted to rule Albion. Only a half-wit who couldn't discern his own nose in front of him would fail to see that.

'And if I'd died?' she whispered darkly.

'You didn't.'

'And if I had, would your dreams have died as well? Is that what you mean?'

'I suppose I would have questioned how the gods favoured me,' he mumbled. 'If they had taken you from me, why would they grant me anything else?'

Was her survival some totemic twist to her father's destiny? Why couldn't he just be happy that she lived without making it about him and who he wanted to be? A bubble of anger rose in her chest, and she was about to launch into a righteous tirade when the strangest thing happened. The bubble stopped. It was like she could feel it, there in her throat, stuck. But no, it wasn't stuck, just still. And then it quietly popped, and the anger was gone. The perfume of the blossom filled her nose again, and she heard the birds clearer than before.

'I wish you weren't so angry, Father,' she said without guile. 'There is more to life than conquering and butchering.'

Whatever strangeness had befallen her in that instant had not gone wholly unnoticed by her father. He looked at her quizzically, as if he too had expected the volley of vitriol that her briefly reddening face had promised. He seemed surprised at the calmness that had fallen over her.

'Pasha, I do not want to spend my days with sword in hand, drenched in the blood of others. People bring violence to us, and there is no response other than in kind.'

Her father was speaking earnestly, and Pasha studied his face. 'And we are hurt,' she encouraged him.

'We are. Deeply. The scars are plentiful and will take time to heal. We have lost a great many of our people. And we will lose many more to the marauders from the north and west if we do not stand together.'

'We must fight,' Pasha murmured with a hint of bitterness. She did not disagree that her people should defend themselves, but the words felt ugly in her mouth, and the thought of more death sickened her to her stomach.

'I do want our people to live in peace.' Her father touched her face gently. 'I want our nation to be great again and be full of peace and prosperity and happiness.'

'You fight for peace?'

'Yes, I suppose so. If you desire peace, you must prepare for war. My father used to say that. I think it was a Roman that said it first, though.' He took his hand away from her face, smiling kindly at her.

'I'm sure it was.'

A knot grew in her stomach.

And then a messenger arrived with some urgent matter that demanded her father's attention, and that was that. Vitalinus was gone.

The knot remained, like a seed, and she wondered for a moment if she could be with child, before quickly realising that was impossible. She had been alone too long, sick too long. This was something else.

It was a need.

* * *

121

He summoned Ossian the moment he had heard what the messenger had to say. The Dalriadans had made incursions on their northern reaches. That wasn't what angered him, though. That was to be expected. Erc was a quarrelsome shit, and it was only ever going to be a matter of time before he started expanding the little kingdom he'd been carving out in the north-west.

'You wanted to see me, Vitalinus?' Ossian breezed in. The druid was probably the only person that didn't ever refer to him with some kind of title. He'd done it once and Vitalinus had thought it sounded insincere, so suggested he reserve it only for addressing him in front of others. Since Pasha's miraculous recovery, which surely owed a great deal to whatever magic and ministrations the old man had conjured up, Vitalinus had made Ossian his official advisor and closest confidante.

'The bastard council has gone behind my back,' Vitalinus spat. His kingdom might be limited to Cornovia, but his fingers were long, and he had loyal subjects in all corners of the island.

'Of what are you speaking?'

'They've written to the Romans. The Romans! Asking—no, begging–for help.'

'They?'

'Well, it doesn't take a druid to figure out who.' Vitalinus didn't even try to hold back his rage. 'Shall I spell it out for you?'

'By all means. Though you need not vent your spleen on me. I am not responsible.'

'Who is loyal to me?' Vitalinus reached for some wine and sloshed it into a cup.

'The council is twelve. Besides you and Vortimer, who now wields power in Dumnonia, your friends include Triffyn of Dyfed—'

'Yes. He has suffered the Hibernians as well, but would not run to Rome for help.'

'Dunvallo in Bernaccia, and Cunedda of the Gododdin.'

'Both harassed by the Kaldi, but yet they believe in me.' Vitalinus paced.

'I know not what side Ceneu favours.' The druid scratched his head.

'He barely knows his arse from his elbow, but I do not think he would stoop to this.'

'So, that leaves Sextus of Londinium.'

'What's left of it,' snorted Vitalinus. 'That pompous little Roman cunt just wants a good supply of handsome, young legionaries.'

'Appius in Eboracum, if the plague has spared him.'

'I'll wager it has.'

'Titus of Ceint,' Ossian smirked.

'Then Elaf, Nudd, and the giant fucking onion.' The Onion, Einion of Calleva, was as colossal a man as Vitalinus was aware had ever walked the island. 'Why is it, do you think, that those who have the least to fear from the Kaldi, the Hibernians and now the fucking Dalriadans, are the ones who go crying back to Rome?'

Ossian shrugged.

'Maybe Ceneu can be persuaded to let his idiot son, Pabo, wed Pasha. That would even things up a little.' Vitalinus poured more wine and slumped down on a bench. 'It's not enough, though.'

'Might I offer some advice?' Ossian crept closer.

'It's what you do, isn't it?'

'You don't want help from the Romans?' Ossian began.

'I don't mind help, but I don't want the Romans.'

'Because if they did return—?'

'If the Romans reinstalled themselves here, and they'd have a fair bit of rebuilding to do, I'd be, well, I wouldn't be king for long, would I?'

Ossian pushed his hands together, letting his fingers intertwine, looking upwards as he thought.

'But what if I did what the Romans would do, anyway?' Vitalinus didn't wait for the druid's words of wisdom. He stood up, determined.

'Where are you going?'

'To The Wrekin,' Vitalinus grinned. 'There's a Jute there I'd like a word with.'

Woad

Derelei left the old women tirelessly grinding the dried woad leaves into the blue powder that would adorn the warriors' faces and bodies in the raids to come and strode up the slope away from the loch. The village was a hive of activity, with weapons being made or sharpened, calves being born, and the land prepared for planting. And there was a lot of talk of boats.

Drust had stuck to his plan and had entered discussions over the winter with Brude, another chieftain. Brude's lands bordered the estuary, and he had already begun building boats that could brave the coastal waters. Drust was more than happy to promise him several warriors to bolster his fleet, intending himself to be among them. He had naturally asked Derelei to sail as well.

She distrusted the sea. The loch made sense to her, as deep and dangerous as it could be, but the idea of ever losing sight of dry land was something that frightened her. She had agreed, but was far from happy about it. The forest, on the other hand, with its bounty of game, was a landscape she could feel at one with.

She clutched her javelin in her hand as she looked behind her before disappearing into the trees on the banks high above the shore. It was a gloomy day, and the water looked grey. She hoped the clouds would break before she returned home. There was nothing more beautiful to her than seeing the loch glisten like a silver ribbon in the sunlight. Her spirits, previously leaden, lifted as she found her solitude in the woods.

She didn't particularly mind if she was to go home empty-handed today.

It wasn't usual to hunt alone, but Derelei wasn't one to either avoid risk or obey tradition. A bear or a wolf would present a problem, as could a boar on occasion, and she was unlikely to take down a stag on her own, but she was not afraid. She knew every branch and trunk of these woods and could tell apart any set of tracks or stool.

What she hadn't prepared herself for was Irb. He appeared almost from behind a tree.

'Hunting alone?' the idiot asked.

'What is it to you?' Derelei was so accustomed to being curt to Irb, it had almost become a stock response.

'I think it's time you and I became a bit more familiar.' Irb lurched towards her.

She stepped back nimbly and lowered the point of her spear. 'I think it's time you fucked off home, Irb.'

'You plan on using that on me?' He waved a gigantic hand at the javelin, a stupid grin on his face.

'Sure. Why don't you bend over? I've got a good idea where to put it.'

He guffawed, and Derelei was taken aback. Irb did a lot of things, but she had rarely heard him laugh. And in the moment that she was distracted by this thought, his hand grabbed the spear just below the point. He tugged it hard, pulling it free from her grasp and almost pulling her over forwards. As she sought to regain her balance, he idly swung the weapon and caught her on the side of the head with the end of the shaft. She fell to the ground, dazed.

And he was upon her.

'Get off!' She screamed, but this was no longer a fight she could win. He pinned her to the ground with his bulk and caught her flailing arms by the wrists, shoving them together into the soft earth above her head.

'I like a bit of fight in a woman,' he spat as he looked down at her cruelly, and his other hand found her neck and squeezed until darkness started to cloud the edges of her vision and her body went weak.

'Irb,' she mumbled his name helplessly. 'Stop!'

He grinned back at her, freeing her wrists to pull at her clothes. He was clumsy, already smirking at what he must have felt was an eventual and well-deserved victory. She had rejected him more times than she could remember, and he clearly wanted to make her pay for that.

As he fumbled to free himself from his own clothes, she summoned what strength she could and reached down to her belt for the dagger she always kept there. He saw it coming too late. He could never get up quickly enough. She brought the blade up hard and sliced into and through the front of his neck. His eyes popped in surprise, and she pulled the blade free, ripping his throat wide open in a furious geyser of blood that sprayed over her face. And he rolled off her, his hands reaching for the mortal wound, trying to close it.

He was dead within a minute.

* * *

She told Drust as soon as she got back to the village. He sent a few men to fetch Irb's body and bring it down the hill to the village, strung between two poles. The gash to Irb's throat was so deep that his head had threatened to come clean off, so they'd supported it with extra twine.

Derelei was shaken by the incident and had washed Irb's blood from her face before reporting the news to her uncle. She could see that he believed her. And why shouldn't he? Everyone knew what Irb had been like, especially in his pursuit of her. Everyone, apparently, except his sister. Modwen.

'I was out hunting with my brother,' Modwen explained to Drust and a few others in the crannog. 'He stopped for a rest and was sleeping beneath a tree. I went off foraging. And when I came back, I saw Derelei sneaking off, with her blade bloodied, and poor Irb's throat ripped open by her.'

'That is consistent with what my niece has told me,' Drust responded drily.

'She said they fought,' Modwen continued. 'His throat was slit, and there's not another mark on him. Or her! Does that sound like a fight to you?'

126

Drust sighed deeply and a sense of dread bubbled up in Derelei. She glanced at her aunt, Aife. Aife looked at the floor. She knew what was coming too, no doubt. Drust wasn't a young man, but he still wielded a sword as well as any man or woman there. And, as legend went, he was undefeated in over a hundred battles. Such a man was keenly aware of his masculinity and his appearance of power, and Aife was not ageing well. Her hearing was poor, and she walked with a limp and a grimace that suggested chronic pain. While Drust could lift a sword, he would feel the need to keep his cock wet as well. And Modwen, half his age, was more than happy to accommodate him.

'Modwen,' Drust began wearily, 'what would you have me do?'

'Justice.'

* * *

The druid, Cailtram, was later called upon to pass judgment, no doubt well briefed by the chieftain. It was to be death. A life for a life. Derelei's heart hurt. Drust would sooner condemn his own niece to death than exchange the warmth between Modwen's legs for the easy attention of some other gullible maiden.

Wroid, pain-faced, looked over at Derelei when the sentence was passed. She grimaced back at him apologetically, knowing how deeply he wanted to save her from Irb one last time.

'You could have beaten him with one hand behind your back,' he whispered to her as she was led from the crannog. 'I'm sorry.'

'So am I.'

They took her beyond the first line of trees, to the drowning pit. A gnarled oak stood over it, with sturdy branches that could support a man's weight if he transgressed in such a way as she had, and mossy roots that arched out of the earth like clawed fingers clinging to the hillside.

'The spring rains will hopefully make your suffering short lived.' Drust could barely look her in the face.

If he had, she would have spat in his treacherous eyes.

She looked around for Wroid but could not see him. The hole, a few feet across at the top, disappeared down into the earth. She knew that the rain would come, and the freezing water would rise over her head, but it felt to her instead that she was to be eaten alive.

Cailtram nodded to Modwen, who had insisted on being there, and she lowered a thick rope into the waiting maw. Derelei needed no shove to her back or firm hand on her arm. She walked to the edge of the pit and looked down. She wanted no ceremony, no platitudes, no lyrical condemnation based on lies. Cailtram opened his mouth to say something and Derelei threw him a look that promised she'd come back for him from the other world and cut his throat too, and he quickly swallowed whatever ill-chosen words he was about to utter.

She dropped to the earth and lowered her legs into the hole, her hands firm on the rope. 'This hole cannot ever be as deep as the hope I have that this is your last year of raiding and pillaging and murder.' She didn't lift her head, but spoke to her own hands, as if the words spoke more of her own destiny than to Drust, their intended audience. Him and the rest of them. *They could all fuck themselves.*

She lowered herself into the enveloping darkness, stopping after a while to look up at the diminishing disc of light that was all that was left of her world. A head peered down at her, but she could not make out whose it was. As she descended, she could feel the temperature dropping. The walls of the pit were sheer, wet earth, devoid of handholds bar the odd root or two, but never enough to make climbing out of there an option once the rope had been withdrawn. She tried to remember the last time a woman had been consigned to this hole and figured it was several years before. She had been younger then, and as short on empathy as many still were. But as the dank walls closed in on her, she finally felt afraid and wished she had been vocal back then. No woman deserved this punishment. What idiot deemed this a less traumatic execution than hanging; the equivalent punishment for men? She'd have taken the noose in a heartbeat.

Her feet found water. Instinctively, she pulled them up, away from the freezing embrace, but her hands and shoulders hurt from the climb, and she knew she would have to at least let the water take her weight for as long as she could hold on. She extended her legs downwards and was surprised that her feet quickly found firm ground. She was wet only to her knees. How long would she be down here? Could she possibly starve to death before she drowned?

The rope was suddenly jerked upwards and away from her. She couldn't even see it in the gloom, but the rough twine burnt at her desperate hands as she reluctantly let it go. And she was finally, and horribly, alone. She craned her neck to look up bitterly at the speck of daylight far above her, and a rock she had barely even realised she was standing on gave way underneath her. She dropped into the water for a moment before righting herself, her hand reaching into the freezing soup to feel the offending object. It was smooth, with two holes.

She dropped the skull in horror and sobbed suddenly. There were bones down here, she admitted to herself. And in time, hers would join them.

She looked back up at the fading light. And she screamed.

Green and Wide

The one good thing about everyone thinking you a simpleton was that you could go anywhere and do anything. It had never really escaped Erbin that people viewed him a certain way. They sniggered at the ways he said things, even just at the way he walked past them. He knew full well that his inherited title was effective in name only. Did they really think he wasn't aware that the Cornovian was running things now? He didn't even mind. Vortimer, with Lamorna at his leash, was far better suited to the role than him. Let him go running sword in hand to the beaches every time the Hibernians made landfall.

He could pass all but unnoticed around the fort, save for the snickering and whispered jokes at his expense, and he saw and heard far more things than anyone would have ever supposed. The Dumnonians grumbled a lot. That was to be expected. They were outnumbered now by Vortimer's men, and significantly outclassed. But again, when the red-haired raiders came, the Cornovians were the ones that laid down their lives to keep his people safe. He had begun to understand his father's quiet and cruel shrewdness and found a new appreciation for the man. *What if he had lived?* And every time that question reared its ugly head in his thoughts, the feeling of disquiet returned, nagging at him. He was certain that Vitalinus, for all his smooth talking and bravado, had played a part in the old man's death. Not to mention that slimy druid who had high-tailed it away with him before Custennin's burial.

And the more he thought about it, the more he realised that, although he tolerated Vortimer doing the dirty work of commanding the defences and taking his sister to bed, it was he, Erbin, that rightfully needed to rule in Dumnonia.

'You don't find it at all suspicious?' He quizzed Lamorna one morning on the ramparts. 'Father wasn't a fighter, but of the few men lost to the Hibernians that day, you don't think it odd that one of them was the man who was probably last to the fight, anyway?'

'No, I don't find it at all suspicious,' she retorted tartly. 'I don't much care for what you are insinuating either.'

'I'm not—'

'You are, and we both know it. Vortimer is a good man, and Vitalinus did us all a great service.' Lamorna huffed away briskly.

It was days later, in his usual half-invisible state, that he overheard a conversation between two of the Cornovians that purported to confirm his suspicions.

'The poor bastard,' the gruff one, Maddock, muttered. 'Like it's not enough that his father gets gutted by someone other than a fucking Hibernian, if you take my meaning, the simple sod has to watch Vortimer lording it over everyone.'

'What do you mean, not a Hibernian?' A fat, older soldier Erbin didn't know answered.

'Were you not bloody there? On the beach that day?'

'Aye, but I had my hands full.'

'Well, course so did I, but I swear I saw none other than you-know-who slip a blade into the old man's belly.'

'Who?'

Maddock lowered his voice to a coarse whisper. "Bloody Vitalinus, that's who.'

The men fell quiet. Erbin didn't move a muscle.

'Fuck me,' came the eventual response.

'Exactly. And now his son, who fuck only knows if he knows, is fucking the daughter, and the idiot boy just flounces around without a care in the world. I swear you couldn't make it up.'

'Leave it out, Maddock.' The newly appointed garrison commander joined the conversation, to be met with raucous jeers.

'Ah, the green-eyed monster woke up. Alright, Jac?'

There was more cheering and laughter. Erbin slid away. He knew, no matter how much it fitted with his own theories, that the talk of murder could be entirely salacious, little more than fire-side gossip. But what of Jac? It wasn't the only suggestion he'd got from his snippets of overheard conversations that Jac had romantic aspirations towards his sister.

Erbin had found a potential ally.

* * *

Vortimer watched his wife undress. He was already naked, cup of wine in hand, reclining on the soft furs of their bed. Since the uneasy consummation of their marriage, he had grown in confidence as both a leader of men and as a husband. Dumnonia finally agreed with him.

'Must you watch me so hungrily?' Lamorna smirked at him.

'I am a man with an appetite.' He grinned back at her.

She descended over him, her nipples raking his chest, and kissed him softly. 'Is that what you call it?' She wrapped her fingers round his cock.

He put aside his wine and pulled her closer, rolling her over so he was on top. She drew him into her immediately.

'I have something to ask you,' she murmured into his ear once they had finished.

'Wife, you are insatiable.' Vortimer smiled, his eyes closed.

'Did your father kill my mine?'

Vortimer opened his eyes. 'What? What do you mean?'

'It is a simple question. I mean no offence. In some ways, I would be happy to know that was the truth.'

Vortimer pulled himself up onto his elbow. 'Your father was slain in battle. By the Hibernians who plague our shores.'

'Yes, yes, I know. But was he?'

Vortimer was lost for words. He had been at the battle and had seen no such thing.

'Never mind. You have answered my question.' Lamorna stroked his chest and closed her eyes again.

'I should be insulted that you even ask,' Vortimer stammered.

'And are you?' She drawled sleepily.

It was entirely possible that Vitalinus was responsible. Vortimer knew his father well enough to know that there was little he was incapable of, if it meant getting what he wanted. But still, this was not the kind of rumour that he needed to get around the fort. 'Your father was killed by Hibernian raiders in defence of his people,' he told Lamorna. 'I don't want to hear otherwise again.'

* * *

Despite his sudden and unexpected elevation, Jac still liked to take the early morning sentry duty at the gate. He felt it kept his senses sharp. Knowing that he was awake and alert while most of the men lay fast asleep set him up for the day and helped him feel that he was earning the trust placed in him.

It was still bloody cold before the sun came fully up, even well into spring, so he was more than glad of the brazier that still smouldered next to him. He poked at it and stirred up the embers, coaxing a little flame to dance back into life.

'Jac.' A thin voice came from behind him.

He turned to see Erbin and immediately stood tall. Even if he, like pretty much all the men, answered to Lord Vortimer, Jac knew that Erbin carried on the line of his father. It wasn't his fault he was young. Or, as the men liked to say, a simpleton. 'My Lord Erbin,' he said, bowing his head slightly.

'Why do you stand guard? Aren't there other men to do it?'

'There are. I like this time of day.'

'Me too. Can I ask you about my father?'

'I did not know him,' Jac said falteringly. Erbin had a way of changing the course of a conversation in a heartbeat. Most thought it was a symptom of his distinct lack of intelligence, but Jac wasn't so sure.

'No, of course,' Erbin continued, his brow furrowed as if his thoughts made his head hurt, 'but you fought with him.'

'Sorry, I didn't. I wasn't on the beach that day.'

Erbin's head sank to his chest. 'Oh,' he said. 'I hoped to hear of how he fell.'

'Sorry,' Jac repeated.

'What do you think of my sister?'

Another change of tack. Jac weighed his answer. 'She is a fine lady,' he stated simply. 'A model wife and, if the gods will it, she will be a fine mother too.'

Erbin smiled thoughtfully. 'I've heard it said that Vortimer's father stabbed my father on the beach that day. He killed him. I don't want vicious rumours circulating among the men.'

Jac had heard the same story, and it appalled him. 'I will see to it that there is no more of such talk,' he promised.

'Thank you, Jac. I like you.'

'Thank you, Lord Erbin.'

Erbin turned as if to leave, then paused. 'It would be awful if it was true, wouldn't it? My sister married to the son of the man that killed her father. And if she bears him a child, who will say what happened between its grandfathers?'

Erbin walked away before Jac had time to reply.

* * *

Over half a year had passed since Petroc's abduction. Joceline had naturally feared him butchered. The last image in her mind was him in his father's armour, wielding his father's sword, prepared to battle the raiders alone. But Vortimer had assured her that nobody remotely matching his description was among the dead. The Hibernians took men and women who were in their prime as slaves. And that meant, as far as she could know, that he possibly still lived.

Her heart was a maelstrom, unable to grieve unless she knew him dead, afraid for him if he was alive, frustratingly helpless, and horribly alone. Lamorna offered some companionship, but she was, despite her precociousness, little more than a child. She was tender and understanding for her age. But, through no fault of her own, she had no capacity to really empathise with Joceline's pain. And she was wrapped up with Vortimer, her eyes full of him.

Vortimer was closer in age to Joceline, but was as enraptured by his wife as she was by him. The bright firm charms of youth, she mused as she lay curled up in her bed one morning. It would be unfair to expect him not to revel in the supple young limbs and tight childless sex of his bride.

A tear trickled from one eye, and she wiped it away angrily, realising she was feeling sorry for herself. She knew that she cried not for poor Petroc and whatever hideous mistreatment he was suffering across the sea, but because she felt alone. She wasn't old, by any means, but already a widow whose only child was gone forever. Her home had been razed to the ground, and she had found sanctuary in this wooden fort. And now she was wide-eyed for the lord and green-eyed for the lady, both of whom had extended her nothing but kindness and comfort.

She kicked her blankets away and rose sharply to her feet, raging quietly at herself.

* * *

Joceline brushed past her, barely stopping to wish her a good morning.

'Are you alright?'

'I am fine, Lamorna,' Joceline remarked over her shoulder as she continued walking. 'I am going for a walk. I expect I'll be gone most of the day.'

'Without a guard?'

But she was gone. Lamorna knew Joceline enjoyed solitude. She didn't much care for it herself, certainly not since her father's death. Only back then had she sought refuge from prying eyes and loud voices, from men. She thought briefly of Erbin's question. She had heard rumours, and couldn't care less. If Vitalinus had indeed killed him, marrying his son had been the most perfectly delicious way to dishonour her shit of a dead father. So was letting him ravage her in her father's bed.

And, quite suddenly, Lamorna realised that she wanted to bear Vortimer a child.

Watling Street

L actodurum had been a thriving trading post in almost living memory for some, a small town that had sprung up around a Roman fort, a haven to barrack men marching the long miles up and down Watling Street. It had been a place to buy and barter, its streets filled with wine-soaked legionaries stumbling from brothels and the heady smell of livestock, its air ringing with the sounds of hammer on iron and stretching leather as weapons were forged and armour mended.

The crumbling walls lay silent, portions of them reclaimed by locals who had sought a more rural existence but still needed building materials. Even Watling Street, one of Britannia's greatest highways, had been plundered for its cobbles and was, in places, almost entirely given over to weeds and grass. The Romans had no business coming back to this, Vitalinus thought. Centuries of careful building and organising had been allowed to dissipate. He knew he was in the right.

He had sent instruction, before leaving Viroconium, to Cunedda near the wall. More than accomplished in facing the Kaldi, Cunedda was as Roman a leader as any who remained on the island. He still commanded what resembled a legion of fierce but disciplined Gododdin warriors and was schooled in successful warfare as well as any man. He would be more than a match for Erc's Dalriadans, and his line of defence would keep the northern borders of Cornovia trouble free.

Vitalinus did not doubt Cunedda's allegiance. As younger men, they had stood shoulder-to-shoulder and, while the brash northerner had a voice like thunder and commanded his own army with more than a little tactical acumen, Vitalinus knew him best as a scrapper, a hound that pulled at the leash, waiting for the cry to attack. It just so happened that when he charged into battle, he took several hundred well-trained men with him, all teeth and claws and baying for blood. His absence from the wall would give the Kaldi an opening, but Vitalinus had other plans for them. And, from what he'd heard, they had taken to the seas this year and were raiding further south along the coast. That might end up as an unpleasant shock for Appius if they ventured as far as Eboracum. Let it be so, Vitalinus thought. Maybe then he would accept that help needed to come from somewhere other than Rome.

Vitalinus looked over at Ossian, riding silently beside him. The druid was lost in his own thoughts. Behind him, the comforting sound of hooves on cobbles reminded him of the men he had brought with him. He had been sure to bring the Nobatians, Shabaka and Tsekani, and Zeki the Ethiope as well. He wanted people to see and know that he was not just some nostalgic fool like Custennin, distrustful of anyone who looked different or came from foreign lands. The Romans had made use of men from every corner of the empire, places that Vitalinus knew he would never see, so why shouldn't he do the same? Every man, no matter his size, shape, or the colour of his skin, could fight. And, as often as not, Vitalinus would not bet on a Briton in a fair fight. Britons would not defeat the Kaldi. Not alone. And Rome wasn't going to help.

'How long since you were back this way?' Vitalinus twisted in his saddle and addressed Osric behind him.

'I was somewhere between a child and a man when I last passed here.' The Jute grinned back at him. 'And that was all I did. Pass it by. It was a shithole then, and it's even more of one now.'

He was undoubtedly right.

'Are we camping here, then?' Osric asked, keen to continue the conversation.

'Yes.' Vitalinus tolerated Osric. He wouldn't go so far as to say he liked him. There was a brashness about him that didn't sit well with anyone with cultural aspirations. Osric was a brute, a fearsome warrior who could drink his own body weight in ale, wine, mead, or anything else you put in front of him and still probably stand victorious alone against a phalanx of Rome's finest. He had a terrible sense of humour and would probably lift a sword against you if someone else gave him better reason than you to wield it. He was exactly what was needed if Vitalinus was to take the fight to the Kaldi.

'You know this place is cursed?' Osric scowled.

'Nonsense,' scoffed Ossian, who hadn't spoken in hours.

'You should know better, druid.' Osric spurred his horse forward ineptly, drawing level between Ossian and Vitalinus. Jutes, and most of their Saxon cousins, were not skilled horsemen, by any means. 'All these places are filled with angry spirits of the dead. Mark my words.'

'Why are they angry?' Ossian asked provocatively.

'Because they are dead!'

'That is no reason to be angry.'

'Why did the stupid Romans build with stone? What is wrong with a good wooden wall?' Osric paused to take a swig of whatever was in his water-skin. It was almost certainly not water. 'A wooden wall comes down, you put it up again. No harm done. A stone wall comes down, and it stays down. Chances are it crushes you beneath it into the bargain. Stupid Romans. Making angry ghosts.'

'They are angry because they are dead, and because the wall fell on them?' Ossian taunted Osric.

Osric screwed his face up, confounded and quiet for a moment. 'They are angry because Romans were—'

'Stupid?' Ossian finished his sentence for him.

'Disrespectful.'

It was Ossian's turn to fall quiet.

'We will camp outside the walls,' Vitalinus uttered curtly. He didn't wait for the Jute's approval, but his silence said enough. Osric pulled his horse back and fell back into line.

'Bloody Jutes,' whispered Ossian, with a sideways glance at Vitalinus.

* * *

Osric had been happy to get away from Viroconium. He never went into the town itself, preferring the wooden sanctuary of the fort on The Wrekin to the neat criss-cross of small streets and stone buildings. The plague had only bolstered his opinions of living in such conditions. He had endured the days of pit digging and corpse carrying, of being assailed by the stench of death at every breath and sleeping every night with limbs that ached more than they had after even the hardest fought battle. It got worse when they lit the fires. All that burning and diseased flesh. He yearned for anything else, even the home of his blood.

Then Vitalinus had come to him, asking if he had family among the small enclave of Jutes that he'd heard lived on the outskirts of Londinium. Well, he couldn't claim family, as far as he knew, but he certainly had kin there. The shadowy circumstances of his departure were not something he'd ever talked about, nor was he likely to. As far as Vitalinus knew, he'd left it as a boy and gone in search of glory and battle. It wasn't anywhere worth staying. The few Jutish descendants of mercenaries who had proved themselves in battle beside the Romans had been rewarded with a paltry bit of bog to call home, close enough to the capital to be called upon when needed, but far enough away for comfort. It was poor land where fuck all was ever likely to grow. So that's where they were headed. Fucking Londinium, or near enough.

Osric poked at the fire with his spear, shifting a sizeable piece of wood so that a flame shot up into the night sky. At least Vitalinus had agreed to camp outside the town here. Who knew what was in there? The dark walls stood silently beyond him, full of secrets. He pulled his blanket tighter around his shoulders, half expecting to hear echoes of footsteps on the cobbles of Watling Street, or some wraith howling and rattling from within the town.

'You are quiet tonight,' Zeki, the Ethiope, observed, looking at Osric with searching eyes.

'I can't be the life of the party every day,' grumbled Osric, returning his

140

gaze to the flames.

'Would you like to hear a story?'

'Is it funny?'

'No.'

'Then no, I wouldn't.' Osric grinned secretly. He liked Zeki.

'I do not know funny stories,' Zeki continued.

'Because you don't know how to laugh.'

'I laugh at you.'

'Fucking everyone laughs at me. I'm funny.'

Zeki smiled broadly. 'Perhaps you should tell a story, then?'

Osric lost himself in the dark centre of the fire for a moment, then asked quietly, 'have you heard of Eryn Boal?'

Zeki shook his head. A few of the other men, sensing a change in the mood, stopped their conversations and leant their heads in Osric's direction.

'Eryn was a young woman from these parts. She was renowned for her long copper hair and beautiful face, and for her laugh that chimed with the music of a busy rivulet on a summer's day. She had never an ill word to say about anyone and was the envy of every other young maid. And an object of desire for every man that set eyes on her.' Osric took a long draft of mead and wiped his mouth with the back of his hand. Everyone nearby was listening now.

'One day a stranger came to the village, a handsome young man called Boal who entertained the people with his stories and songs. They listened to him until the sun came up, happy to feed and water him, and offer him the finest of their beds to sleep in. Eryn was so rapt with his tales that she found herself falling in love with this stranger. And he needed little encouragement. Having watched her closely through the night, he was more than a little enamoured with her as well.'

'I never took you for a romantic, Osric!' a voice interrupted from the darkness, met with a chorus of disapproval.

'Shut up and let him tell his story!'

Osric smiled, leaning over the glow of the fire. 'They were married, much to the anger of all the men of the village. And the very next day Eryn found Boal lying by the river, his head smashed open by rocks. And she knew it had been murder. She was so distraught, so betrayed and lost, that she waded out into the river, that river not far from here that we crossed this afternoon, and she drowned herself.'

Several gasps filled the night air. He had taken them by surprise.

'A fine story, Osric,' another voice called out.

Osric held up his hand. His story was not done. 'The village grieved the loss of Eryn Boal for a while, but soon forgot her. And in the months that followed, the young men of the village began to wash up dead on the banks of the river, their bodies pale, bloated and waterlogged. Drowned, as she had been. The whispers began in the night-time, hushed talk of a beautiful woman whose laughter was like a dozen tiny bells, or the twinkling of a mountain stream, a woman with long green pondweed hair who would call for help from the cold water, and lure brave and lustful men into the river's dreadful grip, and then laugh as they gasped their last breaths.'

The surrounding men were silent. Zeki stared at him, wide eyed.

'Eryn Boal avenged herself on every man, not just the men who had killed her love, but any man who lusted after her. Soon nobody would go near the river at night. No man could claim to have seen Eryn Boal and her green weed hair and live to tell the tale.'

The fire spat and cackled and threw up a few glowing embers into the night sky.

'Stay clear of the river this night is all I am saying,' Osric muttered darkly, and took another drink. 'She's a monster, and drowning is no way to go for a proper warrior.'

'Hold on,' a youthful voice called out waveringly. 'You said no man saw her and lived. How do you know what she looked like?'

Osric drank. He took his time, eventually draining his cup and exhaling loudly. 'Who said that?'

'I did,' came back the uncertain reply.

'I'll tell you how I know.' He paused. 'I know, because I killed the green-haired bitch with this very knife.' He drew his long-bladed seax from its sheath, letting the deep red of the fire catch on its gleaming edge.

There was a moment's silence, a group sense of awe, until Osric's bellowing guffaw broke it. And suddenly there was laughter around the fire.

'I think I've a lock of her hair here somewhere.' Osric pulled up a handful of grass from beside him, to more peals of laughter.

'That was a funny story.' Zeki slapped his leg and grinned widely at Osric.

'Like I said,' Osric smiled back at him, 'fucking everyone laughs at me.'

* * *

Ossian slunk away from the merriment and into the night. The men were in high spirits. Good. After the winter they had lived through, they needed to feel life coursing through their bodies now. They were few, and there was a mountain to climb. Doubtless the Kaldi were already slaughtering Britons north of here, and all Vitalinus' best efforts would be worthless if he couldn't find allies. The plague had decimated the stock of fighting men as well as stolen away the lives of women and children. Osric was wild, but he was strong. Perhaps Vitalinus was right. Perhaps they did need more men like him.

Only time would tell.

A Bend in the River

Winter had been a frustrating time for Emrys. Snow covered the ground and Viction was less interested in training in the cold, preferring instead to sit close to the fire in the empty bath, draped in furs, telling tall stories about the arena. He'd been younger than Emrys when the last fights had taken place in Britannia, but could still conjure vivid detail about battles he'd probably never even seen. Not that anyone complained. Emrys, more than anyone, was thrilled with the blow-by-blow accounts, always closing his eyes to better see the dance of the warriors and imagine the shrill clashes of their swords and other weapons.

Emrys had yearned for the spring, passing the short days ankle-deep in the snow and sword in hand, practising against invisible opponents. Neither Rozena nor Carina were keen on the cold, so he had those times to himself. Only once or twice had he spotted Carina watching from the colonnades, poorly hidden behind the hot fog of her breath, and he had doubled his efforts to impress her.

Rozena was quieter than he'd ever known her to be. She spent more time with Krestell, learning culinary skills and about the healing power of various herbs and salves. Not once had she asked to spar with him further after their previous confrontation, though he doubted that the fight had gone from her. She just didn't want to fight with him, he supposed. In any sense.

When spring had come, it had come quickly. The snows melted away rapidly, and the temperature soared for a while. Viction shrugged off his furs and Emrys' lessons resumed with a passion. His mentor looked pleased with his progress.

One warm afternoon, after a long morning of training, Viction announced he had other matters to attend to and declined to teach any more that day. Emrys was sure he had tired the older man out, and put away his sword with a grin, confident that he was that much closer to being ready for an actual battle.

It was a decent walk to the river, a clear trout-rich brook with grassy banks and burgeoning reed beds, and for once he was not there to fish. He peeled off his tunic and threw it against the trunk of a willow that leant out over the slow water, its fronds trailing down onto the surface like green snakes. And then he saw her.

Carina.

Only her head sat above the surface of the water, but he could make out her pale naked body beneath, blurred by the gentle current. He stopped dead. She was looking directly at him.

'It's lovely,' she purred. 'Are you coming in?'

The winter had nourished her. She had grown over the cold months and was probably a couple of fingers taller than Emrys now, and the womanly curves that had only begun to appear in the previous summer had now taken a more obvious shape. This was the first he had seen of her not wrapped in furs for some time. It was certainly the first he had seen of her wearing nothing at all.

'I was going to see if I could catch a fish,' he lied.

She laughed. 'I think I've scared them all away. Sorry.'

He tried not to stare.

'Where's your line? And your bait?' Her feet found the stony bottom, and she stood up. The water was only deep enough to reach her waist, so she folded her arms across her bare chest casually; not all that bothered what he saw. And see he did. He saw the wispy tuft of dark hair beneath her navel, lapped at by the river's gentle water, matted and intriguing. He'd gone through a few changes himself. His voice had changed, and he had new growths of hair where before there had been none, so it was only natural that she should too.

'I forgot it,' he mumbled feebly, not knowing what to say.

'You'd best come in then.' She stooped and slipped forward into the water again, swimming languorously towards the bank. 'I can look away if you like.'

He nodded. And she turned away from him while he discarded the rest of his clothes and stepped into the cool water, his heart pounding. He could see the whiteness of her bare back as she sat on the smooth stones of the riverbed, her arms outstretched. He was only thigh deep when she tilted her head back, dumping her hair into the stream, and looked upside-down at his nakedness.

He gave out an embarrassed cry and dived sideways into the water, accompanied by her laughter. His head went under, and everything sounded far away for a moment. When he found the air again, she was there, smiling in front of him, clear rivulets glistening on her face, her arms still outstretched and her small breasts buoyant on the surface.

'How long were you watching me?' she asked teasingly.

'I wasn't. I swear.'

'I don't mind if you were.' She moved a little closer. And she lifted her hand and touched his cheek, her finger moving delicately over his scar. He didn't know what to do, wasn't even sure what he wanted to do, or what he should do. He felt like he wanted to reach out and touch her, perhaps even kiss her. But before he could do anything, she giggled and launched herself backwards with a splash, nimbly twisting and swimming towards the middle of the river and into deeper water. And for the time being, at least, the moment passed.

Later, when he was in the gardens, he found Rozena huffing beneath a tree. She had seen them returning, wet-haired, from their swim.

'You and Carina are getting on well,' she grumbled.

'You sound jealous.' She clearly was, and part of him revelled in the fact. He had known Rozena his entire life and loved her dearly. It was hard to imagine a time they wouldn't be close. He had always thought she was the one he would share kisses with, but life had changed, and there was something new and exciting about Carina that he found impossible to ignore.

'I'm not. You do what you want.'

Surely she knew he liked her? He always had. He didn't see why he couldn't like Carina as well.

* * *

Her dreams dragged her home. Home to Bernaccia and to her father. He was chopping wood. She brought him sturdy logs from the pile and stood back as he swung his axe down and split them into smaller logs. He smiled at her, and she felt happy.

She wondered where Emrys and Tugen had got to. They had disappeared in the morning, wooden swords in hand, headed for the trees. She remembered the wounded look in Emrys' golden eyes when he had asked about Tugen kissing her. Tugen had indeed kissed her, but it meant nothing at the time or after. Tugen had clumsily leant across the gap between them one day and pushed his closed mouth against hers before retreating with a quiet look of accomplishment on his face. He didn't even know what it meant yet, and she hadn't exactly welcomed the approach. She simply told Emrys it hadn't happened, but she wasn't good at lying, and he just frowned at her in disappointment.

A sudden shriek arose from the village. Her father stood up tall, having just embedded his axe blade deep in a thick log, and looked across the field.

'Wait here,' he told his daughter and left the axe to begin a loping run toward the houses.

Rozena did as she was told. Her father was the only person in the whole world who she obeyed without question. She watched him approach their home and saw among the buildings more figures than she expected. Another scream came. And then she saw the thatch on Tugen's house go up in flames and a tall, slender man emerge from the doorway clutching a flaming brand.

She lost sight of her father, but soon found him again, sword in hand. She stiffened in fear. They were under attack. Suddenly, the air buzzed with shouting. There was the occasional clash of metal, but mostly shouting. Another house went up in flames, and then another. The Kaldi. It had to be.

Her father ran towards her, across the edge of the field, followed by a man who appeared stripped to the waist. When they were close enough, she could see that the man's torso was spiralled in blue swirls and emblems she couldn't make out. She ducked down behind the woodpile, terrified. Why was her father running towards her? Why was he leading this blue man here? Where was her mother?

Her father rounded the woodpile and fell to his knees in front of her. A javelin jutted out of his back, just below his shoulder blade. She screamed. And behind her father, the blue man appeared, sword raised. With a terrible roar, her father whirled around and smashed his blade against the now descending sword, hauling himself to his feet at the same time. The javelin in his shoulder fell free, and she saw blood pour down his back.

'Father!' she sobbed.

He didn't answer, but lunged forward against the blue man. She saw the tip of the Kaldi sword emerge from the middle of her father's back before the two of them fell to the ground together. Her father, still fighting, pinned the blue man to the ground and began raining fists down on his painted face. Rozena covered her eyes and listened to the sickening crunch of every blow. When the punches stopped, she opened her eyes.

Her father hauled himself to his feet and stood over the prone Kaldi warrior, swaying slightly. With a groan, he leant to one side and picked up his sword. With both hands on the hilt, he dangled the point over the heaving blue chest, then plunged it downwards with all the strength he had left. And there he stayed for a moment, quite still, hands clenched on the pommel, knees either side of the blue man, whose last breath rattled bloodily from his lips, before turning his face towards Rozena.

He tried to get up, and half managed it, though he never found balance. He looked at her, but she didn't think there was any focus in his eyes as he tried to walk towards her. Instead, he ended up scuttling sideways, struggling to stay on his feet. She thought she had seen him like that once before, after a celebration and a large amount of ale. That time he had cannoned into the wall of their house and happily passed out, to wake the next morning with what he described as a howling head and a frown that lasted all day.

This time, with blood coursing from his stomach and his back, his legs buckled beneath him and he fell, crumpling like a broken doll next to the logs, and never moved again.

Rozena pulled her knees up to her chin and wrapped her arms around her shins, and cried hot tears until Emrys found her.

But it wasn't Emrys that woke her from her dream. Her eyes snapped open in the dark and she swam back into the darkness of the villa, wondering where Emrys was and why he thought it was perfectly fine to string her along while he got friendly with Carina.

She thought she heard voices in the night. She shook herself to make sure she wasn't still dreaming. There were definitely voices. She looked around her and saw the sleeping figures of Viction, Krestell, and Carina. Up against the side of the bath, Emrys too was breathing slow and deep, fast asleep.

She pulled herself up over the edge of the bath and padded to the doorway and into the corridor. Moonlight beamed in through the windows there and she crept towards one, looking out down the avenue towards Dere Street. And there, on the Roman road, she thought she could see a handful of shadows making their way northwards.

She shivered. The nights were still cool. She strained her eyes and ears but could make out no more of whoever was out on the road, so slunk back to her bed and slept until morning.

* * *

Krestell looked at him with mounting concern.

'I'm not uprooting us,' Viction told her. 'I'm not leaving this house that we have made our own, on account of a few paltry Angles.'

149

'We've hardly made the house our own,' Krestell argued. 'Half of it is falling down around us and we huddle and eat and sleep in a hard hole where fat Romans used to sit around naked in hot water prattling on about who knows what. Probably which of them had the better-looking slave boy, for all I know.'

'I grew up here,' Viction objected. He wasn't about to leave for anyone, no matter how derelict the ludus had become. So, a ragged band of Angles had made camp some miles up Dere Street from the villa. They would be like the rest of the Saxon kind, too superstitious to trouble Roman built domiciles. 'This is our home,' he stated firmly.

Despite his projected confidence, he had immediately, after discovering that the Angles were nearby, gone and begun sharpening his swords and other weapons. But it was only a precaution, he told himself. They needed tending to anyway, and it was undeniably his responsibility alone to defend his family if such action was necessary, which it wouldn't be.

'You are one man,' Krestell reminded him quietly, as if she sensed that the argument, such that it was, was all but over. 'Emrys and Rozena do not need to be orphaned again.' Like his wife, he counted Emrys and Rozena as part of the family now, happy that they had remained with them, and he had quietly sworn to himself that he would protect them as if they were his own.

It was then that Emrys burst in upon them and silenced the dispute. 'Rozena has gone,' he blurted out, clearly alarmed.

'What do you mean?' Krestell asked quietly, always the calming influence.

'She has left us. Left me.' Emrys kicked at a pot angrily.

'I'm sure she has just gone for a swim or a walk in the garden,' Krestell continued.

'No. She has gone. I know it.'

'How are you certain?' Viction asked.

'Because my sword is gone, too. Well, it was her father's sword. I took it. Pulled it from the man that killed him. And now it has gone. She has taken her father's sword back and left me.'

Emrys' amber eyes filled with tears, furious and afraid.

Jutes

The leader of the Jutes was a man called Egbin. He was a large man, probably ten years older than his kinsman, Osric, but clearly carrying with him that decade's additional indulgence in ale, and considerably less fight. The community, such that it was, was little more than a cluster of wattle and thatch houses that looked in danger of collapse, squashed together on a narrow isthmus of dry land between acres of swamp. Sitting in what purported to act as some kind of mead hall, Vitalinus counted barely a dozen men of fighting age, and imagined the deadliest thing they had ever wielded was a sickle. Some of the women looked more dangerous. And the rest were children, dirty faced and dressed in rags. Vitalinus tried to conceal his disappointment.

'Why should we trust you?' Egbin slurred, looking to Osric to translate. 'We are Jutes. We are born warriors. But we have had little to fight for here.'

'They are farmers, as we all are when there's nobody to kill,' Osric embellished quietly. 'Their grandparents were mercenaries, but these men have barely picked up a seax in their lives.'

'So why are we here?' Ossian hissed at Osric.

Vitalinus held up his hand, silencing them. 'Tell Egbin that Albion needs warriors. And all faithful warriors are naturally to be rewarded with land that will yield proper sustenance, not pushed out to some bog out of the way of Sextus and the other preening idiots of Londinium. I offer glory and gain, in return for your swords.'

Osric relayed the message, and Egbin sneered. 'What makes you different from those Britons? And do you now speak for them?'

'This is ridiculous,' Ossian mumbled beside Vitalinus. 'Are we really having to beg a handful of farmers to come and die for us?'

'You have families, kin, across the sea? Perhaps they would like to share in the spoils of war here?' Vitalinus continued. 'Yes, I speak for Albion,' he lied, 'and all Britons.'

Vitalinus shifted uncomfortably. It had been a long ride, though uneventful, from Lactodurum. They had passed the northern reaches of what remained of Londinium. Its streets were long emptied, its inhabitants scattered to the villas on the outskirts of the town. Somewhere nearby Sextus held court, likely surrounded by young men who still stupidly aspired to be Roman, struggling to understand what a hypocaust was while they oiled themselves up incessantly, and vied for their master's attention.

And yet here he was, Vitalinus, self-proclaimed king of Cornovia, pretending to be the high king of all Britannia, of an Albion that didn't even exist, sitting in a mud hut in a fetid swamp trying to persuade a fat Jute that his barren farming community was the key to defeating the Kaldi and creating a better world.

Egbin snapped his fingers, and a woman, presumably his wife, filled his drinking horn with more mead. 'I suppose we could send a boat,' he mused, then addressed the hall. 'Anyone fancy sailing back over the sea?'

Nobody leapt at the chance.

'It's pretty unlikely any of them have ever even been to sea,' Osric muttered to Vitalinus, who was growing weary of the proceedings.

'All the more for us then, eh, lads?' Egbin's words were met with a muted response. He shrugged a faux apology at Vitalinus.

'Perhaps I will sample your mead.' Vitalinus tried a different tack.

Egbin grinned and waved his hand enthusiastically. His maybe-wife rushed forward and handed a horn to Vitalinus before sloshing the sweet-smelling drink into it and over his hand. She smiled vacantly at him, in what was perhaps some form of apology. He lifted the vessel to his lips and took a sip. It wasn't altogether unpleasant. He was aware of Egbin's eyes on him, so took a bigger sip. Some spilt on his short beard, and he wiped it away with his hand.

'You Britons can't fight, can't drink. What can you do?' Egbin's mood had improved. He was getting garrulous. A ripple of laughter circled the mead hall.

'We do both well, but plague has recently deprived us of many hands that would have held a sword, and our enemies do not wait for us to repopulate.'

'I don't suppose you're much good at that either,' roared Egbin.

Vitalinus waited for the laughter to subside before looking to Osric for translation.

'They wouldn't even know how to form a shield wall,' Osric scowled, his usually proud face downcast. 'We have wasted our time.'

'I think we've heard enough,' Ossian agreed.

Vitalinus rose slowly to his feet, looking around at the Jutes, some still chuckling to themselves. 'I thank you for your hospitality,' he uttered curtly, and turned his back on Egbin. Let them rot in their swamp, he thought.

* * *

Osric was ashamed. It was not a feeling he was accustomed to. His kin hadn't even looked at him as if he were one of them, something he felt he should be furious about, but he was relieved. He was not one of them. They were not Jutes any more. Grown fat and lazy and useless, barely deserving the scraps thrown to them by Sextus and the Britons of Londinium or the shit-heap of land that no real Jute would be proud to call home, they could barely even call themselves farmers. More importantly, they didn't remember him.

Vitalinus' face was stormy as he readied his horse. He had said nothing since they'd left the mead hall. And Osric didn't blame him. He half expected to be told to fuck off and stay here with the rest of the Jutes. If that happened, he'd fuck off, sure, but he'd go anywhere else but here. He set about sorting out his own animal.

'Osric.' Someone called to him quietly in an unfamiliar voice. One of Egbin's young farmhands was furtively scuttling across the mud between him and the mead hall.

'What do you want?' Osric demanded gruffly, thinking he'd sooner cut off his own arm than talk to any of those poor excuses for Jutes.

'A word. If you will. I can help.'

Osric snorted. 'It's not harvest time yet, whelp.'

'I will sail east. To our home.'

The word struck a nerve. There was still a land over the sea, a land not even Osric had seen, but a land nonetheless where surely some true kin of his still stood proud.

'My name is Wulfric. I can sail. My brothers and I have a boat.'

'Well, Wulfric, I suggest you take it and go fish for something edible to have with whatever shit you grow in this bog.'

'I am serious,' Wulfric insisted.

'So am I. Now, fuck off.' Osric scrambled up onto the back of his horse, cursing at the animal for not standing still.

'Egbin has no vision. He thinks it is better to be the big fish in a small pond than have other Jutes around him.'

'It's more of a mire than a fucking pond, boy. And Egbin is a fat cunt that couldn't swing a sword, even if it was all he had to cut up his cabbage.'

Wulfric nodded in agreement. 'We will go anyway,' he muttered. 'I just wanted to tell you, so you could tell the king. We will return with men.'

'And I'll be married to his daughter before the year is out. Good luck to you.' Osric kicked the flank of his horse, which refused to move.

'You don't remember me, do you?' Wulfric asked.

'Should I?'

'I was only a child when you—when you left. But I recognised you. I remembered your name, even if Egbin did not.'

'I was outlawed, named a wolf,' Osric corrected him bitterly, 'and no, I don't remember you, and I shan't lose sleep trying to.'

'It was wrong—what they did to you.'

Osric darkened. He hadn't been back here in nearly fifteen years, and with good bloody reason. He glared at Wulfric, imagining how it would feel to split his skull open. Not that the lad deserved it. For all Osric knew, Wulfric was well meaning, perhaps even capable of what he claimed. But in that moment, he just represented a chapter of Osric's life that he had happily left behind.

'I meant no offence.' Wulfric took half a step back, as if reading Osric's mind. 'For all that it matters now, I was glad for what you did.'

'I'll give Vitalinus your message.' Osric drove his heels into the horse's flanks again, and this time it responded.

* * *

The ride out of the swamp was a relief. Ossian hadn't much enjoyed the soreness of being in the saddle before, but he positively relished it now. The Jutes were a lost cause.

Vitalinus rode silently next to him for a while, deep in his own thoughts and uninterested in counsel. There was little Ossian could think of to sweeten his mood. They didn't know the full extent of the plague across the island, but there was little chance that enough capable men could be raised to counter the threat from the Kaldi. And Vitalinus needed a persuasive victory against the foreign invaders to make any headway towards uniting the tribes.

'Ossian,' Vitalinus broke the quiet. 'I want you to return home. Zeki and a few other men will see you safely there.'

Ossian nodded. 'And where will you go?'

'Calleva. I need to talk to The Onion. And I'll need Osric with me, and probably the Nobatians as well.'

'But not me?' Ossian, for once, whilst he didn't quite consider Viroconium his home, was quietly happy to be returning to there, but wanted to at least sound disappointed.

'Diplomacy is not my intent. I hope not to need your sage counsel. I fear a show of strength, however, may be required, and I suspect Osric might be keen to flex his muscles now.'

'I don't blame him,' Ossian sneered, but got no more words from Vitalinus. Ossian hoped he was not becoming doubtful of his calling. Albion awaited its leader, and Ossian was as certain as a man could be that Vitalinus was the man to take up that mantle.

The Drowning Pit

Wroid cursed himself that he hadn't got there sooner. Drust had waylaid him the first evening after Derelei had been condemned, and had been unusually friendly, wanting to share ale and stories with him until they had both fallen into a drunken slumber. If he hadn't thought anything strange about that at the time, he certainly did on reflection. The next day he had felt eyes on him, watching his every move. It made sense. His affection for Derelei was no great secret. It also rained, which made him afraid for her.

He waited until long into the night. The rain had passed, and it was cold and clear. The moon was haloed when visible, a brisk wind blowing clouds across its face at regular intervals. The loch lit up with its reflection, then darkened again. Fickle as Drust's moods, Wroid mused as he took a precautionary circuitous route to the drowning pit.

By the time he got there, he was exhausted. The rope he carried was not light.

'Derelei,' he whispered hoarsely. There was no answer. He knelt by the side of the pit and peered down into the darkness. 'Derelei,' he called again. But nothing came back.

After carefully looping the rope around the trunk of the hanging tree, he began to lower it into the hole, his hands shaking with anticipation. He had no idea how much rain needed to fall to make the pit true to its name. She wouldn't have starved to death yet, but he wondered how long she could survive the cold, drenched in near freezing water and untouched by any sunlight.

'Climb if you can,' he called into the darkness. 'Please.' He lay on his front, gazing downwards, feeling the chilly pull of the deeper earth. It was a horrid, dank mouth that Derelei had been fed to; a muddy wet throat that had swallowed her. Wroid rested his hand on the thick rope and let his head drop, almost wanting to let himself slide into the blackness and be with her, even if only in death. He was too late. The rain in the day had done for her. He should have come sooner, regardless of consequence.

The rope moved slightly. Or did it? Wroid was suddenly alert, so alert that he immediately wondered if he had imagined the movement. It was still now.

'Derelei?' He whispered. 'Are you awake?' He realised that, even if she were alive, the chances of her still being conscious, given the cold, were slim.

The night fell silent again.

Then the rope moved. It twisted under his light touch, the rough sinews of hemp grazing his palm. Derelei lived. Wroid strained his ear to the hole for any cry.

A thin voice rose from the depths of the earth. 'Pull,' it said. He hauled himself quickly to his feet and heaved the rope upwards. It was weighted, mercifully. Hold on tight, he willed her, as the rope coiled behind him.

A pale hand appeared at the brim, grabbing suddenly at a wayward root from the hanging tree. Derelei's face followed, twisted with effort, as she pulled herself free from her would-be tomb. Her legs scrambled up too, and she rolled clear of the hole's clutches. Seeing her safely out, Wroid ran to her and pulled her to him and even further away from the pit mouth.

'I thought I was too late,' he breathed into her long hair as he held her close. He might as well have been telling her he loved her, he realised, and laughed suddenly. 'Derelei.' He had no more words to say in that moment than her name, which he lovingly repeated against the chill of her cheek. 'Derelei. Derelei.'

She wriggled free of his embrace eventually and looked at him in the moonlight. Her hair fell like snakes, sodden skeins that curled around each other, framing her sharp face. She pulled at the rope that she had tied around her waist and freed herself.

'You took your time.' Her smile was pained, but her humour was unhurt.

'I had to get drunk with your uncle first.' He grinned back at her, unable to stop himself from touching her cheek.

Her eyes flashed. 'I should kill him.'

'Probably.'

'I will kill him.'

'You need to get far away from here,' he told her. 'You can't ever come back.'

She looked at him, studying him for a while, then shivered.

'Oh, here.' He handed her a carefully tied bundle of warm clothes. 'There's a sword and javelin, a dagger, and some other bits in there, too. Some food. I'm sure you're starving.'

She pulled at the ties and let the weapons fall to the ground. Food and warmth were the first priorities. She found the bread and meat and wolfed it while she pulled the clothes around her. 'We,' she said with her mouth full.

'We what?' Wroid asked.

'We need to get away from here. You're coming too.'

A pain shot through Wroid's heart. There was nothing in the world he wanted more than to walk away with her. He loved her completely. But he could not.

'No. You must go alone.'

'Drust will kill you when he finds out what you've done.'

'If he finds out.'

'He will.' Derelei put the bread aside and looked at him earnestly. 'Come with me. Please.'

'If I go with you, they will know you are saved, and they will hunt us like wild animals and let the dogs eat our hearts.'

'We'll take our chances.' Derelei put her hand on his.

Even in that icy touch, he felt the warmth he had long wished to feel from her, and he almost changed his mind. 'No,' he said. 'You must go. As long as I am here, everyone will assume you dead, here in this horrible hole. It is the best chance you have.'

Derelei's eyes filled with tears. Wroid couldn't even imagine what she had gone through down there, waiting for the rains to choke the life from her, but he felt sure that her pain in that moment was not dissimilar to that which he felt. His words were meant to send her away from him, but his heart screamed to hold on to her, so he moved forward and threw his arms around her again. She sobbed quietly, and he felt her arms circle him as well. And, for a moment, he was happy.

'Go south,' he whispered. 'I will follow when it is safe to do so.'

She broke away and nodded.

Then he kissed her.

* * *

The west side of the loch was slow going. The bank rose sharply from the water's edge and didn't stop climbing. More months of the year than not, the tops of the hills that loomed over the loch were at the very least dusted with snow.

Derelei had set off at little more than a hobble, her legs numb from the cold water of the pit, but soon found her usual agility. She ran steadily, happy to feel the warmth that the exercise provided. Like any good Kaldi warrior, she travelled light. What she carried, she owed to Wroid. A small sack of provisions hung from her shoulder, a dagger hung at her waist, and her javelin sat lightly in her hand as she ran. And the sword? *Oh Wroid, what did you do?* The sword that was strapped to her back, its perfect blade lovingly bound in deer hide, was one of Drust's. Wroid had stolen it in a moment of drunken bravado the night Drust had plied him with ale, the night Derelei had languished in that hole.

It was perhaps an unnecessary risk, but Wroid had pointed out that Drust would never connect her with the missing blade. But he would surely miss it. The gods help the poor bastards that would have to listen to his inevitable tantrum. And who wouldn't miss such a weapon? It was a sword of immaculate craftsmanship, strong and keen and wielded in many, if not all, of the hundred battles Drust was reputed to have fought. And won. One day, Derelei swore to herself, he would be reunited with it, and his winning streak would come to a bloody end.

Leaving Wroid had been hard. She didn't feel about him the way she knew he felt about her but, when she had felt the rope knocking against her barely conscious body—knowing it could only be him at the other end—she knew she would have gladly given herself to him every night for the rest of her life. But he was right. If he had come with her, their freedom would have doubtless been short-lived.

Head south, he had told her. To what, though? It was several days hard walking to the wall and beyond. She knew that well, as she knew the way. But she couldn't imagine a warm welcome in Bernaccia. Perhaps she could hide away in some ruined croft in the highlands for the rest of her days, far enough away from any Kaldi that might recognise her, but the thought repulsed her. She was young, vibrant, skilled, and now bitterly turned against her own kin. Drust's betrayal of her—for the sake of a fucking mistress—ate deep into her. She needed to believe that she could one day have the chance to bury his own sword in his chest, and the only way she could imagine that happening was if she took up arms against him. She would need to make friends of her former enemies.

Or die trying.

* * *

It was supposed to be summer. The solstice was nearly upon them, but still the wind could find its way into your bones. Tugen, on watch duty, looked northwards and wondered if Emrys and Rozena had found a warmer sanctuary.

He thought of his friend most days, usually when alone and looking out over the lands that held the Kaldi threat. Emrys had saved his life, yes, but more than that, he had always been like a brother to him, warm and loyal and strong. That day, when the Kaldi attacked their village, was etched in Tugen's mind. He dreamed of it more often than he liked to think about it, but it was always there; the flames, the blackened bodies, the smell of blood, and Rozena's tear-stained face. He had seen his murdered parents, their bodies still aflame and swaddled in dark smoke that stung his crying eyes. And before that, before any of that, he remembered fighting Emrys in the woods, and the bear with its yellowed claws and dreadful roar.

But most of all—and perhaps it was just his mind's way of putting a face to the evil that had changed his life forever—he pictured *her*. He saw that painted blue face every night. The Kaldi woman who had brazenly attacked the bear and spared Emrys' life. Why had she spared him? Why had she not killed them both?

Zala, who Tugen had grown closer to, told him it was because she was a woman. And women don't kill children. Not even Kaldi women. Tugen had resented being described as a child, even if the Kaldi woman hadn't even seen him. And Emrys was no more a child than him, even back then.

'He was waving a wooden sword at a bear!' Zala had laughed at him. 'Why would she want to kill him?'

'So, if he'd had a real sword that day, he'd be dead now, and me too?'

'Probably.'

'Maybe you're right,' he admitted, still stinging from her laughter.

'Well, I'm glad you're not,' she moved closer to him, her dark, smiling face nuzzling into his shoulder.

'Right, or dead?'

'Both.'

Tugen had found himself a new family, and he was happy as much as he wasn't. Kiros had taken him in almost as another son, though Negasi was always going to get pride of place. Kamali was as kind and nurturing as any mother could be, and Zala was, well, she was like nobody Tugen had ever met. He had been blooded in the hunt and had ascended in responsibility to take the watch over the northlands, at least in daylight.

The wind whistled over the flat land, blowing its icy fingers between his ribs. He scrunched his face up, struggling to see against the gust. That's when he saw her. At first, he saw a lone figure, tall and slender, walking in a direct line towards him, towards the wall. Its arms stretched out to its sides, hands holding weapons in an obvious gesture of surrender. As the figure neared, he determined it was a woman. A Kaldi woman. Her face was not painted, supporting her passive approach, but her physique and gait were unmistakable.

A sudden feeling rose in Tugen's chest, a dreadful sense of familiarity. It was the woman from his dreams, the woman who had saved Emrys from the jaws of the beast, the woman who had spared them, the woman who, with her savage kin, had butchered his parents, Emrys' parents, Rozena's parents. He blinked, wanting to believe that it could not be possible. His heart pounded faster as he strained to see her face better.

It was her.

The OldWays

He saw her coming from the rampart, and his heart soared. He had longed to see her since hearing of her miraculous recovery, but she had not come. He had wanted to manufacture some reason to insinuate himself into the palace, to glimpse her, to remind her that he still lived and breathed too, that his heart was still hers. But he knew his place. She would come to him when she was good and ready, he had told himself repeatedly, and here she was.

The sickness had left no marks upon her. She was as beautiful as she had appeared to him the night before he had marched south for Dumnonia. The blackness of her thick hair still hung loosely around her pale face. The arch of her brow was as pronounced as her cheekbones, and her lips were as full and ripe as ever.

He met her at the gate, having deftly slid down the ladder from the top of the walls, and beamed at her. It was all he could do not to run and gather her in his arms.

'Thank the gods you live.' He stepped towards her.

'Oh Selwyn, it is so good to see your face again.' She glanced around, noticing the men of the fort looking in their direction. 'Is there somewhere we can be alone?'

He led her to his private chamber, little more than a lean-to against the fort's wall, but his alone as commander of the garrison. And he took her hands in his. 'It has been so long since I have seen you. I feared that night would remain in my memory as the last vision of you.'

She looked at him gently. Gently. That was odd. She had not been gentle that night, not especially. She had been wild and passionate, finally yielding to a temptation that had grown over months of seeing each other in passing, secret looks and smiles, the scantiest of words exchanged in hushed tones. He had always known her to be spirited and free. That was why he had admired her from afar for so long. And when she had returned his attention and crept from her father's villa in Viroconium out across the fields to meet him, he had felt truly blessed. They had lain pressed naked together under a great mound of furs, and he had dared to dream that they could be together.

'You must have been so scared.' He squeezed her hands a little, wanting to pull her towards him and rekindle the passion. 'What a horrid experience.'

'I had it easy.' She smiled simply. 'My life hung in the balance. I was lucky enough to live. Many others weren't. I feel for you. I know you had the awful job of burying the dead.'

And more, he thought bitterly, remembering the stink of the pyres. 'You are strong,' he said, 'and beautiful as ever.'

'Selwyn.' She looked downward, avoiding his eyes. 'I want you to promise me something.'

'Anything. I love you.'

She lifted her head, and her eyes were startlingly clear. 'Don't follow my father into the abyss.'

'What do you mean?' Her words surprised Selwyn.

'You go where he tells you to go, fight who he tells you to fight. It doesn't have to be that way.'

'Pasha, your father wants the people to be safe and strong, and live in peace.'

She sighed lightly. 'Yes, he told me as much.' Pasha's eyes shone, burned almost. Was that the passion he had seen before? 'How many people need to die before that happens? I don't want you to end up in a field of blood.'

'I won't. I swear.'

'Don't promise things you can't deliver.'

Selwyn knew he would run away from it all in a heartbeat if she were to go with him. He wanted to tell her so, but the words hid from him.

'I can't see you again, Selwyn.'

He stared at her. Into her gleaming eyes.

'I'm sorry. Truly.' She pulled her hands free and raised one to his cheek. 'My path is not yours. Not any more.'

His mind flew to the night he had spent with her, to the feel of her flesh on his, to the fire that danced in her eyes, to the sparks that leapt between her lips and his, to the promises that he had made, and that she had made.

She was wrong.

'We made oaths,' he blustered.

'We did. I was wrong.'

'No,' was all he could mutter.

'I'm sorry.'

* * *

Life was slowly returning to something like normality in Viroconium. The streets were clean, though they lacked the bustling, noisy crowds of people that had constantly filled them. Even the market was muted. Stalls stood empty, shelves bare, and unwanted wagons had been tidied away into a neat line along one side of the square. Too many had died, Sevira thought sadly as she looked out of one of the villa's windows that offered a view of the main thoroughfare.

Ossian was at the gate; she had been informed. The druid had returned.

'And my husband?' she had asked her servant.

'He is not there.'

Only for a moment had she thought something terrible had befallen him, and her heart had leapt in fear. But no, doubtless he had pressed on in pursuit of some other important business. Ossian, she had little doubt, would not have returned to Viroconium if Vitalinus no longer lived.

The druid was not an easy man to like. And yet he had saved her daughter, so she was indebted to him. And her husband trusted him, so she would have to as well. He had about him an air of knowing, of stout belief in some inevitable course of events that he could not possibly know. Vitalinus was a secretive man, with hidden ambitions and thoughts, capable of wickedness as easily as of greatness, but she knew his heart and could hear his unspoken words. Ossian, on the other hand, was a clear lake on a sunny day. No matter how long you looked, you could not see what lay beneath the surface.

She had him meet her in the garden, her favourite place. It was hers, and she felt empowered there.

'Vitalinus has gone to barter with Einion in Calleva,' he told her curtly. 'He wished me here to help you with governance.'

'And I am glad you are here,' she said slowly, conjuring some regality. 'I managed just fine when he was on his errand to Dumnonia, but I confess these are strange times. Your assistance will be appreciated.'

Ossian nodded; his head bowed for a moment longer than Sevira liked. It was that kind of gesture, the calculated hiding of his face disguised as sycophancy, that raised her heckles.

'How did my husband fare with the Jutes?' she asked him.

'It did not go entirely to plan,' he answered unhelpfully, 'but we will find a way.'

Sevira was wearying of him already. 'I believe Pasha was looking forward to your return.'

Ossian's face twitched slightly, the tip of his mouth curling up slightly. 'I trust she has remained in good health?'

'She is as well as she has ever been, and we have you to thank for that.'

'She fought the illness. She may thank herself. I merely watched over her.'

'Regardless,' Sevira said with the last of her patience, 'I am grateful. Forgive me, Ossian, you must be tired from your journey.'

'A little saddle sore, I admit.' He smiled at her genuinely, though maybe it was his own relief at the opportunity to end the conversation.

'Go then, refresh yourself, and eat and drink. We will talk more later.'

He backed away a few steps, with a deference more like mockery, then turned and left the garden.

* * *

She could feel the dead beneath the ground. She could almost hear them. They were at one with nature again. At peace. *Poor Selwyn*, she thought briefly. He was not at peace, and nor would he ever be.

Pasha closed her eyes as she walked the straight path back towards the gates of Viroconium, letting the spirits guide her. Fragments of her dreams flashed through her head. Selwyn, mortally wounded and surrounded by corpses in a field that ran with blood. Her mother, wandering, lost in a cave. Her father, surrounded by fire, was finally afraid. A wolf, with filthy slavering jaws, that grinned and grimaced and ground its teeth. Ossian, his smile vanishing in a rare moment of astonishment.

Ossian. She needed to talk to the druid. If anyone could understand what she needed, it was him.

IV

VINCIT QUI PATITUR

'Gutta cavat lapidem'

'Dripping water hollows out the stone'

(Ovid)

Master and Student

Ossian looked the Ethiope up and down slowly.

'He's one of the best men we have,' Selwyn announced. He didn't like the way the druid looked at Zeki.

'Yes, but are you sure he can be trusted?' Ossian asked quietly, though still perfectly loud enough that Zeki could hear.

'Of course he fucking can,' Selwyn snapped. 'I'd trust him with my life, and I'd trust him with the boy's as well. I might even trust him with yours.'

The druid had asked Selwyn to train Vitalinus' youngest son, Catigern, to show him how to fight. Under other circumstances, Selwyn would have jumped at the chance to spend the extra time in Viroconium. Close to Pasha. But Pasha had made it clear there was nothing left there for him.

'Might I remind you I am here with the full authority of Vitalinus?' Ossian clearly didn't like Selwyn's choice of words any more than he did his choice of tutor.

'His authority, yes. I know,' Selwyn sneered, 'and that's all.'

'He will hear of your subordination.'

Selwyn laughed, surprising himself. Mirth had not come readily to him recently, and laughter was a stranger. 'Tell him, druid. I command here, not you. If you don't want Zeki, you can train Catigern yourself. I'm sure he'll be glad to learn what flowers are best to aid a good night's sleep.'

Ossian bristled. Selwyn knew he was treading dangerously. Insulting a druid was not something to be done lightly, but he didn't really care.

'He will do.'

Selwyn looked at Zeki. 'It may not seem like it, Zeki, but I mean to honour you with this task. Are you happy to train Vitalinus' son, to show him all you know?'

Zeki, who had remained expressionless for the last few minutes, smiled warmly at Selwyn. 'I am honoured. I will teach the boy well.'

'You will not refer to him like that,' Ossian spat, and Zeki's smile disappeared. 'His name is Catigern. And you will call him that, or something else befitting.'

'Young master?' Selwyn teased.

'That would be fine.'

Ossian wasted little more time on The Wrekin and headed back to Viroconium, leaving instruction for Zeki to report to the villa the next morning. Selwyn's shoulders dropped the moment the druid left.

'You do not seem yourself,' Zeki said quietly.

'I'm tired.' He was. He hadn't slept well for days. 'I'm sorry for burdening you with this extra duty, Zeki.'

'Do not be sorry. It truly is an honour.'

'Fuck honour.' Selwyn reached for a jug of ale and poured a cup.

'I thought honour was what bound us all together?' Zeki smiled, holding out his hand. 'We do not fight alone. We do not die alone. And we certainly don't—'

'Drink alone.' Selwyn laughed again. 'Don't use my words against me.' He poured Zeki a cup.

'Your heart is broken.' Zeki frowned slightly.

'Oh, fuck off. Is it that obvious?'

'Probably not to the druid. He just thinks you are impertinent.'

'He really can fuck off.' Selwyn took a long drink. 'Catigern's a good lad, though. He'll learn fast.'

'You should know something,' Zeki spoke quietly, seriously. 'You, not Vitalinus, are the reason that we all fight the way we do. The men love you.'

Selwyn raised his cup in thanks, a sad smile spreading across his face. 'Thank you, Zeki. Truly. Though, as you rightly pointed out, it is not the love of men that I am missing.'

'Nevertheless, it is that love that will give you true purpose. Women are often a mirage.'

'A mirage?'

'An illusion. Something that appears beautiful. Something we think we want or need. But in the end, they always disappear.' Zeki looked down, as if concerned he had talked too freely.

'Mirage,' Selwyn mused as he refilled their cups. 'It's a pretty word.'

Encouraged, Zeki continued. 'Imagine a perfect reflection in a lake, appearing almost real enough that you could reach out and touch it.'

'We used to throw stones into the lake where I grew up. I saw little but ripples.'

Zeki nodded sagely. 'Quite so. Quite so.'

* * *

Zeki warmed to Catigern quickly. He was more man than boy already; tall and strong, and with looks and a smile that would no doubt prove a hit with the women. He spoke softly, but measured and confident, as if he had already worked out that shouting was often just the bluster of a man who doubts himself.

'I don't really want to learn to fight,' he told Zeki honestly. 'Surely there's more to the life of a man than knowing how to kill another man.'

'That you even make such an observation is proof that there is,' Zeki said after a moment's thought. 'But it is my task to teach you.'

Catigern fell to his haunches, letting the dull training blade rest against his thigh.

'It won't be all sword play, young Catigern,' Zeki promised.

'No? What else will there be?'

'Stories. Poetry. Song. Like you, I take no great pleasure in the simple act of wielding a sword and trying to kill a man.'

'It seems like that's a pretty important part of fighting,' Catigern moaned.

'Your father does not always stand in the centre of the battle.'

'So, I am to be trained as a leader of men? Trained to stand on a hill and look down over men killing other men? That sounds even worse.'

'No.' Zeki sighed gently. 'The greatest victories are the ones with the least amount of bloodshed. Isn't that a trick worth learning?'

'It sounds like delusion to me.'

'Pick up your sword,' Zeki instructed.

Catigern wrapped his fingers around the hilt of his weapon and stood up. He was already a few inches taller than Zeki, and as broad.

'Now try to hit me.'

'Fine.' Catigern stood, poised. 'Pick up your sword, then.'

'No.' Zeki grinned. 'I am not trying to hit you. You are trying to hit me.'

'You're unarmed.'

'Yes. Now attack.'

Catigern scowled. This clearly wasn't what he'd expected. He waved his sword limply in front of Zeki. Zeki did not move.

'I said attack.'

Catigern took a tentative step forward and extended his arm, thrusting the sword weakly towards Zeki's chest. Zeki rocked to one side, and the blade did not make contact.

'Again.'

Another thrust, harder this time. Zeki sidestepped. Catigern sighed, frustrated, and put a bit more effort into his next attack, a broad swinging arc that Zeki effortlessly avoided by leaning back.

'Come on,' Zeki goaded Catigern. 'If you lay the blade on me, we'll finish early.'

The boy attacked again, with a grunt of frustration. Again and again Zeki sidestepped, ducked, and eventually even jumped every attack that Catigern made. Within moments, Catigern was breathing hard, his efforts doubled and doubled again. Zeki was wary of humiliating the lad, so decided the lesson ought to end. Catigern's blade flashed in a wayward arc that, had the edge been keen, could have easily severed any man's head from his body. But Zeki was equal to it. He ducked low and rolled nimbly backwards, putting a few yards between them in a heartbeat. Neatly gathering his own sword from the sand, he raised a single parry to Catigern's next attack. And, as the blades clashed, Zeki leant forward and forced both blades upright between them, before twisting his and wrenching Catigern's from his grip.

'How did you do that?' Catigern looked at his weapon on the ground. 'How did you do any of that?'

'That, young master, is what I am here to teach you.' Zeki studied the young man's face and saw it contorted in confusion. 'That will do for now. Go and think about what you have learned today.'

'I will.' Catigern nodded, still frowning.

* * *

It was a hot day. Ossian had cooled off in the river a mile or so from the walls of Viroconium, far from the noise of other people. The chill of the water, however, had made his limbs ache a little. Resting for a while in the dappled shade of the bank, he spotted some comfrey growing and set about digging up its roots with the small, curved knife he always used in foraging.

'It's a beautiful day,' a voice came. He looked up and saw her.

'Pasha.' He smiled. There weren't many people he would have been happy to see in that moment, but she was one of them. 'How pleasant to see you!'

'What are you doing?' she asked innocently.

Ossian looked down at the comfrey root in his hand and pushed it into a small sack that hung at his waist. 'Just collecting useful plants.'

'What does that one do?'

'Comfrey?'

'Comfrey,' she repeated, as if making a mental note. 'Yes, comfrey.'

'My hands are not as supple as they once were. The bones hurt sometimes.' He paused, suddenly conscious of divulging to her the symptoms of his age.

'And this helps?'

He nodded.

Pasha was the picture of good health. Her skin glowed and her eyes shone, and her lips curled into a smile as sweet as any he had ever seen. Even the sweat that beaded on the curve of her breasts he could see between the folds of her loose robe glistened with life. He remembered briefly how she had looked in the winter, drenched in stinking sweat and pus, her black hair matted and stuck to her ghostly white face. He remembered undressing her and tending to her weeping wounds, applying salves to places that should not be seen by anyone but a lover. He had seen her draped in imminent death, and he had brought her back. To this. She was magnificent.

'I see Catigern has a new tutor.' Her words wrenched him back to the present and reminded him of the unpleasant exchange with Vitalinus' attack dog, Selwyn. The insolence of that man.

'You disapprove?'

'Of what?' Her face remained serene. She did not disapprove. And why would she?

'Nothing. What of it?'

'Well, I want a tutor as well.' She smiled at him, her body swaying in some childish affectation.

'You want to take up arms? Your parents would not allow it.'

'No. Ossian. You saved my life.' She took a step closer, her eyes suddenly earnest, almost urgent. 'I want you to teach me everything you know. All your magic.'

Ossian was surprised. He looked away for a moment, into the slow-moving water of the river. He hadn't passed on any of his knowledge to anyone, though he had spent years of his youth learning from other druids. Other druids. Where were they now? He hadn't seen any of his kind in a decade, at least. Perhaps it was time to school another. He looked back at Pasha, at her wide dark eyes, and saw something in them, a hint of fire perhaps.

'Then that is what I will do.' He smiled thinly. 'Though the first thing you must know is that there is no magic.'

She frowned, not in disappointment, but almost in disbelief. Ardent disbelief.

'I see things in my dreams,' she whispered conspiratorially.

'Well,' he replied in kind, 'maybe there is just a little magic.'

Calleva

The forest went on forever. Osric was clearly sick of it.

'Wait until you set eyes on Einion. He's as big as an oak,' Vitalinus muttered in response to the Jute's complaints.

'And you want me to fight this giant? This Onion?' Osric asked.

'I truly hope it doesn't come to that.'

'And if it does?'

'Then we'll find a way for you to win.'

That was about the size of it. And it probably would come to that. Einion was renowned for insisting on resolving matters of diplomacy with combat, often deadly. Considering his size, and skill, The Onion usually got what The Onion wanted.

The Atrebates, Einion's people, were an influential tribe. They had always maintained good relations with Rome and were both progressive in their acceptance of Roman ways but also proudly defensive of their old ways. If anyone could swing Vitalinus' position in the council, it would be Einion.

'Why must we be bound to these stony paths?' grumbled Osric. 'I think my mount enjoys it about as much as I do.'

There was no denying that the horses would prefer softer ground, but the Roman road was the most direct route to Calleva. When the trees finally thinned out, the town's walls loomed ahead of them. It was as impressive a settlement as Viroconium. Perhaps even more so, although the walls were showing signs of wear. Vitalinus spurred his horse forward towards the gates.

Vitalinus was granted a private audience with Einion, leaving Osric and the others milling about in what had once been the forum.

'I did not put my name to it,' Einion referred to the crawling missive sent to Aetius, Rome's favourite son and commander of its legions in Gaul. 'But if they do decide to come back, there's plenty of work to be done here.'

'And in Viroconium,' smiled Vitalinus, happy to find some common ground. It wasn't entirely true. Viroconium had been well maintained. Calleva was, slowly but surely, going the way of Lactodurum.

'Can you believe there used to be several thousand people living here?' The big man asked. 'We're barely a thousand now, and only half of them can wield a sword.'

It was the swords Vitalinus wanted, and the fealty. Even a few hundred good men would aid his cause. 'But you've nobody to fight,' he teased.

'And that is why you are here,' Einion grinned. He lay back on the long bench. Naturally, he had taken over the Decurion's residence, enjoying a parody of Roman opulence within the cracking walls. 'You want to proclaim yourself high king, and take away my strongest men to battle the Picts in the frozen north lands.'

'I have always admired your ability to completely undermine the process of diplomacy.'

'Oh, fuck off. Why should we tread carefully around each other for half a day, muttering pleasantries, and breaking bread, when we know exactly what each other wants?' Einion leapt up, suddenly towering over Vitalinus. 'That said, we do need some wine.'

'You have me at a disadvantage.'

'How so?' Einion found a jug and sloshed its thin red contents into a couple of cups.

'I don't know what you want.'

'I'll tell you what I don't want. I don't want the Romans to come back, even if they promised to just rebuild all the shit that's fallen down.'

'Thank you.' Vitalinus accepted the wine gratefully. His mouth was horribly dry.

'I also don't want to lose kin in a war against an enemy that they would never otherwise see.'

'You don't think the Picts, the Kaldi, would venture this far south if they were unimpeded?'

'I don't see why they would. How many of them are there? How much land do they want?' Einion settled back onto his bench, making it appear significantly smaller than it was.

'I have no idea.'

'No. No, you don't. You just have it in your head that it should all be yours, not theirs.'

'I want to unite the tribes of Albion. And they are enemies to that cause.'

Einion laughed, spilling wine over himself. 'Really? And here I thought you were just worried they'd ravage Viroconium if you didn't find some extra muscle.'

Vitalinus contemplated his wine, swirling it in small circles. 'You have only told me what you don't want, not what you do.'

'I like a fight,' Einion said, suddenly almost wistful. 'Truth be known, we're all just getting fatter here. A good scrap might be just what we need.'

'Well, that I can give you.'

Einion waved his hand dismissively. Vitalinus let him think.

'If you can best me, you can have my oath.'

'Me?' Vitalinus laughed.

'Yes, you. Why not you?'

'Einion, I am not a young man. I will stand in battle, but I am no champion. You propose a joke, a spectacle to amuse the Atrebates and humiliate me.'

'And?'

'I had hoped for more reason.'

Einion sighed. 'You fucking Cornovians have no sense of humour, do you? Naturally, I do not expect *you* to fight me.' He got to his feet once more, a broad smile on his face, and poured more wine for them both. 'I'm sure you have a man in your ranks who could at least offer me some sport.'

'It is to be sport?'

'What else? Give me a measure of time with your best man. If he still stands when the water runs out, I will join your cause.'

'Deal.' Vitalinus smiled uneasily. That was going to be a tough ask for any man.

'I'll try not to kill him immediately.'

'But you will try to kill him before the water runs out?'

'Obviously. And it will be hard not to.'

Vitalinus wanted to say something cautionary about over-confidence in battle, but there was just no getting around the fact that any fight was likely to be horribly one-sided.

'Elaf and Nudd will give you their oaths as well,' Einion said solemnly. 'If your man stands.' He erupted into laughter.

* * *

Osric had made it his business to fear no man. In battle, at any rate. There were plenty of sharp tongues in men's heads that could do more damage than a sharp sword to a man of virtue. Fortunately for Osric, he neither valued virtue nor cared what any man said of him. His blade was happy to answer any call, and he was yet to meet a man he would be afraid to stand against.

Einion was bigger than Osric had been led to believe, certainly bigger than he had allowed himself to believe. Vitalinus had not minced his words in describing the stature of this giant, but Osric was not one to pay heed to anything that he could not see for himself. This man, this Onion, stood probably a head and shoulders above Osric, and was twice as broad, with arms as thick as branches and hands that could doubtless break a man's skull in their enormous grasp.

'He'll make the earth rattle when he falls,' Osric muttered to himself. 'Still, it might have been better if Vitalinus had won him over with words.'

Shabaka looked at him with a wry smile. 'Have you heard of the porcupine?'

Osric shook his head, words not coming easily.

'It is like your hedge-pig, only bigger. Call it a giant hedge-pig.'

'Hedgehog? The man's as big as a bear.'

'Imagine him filled with arrows.' Shabaka winked at him.

Was that what Vitalinus had meant about finding a way to win? Did he mean to have Shabaka and Tsekani fill him with dozens of poisoned barbs to slow him down? Osric angered at the thought. 'You will let me die if die I must. I do not need your help.'

'You only need to be standing when the water runs out,' Vitalinus said as he approached.

'Tell Shabaka and his brother I do not need their help.'

'Fine. You weren't going to get it, anyway. I just wanted you to think I wouldn't let you die out there. But since you're happy to do so—'

'I'm not happy. Not happy at all. If I weren't so ashamed of Egbin and those other poor excuses for Jutes, I might have even told you to fight your own fucking battle.'

'Your loyalty will be well rewarded,' Vitalinus said, laughing.

Osric grinned back at him. 'If I can live long enough.'

'Indeed.'

'It's a shit plan.' Osric got to his feet. 'Let's do it.'

They had walked from the forum in the centre of Calleva and exited the town through a small postern gate. Just outside the city walls was what had probably once been a spectacular amphitheatre. Its sandy arena was now pitted with thistles and weeds, some as high as Osric's waist, and the stone tiered seating was green with moss and ivy. And yet today promised entertainment, so the amphitheatre was already half full of Atrebates eager to see their leader shed some foreign blood. Most were already drunk, and all were in fine voice.

Einion stood in the middle of the arena, arms outstretched, turning slowly, and encouraging the baying crowd. He was barely armoured. A huge thick leather gilet, studded with iron rivets, hung from his broad and otherwise bare shoulders, but he wore no helmet and carried no shield. The sword in his hand appeared little bigger than a gladius, even though it was twice the length. He's one big bastard, thought Osric.

'Come, Vitalinus,' the giant bellowed, 'where's this champion of yours?

We've not seen sport here for an age.'

Shabaka handed Osric his little round shield, painted in red and white.

'For all the good that's going to do me,' Osric muttered with a thankful nod. He unwrapped his broadsword and took a step forward, glancing at Vitalinus for some last reprieve. All he got was a sombre nod of encouragement. He puffed himself up as tall as he could and walked into the arena.

'What's this? A fucking Saxon?' Einion chuckled. 'I had hoped to give my people a show. And you give me a Saxon.'

It was fighting talk, Osric knew. Not that The Onion needed words to intimidate any opponent.

'Jute,' he called out loudly, quickening his pace towards the middle of the amphitheatre. 'I'm a Jute.'

Einion roared with laughter. 'Same fucking difference.'

Osric tried to think of something witty to come back with, a retort that would encourage cheers of his own. I'll let my blade do the talking, he thought grimly, already doubting that his sword would have much to say in this fight.

'Let it be known,' Einion rumbled on, 'that if this—this Jute—is still on his feet when the water runs out, we will ally ourselves with Vitalinus, king of Cornovia, and make his enemies our own.'

'Fat fucking chance!' A voice called out from the top tier. It was met with a raucous chorus of laughter.

Einion held up his hands, calming the throng, then sought out Vitalinus at the edge of the arena. 'You have my word,' he told him. 'Now,' he turned away again, a mad grin on his face, 'let's see how they bleed in Jutland.'

A tremendous roar filled the amphitheatre, rolling around the stone sides, deafening Osric. The crowd were on their feet, shouting and clapping. Some Romanesque looking official in a long white robe stood by a strange wooden framework that held an upturned amphora over a paddled wheel that was attached to a marker that would rise up a lined vertical bar. A clepsydra, Vitalinus had called it. Osric had never heard of such a thing, but the principle was straightforward enough. This clepsydra thing marked the passing of time. The passing of what little time was left to Osric.

'You are ready?' Einion asked him.

Osric nodded. The robed man pulled at a wax bung in the amphora and released a gentle trickle of water onto the wheel. If only blood would flow as slowly, Osric mused, and turned to face The Onion.

'Then begin!'

Chains

Tugen waited until long after it was dark to go to her. Even in the chill of night, the hilt of his dagger stuck to his clammy hand.

The Kaldi woman had brazenly walked right up to the walls of the fort and presented herself. She had said little, just identifying herself as Derelei, niece to Drust. Drust of a hundred battles. Unsurprisingly, Kiros had immediately ordered her to be restrained, and she was quickly chained to a hitching post in the yard. Tugen had rushed down from his sentry position to watch the proceedings. He observed from a distance, making doubly sure that his convictions were correct. If she wasn't the same woman who had speared the bear while it loomed over Emrys, then she was certainly a close relation.

There was some discussion about this apparent refugee from the Kaldi lands. She was quiet, neither struggling nor complaining as the chains were attached to her wrists. Kiros made it clear that, while he did not yet know what to do with her, they could certainly not risk her running back to her kind with information on the defences and numbers there at the fort. Probably because they were weaker and fewer than an outsider might assume.

Clouds obscured the moon, giving Tugen the cover of darkness as he padded across the yard towards her quiet silhouette. A loud snort came from behind him, within the hall, causing him to stop in his tracks. He stood there, motionless, waiting until he was certain nobody else was awake. A rasping snore comforted him, but in that moment, a pang of doubt flashed into his mind. And with it, Zala's face. He was certain she would not approve of what he was about to do.

He had grown closer to Zala. He patiently endured his reading lessons with her mother just so he could justify going to Zala for additional instruction. Really, he just wanted to be near her. He wanted to see her green eyes look at him. He wanted to kiss her dark skin. She was paler than her father, as was Kamali. Kamali's mother had been a Votadini, understandably enamoured with an Ethiope warrior, and doubtless Zala's green eyes had come from her. Tugen knew his affection for Zala was well known among the rest of the fort. Even Kiros had commented, suggesting that they would likely one day be married.

Kiros was good to Tugen. Would he still think so well of him after tonight, Tugen wondered. Probably not. He gripped the hilt of his dagger tighter, his jaw stiffening with resolve. If it must be so, then let it be so.

The moon re-emerged from the clouds, dropping pale light onto his quarry. He strode across the rest of the distance to the hitching post with extra purpose, and lifted her head up by her hair, his blade quickly finding the pale flesh of her exposed neck. One small move would do it.

She looked up at his face, expressionless. Nothing in her eyes cried out for mercy or explanation. They were just sad.

'I want to look you in the eyes as you die,' he told her through gritted teeth. He had let his murderous ambitions simmer all day. The sight of her face was more than enough to bring all the rawness bubbling violently to the surface.

She looked back at him. Blank. He felt sure she would have just quietly nodded and accepted his sentence, had his blade not been hovering against her throat.

He grunted in frustration. 'You don't understand me, do you, bitch?' Why should he expect this wild woman to speak his tongue?

'Why do you wait for nightfall,' she asked quietly, 'to murder me?'

He was taken aback. 'You speak our tongue.'

'We are not savages,' she whispered, as if she had read his mind.

'You and your people slaughtered my family,' he spat, quickly emboldening himself. He had not anticipated a conversation.

'My uncle is much aggrieved.'

He didn't know what he had expected. Repentance? Surely not. Gloating? Perhaps. But she seemed reluctant to offer either apology or brag.

'He feels he has something to prove. He feels he is owed.'

'Owed?' Tugen asked.

'Are you going to use that knife or not?' Her eyes searched his.

'Yes,' he answered.

'Then why should I talk more to you?'

He pulled the knife back a little and relaxed his hold on her hair. She wasn't going anywhere. He could kill her at any moment. What harm was there in letting her believe he intended to spare her?

'You're transparent, even for a child,' she said plainly, though the word 'child' stung him. 'You still intend to murder me.'

'You spared my friend,' he blurted out. 'You killed the bear that was attacking him, and you spared him. You hid him from your kin. Why?'

There was a flash of recognition in her dark eyes. She remembered, alright. She looked away into the night. 'You were the other boy.' She almost smiled. So, she had seen him as well. Which meant she had knowingly spared them both, not just Emrys.

'Yes. Tell me why?'

'Why?'

'You had just murdered everyone dear to us. Why save us?'

She looked at him, her eyes soft. They glinted, as if tears were forming in their corners. 'We do what we can.'

'What does that mean?'

'A moment of honour goes a long way to repairing for a lifetime of horror.'

Tugen looked at her, not really comprehending. Not only did she speak his tongue, she spoke it better than him.

'What do you live for, boy?' she asked him quietly.

'Revenge.'

'And now you can have it.' She smiled at him, offering herself freely. He felt the knife in his hand, ready to taste her flesh, but suddenly nothing was clear to him.

'And you? What do you live for?' he asked her.

'I too would be happy to breathe a while longer so that I may put an end to my uncle. But I live for love as well.' Her eyes saddened, and Tugen thought of Zala.

'Why did you come here?'

'To warn you about Drust. He is coming. With more warriors than you can imagine. It won't be a raid. It will be a war.' She looked at him earnestly. 'I want to join with your people against him.'

'I can't see Kiros allowing that.'

She stared at him, then sighed. 'No, I suppose not,' she said eventually, then dropped her head. 'I'm tired, boy. If I fall asleep, you just carry on and do what you must do.'

And she spoke no more.

He looked at her for a while, at her dark hair fallen over her face. He took half a step back and contemplated her lean, muscular body. She was not the mindless murderess he had expected, even wanted, to find. But she and her kind had burnt his parents alive. She had to pay for that. He tensed his fingers on the dagger's hilt, trying to steel himself. But his hand responded by shaking, by rebelling against his inner sense of necessary justice. It didn't want to do it. It didn't want to be sullied with blood. Not like this. She was no wild boar falling on his blade. She was a woman. She had spared his life before and now wanted to fight alongside him. His heart pounded and his tremulous hand grew clammier.

'Tugen,' he eventually whispered, as he sheathed his dagger. 'My name is Tugen. I will not kill you. Not tonight. I'm not sure about tomorrow. But it won't be tonight.'

But she was asleep.

* * *

It was still dark when something awoke Zala. A noise. Something unfamiliar, not the snoring of her father. That she could hear, faithful as ever. But no, there was something else, further away, perhaps outside the wall. It sounded like someone crying.

She slipped out from under the furs and padded out into the night. There was a glimmer of cold light to the east, but nothing more. It was enough for her eyes to adjust to the gloom, so she skirted the wall with her hands grazing its cool timber, searching for the source of the sound.

She knew instantly that the hunched figure sitting against the wall in the cold was Tugen. She crept towards him and sat down beside him, saying nothing, and waited for him to notice her. He lifted his head from where it had lain, cushioned on his crossed arms. His legs were bent at the knees, pulled up close to his chest, as if he had made himself as small as possible. And his eyes were red with tears. He looked at her.

'Is she dead?' Zala asked simply. He hadn't told her that the Kaldi woman was the one he had talked about before, but she knew from his behaviour all day that there was something significant about the new arrival. His eyes widened slightly, revealing his surprise at her intuition and confirming her suspicion.

He shook his head. 'No. I couldn't do it.'

Zala found his hand with hers and squeezed it. She loved him. It was that simple. And she felt his pain as though it were hers. 'Good.' She shuffled a little closer to him. Her mother, more practical than her father, who had simply observed that perhaps she should marry Tugen one day, had taken her aside a few days ago and schooled her in romantic ways. A father would never tutor his own daughter in the art of seduction, but a mother could.

'You'll know when the time is right,' she had told Zala. And had proceeded to explain a few simple truths about men and their desires and needs. Zala had been surprised to learn that there was more to it than just men, overcome with lust, sweatily grinding and grunting. And women serving the needs of those men.

'They need to feel like men,' her mother had said, 'often when they are at their weakest. That is our power over them. That is how we get what *we* want.'

Zala drew Tugen's hand towards her, into her gown, against the smooth flesh of her breast, and held it there, gliding it across herself. She felt her skin prickle and rise in goosebumps. She closed her eyes, revelling in the sensation, waiting for his hand to spring to life and administer its own attentions.

'Touch me,' she whispered encouragingly, and felt his fingers move. She felt his hand cup her firm flesh, squeezing gently, nervously. She turned to him, eyes half open, and leant towards him. 'Kiss me,' she breathed into his already open mouth, and their lips met for the first time. She pushed her tongue out against his, twisting against it, tasting him, pushing his tongue into an animated response. His hand squeezed her a little harder, and she moaned into the kiss, and reached up to put her hand on the back of his head. She held him there while they kissed, keeping him where she wanted him.

There was a hint of gold in the sky when she finally pulled away. The warm light fell on his tear-stained face, glistened on the wetness around his eyes. She had never seen anything so beautiful in her whole life. She laughed, finding her eyes flitting between the two of his as if uncertain which one she should look into. And he laughed in reply, his hand still lingering on her breast.

'I'm glad too,' he whispered. 'I'm glad I didn't kill her.'

And she knew that one night, before too long, she would give herself to him entirely.

* * *

She woke from a deep sleep. The sun was up and palely warming her face. She had dreamt of Wroid, of his arms and his eyes. In the light of day, her thoughts stayed with him for a moment. She worried for him. Here she was, chained to a post amid a legion of angry Ethiopes, facing certain death, and she was concerned for Wroid. His death, if it came at the hands of Drust, if any discovery was made of his part in her escape, would be horrible. Violent and unspeakable. Drust was not known for his clemency.

And then she considered her own plight. She had expected this much. Why would this ragged legion treat her with anything other than contempt and distrust? For all they knew, she was an assassin, sent to kill their leaders. Not that she'd have just walked up to the gate had that been the case. At any rate, she had little doubt that when they stopped debating what her hidden agenda might be, they would deem their own lives simpler if hers were just extinguished.

But the Briton boy–Tugen, he said his name was–the friend of the one with amber eyes; his coming to her in the dead of night, full of murderous intent, was not something she had anticipated. The thirst in his tormented eyes for revenge was frightening. She had revenge in her own heart, but for betrayal, not for the slaughter of all that was dear to her. She almost felt she deserved to feel his blade bite into her neck and give him some small sense of justice.

She noticed him there, at the back of the small crowd that gathered around her. His face was stony, unmarked by emotion, as he watched her.

'You want to fight with us against your own people?' Kiros spoke. His voice was deep, resonant, just what you'd expect from a leader of men.

'I do.' She answered simply.

'Our women don't fight.'

'Ours do.' She looked into his searching eyes.

He nodded thoughtfully. 'We may appear Roman in our armour, our weapons, but we are not of Rome. We have no quarrel with your people.'

'And I have none with you.'

'Yet your people kill, you burn, you destroy. Why would I ever be minded to trust you?'

'Drust carries generations of hatred in his blood. He wants to cause suffering.' She answered truthfully.

'And you do not?'

'I wish to kill Drust.'

'Your uncle.'

'My uncle, yes.'

Kiros scratched his face. 'Why does he raid lands far south of his own?'

'Drust believes we were driven north by the Romans from lands that were once ours. We chose freedom from the Romans, not surrender.'

Kiros chuckled. 'He raids further south than I'll wager your people have ever set foot.'

'Like I said, he wants to cause suffering.'

'And you would end it?'

'Give me my sword back and I will.' She pushed her chin forward proudly. She was a warrior before anything. Being robbed of her sword, even if it had been stolen from Drust himself, was a dishonour.

Kiros looked her up and down, taking stock. 'You will show us what you can do. It might be that, if freed, you would run back to Drust and tell him all you have seen. We are few. We are easily overcome. Maybe. It might be that you would slit my throat before doing so, to cut off the head of the snake, perhaps.' He smiled, as if he revelled in taking such a chance. 'But I would see you fight. My best man.'

'Give me your best three men,' she answered with a smile, 'if it will earn me my sword back.'

Kiros looked at her, and his smile broadened into a grin, and then into a laugh. 'Staves, bring staves. Four of them.'

* * *

Tugen watched Derelei disarm and disable the three finest fighters in the fort. She didn't even break a sweat, and she didn't injure any of them significantly. She wielded the wooden staff with a grace he had never seen before, her movement fluid and controlled. The men had come at her with no quarter intended, aggressive and masculine, and she had responded with a dance.

She confused the first man who came upon her so much that he dropped his staff in the mud almost immediately, his knuckles bruised. She swept the second from his feet before he got within arm's reach of her, and quickly bloodied the nose of the last man, though Tugen was sure that was

192

a miscalculation. She was so intent on defeating them without a show of blood. And yet it was only a broken nose, nothing that would hinder one of the three best fighters they had from taking up arms that day, should the need arise. She was left standing, staff poised and ready for a reprise, motionless and alert.

The men all gathered themselves up and picked up their staves, ready to visit upon her some macho retribution for their humiliation, which Tugen was quite certain would never come to pass. But Kiros held up his hand and called a halt to the proceedings.

'You shall have your sword,' he announced. 'And I would like to hear more of Drust and his plans.'

Derelei nodded, finally letting a long breath out of her puffed up chest, and relaxed. She threw the pole into the mud dismissively. Then she looked up, straight at Tugen. Tugen swallowed. She must know that it had been him who had gone to Kiros. She had to realise that he was the reason she had not been simply and summarily executed.

She nodded at him, a corner of her lip curling up into a smile of respect. She knew. He had left out what she had said about love. Revenge was a convincing enough motive for Kiros.

He nodded back.

Fruit on the Vine

The morning sun was fierce, so fierce that Lamorna, who had ventured a short distance from the fort to find fresher air, took shelter in the shade of a wizened old tree, one permanently bent to the wind that blew up from the sea. She had awoken feeling a little nauseous, no doubt down to her overindulging on cheese the night before. The noise and the smell of the men around the fort had been more than she could stomach, but now even the sun was causing her discomfort.

'My lady,' a voice called out in a slightly whispered cry. Just what she didn't want. It was Jac. He was pleasant enough to look at and bright enough. He'd impressed Vortimer, so he couldn't be all bad. She just didn't want any company.

'What is it, Jac?' Lamorna asked as patiently as she could.

The boy was pleased that she knew his name. 'Jac, yes, thank you, my lady,' he blustered. Obviously, she knew his name. She had caught him looking at her often enough, and he oversaw the garrison too. She wasn't blind or stupid. 'I wondered if I might have a word.'

'I was rather enjoying a brief respite from the clamour of the fort, but I'm sure if you came all this way from the gate, then it must be important.'

He smiled mawkishly, bending his head slightly in deference, but still having a good look at her. 'It is, my lady, and a matter I wanted to discuss in private.'

'Should you not take your private matters to Vortimer?' she asked hopefully.

'Yes,' he answered curtly, as if she had touched a nerve, 'but not this one.'

She sighed heavily, not even trying to hide her disappointment. 'Go on then, what is it?'

Jac hopped a little from one foot to the other, as if trying to find some perfect balance with which to deliver his mind.

'Speak,' she prompted him.

'It regards your husband,' he stuttered uneasily, 'or rather your husband's father.'

Lamorna's heart sank. It had always only been a matter of time. 'Again, Jac, perhaps you should talk to my husband or, better still, not talk at all.'

'I'm afraid my conscience won't permit me to remain quiet any longer, my lady.' Jac looked close to tears. His cheeks were reddening, and his eyes appeared shiny with moisture. 'It is well known among the men, my lady, that your husband's father, my lord Vitalinus—he killed your father, my lady.'

'Silence, Jac.' Lamorna held up her hand to stem the flow of his words. 'You don't know what you are saying.' They were all talking about it. Even now. 'What loyalty do you have to my father, or to me, that you feel the need to spread such lies?' She felt panic and anger jostling for control of her.

'To your father, none, my lady. But to you—'

'You are sworn to my husband, if not still to his father as well, are you not?'

'I am, my lady,' Jac blustered, suddenly lurching towards her. 'But I have honour, my lady, and so do you. You have been wronged.' He grabbed her by her shoulders, looking into her face imploringly.

'And what?' She tried to pull away, but his fingers gripped her tightly. 'You would defend my honour? Unhand me this instant.' She stepped back, twisting her body to free herself from his grasp, but fell back onto the ground. Jac came after her, blocking out the sunlight as he leant over her.

And then he was gone.

Lamorna blinked against the overhead sun, recovering her vision. Only to see that a few men were now gathered around her, and Vortimer had a firm hand on Jac's arm.

195

'What is this?' Vortimer demanded gruffly. He was only half dressed still, his shirt open above his breeches. And he was unarmed.

Jac pulled himself free and backed up, squaring off against Vortimer, suddenly tongue tied. His hand quivered, probably just instinctively, above his scabbarded sword.

'Speak,' came another demand. Vortimer pulled a sword from the scabbard of a soldier that stood nearby and levelled it at Jac. 'Speak now, Jac. From where I stand, you were laying hands on my wife.'

'I am not hurt, husband.' Lamorna spoke up.

'What business did you have with my lady?' Vortimer pressed on. Jac remained silent. 'Nothing? You spoke of nothing of importance with her? Did you mean to court her?'

Jac shook his head.

'No. That would be ridiculous. So, what then?'

Nothing.

Vortimer lowered the tip of his sword and glared at Jac. Lamorna thought she saw a little bitter disappointment hidden behind his anger. 'Take his sword and bind him.'

A couple of the men quickly obeyed. Jac didn't put up a fight.

'He meant no harm,' Lamorna muttered.

'I heard exactly what he said,' Vortimer hissed, then strode to within an arm's reach of Jac and looked him in the face. 'And for your traitorous words against my father, and against my family, and for assault upon my wife, I have no choice but to sentence you to die.'

Lamorna watched as Jac was marched back toward the gate.

'I'll do it myself,' Vortimer called after them, 'just as soon as I am dressed.'

* * *

The earth of the courtyard, exposed to the elements and all too often a mire that needed careful negotiation, was caked hard. Jac knelt there, head bowed, contemplating his impetuous behaviour. He wanted to curse out loud. But he had not been wrong. He knew he had acted because of his uncontrollable desire for Lamorna and knew that it was lunacy to have expected her to see him as anything more than the commander of the garrison. But he had not been wrong. He could have probably foreseen how his actions would have provoked an unfavourable response from Vortimer.

But he had not been wrong.

She had been wronged. Erbin had been wronged, too. All Dumnonia had been wronged. He wasn't sorry for saying what had to be said. And he would pay for it with his life.

'Bloody fool,' Maddock muttered nearby. Clearly, he didn't share Jac's principles.

Jac looked up, smiled sadly at Maddock, and behind him saw Vortimer emerging into the sunlight, his own broadsword now at his side and his hand ominously resting on its hilt. Lamorna trailed behind him, her face stony. She hung back a little as Vortimer strode towards the centre of the courtyard, where Jac knelt.

'As acting Lord of Dumnonia,' he began solemnly, loud enough for all the men, and Lamorna, to hear, 'I sentence you to die by the sword.'

The bright sun hit the smooth metal of Vortimer's blade as he drew it.

So be it, thought Jac, and he bowed his head again.

'Stop.' A weak voice rang out in the silence that had fallen over the men.

'Go back inside, Erbin,' Lamorna blurted out.

Vortimer paused with his sword raised. 'Let him watch. He needs to learn what it is to rule.'

'I am learning. From your mistakes,' came Erbin's response. 'Lower your sword.'

'I rule here, Erbin, until you are of age.' Vortimer said wearily. 'Perhaps you should do as your sister says and go back inside. You are not ready.'

'This man does not deserve to die,' Erbin persisted.

'He spoke treacherous words.'

'Against your father. And your father does not rule here. Not yet, as far as I know.'

There was a murmur among the men. Jac lifted his head a little to observe the confrontation.

'He does not. But I do, in your stead.'

'Do you? Or does my sister?'

'Tread carefully, Erbin.' Vortimer's hand clenched on the hilt of his sword.

'If you kill him, I suspect you must kill most of your men.'

'What are you talking about, boy?' Vortimer was losing patience.

'He wasn't even on the beach the day my father was killed. He can't know who killed him.' Erbin walked closer to Vortimer, brazen and unafraid. 'It is your men that spread the rumour. Jac only did his duty and reported it.'

The murmurs of the men grew louder. Vortimer lowered his sword a little.

'Perhaps you saw who killed my father?' Erbin's voice took on a taunting tone.

'No,' shouted Vortimer. 'I was too busy risking my life to protect your weak people and your barren fucking land from the Hibernians. You're very welcome, by the way.'

Erbin looked down, quieted by Vortimer's temper. He stepped back slowly. 'So, you admit they are my people,' he said quietly, 'and it is my land. Not yours.'

'Shut up, Erbin.' Lamorna rushed forward, standing close to Vortimer.

'I will not. Jac is a good man. I like him. And he was only doing what he thought was right.' Erbin puffed up his little chest and looked straight at the reddening Vortimer. 'Are you going to behead every man here? Why don't you ask them all who they think killed my father?'

Vortimer glared at Erbin. His hands trembled with anger.

'You are here to advise me. Not to be an executioner. I rule here, my Lord.'

Vortimer held his gaze, his brow furrowed. 'I speak to my own men, men who follow me and follow my father, Cornovian men good and true. If I hear any of you uttering these lies about my father, I will not be turned again from purpose. I will kill you.' And with that, he slid his sword back into its scabbard and turned on his heels. Lamorna reached for his arm, but he pulled away roughly. Erbin watched him go, a triumphant smile on his face.

'Lucky bastard,' Maddock spoke up again, and Jac slumped forwards onto the hard earth, his heart racing. He was spared. For now. He rolled onto his back and looked up at the deep blue of the sky.

* * *

Joceline had not witnessed the events in the fort earlier in the day, but she had heard whispers since about how Vortimer had been humiliated by the boy, Erbin. She was surprised to hear that, but was even more surprised when, after nightfall, Vortimer came to see her in her chamber.

'I wondered if I might entreat you to give me some company.' He was slurring his words slightly. The half-empty cup in his hand offered an explanation. She had already had a fair amount of wine herself, as had become her custom, a way to drown out the ghosts that haunted her. 'I am sick of this place, and I'm sick of this shit wine. And I apologise for talking this way to you.'

'You could accompany me for a walk perhaps,' Joceline offered.

'But I'm tired,' Vortimer grumbled, and sat down.

'Then you should go to bed.'

'Maybe I should,' Vortimer said with surprising sobriety, eyeing the furs.

'With your wife,' Joceline suggested reluctantly. It felt like the proper thing to say.

Vortimer frowned. 'I'm sick of them all,' he muttered, 'of her, of her brat of a brother, of this whole fucking place. I didn't want any of this.'

Joceline came to the realisation that Vortimer wasn't about to leave anytime soon, so she filled his cup and poured another for herself. As she poured the wine, she remembered a story her father had told her when she was younger about a fox trying to eat some grapes high on a vine. Unable to reach them, and not wanting to admit defeat or show his frustration, he denounced them as unripe and claimed he didn't want them after all. She briefly contemplated narrating the fable to Vortimer, but decided against it. Instead, she sipped her wine and looked at him calmly.

'There must be something you want in this place?' she murmured, offering the slightest hint of seduction hidden behind her innocent tone.

It worked. He looked at her with lust in his eyes. And why wouldn't he? She was certainly riper than Lamorna. She stepped back, slowly sinking onto the bed of furs, her robe parting to reveal a bare leg. He needed little more encouragement. He set his cup down and shed his clothes in no time at all. In a heartbeat, he was standing naked before her, his cock already nodding with appreciation of what was on offer. Joceline had not been with another man since her husband had died the year before, not even really entertained the idea, but her life was no longer the life she had chosen. Her husband was dead. And her son, if still living, was enslaved in Hibernia. She had been surprised at the desire she felt for Vortimer not long after being given sanctuary here, and had dutifully suppressed it, but she could deny it no longer. She pulled her robe up over her thighs and undid the sash that bound it together. As he descended towards her, she realised he was no more interested in whispering words of love to her than she was in hearing them, so she wriggled out of her robe completely and twisted herself, as naked as him, onto her hands and knees.

Let him have her.

* * *

Vortimer awoke to a pounding in his head. As he opened his eyes to daylight, memories of the previous night flashed in front of his eyes. Joceline. Her steely grey eyes, heavy lidded, staring into his. The warmth of her flesh. The wine on her lips. He closed his eyes again, letting the images linger.

Lamorna stirred next to him. He had at least made it back to his own bed. She moaned as she awoke and stretched her arms and legs. He opened his eyes again to see her observing him. 'I fell asleep before you came to me,' she offered, almost by way of an apology.

He shook his head ever so slightly. 'It is no matter,' he whispered. His mouth felt dry and tight. He screwed his eyes closed again, not to recapture the memories of the night before, but to evade the light of the morning.

'I'm glad you spared Jac,' Lamorna murmured next to him.

'I'm not sure I'd describe what happened as me sparing him,' Vortimer said gruffly. 'Your idiot brother made a fool of me.'

'He's no idiot, Vortimer. He's just different.'

'He's a fucking thorn in my side.'

'And he does rule here, no matter how much both you and I would have it otherwise.'

Vortimer looked at her, at the innocence of her face, and frowned. 'Jac should die for what he said, and for laying hands on you.'

'Why?' Lamorna propped herself up on her elbow. 'He said what everyone knows.'

'No,' Vortimer growled. 'I don't want to hear it.'

'What? That your precious noble father gutted mine on the field of battle? So what?'

Vortimer pushed her back onto the bed, his hand lightly covering her mouth. 'Enough, woman.'

'You stink of wine.' Lamorna screwed up her nose. 'And I'm glad he's dead. I'm glad Vitalinus killed him. And I'm glad—'

'I mean it.' Vortimer felt a surge of panic, alien to him, blossom angrily in his chest. His stomach churned, threatening to eject its contents. 'Be quiet, Lamorna, please.'

'You're becoming as bad as him.' Lamorna pushed his hand away. 'Father used to drink too much wine too, before he bedded me.'

Vortimer pulled back, horrified. There had been talk. There were always rumours. To hear it from Lamorna's own mouth made it real, however, and he was not ready to hear the truth. He rolled away from her, disgusted, appalled at her but also still assailed by visions of Joceline's nakedness, of the still fresh sensation of being inside her. Surely, he was going to throw up.

'Please don't be like him,' Lamorna implored him, and she too suddenly looked pale. 'You're better than him. Please.'

'I need some air.' Vortimer gasped and hauled himself to his feet. He was still in whatever clothes he had scrambled back into after leaving Joceline. The room swayed around him as he felt for the wall to lean on.

'Where are you going?' Lamorna got up on to her knees, her long hair knotted around her head, her eyes now soft with tears. 'Stay.'

Vortimer felt his heart beating faster. He was sure he was sweating. He needed water. 'You,' he began, wanting to vent spleen about her father, her, Erbin, the whole of Dumnonia. He'd done that already, he realised bitterly. He'd done just that when he'd angrily emptied his seed into Joceline the night before. Who was he to judge anyone? It was this place. It was poison. This shithole, forsaken by the gods, barely even raided any more by the Hibernians, this barren fucking land with its windy moors and cruel cliffs and cold sea. He wanted none of it.

Lamorna retched violently and emptied what little was in her stomach onto the middle of the bed. Her body spasmed as she drily coughed up a pitiful amount of bilious fluid onto the furs. Vortimer looked on, frozen in horror, until eventually she looked up at him, her hair hanging in damp ropes around her pale face. She smiled thinly.

'I am with child,' she breathed.

Tempus Fugit

As a big man, Osric was not used to being the light-footed one in combat. But he was certainly glad of what agility he possessed. Einion was formidably large, and mercifully slower than the Jute. They'd made a few feints and lunges towards each other, and Osric had rolled clear of the flashing blade. He walked now in a wide circle around the colossus, hearing Vitalinus' words in his head, 'you just need to be on your feet when the time runs out.'

But how long was that? Osric had no genuine sense of how long it took however much water there was in that contraption to flow over that wheel thing. In a fight like this, a minute could feel like an hour. And he didn't fancy his chances to last too many of them. The crowd was already restless, hurling taunts at him. Some had even started chucking rotten food at him. His circling of The Onion needed to narrow, or he was in danger of someone in the crowd throwing something sharper and weightier in his direction.

Einion just stood firm in the centre of the overgrown arena, tracking Osric's movement. His hand flexed on the hilt of his blade, and his confident smirk never faltered. Osric was not one to shy away from a fight, and it was only because of his master's specific instructions that he had not already charged in, summoning the power of his ancestors, and engaged the giant in direct combat.

'I think we ought to change the rules,' bellowed Einion. 'If you're going to prowl around the edge of the arena like a scared cat, we can hardly call this a fair contest.'

'You can't change the rules now,' Vitalinus shouted.

'I'm joking.' Einion chuckled. 'I'll get him before the time runs out. I've known a few Saxons—sorry, Jutes—in my time, and they don't like to keep their blades clean for long. I'm sure your man is no coward.'

Osric's blood bubbled at the word. Even he knew that The Onion was baiting him. And it was working. He wanted to fly at him, to trust his sword to do its work. He might not live, but he would not be disgraced. Gripping the strap of his shield a little tighter, he wondered if his relative speed was enough to turn the advantage his way. Perhaps someone even nimbler, like Shabaka, would have been a wiser opponent to this lumbering foe. Shabaka moves like a hare, Osric mused, and strikes like a viper. Perhaps he should be Vitalinus' champion.

Half a brown cabbage struck Osric full in the face, riling him further. He didn't care what these Atrebates thought of him, and they could throw all their spoiled food in his face for all he cared, but the growing sensation of being judged a coward was fast proving too much for him. Taking a step inward, away from the baying crowd, closer to Einion, he continued circling. He lifted his sword, signalling an intention to attack, and narrowed the circle further still. Einion was supremely confident. That much was clear. Osric waited for what he thought was a moment of distraction, a shout from someone in the crowd that seemed to amuse his opponent, then he charged.

The Onion was quicker than he looked. His blade swung in a mighty arc towards Osric, who raised his shield instinctively to catch the blow. Einion's steel smashed into, and through, the wooden obstacle with little trouble, shattering the shield around Osric's arm. Osric wore the blow stubbornly, his bones rattling from the impact, and threw the remains of his shield amongst the weeds as he tried to regain his balance.

But the blade was back again. Einion's sword slashed back the other way, and Osric ducked as best he could. His feet folded and he felt himself falling towards the earth, but not fast enough. A splash of fiery blood flashed across his cheek, surprising him. Mustering as much agility as he could, he rolled away from the reach of further attack and righted himself.

He could feel wetness on his cheek, but oddly, no pain. Reaching up and across his face with his now useless shield arm, he touched his fingertips to his cheek. There was blood. He felt higher, seeking the source of the blood, needing to know what wound he had sustained.

His right ear was missing, the useless fleshy appendage entirely severed. He looked up at Einion to see him laughing and suddenly wanted nothing more than to wipe that smirk off his self-satisfied giant face. He steadied himself, standing his ground, and invited the next engagement.

The Onion came at him, his sword swinging viciously from side to side, great swathing attacks that would probably fell a tree. Osric did his best to dodge them and parried when he was able. He could not keep it up for long. Each shrill clash of their blades rattled him to the core, and he feared either his sword would break, or his arms would. He realised he was being forced backwards, towards the edge of the arena. He was being slowly cornered in the round and humiliated.

Desperate, he offered another parry, his knees bent against the force of the attack, then dropped and tried to roll away from his disadvantaged position. A sharp sting to his right thigh told him he had not been quick enough. Einion's blade had found his retreating limb and drawn blood again. He rolled free and hobbled backwards into the middle of the arena before his leg failed him. He dropped awkwardly, sideways, onto the dirty sand, feeling the blood ebb from his newest wound.

'Get up,' Vitalinus shouted. 'Get up now!'

Osric glanced at the clepsydra, its marker nearing the top of the pole on the right. The flow of water was surely ending soon. He needed to be on his feet. Einion was soaking up applause from his sympathetic crowd, so Osric leant on his sword as he pulled his numb leg up out of the sand and the weeds and tried to stand.

The Onion clearly wasn't interested in losing at this stage. Once he'd turned and seen Osric struggling to his feet, he strode purposefully towards him, his sword already raised. Osric focussed. He exhaled slowly, his mind searching for clarity. Einion was a slasher. There was no finesse to his sword play. It was brutish and powerfully effective, but it relied on the reach of his long arms. A shorter armed man using such aggressive technique would lay himself open to easy counterattack. Romans favoured the point of the sword to the edge for that very reason.

The blade came at him as he struggled to stay on his feet. Parry. It came again, from the other side. Duck. And a third time, lower down, aimed at his weakened legs. He parried again. Einion gathered his breath and prepared to continue his attack. It was so obvious. Osric parried one more, barely able to keep his hands on his own sword under the force of the attack. Einion's blade came back from the other direction and, as Osric ducked, he lunged forwards a full stride, pushing his blade out as far as he could in front of him, aiming its tip at his opponent.

And it found flesh. It sunk several inches into Einion's exposed side. The Onion howled, probably as much surprised as pained, and lashed out at his attacker with his enormous fist. Osric, dazed, found himself suddenly prone on the sand again, his sword dropped beside him.

'Get up!' Vitalinus screamed with an urgency Osric had never heard from him before.

Einion was too busy looking over to the clepsydra to notice Osric pulling himself first to his knees and then to his feet, doing so just seconds before the Romanesque official shouted, 'time.'

He had prevailed. Somehow, he had prevailed.

* * *

The Jute had done it. Osric was a little worse for wear, and an ear short, but Vitalinus suspected he would make his deformity the subject of lust rather than revulsion when regaling women with his tales of battles fought and won.

Vitalinus had marched into the middle of the arena both to thank his champion and to ensure Einion was still fit to keep his oath. He needn't have worried. The Onion, despite the steady flow of bright red blood from his side, was beaming from ear to ear as he gathered the beleaguered Jute into his arms like he was cradling a small child. Osric was usually the giver of great bear hugs to the other men, not the recipient. But, next to Einion, he looked anything but bear-like.

'Your Jute is a fine champion, Vitalinus,' Einion bellowed, releasing Osric. Osric looked a little unsteady on his feet, but his smile was back, too.

'I never doubted myself.' Osric grinned.

'Sorry about your ear.' Einion sounded sincere.

Osric shrugged. 'I've got another one.'

'And I believe I have more of the council behind my cause than against it.' Vitalinus needed confirmation.

'You always did,' laughed Einion. 'I just wanted a good scrap, and this man here,' he slapped Osric on the back, knocking the wind out of him, 'he gave me as good as I've had in quite some time.'

So, The Onion had always intended to back him. Vitalinus felt his heart swell. Finally, he could get on with creating his own Albion. He could take the fight to the Kaldi and preserve the Briton way. If it had needed a Jutish ear to seal the deal, that was a modest price to pay.

'Osric.' Einion put his arm around the Jute's shoulders, 'I have some fine purveyors of restorative medicine here in Calleva. I am afraid there is little they can do for your ear, but they will dress your wounds and stave off any rot. They also happen to be fair of face and round of bosom. You shall be my guest of honour tonight. Once they have tended to you.'

Osric couldn't have looked less pleased if he'd tried. 'If there is ale or mead to be served, the honour will be all mine.'

'More than even you can drink, my friend, which I am sure is plenty.'

Vitalinus was already scheming, already considering his next move, now that his opposition was outnumbered. He had further need of Osric. 'Osric, before you surrender to any curative caresses, I would have a word.'

'The high king means to give you your well-earned reward,' Einion chuckled, 'as if you need more than I have offered.'

Vitalinus smiled thinly, and Einion took the hint. He bowed his head slightly and stepped backwards. 'I should have my little scratch tended to as well,' he said as he turned away.

The crowd was already thinning out, heading no doubt to the tavern or whatever street vendors might ply them with more ale. Shabaka, Tsekani and the Cornovians waited on the edge of the arena, joking amongst themselves. Vitalinus didn't suppose anyone had believed Osric would survive.

'How is your leg?' he asked Osric.

'It's nothing.'

'A scratch?'

'Compared to wound I gave The Onion, yes.' Osric looked pleased with himself.

'Though he still has two ears.'

'Yeah, but he wasn't as pretty as me to begin with.'

Vitalinus smiled. He could afford to. The victory wasn't just Osric's. Or his. It was bigger than that. Even if the fight had been a formality—he would have already had the support of the Atrebates, and with them Elaf's people and Nudd's people—it had been a necessary formality. It was just Einion's way of doing things.

'So, my reward?' Osric asked.

'It will have to wait.' Vitalinus smiled apologetically. 'I'm afraid being so highly valued comes at its own cost. I have further need of you.'

'Not today, I hope.'

'No, not today. You shall have your healing.'

'What then?'

'I need you to go to Eboracum.'

'What the fuck for?'

Vitalinus could never imagine Osric bowing and scraping to any man, but his gruff loyalty and affinity for a good fight were undeniable.

'There's a community of Angles there. I need you to get them on our side.'

'You want them to fight for you?'

'I need them to fight for me.'

Osric's smile had faded while he thought. A frown stretched across his brow. 'I think I can manage that.'

'Excellent.'

'They're probably itching for a decent fight, anyway.'

'They can kill all the Kaldi they want when it comes to it.'

Osric's mouth turned up slowly into a fresh grin.

'Take the Nobatians with you. I will find more guards here for my journey back to Viroconium. Oh, and if you happen to see that posturing prick, Appius, feel free to slip your seax between his ribs with my regards.'

Butterfly

The streets of Eboracum were quieter than Viction had ever known them to be. It had been some time since he'd been there and, in that time, the plague had clearly left its devastating mark. He hadn't been a regular visitor there since his father had passed. There had been little need. He and Krestell had the villa and its gardens. He hunted, and she cultivated. And that was enough.

Childhood memories came to him of bustling, stinking, cobbled roads lined with vendors and veterans, purveyors of pleasure he didn't begin to comprehend, craftsmen and women, the intoxicating aromas of spices and cooked meat, and his father's hand leading him through the throngs of people. It was still a Roman town then, though his father had earned his freedom from the dying arena, and the legions were beginning their exodus.

After the plague, there was little left to suggest that the town had ever thrived. What had once been a market, crammed full of every kind of food you could imagine, was now an open square with a handful of rickety tables offering a meagre selection of breads and fruits and some skinny looking rabbits strung up by their hind legs. The cobbles, once in turns dusty and wet with blood and wine, were now dotted with weeds that had grown unchecked for several months.

There was no sign of Rozena here. Wherever she had ended up, Viction hoped it was not here, hoped that there wasn't some creaking hovel still reeking of its recent deaths that offered her a bleak shelter. The villa was overgrown and run down, too vast for him to maintain properly, but it was homely. He couldn't imagine living in this ghost town. But Emrys had begged to come here, to see for himself. The boy was distraught. He clearly blamed himself for her departure and feared the worst.

They had passed, at a safe distance, the growing Angle encampment on the northern reaches of Eboracum. Emrys had even suggested she might have gone there. If pushed, Viction couldn't decide which would be the worse fate for her. Here she might starve or become ill. And if she had fallen foul of the Angles, with their primitive ways—he didn't dare even think about that.

'Where else could she have gone?' Emrys asked him. His eyes, red from earlier tears, were plaintive. He was lost without her. They had searched the immediate surroundings of the villa in all directions for several days, worrying initially that something unfortunate had befallen her. Viction had half expected to find her body, an eventuality that he dreaded more than anything, but now realised that the painful truth of the matter might be of even less solace to poor Emrys. Her death would be cruel, but it could be understood. Her disappearance, apparently wilful, left the boy with crushing feelings of guilt. And Viction had a good idea what drove those feelings.

Carina. He knew his daughter was enamoured with Emrys. She was young, but old enough to feel the stirrings of womanhood. He was a good lad, Emrys. He had an old head on his shoulders, or so Viction's father would have said. Old before his time. He had seen too much already. But his quiet intensity, his intelligence, his aptitude for learning, and his surprising skill with a sword—Viction didn't need the prescience of a seer to know that the boy was destined to have a lot more twists and turns in his life. And probably a lot more tragedy. Viction would have normally already been considering Emrys a good match for Carina, as he knew his wife did, but his instincts warned him otherwise. Emrys, unwittingly, in the shadows of his amber eyes, already showed a destiny beyond this little part of Britannia.

'I do not believe she is here,' Viction uttered with a mixture of sadness and relief. He wanted to leave the town, and the sooner the better.

'Nor I,' Emrys huffed. 'What about the Angles?'

'That's a nest of wasps I'm not keen on prodding.' Viction didn't trust them one bit. He had spent the time since he became aware of their presence building up his strength again, training and practising with a variety of weapons. He had trained Emrys harder too, but for his own good rather than the boy's. Training was an excuse. There was every possibility that Rozena's absence had something to do with the Angles, but he didn't want Emrys to believe that. He would deal with that on his own.

'But if she is there?'

'She isn't.'

'How do you know?' Emrys persisted.

'Emrys.' Viction sighed. 'I think we need to accept that she has gone.'

'But why?' asked Emrys. But the guilt and grief written on his stricken face betrayed the fact that he knew precisely why she had probably chosen to leave.

'She's tough. She's resourceful, and as far as we can tell, she is still alive.'

'For now.'

'Yes, for now.' Viction laid his hand on Emrys' shoulder, squeezing it slightly. 'Let's go home, son.'

* * *

The night was clear and balmy. Emrys ventured through Krestell's garden and into the field beyond, away from the cool darkness of the villa. Its quiet silhouette stood behind him as he craned his neck up to gaze at the stars. The moon sat full and bright too, and when he looked down, he saw that he cast a slight shadow, and he was oddly glad for the company, such that it was. He had wanted to be alone, away from the others, driven to solitude by the enhanced feeling of loneliness that being around them had brought out in him. He missed Rozena.

Emrys lay down on the grass. The dew was light, but it made the earth refreshingly cool. He stretched his arms out to his sides and looked up into the night. Where was she? He tried to picture her looking up at the same sky, at the tiny pinpricks of light. He suddenly felt tiny, dwarfed by the immensity of the winking darkness above him, painfully aware that there was so much more to the world than he had seen. And he ached to know what else there was out there. How strange the Kaldi were to him. The woman with the painted face came to his mind, her dark eyes imploring him to run and save himself. She was no savage. He wondered what other peculiar people inhabited the world, and he wanted to know them. And then he felt more alone again. Sadness slipped over him, and he closed his eyes. And, unbidden, images of Carina came to him.

Carina, naked in the river. Carina, promissory smile on her full lips. Carina. Begrudgingly, he opened his eyes, feeling a stirring of arousal. He didn't want to desire her, only Rozena. Rozena, who he loved deeply. But there was something in Carina that excited him. He had pleasured himself to the vision of her in the water that day when her wet limbs glistened under the summer's sun. He had seen more of her than he had ever seen of Rozena, and no matter how much he wished it otherwise, he still wanted her. His eyes fell closed again, as he submitted to the arousal and allowed the memories of her nakedness to fuel his yearning.

'What are you doing?' Her whisper shattered his imaginings. He opened his eyes to her face, leant slightly over him, smiling inquisitively.

'Nothing,' he lied. 'I came here to be alone.'

'I can see that.' She sat down beside him.

'Does your father know you are out of the villa?' Emrys couldn't think of anything better to ask her.

'He's asleep. And I can go where I please, just like you.'

Emrys sat up, needing to feel less exposed. 'What are you doing here?'

'I came to find you. You looked sad.'

He was sad, but he was also excited. 'I'm fine,' he shrugged off her apparent concern.

'And I wanted to kiss you.' Her hand found his thigh and rested there gently, like a bird settling on a branch. He only just stopped himself from flinching at the slight touch. 'Can I?'

He struggled for words, and her fingers stretched out on his leg, brushing against his hardness. She leaned close to him, her lips parted, and closed her eyes. She was right there, waiting for him to touch her back, waiting for his mouth on hers, waiting and wanting to hold his cock in her hand. Every fibre of his body screamed at him to throw himself upon her and give her everything she wanted. Everything he wanted. He wanted to know how it felt to be naked with her. He wanted to be a man.

'I can't,' he said with a long exhale, realising he'd been holding his breath. Not while he didn't know what had become of Rozena. 'Not yet.'

* * *

She hadn't really intended to stay gone. She wasn't sure where she thought she was going. Eborakon, perhaps. She had felt stifled. Apart from the others. And since Emrys, probably unwittingly, seemed keener on Carina than he did on her, nothing else held her to the crumbling villa by Dere Street. Let Carina have him, she told herself. Rozena pined for more of a sense of community, of bustle, of life. Emrys had a purpose. The gods only knew what, but it served her poorly. He was always so earnest about his need to learn and better himself. Rozena wanted the trivialities of day-to-day existence. She wanted to wake and work, play, talk about nothing, and laugh (how she missed laughter) and then, when the sun went down, she wanted to be so tired that she would sleep through the night until the sun arose again.

She had taken her father's sword from Emrys, not as a trite snub, but simply in case she needed to defend herself. She was small, and a girl, but she knew how to swing a blade a little. It would be far better, she reasoned, to take off an arm or two (or at the very least draw blood) before she was killed than to be someone's pathetic and hapless victim. She would never beg for mercy, however unbecoming it was for a girl to lift a sword. Why should she?

A few days after her early morning departure from the villa, having walked mostly southwards and passed warm nights under the boughs of trees, she found herself in a scratchy area of scrubland. The field was thick

214

with thistle and nettle, and something of a hedgerow cut a straight line across it. A few stones lay almost hidden in the embrace of the weeds, suggesting that this was once some kind of homestead.

It was a warm afternoon, and she paused in the shade provided by a buckthorn bush in the broken hedge. Her sleep the previous night had been interrupted by a particularly vivid rendition of her recurring nightmare about her father being killed, so she dozed off almost as soon as she lay down.

When she awoke, she opened her eyes to a leaf, yellow-green, opening and closing in front of her face. Blearily, she watched its veins moving up and down. The air was still and quiet, free from anything that might cause alarm, but she scowled at the strange behaviour of this part of the buckthorn. Only after a moment or two, once her eyes had become accustomed to the late afternoon light, did she realise what she was looking at was not a leaf at all. It was a butterfly. Its wings perfectly matched the foliage on which it sat, in both pattern and colour. She watched as it aired its leafy wings, gently opening and closing them. When they were open, the sun shone through them, and she saw that the butterfly was more yellow than green. And she couldn't help but smile.

It was at that moment that two men and a woman burst through the bushes. They carried spears and wore short swords on their waists. Even the woman. All had blonde hair; long, tied in plaits on top of their heads. The most obvious difference between the men and the woman was that she had no beard. Rozena was quick to her feet before they even noticed her, her father's sword held aloft in both hands in readiness. The men raised their spears when they saw her, and Rozena realised how useless her sword was likely to be.

'Who are you?' the woman asked, with a clipped accent that Rozena did not recognise. Did she command the men? Did she speak for them? Rozena looked down the length of her blade at the blonde woman's face. Below piercing blue eyes, her sharp cheekbones jutted out over her full lips and rounded chin. It was a noble, yet attractive, face. Her stance was quietly aggressive, but there was nothing savage in her voice. She was beautiful. And the men that stood either side of her looked the same. One had plaited his beard into a single cord that dropped earthward from his chin. His eyes were of such a pale blue that they almost lacked colour altogether.

'Who are you, girl?' The woman repeated herself. 'And why do you raise a sword to us?'

'Why do you raise spears to me?' asked Rozena boldly, eyeing the sharp tips that pointed at her. The woman glanced to either side, at the two men, and they lowered the spears. Rozena lowered her blade, too. Gladly, as it was already starting to feel too heavy.

'You are a Briton girl, yet you carry a sword,' the woman observed, appearing confused.

'And what are you?'

'We are what you know as Angles. I am called Edoma, and these are my brothers, Wigo and Wine. We are hunting. Now you?'

'I am Rozena, from Bernaccia,' Rozena began, 'and I don't know what I'm doing. I'm looking for something.'

'As are we all.' Edoma took a step forward, motioning to her brothers to stand back. 'You know how to use that? Or did you steal it?'

'I am no thief.' Rozena felt herself reddening. 'It belonged to my father before the Kaldi murdered him. And yes, I know how to use it, so don't come any closer.'

Edoma smiled, and it could have been a friendly smile. She was clearly unthreatened, but she held up her hands submissively, anyway. 'I have no desire to test your ability. It is a fine blade, and I'm sure you can handle it well. I was not aware that Briton women wielded swords.'

'This one does.'

'Perhaps you can teach me.'

'Maybe.'

'You look hungry, Rozena. Would you like to come with me and eat?'

'Where?' Rozena was famished.

'We have a settlement not far from here. Come. My brothers will go on with their hunt, but you come with me.' She held out her hand, palm up, and smiled warmly.

'Thank you,' Rozena said quietly.

Edoma muttered something to Wigo and Wine in a language Rozena could not understand, and the two men nodded and took off across the field. 'This way.' She turned.

Rozena looked around at the foliage of the buckthorn, hoping to see the yellow butterfly again for just a moment. But it was gone, or had at least hidden itself successfully from view. Her stomach grumbling, she fell into step behind the Angle.

Celebrations

Word of her husband's triumphs had already reached Sevira in Viroconium. She could barely contain her excitement at the prospect of his return and had ordered preparations for the biggest celebratory feast the town had ever seen. Coloured linens were hung from the fronts of houses, shops, and official buildings. She had even been out to see Selwyn at The Wrekin and instructed him to ensure that the fort underwent rigorous maintenance. Every blade and every link and chain and scale and stud of armour was polished to gleaming. For the first time since the pestilence had decimated the town in the winter, Viroconium was fully alive.

He came to her in her bedchamber after dark, surprising her with his muted arrival. She had expected, wanted even, to welcome him through the gates with a cheering throng of townsfolk. But he had sent no warning of his imminent arrival.

'I left the men at the hill and rode here alone,' he explained to her as they embraced. 'I snuck through the gate unnoticed. I wanted to share my glory with my wife before anyone else.'

'That doesn't say much for the guards.' She pulled back and looked at him. Several wisps of new grey were threaded through his long hair. She liked them.

'I'll have them executed tomorrow,' he joked.

'I don't suppose they even recognised you. It's been too long,' purred Sevira.

'Far too long,' he agreed, touching her face tenderly.

'So, I should call you High King now?' she teased. Her hands opened his tunic and found his bare chest.

'You should.' He lifted her chin and kissed her. She yearned for him, as she had done for an age. She responded to his kiss forcefully, quickly eliciting a heightened passion in him. He squeezed her body against him and pushed his tongue deeper into her mouth. She wriggled free and dropped silently to her knees.

'You said something about sharing your glory.' She looked up at him hungrily. 'Let's have a look at it, then.' Sevira had rarely knelt before him, rarely offered him the pleasure of her mouth. She was a proud woman, of mixed Roman descent, as driven and ambitious as her husband, and she had never been one to bow to a man simply because of his gender but, in that moment, she could think of nothing she wanted to do more than prostrate herself beneath the man she loved and admired. Her husband. The high king. In no time, she was sitting back on her legs, looking up at him. His chest was puffed out, his chin pointed forwards, and his cock up. She held it reverentially, working it gently as she watched his eyes slide shut, then lifted herself up onto her knees and lowered her mouth onto him.

She needed no great lover's expertise to bring him to completion in a short time. He was clearly bursting. His appetite was such that only moments after she had swallowed his seed, he was up and ready again. He hadn't displayed this kind of virility since they were much younger, since he had courted her relentlessly. She lay back on the bed and welcomed him into her, wrapping her legs and arms tight around him as they fucked, biting his ear with a guttural growl as she too climaxed.

She was consumed by the aura of power that he exuded, now more than ever. High king. And she was his wife. Everything they had talked about for years was coming to pass. And why shouldn't it? He was unfaltering in his ambitions, uncompromising, a fighter and a leader. Albion was no longer an ideal, an impossible dream. It was an almost tangible reality. And she would help him rule.

After they had made love a third time, she lay breathless on his heaving chest. His hair there was matted with their sweat, and she idly twisted it into wet spikes.

'I will need to go back to Londinium, or somewhere near there,' he said after a while. Sevira took her hand from his wet chest and sat up with a twinge of resentment.

'Why?' She knew why. He needed to assemble men from all corners of the island in readiness for the inevitable hostilities. He needed to be somewhere more central. He needed to rule. What he didn't need to do, in that moment, was say anything about leaving again anytime soon.

'I'm sorry,' he muttered, as if he understood her sadness.

'Am I to stay here?' The mood was broken. She half wanted to. Viroconium was home. But so was he. He sighed, and his answer was clear. He was preparing for war. It was no place for her.

Sevira rose from the bed and threw on a robe.

'Don't be angry, Sevira.'

'I'm not,' she lied. She was trying not to be, at least. 'I'm really not.' She poured some wine for them both, quietly telling herself to enjoy the time she had with him.

When she turned back to offer him his cup, he was asleep.

* * *

He would have liked some warning that Vitalinus had returned.

'The Onion still lives, then?'

'Yes, Ossian,' Vitalinus smiled. 'Einion supported me already. He just wanted a spectacle for his people. How go things here?'

Ossian rubbed his hands together. They ached from foraging and teaching Pasha the day before. Pasha was a formidable student, already versed in healing herbs and a wide variety of potions. She pestered him daily about her visions, but he always played them down. It was possible she possessed some power, but it was too early to nurture it. Besides, he enjoyed spending time with her. But Vitalinus did not need to know about that.

'All is well here,' he answered. 'All the better for your triumphant return.'

'It is good to be home.' Vitalinus was in excellent humour, invigorated. 'It is a glorious day.'

'You have something on your mind, Ossian. I know you enough to know that.' Vitalinus couldn't have appeared more receptive. 'Speak. Tell me.'

'You are most perceptive, High King.' Ossian gave him his title with a sense of self-satisfaction. 'And you have begun to achieve what I only half believed might be possible.'

'Albion.'

'Yes. We are a step closer.'

'I will crush the Kaldi.'

Ossian nodded thoughtfully. 'We will still need more men.'

'I'll find them.'

'And you might consider being less Roman and more—'

'I am a Briton.' Vitalinus insisted.

'Yes, you are. In here.' Ossian deigned to place the palm of his hand on Vitalinus' chest. 'Albion needs a king with a name that inspires, a name that fits the new times. All this island knew for centuries was Roman rule, and then chaos. We must reorder the chaos that has consumed us for our lifetimes before we can call it Albion. We must find you a name that will unite the people behind you.'

Vitalinus was quiet. Ossian wondered for a moment if he had caused offence.

'You are right, druid. There is no place for Rome on this island.' Vitalinus paused and took a breath. 'I shall be known as Vortigern.'

'Vortigern, High King of the Britons.' Ossian smiled. It was a good choice. He suspected that the man he would now call Vortigern had already given this matter some thought.

* * *

The streets were bathed in summer sun and lined, several layers deep, with cheering and smiling people. Vortigern, as he was now to be known, revelled in the attention of the crowd. These were his people, his immediate people, the people he had grown up with and lived amongst since the Romans had left. His triumph was unilaterally recognised in Viroconium. He sensed in the air a feeling of great anticipation for the future. These loyal subjects would witness him build his Albion around them. Even if he had to command his men from closer to Londinium, or ride the length and breadth of the island, this is where he would return when he had forced peace upon the new nation.

Hands reached up to him as he passed on horseback, heading a small column of mounted men parading towards his villa where the feast awaited. He let their hands brush the flanks of his horse, raising his arm in salute to the throng. 'Vortigern,' several voices called out, voicing their approval of his change of name. The proclamation had gone out immediately after he had spoken to Ossian that morning. Soon, the entire island would know his name. And his enemies would learn to fear it.

Outside his villa, Vortigern twisted his body towards the crowd and raised his hands with a grin, then turned into the courtyard and left the townsfolk to their own inevitably lengthy and debauched celebrations. Standing waiting under the colonnade were Sevira, Pasha, Catigern and Ossian. He smiled at them and dismounted. Behind him, Selwyn slipped from his own horse and approached.

'Vit—' he began, then corrected himself. 'King Vortigern, apologies. Should I remain with my men at the gate?'

'No, Selwyn. You will feast with us. And see that the guards are well fed as well.'

Selwyn nodded sombrely. 'As you command.' He turned away towards his men.

'Selwyn,' Vortigern snapped. 'What troubles you?'

Selwyn spun back to face him. 'Nothing.'

'Nothing?' Vortigern asked lightly. 'Really?'

'I am a warrior,' sighed Selwyn. 'Nothing more. I apologise if I am short of mirth. My mind is already on the battles we have ahead of us.'

Vortigern clasped him by his shoulders and looked into his eyes. 'Put those thoughts aside until tomorrow at least, old friend. Today we celebrate.'

Selwyn nodded, forcing a smile, then excused himself.

'Husband, my king.' Sevira approached, wrapping her arms around Vortigern's neck and kissing him. She still had a look in her eye that suggested she was looking forward to a further display of his newfound virility. Behind her, Pasha smiled thinly at him and Catigern beamed.

'Pasha, Catigern,' Vortigern called. 'Come.'

Catigern walked purposefully towards his father and clasped his arm in a manly fashion. 'Father,' he smiled, 'I have been training hard. I will fight beside you.'

'That is excellent news! But not today, my boy. Today you will eat and drink beside me, and I will tell you of my adventures. Pasha?'

Pasha was several paces behind Catigern, her face impassive. 'It is good to see you again, Father,' she mumbled.

'Pasha, kiss your father,' Sevira instructed. Pasha stepped forward obediently and kissed Vortigern on his cheek. Her face felt cold against his.

'Are you well, my daughter?' he asked, concerned.

'Quite well, thank you.' She forced a smile. He looked at her, trying to read her face. 'I'm fine,' she reiterated.

'Then let us feast,' Vortigern announced loudly, for everyone to hear.

* * *

The spread of food was impressive by any standards, and owed more than a little to Roman tastes, an irony that Pasha quietly enjoyed. Her father had cast aside his Roman given name, desperate to appeal to some sense of collective identity among the fragmented peoples of the island. Yet, as poorly travelled as she was, Pasha knew from just her experience of life in Viroconium that this was surely a dream, an exercise in vanity. What could her father hope to do differently from any other leader that had come before? He would bear arms and vanquish enemies and surround himself with nice things and play at being a king. People would band behind him while he was victorious, whimsically casting aside their own differences if there was a common enemy to focus on. But would the sick be cured? Would the hungry be fed?

Several respected individuals from the townsfolk, those more familiar with opulence, had been invited into the villa for the celebrations. They sat around now, gorging themselves on roasted swan, woodcocks and pigeons, wild boar and deer, plums, damsons, myrtles, quinces, cheeses, almonds, and freshly baked breads. Wine and ale flowed freely and copiously.

Pasha glanced over at Selwyn. He looked miserable and was clearly avoiding her looks. She felt a pang of guilt for rejecting him, but only because of the pain she was clearly causing him. He was destined to fight and fall for her father. Could she change that? She didn't think so. Her path was taking her somewhere else. She wasn't sure exactly where but, for now, she was content to dedicate her waking hours to her education at the hands of Ossian.

The druid sat dutifully close to her father. She didn't particularly like the old man and was aware of his lecherous attention. She just wanted to know everything he knew, and more. Even if that meant suffering his lingering eyes as his acolyte for a time.

There was more than a war coming.

The Seven

The fires were too many to count. Like tiny beacons, they receded into the darkness along the ridge as far as Wroid could see. The Kaldi were finally amassed. Drust had united the seven tribes, having successfully whetted their appetite for death and destruction and the promise of better lands. Before the sun had set, Wroid had gazed in awe at the sheer number of men and women, laden with steel and hatred, that had gathered to lay waste to the Britons.

There were more flames on the slopes below, some among the ruins of the Roman fort that used to hold the entrance to the valley. While two of the seven tribes waited on the banks of the Forth, ready to follow Brude out onto the sea and down the coast, the other five were here, camped by Grim's Dyke, near the broad earthen base of the northern of the two walls built by the Romans to keep their kind out. Grim had smashed a hole in that wall generations before, so the tale went, and the Romans had retreated behind their stone wall. But they were gone now, and even that wall presented no real obstacle to any Kaldi that wanted to venture southwards.

Wroid had heard some of the tribesmen refer to the broad ditch as the Devil's Dyke. But he didn't know what or who this devil was. As far as he knew, it was Grim's and Grim had been a fearsome Kaldi warrior. Something he was supposed to be as well. But he had little taste for what was to come. He liked his life, such as it was, on the banks of the loch he had called home all his life. Would he feel different, he wondered, if Derelei was here beside him? Had she not been wronged and condemned

225

to die, would she still be eager to draw blood with the rest of the Kaldi? More importantly, where was she now?

They were all already daubed with woad, decorated in their blue war paint, covered in the intricate designs that would capture the power of the gods and instil fear in their enemy. Sitting back from the nearest fire, Wroid could see the orange light on the faces of his comrades who sat closer. He watched quietly as it flickered ominously across their painted visages. They talked freely, brazenly confident that nothing in the shadows could hurt them. They were already in lands that used to belong to the Votadini—now to the Gododdin—warriors entrusted by Rome to keep the Kaldi at bay. Even they were gone now.

Derelei.

Her kiss haunted him. He had spent every moment of his life since becoming a man, and some before, doting on her. He had risked his life to free her from Drust's unjust punishment, from that terrible hole. Not that he wanted thanks for that. He'd do it again and again if the need arose, in any manner necessary. Because he loved her. It was nearly enough to know that she was, hopefully, alive and free somewhere. Anything was better than the judgment that had been dealt her after Irb's well-deserved death. And Wroid was glad he had altered that fate. Yet here he was, on the eve of marching in the largest company of Kaldi warriors ever assembled, on the cusp of a glory that Drust had been talking about for as long as he could remember, a proud moment for his people, and all he really wanted was that kiss. Again. Well, he wanted more than that. He wanted a life with Derelei, a life of peace and tranquillity, nestled in the bosom of the highlands, with the cold and clear water of the loch nearby and the gentle lowing of the cows on its banks and a crackling fire to warm them on the winter nights. He wanted to lie, woad free and sword scabbarded, with his arms around her naked body and the stars pricking the darkness above them. He wanted her kiss. He wanted a family. And, knowing that was never going to happen, he didn't care if he lived or died in the coming battles.

A garrulous laugh drifted through the dark air, between the sparking embers that flitted up into the night sky like fireflies. Drust. Even his laughter rose above that of other men. Wroid pulled his blanket around his shoulders and drew his legs up towards his chest. They were tired from the days of walking he'd already endured, and his mind was weary, too. Sleep couldn't come too soon.

* * *

Drust pulled playfully at Modwen's copper braids. The blue spirals that curled across her cheeks inspired no fear in him; they aroused him. He'd have her again before the night was out. Some warriors abstained on the verge of hostilities, not wanting to diminish their potency or dilute their masculinity. They feared the loss of their manly essence might lessen their power in combat. Drust, on the other hand, was supremely confident. He was Drust of a hundred battles, so the bards sang, and if he wanted to rut the night before a slaughter, then rut he would.

Modwen didn't mind. She smelled of it, and was naked under her thick cloak, the cloak that he had wrapped around them both as he had speared her on himself moments earlier. He was Drust, chieftain, warlord, undefeated. He didn't care who heard the slap of her flesh on his, her squeals of ecstasy as he filled her, or his guttural grunt as he emptied his overflowing potency into her hot womb. Let them listen, he thought. Let them hear what it is to be a ruler of men, with power enough to pleasure his mistress on the eve of battle.

Drust felt himself harden again, felt his pulse quicken. He kissed Modwen hard, biting her lip until her blood bubbled hotly into his mouth. She growled back at him; her nails digging into the hard flesh of his shoulders. He savoured the taste of her on his tongue, liking the sharp metallic flavour that brought flashing images of swords and hewn limbs to his mind. He imagined taking her in the immediate aftermath of a battle, both steeped in the sticky blood of their enemies, naked on a pile of the dead. He imagined her cries mixing with the moans of the mortally wounded left there to perish. He imagined her back arching against him as he pulled her hair in his fist and skewered her from behind. He imagined the field of blood and mud and excrement all around them, littered with half dead Britons, limbs and heads and broken spears, a feasting murder of crows cawing in the fading light as he emptied his hot life into her.

Drust pushed Modwen to the ground, face down, and lifted her cloak to expose her chalky rump, possibly the only part of her not lined and spiralled with the blue woad. She lifted it dutifully, hungrily, growling, and her stench wafted up towards his nose and open mouth. He gripped her hips in both hands and aimed for the heat that rose to meet him. Then he saw Cailtram approaching.

'What?' he bellowed angrily, not even bothering to conceal his engorged member.

'Would you prefer I returned later?' Cailtram smirked at him.

He liked the druid, and though he would have gladly replied in the affirmative, and told the young mystic exactly where to go, his arousal was already on the wane. 'No. Speak, druid.' Drust sat back on his haunches and covered himself up. Modwen did the same. 'We'll have time enough for that later.'

Cailtram nodded and approached. 'I have reports from our scouts.' He nodded towards Modwen, who leered back at him, perhaps even more aggrieved at the interruption than Drust.

'And? Is it all good news?'

'Mercifully, yes.' Cailtram took a seat. He reached for a skin of ale and took a long draught. 'There is no sign of Cunedda.'

'None?'

'The fortress at Eidyn is all but deserted. The garrison there will cower behind their walls as we pass. They would not dare challenge us.'

'Where is he? Where have the Roman-loving whelp's fancy legions gone?'

'My sources tell me he has gone south and west to repel the Dalriadans.'

Drust roared with laughter. It couldn't be better news. The Dalriadans were already encroaching on Kaldi lands as much as on those of the Britons. They were more than a nuisance. If Cunedda and the Gododdin had gone off to challenge them, it was possible he could kill two birds with one stone.

With no stone, really. Let them kill each other. It was a double victory.

'It is hard to believe,' Cailtram admitted, 'although it may not be as fortuitous as it seems.'

'It's fucking perfect,' roared Drust. 'I don't have to worry about Erc and his Scotti bastards raping me in my arse while I'm face to face with the Britons. What's not to like?'

'It is unlikely that Cunedda took it upon himself to abandon Eidyn in favour of picking a fight with the Dalriadans.'

'Meaning?'

'Meaning he may well be doing someone else's bidding.' Cailtram took another drink.

'You think the Britons have stopped squabbling amongst themselves?'

'It is possible.'

Drust pondered. So what if the Britons had found themselves some king to unite behind? There was no army waiting for him. It didn't make sense.

'I imagine you have arrived at the same conclusion as me,' Cailtram offered.

'I have?'

'If Cunedda has been ordered away from here, and even if the Britons are united, they are not ready for our offensive. Not yet, at least. They are more worried about a few Dalriadan pirates.'

'Then they are in for a surprise. They're lost without Rome, anyway. We'll catch them in their beds, praying for the legions to return, and slaughter them all.'

'The omens are good,' Cailtram smiled in agreement. 'The weather is set fair and Brude's boats will do well at sea.'

Drust plucked the skin of ale from the young druid and took a drink. 'We have waited for this day for generations, druid. Our people have endured much hardship. Now I will lead them into a new world.' He passed the skin to Modwen. 'Soon we will pick our teeth clean with the finger bones of the Britons.'

'There isn't an army on this island that can stop us,' Cailtram agreed.

Drust hauled himself to his feet and beckoned to the young druid to do the same. 'Come here, my friend.' He opened his arms wide. Cailtram stumbled to his feet and fell into a great bear hug. Drust's arms clamped around him and his hands battered his thin back.

'The gods have seen fit to allow me to witness your glories,' Cailtram stammered, 'to see our people triumphant at long last.'

'Yes, yes,' growled Drust dismissively. 'The gods be thanked. Though I think you'll find it's mostly my doing.'

'We all live by the whims of the gods,' Cailtram reminded him.

Drust pulled his arms away and rested his hands on the druid's shoulders. 'We do. I, however, am also at the mercy of a beautiful young woman who demands my attention.' He glanced over at Modwen, who flashed him a lascivious smile.

'Of course,' Cailtram nodded.

'And Darlagh? Does she not demand your attention?'

'She readies herself for battle.'

'As do I,' Drust grinned, pulling Modwen closer. 'As do I.'

Cailtram took the hint. He rose to his feet and slunk back into the darkness, as Drust slipped his hands inside Modwen's cloak and gripped her warm, welcoming flesh.

Britannia was ripe for the plunder.

V

HOC EST BELLUM

'War must be, while we defend our lives against a destroyer who would devour all; but I do not love the bright sword for its sharpness, nor the arrow for its swiftness, nor the warrior for his glory. I love only that which they defend.'

(JRR Tolkien)

Severed Head

There were two well-told tales about Verulamium. Selwyn had heard them both on the long ride down Watling Street. The first was a sentimental harkening to days of glory when Boudica and her army of Iceni had sacked and burned the Roman town. Even though the chariot-driving queen was long gone, and Rome had endured and prospered for centuries since her heroics, there was a sense among the men that, in the aftermath of Rome's grip on the land, this heritage could auger well for this particular location's part to play in the imminent hostilities.

Selwyn was certain that Vortigern, as he now liked to be called, had chosen Verulamium for just this reason. It wore well with the men. It called upon their lineage and their proud spirit. He could have chosen Londinium for the same reason. Boudica had been equally brutal and successful in her assault of the capital as well. But Verulamium was that much further north, closer to the threat, and still rooted enough in the southern lands to be an apt place to bring the tribes together.

By the time they had arrived, Einion was already there, fresh from Calleva. Elaf and Nudd had come north with him, and Sextus had made the short trek up from his crumbling palace in Londinium, accompanied by Titus from Ceint. The chieftains gathered, and Selwyn saw to the men. None of the other tribes had delivered as many spears and swords as the Cornovians, but the combined numbers already amounted to more armed men than Selwyn had ever seen.

They set up camp along the banks of the river Ver, which recalled the second legend of this place. This was where Alban, a follower of the one God, the Christian God, had met his end. Here, Selwyn heard, Alban had offered his life in the place of a Christian priest he was sheltering. His head had been struck from his body and, where it landed, a well had sprung from the dry earth. Utter nonsense, Selwyn mused as he mindlessly tended to his sword. It hadn't had a lot of use of late, and the edge was already keen, but he sharpened it anyway. A time would come soon enough that it would likely need to cleave a few Pictish heads from shoulders.

'Don't follow my father into the abyss,' Pasha had told him, before pushing him into one of her own fashioning. She had abandoned him, denied his love, turned to studies with that odious old druid who could barely contain his lust when he clapped eyes on her. Selwyn had little left except for the promise of battle, the prospect of victory. Of glory. Pasha had warned him against just that, her eyes darkened by a fear she had that he would end up dead in a field of blood. That was hardly news to him. He'd always assumed that was how he'd meet his end, anyway. He was a warrior, a leader of warriors, and his king's ambitions for peace and unity meant a foreseeable future of bloodshed. If, by some miracle, he lived to an age where he could no longer lift a sword, then perhaps he might die peacefully in his bed. But what was the point without Pasha beside him?

For now, he had the unenviable task of marshalling the combined forces. His men would follow him to certain death. But the others were unknown quantities. There was a decent contingent of Atrebates camped already, burly looking men who started drinking heavily the moment they had stopped marching, and who would no doubt fuel their battle cries with even more ale when the time arose. They had a reputation as brawlers and, if Einion was anything to go by, they'd be handy in a fight. If they could be controlled. A few small bands of Regni and Belgae had journeyed north with the Atrebates. Selwyn doubted if they'd seen much in the way of combat, but they would follow their northern neighbours and the giant Onion into any fray. There were a few Saxons among the Cantii that were there, sons and grandsons of the mercenaries employed by Rome years before. Selwyn imagined that they, like Osric the Jute, lived to fight.

The most men Selwyn had seen face each other in battle were maybe forty or fifty on each side. Well matched armies meant carnage. The best battles were won in minutes, not hours, with few casualties. Superior numbers or unassailable terrain decided victories far more clearly than a field of corpses and a handful of wounded men left arguing over who had prevailed. There had to be two hundred men gathered in Verulamium, with the promise of more to swell the ranks, and still Vortigern felt vulnerable. How many Kaldi were there? Whatever battle they were preparing for could easily be the field of blood that Pasha had foreseen.

Selwyn sheathed his sword and reached for a skin of ale. There was no use dwelling on the future. What would be would be. He drank a long draught and lay back on the cool ground to watch the light fade from the sky.

* * *

The basilica at Verulamium had suffered a few fires in its time, and the abandonment by the Romans had left it in typical disrepair, but it was still a fine building. Vortigern gathered the chieftains there.

'Friends, the Romans are not coming to help us.' He began, looking at Titus and Sextus pointedly. He knew they still held out for assistance from the Empire. And yet he knew they didn't really care about the ravaging of the northern lands by the Kaldi. He knew they didn't feel threatened by the savage invaders. Their lands were in the far south, warm, and green and fertile, still dotted with stubbornly standing Roman villas and baths. The only reason the likes of Titus and Sextus wanted the Romans to come back, as evidenced by their names, was because they enjoyed the lifestyle. The legions and the slaves and great Roman minds had built cities on their island, walls, great theatres, and markets. Trade routes that had flourished across the empire had brought them exotic meats and fruits, olive trees, furs, gold, and spices. Slaves kept the privileged few in a state of contented ignorance. But the Romans were gone. And they surely hadn't left because they'd been asked to leave, or because they wanted to go somewhere else.

The empire was in chaos. The legions had been recalled because of other threats to the vast borders of Rome. Britannia, Albion, was on her own.

'I do not take the authority you have entrusted me with lightly,' he continued. 'I know some of you may not see the threat posed by the Kaldi as one that need worry you personally.' Again, he looked at Sextus and Titus, who both glared back at him. 'You think you are safe? Well, you're not. If the Kaldi expand into Bernaccia, what is to stop them moving further south? We already have Dalriadans baying at the borders of Powys, and the Hibernians are being kept at bay from the Dumnonian coast by my son. We cannot afford to sit back and let this be someone else's problem. If we do, we will be driven into the southern sea and will have to swim for refuge in Gaul or Armorica. And who knows what violence could await us there?'

Einion nodded his colossal head in agreement, followed in suit by Elaf and Nudd. Vortigern knew they just wanted a good scrap but was glad of the visible support.

'I chose Verulamium as the place to muster our forces because it has heritage. Heritage we can all be proud of. But our history also serves as a reminder. Yes, the great warrior-queen of the Iceni burnt this town to the ground. Yes, she prevailed, briefly, against the might of Rome. And now it is our town. But I want you to remember that people we may consider as savages, as no doubt the Romans saw Boudica and her warriors, can and will overrun a fortified and civilised settlement such as this. They can and will leave us bleeding in the ashes of our own arrogance.' Vortigern breathed deeply. Even the Romanised chieftains were listening to him. 'And we are many. But we are not enough. And those that live north of here, in the path of the savage invaders, on farms, in villages, defenceless, unarmed, and ignorant of their impending doom—they have no chance. They will be slaughtered and raped. Their houses will be levelled, their lands scorched. And every Briton that dies makes our land, our Albion, one man or one woman smaller. So, we must take the fight to the Kaldi, and banish them from our lands forever.'

'Vortigern, as you now insist on being known.' Sextus spoke up after a moment's silence. 'Do you really think the Picts want to come this far south?'

'My understanding is that their appetite for destruction is insatiable.' Vortigern puffed up his chest. 'Since the Romans left, there is little to stop them.'

'Horse shit,' Titus blurted out. 'The Romans left thirty-some years ago. If they wanted to, the Picts would have already got here.' Titus was a weedy-looking man with a permanently furrowed brow and hands that resembled claws. Vortigern fixed him with an angry stare.

'When is the last time you lifted a sword to protect your people, Titus? When did you last see a village burnt to the ground, littered with charred corpses? When did you last hear the screams of the dying, or the protests of women in the brutish hands of a battle-drunk warrior?'

Titus shrank back, as if afraid of the images of these things that Vortigern had put in his head.

'Make no mistake. They are coming.'

'Aye!' Einion bellowed suddenly, rising to his feet, his sheer size providing an inescapable show of force and support for his king. 'I agree. We take the fight to them. Then you can get back to your shitty villas and back to pretending to be Roman.' He spat on the ground near Titus, who stepped back in alarm.

'And we must stand together,' Vortigern interjected, keen to preserve the fragile peace.

'And are we enough?' Sextus asked.

'Not yet,' Vortigern replied quietly. 'But we will be.'

'How so? Your son, as you have said, is busy with the Hibernians. And Cunedda is fortified against the Dalriadans. Is that not so?'

'It is, Sextus. On my orders.'

'So, you ordered Cunedda to abandon his lands near the wall, near the Pictish rabble, the one man who could have kept the Picts at bay, to take up arms against the Dalriadans? Why would you do that?'

'The Dalriadans were the greater threat.'

Sextus sneered. 'You left Bernaccia and the northern lands defenceless so that your own borders would be protected. I wonder why.'

'I envy you that you have not had to make such tough decisions,' Vortigern snapped.

'Was it a tough decision for Cunedda?'

'He is a warrior. He was happy to take my orders.'

'He is a wily old badger who wants his son to wed your daughter, you mean.' Sextus grinned wickedly.

Vortigern felt himself redden. The little shit was getting under his skin.

'And you put your son in charge in Dumnonia, too.'

'Erbin rules Dumnonia,' Vortigern stammered.

Sextus laughed. 'The idiot child? He rules nothing.'

'You are well informed, Sextus.' Vortigern tried to control his rage. 'It surprises me, given that you fritter away your days in your villa in the company of boys, pretending to pray to your one God.'

It was Sextus' turn to rouge. His fists balled. He wasn't any smaller than Vortigern, but he had never led men in battle and wouldn't have the nerve to start a fight here. 'We maintain a degree of civilisation in Londinium that you pagans have forgotten.'

'Slaves and sodomy,' muttered Einion. Elaf and Nudd sniggered next to him.

'We still trade with copper coins, and we acknowledge the true God,' Sextus blustered proudly, and waggled a finger at a cluster of useless coins that had been pierced and now festooned a necklace around Einion's broad neck.

'And yet you are Roman when it comes to sex,' Einion continued. 'You're a fucking hypocrite. Now shut up and sit down.'

Most men would have taken any kind of instruction from a man of Einion's stature seriously. There wasn't a man in the basilica that Einion couldn't have torn limb from limb with his bare hands if he felt so inclined.

'I make difficult decisions every day,' insisted Sextus. 'The Saxon quarter in Londinium is always the source of trouble. Perhaps we should oust them. I hear from Appius that the Angles are being a nuisance in Eboracum as well. Shall we march against them? That is the threat to the southern lands. Why don't we fight them?'

'Your Saxons fight with us.' Vortigern beamed with relief. Sextus had apparently forgotten that several Saxons from both Londinium and Ceint were camped down by the river, ready to spill Kaldi blood. 'And I expect the Angles north of here will soon do the same.'

'They can't be trusted.'

'I have a Jute among my men who I would trust with my life,' Vortigern said defiantly.

'I can vouch for him. He bested me in combat,' Einion added. That quietened Sextus. Any man that had beaten The Onion in personal combat, even if it was just through surviving long enough to tell the tale, was a man to be respected.

'They'll want land.' Titus muttered inconsequentially.

'And maybe they'll earn it,' Vortigern said firmly.

War Band

The Angles had been welcoming to Osric. More so than his own people, the Jutes. Egbin was a posturing idiot, surely not representative of the stock from which he came. Osric hoped that Wulfric, the young Jute who had promised to sail to their homeland and bring back boats and blades, would prove himself reliable. But for now, the Angles seemed like they might be ready to fight.

'You have never seen your homeland?' Leofric, their leader, asked Osric as he pulled at his long blonde beard.

'I was born here, so no. And I don't suppose I ever will,' Osric admitted with a tinge of regret.

Leofric waved his hand dismissively. 'You don't need to. It's not what it used to be. Even when we're not battered between Romans and barbarians, our crops fail, and the weather is shit. We're better off here, though we could do with a decent scrap. Just to keep our hands in.' He winked.

'You would need to swear allegiance to my king.' Osric was tentative, but he already liked Leofric. He took a long draught of ale, thirsty from the ride up from Calleva. There had been little time to recuperate, and his arse was grateful for the soft fur that he was sitting on. He and the Nobatians had barely stopped for rest, sleeping only short nights by pitiful fires in an attempt to do justice to the urgency that Vitalinus had imbued him with. Shabaka was splendid company, always happy to listen to Osric's fanciful stories. His brother, Tsekani, was quieter, but always rewarded his jokes with a toothy grin.

'We are nobody's vassals,' the Angle roared before smiling, 'but we will pledge our swords and shields to his cause if there is reward at the end of it.'

'I would have thought blood and glory would be reward enough.' Osric smirked.

'But they are not your king's to give. We want something from him.'

'And I'm sure you will get it.'

Whatever the cost. That's the negotiating power he'd been given. They needed extra muscle and steel in the fight against the Kaldi, and trained Briton warriors were few and far between in these parts. Osric glanced at Shabaka beside him and was greeted with only a stern nod. It hadn't been clear how the Angles would react to the Nobatians, but apart from a few suspicious sideways looks, they had made no issue of the exotic archers' presence. There was something quite imposing about their lean and dark physiques, and the undeniable mystique of bowmen commanded some respect from people with a culture of spears and swords.

'I have forty good men and women here,' Leofric said proudly. 'They might look like farmers, but they were warriors first.'

They didn't look like farmers. To a man and woman, the Angles looked like they had only to pick up shields and spears to be battle ready. They were nearly all of good fighting age. There were only a couple of children there, and a handful of elders that might be persuaded to stay at home. Amid the fair hair and pale faces, Osric had noticed the long chestnut brown hair of a Briton girl. She was on the cusp of womanhood, shorter than the Angles around her, but wore a sword strapped to her back. Apart from the colour of her hair, it was the sword that gave her away as a Briton. While Angles, like Saxons and Jutes, always carried a short broad-bladed seax, hers was slimmer and longer. It was too long for her and would have hung low enough to trip her up if she ever needed to run with it by her side. It was too long to be strapped to her back too. She could never draw it in a hurry. But it wasn't how she wore her weapon that was strange; it was the fact that a Briton woman was carrying a sword at all, and that she had become part of this community of Angles.

'How have you been treated by Appius?' Osric asked Leofric.

241

'Coldly,' came the simple response. 'He's a trumped-up little twat if ever I met one.'

Osric grinned. There was a consensus on the Praefectus of Eboracum, as he liked to be known. 'But he leaves you alone?'

'He knows to,' Leofric snarled. 'There's barely a spear to be seen in that pile of rubble they call a town.'

'And yet you remain on the land he has offered you?'

'For now.'

There was something about Leofric's tone that suggested a lack of complete contentment with his current lot. Perhaps the reward of more lands in exchange for a war against the Kaldi was just the incentive he needed. Osric could easily imagine that the Angles would otherwise not wait all that long before looking to extend their territory. Perhaps more of his countryfolk would make the sea voyage from their homeland in search of greener pastures. If they did, they would need more land. Whether they would earn it or take it remained to be seen. Osric quietly wondered if his king's tactics underestimated the bold tenacity of the Germanic people.

* * *

Rozena didn't much care about the comings and goings of a random Jute in the encampment. She would have barely even registered what little difference there was between him and the Angles she had become accustomed to. But the sight of Osric perched uncomfortably on a tall horse heading south after talking at length to Leofric was enough to pique her curiosity. Angles, Saxons, and Jutes weren't particularly fond of horses, and tended to keep smaller ones than the Britons. They were barely bigger than ponies and were used as beasts of burden rather than on the road or on the battlefield. Angles—and Jutes, she assumed—preferred to keep their feet on firm ground. Apart from the dogs they trained to kill, they had little trust in lesser beasts. Even more intriguing to Rozena were the two dark-skinned bowmen, the likes of whom she had never seen before, who flanked the Jute. Who was this man?

'He's an emissary from your high king,' Edoma told her.

'High king?' Rozena echoed.

'Yes. From a place called Viroconium.' Edoma had been outside the wall of the hut, listening to Osric and Leofric's conversation. 'Apparently he's united all you Britons together to fight the Kaldi and we get to fight alongside him.'

Rozena bristled at the mention of the Kaldi, instantly beset by the image of her father's corpse. She couldn't think of a better reason to unite her people. The Kaldi needed to be crushed, once and for all. 'I want to fight too,' she muttered, almost to herself.

'You shall fight beside me,' said Edoma solemnly and Rozena nodded, suddenly more aware of the weight of her father's sword on her back. She had lived among the Angles for a few weeks now and had become familiar with their bluntness. She appreciated it. There was little room for subtlety. There was nothing complicated about Edoma, at least not so far as Rozena could see. The Angle warrioress said only what she thought and meant every word. She seemed to have found Rozena amusing at first and made no attempt to disguise the fact.

'Do you even know how to use that sword?' she had asked the day after Rozena had drawn her blade on Edoma and her two brothers.

'Not well enough.' Rozena had already decided honesty was the best policy in dealing with Edoma. 'But I will fight like a cat if I have to.'

Edoma had studied her, pale blue eyes piercing into her, and nodded with a wry smile. 'I have no doubt of that,' she whispered.

Rozena slept beside Edoma from the first night with the Angles, and it took only a few days before she looked upon her as a big sister. In the days following, they sparred together, and Rozena grew in confidence with the blade. There were no training swords here, but she just knew Edoma wouldn't hurt her. More to the point, she knew Edoma wouldn't allow herself to be hurt by her. The lads watched them spar, whispering among themselves, probably laughing at the dark-haired girl with the oversized sword. But Edoma's brother, Wine, was kinder. His smiles were meant for Rozena, rather than at her expense. She flashed a smile back during a bout, and Edoma scowled at her and bruised her shoulder with the flat of her blade. Rozena crumpled to her knees in shock as much as in pain.

'You're with me,' Edoma told her firmly and held out a hand to help her to her feet.

And Rozena raised her sore arm and fought on, happy to feel wanted.

* * *

An hour after the Jute and his mysterious escort had departed, Wine and a few other Angles staggered back into the settlement. One was bleeding profusely from a stab wound to his shoulder and another limped heavily, a deep gash in his thigh.

'What happened?' demanded Edoma, her brow creased.

'Britons,' grumbled the lame man, instinctively glancing at Rozena, who watched from a little way away. She thought his name was Guthred.

'What Britons?' Edoma pressed. 'Where's Wigo?'

Wine shook his head sadly.

'Killed?' Edoma hissed.

'There were too many of them,' admitted Wine. 'They surprised us.'

'They killed Wigo?'

Wine nodded.

'And they have paid with their lives?'

Wine looked down, ashamed. The Angles had been routed. That was clear.

Edoma's face reddened. 'Then they must. Why did they attack?'

Wine shrugged. He was the youngest of the three siblings. Rozena had liked him until this moment. Now he showed his age. He was like a chastened child rather than a man who needed to avenge his brother's death. Edoma, as the eldest, had no such failings. She marched forward and snatched the spear that Guthred was using as a crutch, almost causing him to tumble into the dirt. She glared at the man with the wounded shoulder, eyeing his seax. The man unsheathed his weapon and passed it to her.

'Go, and fetch me a shield,' she instructed Wine, 'and rouse Cedric and Oswald as well. Are either of you two injured? Can you fight?'

'I'm fit,' sighed a man Rozena knew as Widmund.

'Me too.' Eadgur nodded reluctantly, glancing nervously at the retreating Wine.

'Rozena,' Edoma called.

Rozena walked forwards. 'Yes?'

'Will you come with us?'

'To fight the Britons?'

'To fight some Britons. Yes. Not all of them. I still want to fight the Kaldi with you and your king, but this is personal, not war. Will you stand with me?'

Rozena knew Edoma was testing her, but she had grown close enough to her in the last few weeks that she saw no malice in it. Edoma didn't want to turn her against her own people. She had a score to settle, and she wanted her new friend to fight beside her. Surely that was all. Rozena nodded slowly. 'I don't have a shield.'

'You won't need one. If we have to form a shield wall, you can stand behind it.'

Wine reappeared with a sturdy round shield like those carried by the others. Edoma strapped it to her back effortlessly. 'Guthred, Bedric. Go and get patched up. We shall avenge your injuries as well as my brother's death.'

Cedric and Oswald, bigger and older than Wine or any of his companions, trudged towards them. 'What do you want?' Cedric asked Edoma gruffly.

'Blood,' came the simple response.

And Rozena marched out with the six Angles to take up arms against her own kind.

The Fort

The dawn brought horrors. Voices woke Kiros from his slumber. He stirred for the briefest of moments, with Kamali warm beside him, still groggy enough to not recognise the urgency in the cries. Then came the blast of the horn that meant only one thing.

Picts.

He leapt from the heat of the furs and pulled his greaves and jerkin on in swift motions. 'Negasi, awake,' he shouted. 'Now. To the wall.'

His son was as swift as he to dress and ready himself for battle. Both men, for Negasi was as much a man as any of them now, buckled on their swords and reached for their spears and raced into the cold light.

The sun was barely kissing the stones of the wall that stretched out to the east when Kiros reached the ramparts. Scores of his kin were already there, and the rest were coming fast. They stood, quietly looking northward over the parapets, shivering in the autumn air.

The Picts had come. And this was no roving war band, intent only on the vengeful savaging of innocents and the burning of thatch and home and crops or stealing a few cattle here and there. This was a gathering of great numbers. More than Kiros had ever dreamed even roamed the higher lands. There had to be two hundred, maybe three. And Kiros knew they weren't shivering in the cold. They didn't feel it. Even in the dissipating gloom, through the wisps of mist that snaked ominously across the land between them and the wall, he could make out the painted blue torsos and faces. Three hundred of them, all spears and swords and savagery. Against maybe sixty fighting men on the wall and the women and children down below.

A well-disciplined cohort would have held this fort in days gone by. But he didn't even have enough men to make a Century. The men he had were dressed in odd bits of tarnished Roman armour, armed with old Roman spatha and spears, and they were fierce. But they were not legionaries. And he was no Centurion. Yet, they had one thing in their favour.

The wall.

'Hold the wall. Don't let one bastard get up here.' His words were passed down the line to anyone that hadn't heard him. Why they were even here was beyond him. The wall spread across the country, from coast to coast, and most of the Roman forts that had once lined it at regular intervals had fallen to wrack and ruin long ago. The Picts could have found a thousand other ways over the wall without laying siege to this fort.

He looked down from the rampart. Negasi was there, left in charge of the boys. He had grumbled when Kiros told him to remain behind the front line. But the warriors would need replacement spears. Kiros had asked Negasi to oversee the youngsters supplying arms when needed. It was a vital role, and it kept his son away from the imminent wave of blue-faced demons. The Briton, Tugen, who stood near Negasi, clearly ached to fight alongside the men as well.

'Just you see to it no harm comes to my Zala,' Kiros had told him, his hand resting on the boy's shoulder. And Tugen had nodded with his typical solemnity. Kiros looked beyond the courtyard, beyond the boys, to the glow coming from behind the bolted doors of the hall. Sorrow flooded through him. He knew he had little chance of kissing his wife or holding his daughter again.

What appeared to be a completely naked man broke from the line of Picts. He swaggered towards the wall, his voice raised in sudden jeering aggression as he danced. Long hair flailed around his painted face as he thrust his hips towards the wall in an unmistakable taunt. It was as ludicrous as it was chilling.

From Kiros' right side, someone hurled a spear towards the naked man, towards the druid that Kiros knew was cursing them with every ounce of magic he believed in. He knew it was supposed to be bad luck to show any sign of aggression towards a druid in the throes of his battle incantations and was in part relieved when the spear fell well short. But Kiros didn't believe in bad luck, so another part of him wished the spear had found a home in the naked man's throat. It did, at the very least, cut short the druid's spectacle. He returned to the line of Kaldi warriors in stony silence.

'The wall will hold,' Kiros called to the men in encouragement. 'We have spears, and we have swords, and we can drive these savages back.'

Derelei appeared beside him on the wall, her eyebrow raised at his description of her kin. 'Remember, every one of them is worth three of yours in battle,' she warned quietly. 'And I am only worth five of them. If you have a god to pray to, now is the time.'

'You will stay and fight with us?' Kiros asked.

'There's a particular *savage* I'd like to see on the end of my sword.' She grinned.

Then, as the sun's light and warmth touched the skeins of mist that danced over the ground beneath them and burnt it away, the Kaldi charged.

* * *

Drust was not at the head of the Kaldi advance. Not as far as Derelei could see. Cailtram's traditional exhibition had always seemed so potent, so virile and terrifying, when she had previously stood behind him in the lead-up to a battle. Faced with his naked body flailing in the chilly morning air, she was surprised how little his dung matted hair and body paint and jabbering nonsensical curses affected her. The men she stood beside were equally unimpressed, and that encouraged her. Perhaps this is why the Romans had kept the Kaldi at bay. Perhaps these dark men in their ancient armour really did know how to fight. Perhaps they could hold the fort after all.

Not that she cared about that. She wanted only one thing and didn't care how many of her blued kin she had to put to the blade to get it. Her rage at her former chieftain, which had subsided until then, flooded her again. She wanted to look him in the eye when he breathed his last, when he looked down upon his own sword jutting from his chest.

He was usually unmistakable in the fray. He was a tall man, and vocal. His woad decorations were always so dense, so complicated, and so intricate that his face would appear to be entirely blue. And if you ever got close enough to see the design in the heat of battle, you would likely already have his spear or sword embedded in your guts.

But he wasn't there.

The first wave of Kaldi reached the base of the wall, weapons strapped to their backs as they climbed. Another line formed behind them and began hurling fist-sized rocks and the occasional spear up at the parapet.

'Hold on to your spears,' Kiros shouted next to her. There was no sense in hurling them yet. It was an excellent tactic. A few of the Ethiopes were struck by stones and reeled precipitously on the rampart, blinded momentarily by a sudden flush of blood. Their compatriots caught them, and the line held.

Derelei, who squatted down behind the stone parapet for cover like the men, craned her neck to look down the vertical side of the wall. The climb did not appear too challenging, and the Kaldi would make it to the top easily if they weren't confronted. She glanced at Kiros, who just nodded back at her with a grim smile. At least he knew what he was doing.

And then she could hear the breathing of the climbers on the wall. She could smell them. And Kiros bellowed a command. The Ethiopes stood tall, spears in hand, and jabbed down at the invaders. A few of the Kaldi spears that hissed through the air to greet the counterattack found targets. Derelei saw at least two of the Ethiopes stagger backwards and fall into the courtyard behind them. But the defenceless, climbing Kaldi were easy targets. Those that weren't mortally wounded still fell. Maybe they'd be able to try again, maybe they wouldn't. But they weren't going to assail the wall. Not like this. She searched among them again for Drust. Surely, he had a hand in this.

Another line of blue etched hopefuls began their ascent of the wall, and another barrage of stones and spears pushed the Ethiopes behind cover.

249

Kiros looked at her, his smile a little steadier, a little more confident. But something wasn't right. Drust had to be here.

A scream pierced her from behind, followed by a chorus of more. She turned from the imminent assault and looked down into the courtyard. The first thing she saw was the smoke. Then the flame. The door of the hall had been wrenched open, and a brazier tipped onto the dry straw that lined its floor. Flames were already licking up the sides of the door. Several women had spilled out of the hall into the courtyard, ushering children away from the terrors within.

And then she saw the Kaldi. She guessed there were twenty or more brazenly walking amongst the women, blades flashing. They must have snuck over the wall miles from there, a small enough group to go unnoticed, but large enough to wreak havoc by entering the defenceless southern part of the fort. She saw Kamali, dagger in hand, run at a painted warrior in desperation. The Kaldi warrior brought his sword down, severing Kamali's knife hand at the wrist. Behind Derelei, Kiros roared like a wounded bear. He had seen it, too. And his first instinct was to leap from the rampart into the courtyard and fly at his wife's attacker.

He was too late. Unable to defend herself, Kamali was grabbed and spun around, her assailant pulling her close before drawing his blade across her neck and letting her body fall into the mud. Kiros' sword fell heavily on the assassin's head, cleaving it in two and sticking fast in the bone beneath his neck. But it would be little compensation.

Half a dozen other husbands and fathers leapt from the wall to defend the women and children, but the rest remained. They, like Derelei, knew that the main assault was on the wall. This was a cruel ruse, a ploy to split the defences. She stood in readiness to repel the attack. But another dozen Kaldi had appeared in the courtyard.

Then she saw him.

Drust.

He stood back from the slaughter, watching his warriors at work. He might have been capable of ordering the murder of innocents, but he was not one to partake in such a business. He liked to fight more than he liked to kill. He was waiting.

Kiros, who had pulled Kamali's corpse away from the battle, stood up and shouted angry orders to the men on the wall, calling more swords to his side. A couple of Kaldi warriors fell to his blade in a single swing.

That was all the invitation Drust needed. He began striding towards Kiros, oblivious to the fighting going on around him. And Derelei, less to protect Kiros than to deny him from claiming Drust's life, threw herself down into the fray. She had to get to Drust.

She landed with a roll in the mud and quickly found her feet. Drust's sword was light in her hand, her head swimming with vengeance. Then she came face to face with Wroid. His sword, unbloodied still, hung limp in his hand as he stood unhappily with his back to the wall. Derelei's heart leapt.

'Derelei.' A smile spread across his face. 'You're alive.'

She nodded, suddenly confused. 'Stay there,' she told him. 'Stay alive.'

The spear struck him in the neck. It came from the side, brutally ripping through his jugular, and clattered against the wall beyond. Wroid dropped his sword and lifted his hands to the wound, which quickly coursed with bright red blood. He staggered and dropped to his knees just as Derelei started towards him. A shriek pierced the din of the battle and Derelei glanced sideways, glimpsing a flash of copper hair. Modwen. She had thrown the spear that had done for Wroid and was now running, sword raised, towards Derelei.

There was little time to react. Derelei brought up Drust's sword to parry the vicious blow that would have cleaved her head in two. The impact between the two blades must have jarred Modwen. She took a step back to recover, a sneer curling on her lip.

'He was a traitor,' Modwen snarled, and spat in Wroid's direction.

Wroid had fallen face forwards into the mud, blood pooling around him. He was gone. He had paid with his life for helping Derelei.

'That's a handsome blade, Derelei.' Modwen grimaced. 'Let's see if you are worthy of it.'

It was clear Drust had led Wroid to the slaughter. He must have known all along that Derelei had escaped, and that it was the lovesick Wroid who had aided in the matter. And Modwen still just wanted vengeance for her brother's death.

'It's a pretty notion that Drust's own sword will be the death of his bitch.' Derelei readied herself for the onslaught.

Modwen screamed and charged.

All around them, men and women were fighting and falling. Derelei and Modwen were evenly matched. Where Derelei surpassed Modwen in skill, she had to contend with the perfect fury of a woman bent on revenge. Modwen came at her hard, grunting and slicing, fast and deadly. For a while, it was enough for Derelei to parry the attacks, to wear down her opponent, to wait for the gap always left open by a sword raised in anger.

Modwen overreached, and Derelei was quick to lunge forwards, her sword aimed at Modwen's belly. But Modwen, rare as it was, had manufactured a cunning feint. She must have planned it, because she found her balance and brought her blade slicing down into Derelei's shoulder. It wasn't a perfectly aimed blow, and Derelei's quick reactions were certainly enough to keep her arm attached, but it drew blood. And it hurt. Derelei roared, anger suddenly feeding her as well. She whirled with a renewed energy, knowing that she had to strike fast before she lost blood and became weaker and slow.

Modwen's brief glimpse of victory was taken away from her as Derelei brought another hand to the hilt of her sword, using her strong and supple wrists to produce a dizzying array of cuts and parries. The stiff grin vanished from Modwen's face as she struggled to keep up. Derelei pressed her advantage, pushing Modwen back against the wall until she lost her footing. It was a barely perceptible shift in her balance, the faintest of wobbles, but Derelei seized upon it in a flash. Her sword, Drust's sword, swept Modwen's blade aside. Then she rolled her wrists and brought it in a downward arc that slashed into the side of Modwen's knee.

Modwen's leg buckled beneath her, and she fell sideways. And Derelei was upon her. There was no time for mercy, or for gloating. She needed to get to Drust. She slid the end of his sword up into Modwen's exposed throat where she lay, twisting it with a calculated efficiency. After the briefest glance at her poor Wroid—dead in the mud—she spat on Modwen's corpse and turned to look for the king of the Kaldi.

She turned just in time to see Kiros fall. And her eyes met with his killer. Drust.

And he turned and strode away.

'Fight me!' Derelei called after him in the clamour, but he did not turn. She took a few steps in pursuit but was hemmed in by other Kaldi warriors she did not recognise, and had to fight. Her shoulder was aching, wet with blood, and she found herself in retreat, with Drust vanished from view.

She had failed.

* * *

Negasi had been the first to fall. He spotted the Kaldi first and grabbed the spear he'd been preparing to hand up to the rampart. Desperate to prove his worth as a warrior, he charged with a scream that was lost amidst the shouting from above. The rest of the Ethiopes were far too busy fending off the assault on the wall to see the rear-guard attack.

Tugen watched, mouth agape, fear paralysing him for a moment, as Negasi ran to his death. The Kaldi weren't even in a hurry. They strode into the courtyard, blue faced and arrogant, the man in front stopping Negasi's rush with the sharp end of a spear. Tugen tried to call, to alert the men on the wall, but his voice stuck in his throat. He cursed himself in that moment, hated himself for his inaction. He had dreamed about the day he could kill some of these fiends that had slaughtered his parents but, when it came to it, he froze.

A couple of Kaldi warriors easily forced the door to the great hall, and the next thing Tugen saw was fire. Fire and black smoke. It took Kamali's appearance to stir him into action. As Negasi had done, he grabbed a spear and uttered the best war cry he could muster. And then Kiros was there, landing in the dark mud, sure-footed and powerful.

Kamali died next. Murdered. Her throat slit from ear to ear, just as

Tugen imagined his mother had perished. And Kiros' blade whirled in vengeance, shedding Kaldi blood in a retribution that would never satisfy him.

By the time the huge Kaldi, certainly a chieftain, set his sights on Kiros, Tugen realised they were horribly outnumbered. His thoughts went to Zala. He had to get to her. Skirting around the wooden struts of the hall, he ducked into the smouldering building all but unnoticed. A copper-haired Kaldi glared at him for a moment but passed him by as if he was barely worth the touch of her blade. And he was thankful for that.

He found Zala pulling at loose planks in the rear of the hall, forcing an opening in the wall. She nodded at him, her dark cheeks wet with tears. The look that passed between them told Tugen that she knew her mother's fate. He was sure she could guess at Negasi's, too.

He landed a foot heavily on a rogue bit of wall and pushed it outwards. A hole, big enough to crawl through, opened. She lurched forward, eager to escape, but he caught her by the shoulder.

'Wait. Let me see if it's safe.'

The hole opened into the pale light of morning. But there was no fighting to be seen. He pulled back and ushered her through the gap, following quickly behind. Outside, Tugen suddenly wasn't sure what to do. He felt bad, making his escape, even if it meant seeing Zala to safety. Negasi wouldn't have run.

'You can't help them.' Zala pulled at his arm gently. Her words, though true, cut deep. She wasn't challenging his ability to fight. She just knew the odds were insurmountable, and there was no sense in him dying for her people when he could run away with her. He nodded, and they scurried along the base of the wall, heading for the corner nearest the trees to the south.

Then he saw Derelei.

She sat slumped against the wall, pulling some fabric tight around her upper body. Where it wrapped around her shoulder, the cloth had stained a deep crimson. She was wounded.

'Tugen.' She grimaced as she looked up at them. 'You're going the wrong way.'

'The fort is lost,' Zala blurted out.

'Probably. I'm sorry about your father.'

It shocked Tugen to hear that Kiros must have fallen, but beside him, leaning on him, Zala recoiled at the revelation, her legs giving way for a moment. Tugen held her up. 'He's dead?'

'Drust killed him.' Derelei nodded, grunting as she hauled herself to her feet. 'But he won't live long enough to celebrate his victory.'

'You're hurt,' exclaimed Tugen. 'You won't last a minute.'

'Better to die in battle than in a hole.' Derelei smirked. 'At least I have that.' She tensed her fingers on the hilt of her sword, but it was clear she was in pain. He did not know this renegade Kaldi well, but something had passed between them, and he couldn't stand to see her stagger back into the fray, to a death that surely awaited her. He knew, however, that such an argument would not hold water with her.

'Come with us,' Tugen said simply.

Derelei looked at him quizzically, as if he had suggested the most ridiculous course of action imaginable.

'Please.'

Zala nodded in support.

'But I am a warrior.'

'The best of them,' Tugen agreed. 'And we need you.'

'You?'

Tugen looked at his feet, his shame intensifying in front of Zala. He wanted her to believe him brave and strong, a man worthy of her affections. But he wasn't. He had not fought well. He had not killed a single Kaldi. He was unprepared, and not the man he hoped he was. Not yet. And he wanted Derelei to live, too.

'I cannot guarantee Zala's safety alone.'

'Tugen,' Zala began sympathetically, but Tugen shook his head to stop her.

'I am blooded in the hunt, but not in battle. We need you to protect us. Please.'

'Why should I?'

'You don't go to fight to save your people,' Zala pointed out. 'You want to kill your people.'

Derelei leant her head to one side thoughtfully.

'You don't owe my father anything,' continued Zala. 'But Tugen vouched for you. He saved you.'

'We keep doing that for each other,' Derelei said quietly, clearly still thinking.

'We need to get word to the rest of Britannia,' said Tugen. 'This is no raiding party.'

Derelei nodded.

'I know people in Eborakon.' Tugen smiled at the thought of seeing Emrys again. 'We'll come back and kill Drust. There's always time for that.'

'Aye.'

Zala looked at Tugen, her wet, sad eyes shining with a glimmer of hope.

'Come on then,' Derelei started south. 'What are you waiting for?'

Gladius

The sun had dropped below the clouds, rendering the evening suddenly darker than it had been moments before, and a veil of mist washed over the long grass of the field. Rozena walked a step behind Edoma, the other Angles in an untidy line to either side.

'We'll make him pay,' Wine muttered to her left. The word 'him' struck Rozena as strange, given the tale he had spun of being woefully outnumbered. She frowned to herself, but her desire for quiet prevented her from questioning him or alerting Edoma, who didn't appear to have heard.

The fog thickened, swirling damply around them. The dew had fallen hard, and Rozena felt the chill in her feet. She picked them up a little higher and shrugged the heavy blade on her back into a more comfortable position.

'This it?' Edoma asked as she stopped walking suddenly.

'I think so,' Wine mumbled, stepping forward.

A red wall had risen out of the gloom in front of them.

'Go,' ordered Edoma. 'Silently.'

Wine nodded and hauled himself up on the top of the wall, then dropped without a sound to whatever lay on the other side. Cedric and Oswald followed, both grunting softly as they dragged their fearsome bulks over the obstacle. Widmund and Eadgur followed. One of them cried out from the other side of the wall, probably landing badly on his ankle, and was quickly hushed. Edoma grinned at Rozena.

'Need a hand?' She cupped her hands together and nodded at Rozena's damp feet. Rozena stepped up into them and pulled herself up and over the wall.

There was no fog on the other side. And Rozena's heart sank. As Edoma landed gracefully next to her and waved the war band forward, Rozena suddenly realised where she was. She recognised the gnarled olive tree that she had sat beneath on countless occasions. They were in Krestell's garden. At the villa.

There had to be some mistake.

* * *

Viction had kept his continued search for Rozena quiet from Emrys. He didn't want to endanger the boy. There was every chance that Rozena had fallen foul of the Angles.

He'd encountered a group of them on the far side of Dere Street, young men who were out on a hunting trip but weren't in danger of catching a thing. They were garrulous and loud, well steeped in mead, and more intent on wrestling each other for entertainment than feeding their families.

'Good day.' Viction had picked up a few words of their language in his time in Eboracum. It was a rough tongue with words that stuck in the throat.

The Angles had sobered up when they heard and saw him. A couple reached for weapons, so Viction held up his hands in submission.

'Peace,' he insisted calmly. 'I am looking for a girl.'

'So are we,' one of them blurted, and the Angles sniggered. The tallest of them, his long blonde hair tied in a knot, stood up to face Viction. He pulled at a long, plaited beard.

'I am Wigo. What girl?'

'A Briton girl, so high.' Viction held the palm of his left hand to just above his chest, a fair estimation of Rozena's height. He didn't bother to identify himself. Hopefully, a little disrespect would anger the Angles into giving something away.

'What do we want with a Briton girl?' Wigo sneered. He was a handsome man, but there was a cruelness in his pale eyes.

'I heard she was seen with a group of Angles,' Viction said quietly. He was bluffing, but they had no way of knowing that. A younger looking version of Wigo, behind him, looked down, hiding his face. 'Are you sure you haven't seen her?' Viction pushed.

'Did you not hear me the first time?' Wigo squared up to Viction, his hand twitching near the hilt of his seax.

'I did.'

'So, move along, old man.' The Angle was clearly itching for a fight, a prospect Viction didn't particularly relish. He could maybe take on three of them, but six? And he had no way of knowing how skilled they were in combat.

'She is not to be trusted.' Viction tried a different approach, knowing Angles were prone to superstition. 'She wields the power of the gods, and has placed a fearsome curse on several families, apparently just on a whim.'

There was a ripple among the younger Angles, but Wigo stared steely-eyed back at Viction. 'Your gods are weak and do not scare us,' he spat. 'Do not make me tell you again that we have not seen this girl.'

Viction was sure he was lying, and his anger swelled, overshadowing his assessment of the odds in combat. 'I don't believe you.' His fingers on both hands flexed in readiness. He held his hands up in mock surrender, ready to arm himself, knowing he had pushed Wigo far enough.

Wigo either knew where Viction's weapons were, or he simply paid no heed to the submissive gesture. The Angle's seax was barely clear of its scabbard before Viction had drawn the two sica from their smooth swaddling on his back. The twin blades descended as a blur, their curved edges biting into both sides of Wigo's neck.

Headless, Wigo slowly crumpled to the ground. His comrades reached for their own short swords, caught in sudden close combat with no time to pick up their spears. Viction knew his only chance at victory was speed. He stepped over Wigo's twitching corpse with his twin blades, targeting the first two men at once. One sica bounced off the wooden boss of a shield, but the other found the soft flesh of a shoulder. It bit deep and the Angle roared in pain, dropping his seax and staggering backwards. But Viction wasn't done. He whirled and ducked low, aiming under another shield that was raised protectively. His blade found a leg and sliced deep into a thigh.

And even while Wigo's blood still flowed from where his head had been, the rest of his kind had turned tail and fled. Viction had considered waylaying the one with the leg wound, pressing him for information about Rozena, but he was already exhausted. The speed and severity of his attack had taken its toll. He wasn't the young man he once was and, as the Angles disappeared, he slumped to his haunches and wheezed.

He was sure of one thing. The Angles had Rozena. And he would need to think of a way to get to her that did not involve combat. And he was still pondering that problem later, when they came to the villa, when they brought their vengeance to his family.

It was Krestell's scream that alerted him. He was sparring with Emrys in the ludus when the cry came from within, and in an instant, he knew his wife was dead. The boy looked at him in wild terror, unable to speak, as if he knew the same. And, in the time it took them to turn from each other and race indoors, they were surrounded. Half a dozen Angles appeared from the shadows of the colonnade, axes and swords readied and shields raised.

'Kill them both,' sneered their leader, a woman.

Viction recognised three of them. The one that had hid his head when he had asked about Rozena was there. He stayed close to the woman. And the other two were wide-eyed and clearly anxious. The cowardly whelps had found bigger, stronger friends this time. This time, Viction knew that, without the element of surprise, he couldn't possibly hope to fight them all. Then he saw the blood. Two of the seaxes were tainted with it.

'Go,' he hissed to Emrys as he raised the spatha he had been training with. He had no shield, and though he could use all the help he could get, he couldn't bear to see the boy fall. Besides, there was a glimmer of hope that Carina was alive somewhere.

Emrys looked back at him, his golden eyes burning with fear and anger. He could feel the boy's desire to stand with his mentor and he admired it. He wanted it, too. For a moment, as the Angles advanced on them like hungry wolves, he considered whether the two of them could prevail. And then he dismissed the idea.

'Find a gap and go,' he shouted at Emrys, knowing he would never see him again. 'Find Carina.'

'You killed my brother,' the woman said in her own tongue.

Viction shrugged, pretending not to understand, and raised his sword. The woman was clearly adept, worthy of respect, and the two larger Angles, flanking her with their blood-stained blades, exuded a confidence he had not seen in the group he had previously encountered. They had killed Krestell. They, at least, needed to die. But not yet.

With a speed he hoped would surprise the attackers, he rushed at the youngest two, the two who had seen him fight already. His blade met an ill-gripped shield and smashed it. He followed through with a kick and sent the young Angle sprawling into the sand. The second one was too slow to react, and Viction opened his throat with the sharp tip of his spatha. He spun and drove his sword into the other's chest.

'Go!'

Emrys took the opportunity and ran into the shadows, and Viction turned to face the remaining four. They fanned out, flanking him. He had no choice but to fight them all at once.

* * *

Krestell lay, arms outstretched, one hand almost still reaching for the knife she always used to prepare the meat, a paltry weapon in defence that had done her little good. They had cut a deep gash into her midriff, and she spilt from it. Her eyes were still open, frozen in anguish, horror and fury at the invasion visited upon her.

Emrys couldn't take his eyes off her corpse. A pain knotted his stomach, and he felt angry tears brimming in both eyes. It wasn't the first time he had seen the innocent felled by war-hungry steel. He had run from this before and didn't want to again. He wanted to fight. Seeing Krestell splayed out like that made his fist tighten around the hilt of his sword. He half turned, intent on standing with Viction, even if it meant the end of both of them. But then he saw Carina. Or rather, he heard her.

The Angles had missed her. He imagined Krestell, with the briefest of warning, ushering her daughter into hiding. It was her sob, the faintest noise, wilfully suppressed but just audible, that gave her away. Emrys stole forward, gingerly stepping over one of Krestell's arms, and lifted the cloth of the makeshift tent that leant up against the wall of the bath. Carina's wet eyes blinked back at him.

'Stay here,' he told her, knowing full well he should be telling her to flee with him. 'I need to stand with your father.'

She was shaking with terror, so he wasn't sure if she nodded in reply or not. But her eyes told him she understood. She had to know that he would fight to protect her, that he would do everything he could to not see her lose both parents in the same day, as he had done. And then he realised he could no longer hear the clash of blades. He dropped the canvas, concealing Carina again, and turned just in time to see the Angle woman and another heavy-set warrior emerge into the bathhouse.

Viction had perished. There was no other explanation. Emrys felt a pang of sadness that he wouldn't even have time to grieve for his mentor. The big Angle raised a spear and readied his throwing arm and Emrys lifted his sword defiantly, for all the good it would do him.

'Wait.' The woman held her arm out in front of the spear. 'We have no fight with this boy.'

Emrys neither understood her words nor paid heed to her apparent reluctance to let the spear be hurled at him, so he took a step closer. More than anything, he wanted to put distance between himself and Carina.

'You want to fight me, boy?' The woman spoke in his tongue, moving to stand in front of her burly spearman. 'You want to die today, like your mother and father?'

Any words Emrys had caught in his throat. He half shook his head, wanting to tell her that Viction and Krestell weren't his mother and father, that the Kaldi had slaughtered his own parents, that he would gladly avenge them all by killing her.

'So, lower your sword, boy,' the woman scowled. 'You didn't kill my brother. You don't need to die.'

Emrys couldn't help but glance at Krestell, wondering how she had deserved to die, but he didn't.

'I am sorry for her,' the Angle said abruptly, and maybe even meant it. 'And the other one.'

Confused, Emrys lowered his blade.

'We will go.' She turned her back on him, ushering the man beside her in front of her. 'Wine,' she shouted. 'We are leaving.'

And they were gone.

Emrys turned back to where Carina lay in hiding, pausing only a moment to be sure the Angles had gone, then flung back the canvas.

'Carina.' Her pale face was turned away from him. He knelt beside her and reached out his hand, touching her cheek. It was damp with tears. She didn't move. His eyes scanned down her body, over her clothes. Her dress was stained crimson. He hadn't seen it before, but she had been mortally wounded. As he turned her face to him, her open eyes still bright, he knew she was dead.

It was as though the breath was sucked from him. He belched out an empty gasp of horror, a dry retch that was hurled back at him by the tiled sides of the bath, and his eyes flooded with tears. He fell forward on her and buried his face in her hair, kissing her already cooling cheeks.

Later, when he felt a hand on his shoulder, he barely reacted. He could have happily let someone, anyone, slide a blade between his shoulder blades and pin his corpse to hers.

'Emrys,' a soft voice called to him from far away.

And eventually he lifted his head and looked up. Through the mist of his grief, he saw her face, also streaked with tears, tears he didn't yet comprehend.

Rozena.

Mandrake

She looked at him without flinching. Brazenly attentive.

'It is well known to the wise that men, when slain in battle or killed violently, often defecate themselves at the point of death,' Ossian continued. He paused again to look at Pasha, but her wide eyes barely blinked. 'What is less well known is that they also sometimes spill their seed.'

Pasha barely reacted. The flickering of the brazier in her private chambers imbued her pallor with a warm orange lustre that mirrored the hue of the full harvest moon beaming down outside the walls of the villa. Viroconium was quiet, much of its population out making the most of the light afforded them. It was still a population decimated by the ravages of disease the year before, but the weather had been kind this year and the bounty from the fields was going to sustain the town well through the winter.

'And where the dead men lie, where their flesh and fat dissolve into the hungry earth, where their blood and seed and shit spread into the soil, that is where this grows.' He held up what could easily have been a carved mannequin, a crude rendition of a figure. 'Do you know what this is, Pasha?'

'It's the root of the mandrake,' she intoned.

Ossian nodded. 'And what do you know of it?'

'It produces beautiful purple flowers.' Pasha's lip curled into a provocative smile.

'Yes, yes it does,' Ossian admitted. 'And?'

264

'I heard that when pulled from the ground, it screams in anguish, and anyone hearing the scream dies immediately. Of fear, I imagine.'

'Quite so. The only way to extract this root is to dig a furrow around the plant until the root is exposed.' Ossian leant closer to Pasha, knowing the firelight would add to his theatre. 'You must tether that undisturbed root to a faithful hound and then move to a safe distance and plant your fingers firmly in your ears. Then you whistle for your dog, and the root is safely unearthed.'

'And the dog dies,' Pasha muttered.

'And the dog dies,' echoed Ossian, studying Pasha's face. Her lips were parted, and a spark danced in the obsidian depths of her eyes. She troubled Ossian. He didn't quite know what it was, but there was an undeniable power in this woman. She was only just becoming aware of it, but perhaps her brush with death had taken her into the company of the gods. Perhaps she had brought back some kind of immortal boon from her travels beyond the veil. The way she'd spoken to her mother earlier had surprised him. Sevira had pointedly asked her why she was allowing 'the druid' to visit her private room and had been told in no uncertain terms that it was not her place to make such queries. She was so sure of herself, so strong. And yet so innocent and pliable still.

'No.' Ossian announced after a moment of quiet. 'The dog does not die. And the mandrake does not scream.' He waited for her eyes to widen further still at the revelation, but they did not. 'It's all lies. Lies told by people like me.'

'You want it for yourself.' Pasha said, in an almost whisper, almost seductively.

'Yes.'

Ossian put the root aside and lifted a carved wooden cup from near the brazier.

'What's in there?'

'You already know.'

'Mandrake root.'

'Yes, and mugwort. The reason these nightmare stories about screaming roots proliferate is not merely because people like me want them for themselves. We can't have every lovelorn maiden or randy farmhand plundering such a valuable resource, thinking it will answer all their problems. But even though there is no murderous shriek, it is replete with death. An untrained idiot or even a gifted neophyte could soon find themselves in a never-ending slumber if left to their own devices.'

'It shows us the other world?' Pasha asked quietly.

'It can. It can evoke visions. It can penetrate the veil, as I believe you have already done, and can show us our life's true purpose.' Ossian let the words sink in. Pasha fixed her eyes on the wooden goblet. 'And mugwort will protect the traveller from evil along his, or her, way. And make no mistake, it is a journey.'

Ossian held the cup out, offering it to Pasha.

'Will I come back?' She showed the first sign of unease, moving her body for the first time in a while.

Ossian nodded. 'I will see to it that you do.'

Pasha took the vessel carefully, extending both hands to hold it. She cupped it in front of her and peered into it as if trying to fathom the threat it posed to her. Ossian smiled in encouragement when she looked up at him, then closed his eyes. Let her see that he would join her on her vision quest. He would protect her. He would nourish her.

* * *

The concoction was foul. It was all Pasha could do not to gag. Beneath the already unpleasant earthiness was a horrible bitterness that stung her eyes and nose. Whatever Ossian had used to sweeten the drink was woefully ineffectual. But she emptied the draught in two long gulps, clutching her hand to her chest to try to coax it down. The druid smiled in the half-light. His eyes were firmly closed, but her involuntary little noises of disgust amused him.

She would never admit it to anyone, but there was little she saw in Ossian to like. He was a smarmy, self-righteous man who possessed the wisdom and knowledge she wanted. She knew how he looked at her. She knew her mother saw it too and had tried to offer protection earlier. What was the worst the old man could do to her, anyway? Let him steal glimpses of her womanliness. Let his eyes linger on her curves a little too long. He was old, but he was still human. And if he was helping her because he liked to look at her, then so be it. Pasha was ravenous for knowledge, desperate to comprehend the images that flashed into her mind in the depths of the night. Who else was going to help her do that?

Certainly not Pabo. Pabo, in his moulded bronze breastplate. Pabo, son of Ceneu, the once mighty overlord of Northern Britannia, of the kingdom of Rheged, now old and feeble and a devotee of the Christian God. Pabo, who had come to Viroconium under the pretence of emissary duty, full of stories about the savages in the north and their campaign of destruction when, really, he was there to seek the hand of the high king's daughter in marriage. Pabo, whose commitment to that veiled cause was undermined, as clear as day, by his obvious persuasion towards those of his own sex. Pabo, preening and dull and painfully devoid of any kind of self-awareness. Pabo had potent stock. His grandfather, Coel, was the substance of legends, once leader of the northern men, defender of the wall, and a proud Briton who found a way to serve his own people as fiercely as he allied himself with Rome. Pabo was not his grandfather. He wasn't even his father, or his older brothers. And Pasha had no interest at all in forging a union with him, even if her father marched home and demanded as much.

She felt her eyelids dropping, distantly amused at how heavy they felt and how little control she suddenly had over them. She felt as if she fell in slow motion, sideways, onto the rug near the fire. Perhaps Ossian had smoothed her fall, but she was sure he did not move. He sat across from her, eyes closed and a thin smile on his face. She thought she could see his lips turn up as his face went sideways in her blurring vision. Her eyes closed by the time her head had reached the thick fur of the rug, and only the dancing tongues of fire penetrated her closed lids for a while, until they too receded into blackness.

And from the blackness, a river flowed. A river of dancing lights and dissonant bells. It was as if the rocks that rose dark and wet from the water, if water it was, were strings on which the current played a tune of such randomness that it could barely be called music. And yet, the more she listened to it, the more sense it made. The disparate notes languidly congregated into chords that grew into a kind of harmony that almost fell into melody.

She looked upriver, the landscape opening in front of her as if a mist was lifting from it, as if a blanket was being slowly pulled back to reveal what had been long hidden. A mountain stood beyond, and she felt herself rise and soar over the wet rocks and rushing water, against the flow, observing as the river shrank into a brook, a stream, then a tiny bubbling spring that found its way through fissures and cracks among boulders and rocks that grew bigger as she flew higher up the slope. And then the dark water, a single plaintive note quivering in the thin mountain air, disappeared into a hole in a stone and was gone.

A wolf cried to one side of her, a mournful howl that echoed a deeper part of the chord. Another joined it from behind her, a third note, and Pasha felt herself rise further into the cloud. Looking down, she saw the two lean grey beasts approach each other and look after her, their heads raised in an uncomfortable harmony. And as she rose higher, she realised the river really was flowing backwards. It was being sucked back into the mountain, leaving dry gullies and exposed roots, fish gasping for breath, and rocks that became dry and baked by the sun. And the two wolves lapped at the last of the water as it vanished back into the earth, and then they howled again.

She floated near the top of the mountain, by a jagged knife-edged ridge dusted in snow that rose sharply into a dog-toothed peak. And on a ledge just below the summit crouched an old man with eyes like suns, crying molten gold onto the dusky fur of a great bear, his hand resting on the animal's head as inky clouds rolled over each other to swallow him up and reclaim the mystery.

And she saw, in the depths of those clouds, an occasional flash of light. She heard great swells of thunder rolling around her. And the hot breath of the bear on her face. Only it wasn't the bear. Light seared into her brain, stabbing her behind the eyes, revealing glimpses of a face. An older man. The druid, Ossian. His own heavy eyes swayed for a heartbeat in front of hers and were gone again. And she was no longer flying. She was lying on one of the hot dry boulders by the dried-up river; her back arched against the curve of the stone, a weight pushing her down. Something pushing into her. Invading her. And the black clouds descended into the valleys, their darkness smothering all noise, all movement, obscuring everything. Everything except the invasion.

Until even that subsided, slipping away from her into nothingness.

Until she awoke, ears thick with her own heartbeat, in the half-light of the dying brazier in her room.

Alone.

* * *

Catigern had begged Zeki to take him with him. Perhaps he thought there was some promise of glory. Zeki was proud of the boy and his excellent progress with sword in hand. When they first started their training, Catigern had shown more mental fortitude than anything. He hadn't exhibited any desire to fight. And perhaps he still didn't. Not like some men. Lesser men, those who didn't question their own existence and the world around them, fought only for the primal thrill of violence. They thrived in the shedding of blood and became stronger in survival. Catigern took no delight in the violence itself. He had taken to combat as if it were an intricate dance, an exercise in strategy and stamina, fed only by physicality and skill. Now, with that ability well honed, he had the presence of mind to realise that he could be a formidable opponent not with brawn, but with brain.

Whether he could hold his nerve in the thick of battle, surrounded by the horror of death and dismemberment, Zeki was not sure. Ready or otherwise, it was not Catigern's time to leave Viroconium. Zeki had been tasked by Ossian, the druid's terse instruction blessed by the slight nod and smile of Sevira, with relating important news to Vortigern.

News had come from the north, brought on the back of young Pabo, son of Ceneu. The Kaldi were pressing southwards, undeterred by the encroaching season. Their progress would be slowed by the weather, but they were clearly intent on reaching warmer climes.

As he guided his horse along the now familiar Roman thoroughfare, heading for Watling Street and onwards to Verulamium, Zeki was sad to leave his duties in Viroconium but glad to be bound for the company of his brothers in arms. There was a fight coming, and honour to be had. He did not want to be sparring in the comfortable embrace of the high king's villa when there was a war to be fought.

'Tell the high king he needs to move his men northwards,' Pabo had stammered, clearly unused to speaking in the presence of strangers. He was a strange young man, handsome and tall. The sheen of his breastplate, strapped tight to his thin chest, was enough to let Zeki know that the man had never had to raise a sword in defence.

Pabo had glanced at Zeki several times. Searching looks, arrogant almost. Zeki was used to attracting a variety of curious glances. He looked different to most men here. Some looked at him in horror, some in fascination. Some in irrational loathing. But Pabo had looked at him with a quiet hunger, like a warrior might look at a well-crafted blade or a prize stallion. He had looked at him like he wanted to possess him. And perhaps, had Zeki not been quickly sent on his current mission, he might have let Pabo have him. If that's what he wanted.

In Bloom

B
eside him, Joceline slept. In a while, he would get up and leave her bed and return to Lamorna. But not yet. There was little appeal to the marital bed. His young wife was round with child. Her sleep would be fitful, disturbed with the need to empty her bladder in the frosty night. She would squat in the corner and moan with effort as she expelled what little fluid had been trapped in her bladder by the movements of their unborn child. And he would pretend to sleep.

He wasn't proud of himself. He knew he should be by Lamorna's side. He knew he should leap from the furs and offer any help he could. But he was lost in his own selfish malaise. He could admit that at least to himself and perhaps, by proxy, to Joceline, who selfishly revelled in his absenteeism from his marriage. He studied her still face. It looked to be carved from stone and was smooth like the pebbles on the beaches. Her pale grey eyes were closed, but skittered a little from some dream she was having. He didn't suppose it was a good one. The sadness in Joceline was deep-set. Her mouth turned up into a genuine smile only when she was in the throes of physical pleasure, as if only that intensity could blind her momentarily to the tragedy that she wore like a veil, day in and day out. How strange that here he was, in the arms of a woman who had lost her only son, too disillusioned with his own life to spend his nights with the woman who carried his child.

Her eyes captivated him. The paleness of their grey hue belonged here. It was like an extension of the sea on a windless day in autumn. And yet she begged him to take her away from Dumnonia. Anywhere but here. And

271

most of the fibres in his body screamed at him to do just that. Anything to get away from this backwater. The Hibernians were barely a nuisance any more. He suspected they had turned their attentions northward. He half wanted them to wade ashore just so he could draw his sword.

In the meantime, Vortimer trod water. He would await the birth of his child and while away the darker hours of winter with Joceline. Whether Lamorna knew of his trysts didn't hugely matter. She was to be the mother of his child. Their child would inherit this awful place. But the child would be a direct descendant of the high king. Vitalinus, or Vortigern as he had apparently now pronounced himself, had known exactly what he was doing. He had subdued the troublesome and fiercely independent Dumnonia and bound it to him in blood. None of this was consolation to Vortimer. Nor, if he was honest with himself, was the embrace of the woman who lay next to him. It had offered a glimmer of comfort, of warmth, but he had once had that with Lamorna, too. It would fade, and he would be lost again.

Sighing, he pulled himself free from Joceline's loose embrace and stood up. He glanced back down at her pale exposed skin, almost luminous in the moonlight that fell over it, and felt a carnal urge again. He shrugged it off. Perhaps that was all it was. He covered her up and dressed himself, pausing only to stir the fire before leaving her.

A frost had already fallen, and his feet crunched lightly through it as he made his way across the courtyard in the pale light. A single brazier burned near the gate, and a couple of hunched guards clapped their gloved hands together for warmth, stirring up a spiral of glowing ashes that darted up into the starry sky. Poor bastards, he thought. This was their life. He wondered what dreams they harboured. Did they want to be anywhere but here as well? The rising embers led his gaze to the rampart and the solitary figure silhouetted there in the moonlight. He knew it could only be Jac.

Perversely, Vortimer decided he would impose on Jac's nocturnal vigil. He climbed the slippery steps and approached him. 'Anything to report?'

Jac turned to him, his face shadowed. 'Nothing, my Lord. What brings you out in the cold?'

'A sleepless night and the promise of fresh air.'

'The lady is well?'

'She is, thank you.' For a moment, Vortimer wondered if the lad was insinuating something. There was every chance that his dalliances with Jocelyn were not as secret as they could be. Perhaps there was some barb in Jac's apparent courtesy. And yet, Vortimer mused, probably not. It was clear to all, including him, that Jac regarded Lamorna fondly. Lustfully, perhaps. How it must gall him to see her bloated with child and bound to another man. 'All is well with the men?'

'As ever, my lord.' Jac looked out onto the moon-blanched moors as if searching for a shadow. 'There has been no more talk.'

Vortimer nodded. He knew well that Jac was at the centre of that talk, spurred on by the brattish simpleton, Erbin, who no doubt promised him wealth and glory if he were to seize upon an opportunity. Well, let him have that opportunity, Vortimer seethed. Let him try to hurl his Lord and master from the walls of the fort. Let him try.

But Jac was impassive. Older, wiser. Perhaps his impetuosity had waned at the near threat of execution.

'The Hibernians are long absent,' Vortimer changed the subject. 'You must be aching to draw your blade?' Jac had shown great promise in battle, but Vortimer's tone was more provocative.

'Aching is not the right word,' Jac said quietly. 'Like most men, I would prefer to avoid bloodshed. But perhaps I do feel the warrior in me calling out for action.'

'Indeed?'

'Can a man be content to always watch?'

'It depends on what he is watching, I suppose. And what action he feels compelled to take.'

A breeze sprung up, icy and brisk, and Jac pulled his furs closer about him. 'I just watch and wait, my Lord. I watch. And I wait.'

* * *

Lamorna was enjoying her pregnancy. Her bladder had rebelled and her back ached but, once she got comfortable, she was happy to let her mind wander. Her hands idly rested on the growing roundness of her belly, and a smile sat easily on her lips. Even the intrusion of Joceline one morning did little to dampen her spirits.

'How are you feeling?' Joceline's insipid eyes flickered towards Lamorna's middle, as if to accent her query.

'Never better.'

'I had terrible sickness with Petroc. The old women told me it was a good thing.'

'Then all is well with me, too.' Lamorna smiled at the other woman. It was hard, even knowing that her husband took refuge in the arms of this sad-eyed widow, to truly hate her. They shared the fault, but Joceline's air of tragedy was justifiable, especially to an expectant mother. Already widowed, the poor woman had lost her only son to the Hibernians. What greater pain could a woman endure?

'I just wanted to tell you,' Joceline said coolly, 'if there's anything you need, please ask.'

Lamorna nodded regally, her head held high. Let her husband warm the widow's bed. He would tire of her soon enough. 'Thank you, Joceline.'

Joceline smiled thinly back at her.

'Actually, perhaps you could do something for me.'

'Yes?'

'I'd quite like to take a short walk. Outside the walls.'

'Are you sure?' There was an air of subdued panic in Joceline's question, as if she was scared that someone might see them together. As if Vortimer might see them together and worry that his poorly kept secret had been spoiled by the solidarity of women. Oddly, that was exactly what Lamorna wanted to happen.

'Quite sure. I am more than capable. It's just that it's quite muddy on the way and I'd rather not slip and fall. If I could take your arm?'

Joceline's grey eyes flitted again, her thin lips pursed. 'Sure,' she agreed, and helped her out into the thin, cold air.

'I am certain I will have a son,' Lamorna announced as they trod carefully through the mud towards the gate. Most people in her position would wilfully believe they were going to produce a male heir, but Lamorna was less than happy about her supposition.

'I am sure you will,' Joceline answered with predictable sycophancy.

'I'd rather have a girl.'

Joceline had not been expecting that. 'What? Why?'

'Girls are better,' Lamorna said with a sly grin. 'Don't you agree?'

A smile flashed across Joceline's face. Perhaps she could be a friend—once they'd moved past the small matter of her infidelity. There was still life in her yet.

'Men are just so predictable and plodding,' Lamorna continued. 'They never disappoint by always disappointing.'

Joceline's smile faded, and Lamorna regretted her words. She had not meant to insinuate anything, but it had come out anyway, unbidden.

'My mother said I kicked like a mule in her belly. Erbin was quiet as a mouse.'

Joceline composed herself. 'I would have thought it would have been the other way around,' she offered wisely. 'Boys are usually the kickers.'

'And yet, look at me. And look at Erbin.'

'And your baby. Does he kick?' Joceline asked, half smiling again.

'Like a mouse.'

They reached the gate. Jac, who had been sitting on a barrel near the dancing flame of a brazier, leapt to his feet with hungry eyes. Lamorna knew full well that the boy (boy, he was still a couple of years her senior!) believed himself in love with her. She pushed out her belly and rested a hand on it, letting him see her fecundity, knowing it would arouse and appal him in equal measures.

'Ladies,' he barked with nervous deference. 'How can I help?'

'You can open the gate, Jac. We're going for a walk.'

He could barely conceal his confusion at seeing them together, evidence enough that her husband's dalliances were anything but secret.

'Yes, my Lady Lamorna.' He signalled one of the men to open the gate. 'I would recommend an escort. I could accompany you?'

'That won't be necessary. Thank you, Jac. Joceline here is all the protection I need from the odd patch of mud or a slippery stone. I won't go far, I promise.'

Jac half bowed, his face already reddening from being near the object of his infatuation. Lamorna glanced at Joceline as they walked out of the fort, and the two women shared a smile.

* * *

Jac turned his eyes upwards, finding Erbin at his usual spot on the ramparts. Watching. The boy saw and heard everything. What he lacked in popularity, he certainly made up for in intelligence gathering. He was shrewd and devious and would probably make a better ruler than any man in Dumnonia if he could garner enough support. He was no idiot, Jac realised, despite the echoes of the taunts that had followed him through his childhood. Erbin was a spider in the middle of a web and was not to be underestimated.

Jac was also painfully aware that Erbin was manipulating him. The boy was more than bright enough to have spotted the affection Jac felt for his sister. It was a fool's dream, but there was a glimmer of promise, an insinuation of reward for loyalty. If Vortimer could be deposed, exposed as the son of a murderous tyrant, revealed as a wayward husband, his honour brought into disrepute, then—and only then—could Erbin take on the mantle of Dumnonia without fear of challenge.

Erbin had all but promised Jac a position at his side. Jac was already in charge of the men, a promotion afforded him by Vortimer on the strength of his battle prowess, but what other strings could Erbin pull? What other rewards could he bestow on the shoulders of his most loyal supporter? Jac still dreamed that, if something were to befall Vortimer, he could find his place beside the beauteous Lamorna.

He watched her walking along the perimeter wall, Joceline by her side. Just the sight of her hair, hanging to her waist, was enough to quicken his pulse. What would Erbin have him do? To challenge Vortimer in any regard would be suicide. Vortimer's skill with a sword was undeniable. And the men revered Vortimer. He was as popular as any leader could be. When the Hibernians were raiding, he had led from the front, totemic.

Jac's shoulders slumped. If it weren't for the fact he desired Lamorna, or that Vortimer was wronging her, or even that Erbin had all but lain promises of her hand at his feet, he would have no grievance with his lord and master. Vortimer's father had shown fault, and Jac hoped that justice would one day prevail in that regard, but Vortimer himself had been nothing but good to Jac. He had threatened to execute him, but with just cause.

No, he could not challenge Vortimer. Not for his father's sins. Not because of the lady Joceline. And not on behalf of Lamorna's honour. Besides, Lamorna still adored Vortimer. He could not win her affection by deposing her husband. Even Erbin could not promise that. It was horrible enough to recall how she had recoiled from his touch that day. No, the only way to accomplish his heart's desire was to be there in support of Lamorna in the event of Vortimer's mysterious and tragic demise.

He would have to murder him.

Discontent

With the first snow came a blizzard of bad news. Not even the welcome return of Osric and the Nobatians, with the positive prospect of alliance with the Angles, could warm the chill brought by several other emissaries.

Vortigern sat with his head in his hands. A half-empty cup of wine sat beside him.

'We have the winter to regroup.' Selwyn was doing his best to remain positive. He sat to Vortigern's left, and across the table from Osric. The villa in Verulamium was comfortable, but it wasn't home. It lacked a woman's touch.

'Tell that to the Kaldi,' Vortigern spat bitterly.

The Kaldi, apparently, were less affected by the winter's cold than everyone else. A messenger had ridden into the town a week earlier, gaunt and barely conscious, bringing ill tidings from Dunvallo in Bernaccia. While the barbarian horde had at least slowed its relentless progress southwards, they were still devastating villages and smaller settlements. The amassed tribes had splintered into roving war bands that were not content with stealing a few head of livestock to feed their multitude of mouths. They weren't staging full assaults on the northern towns, but they were murdering and raping and pillaging and burning wantonly. Was it just opportunism? Were they just killing two birds with one stone? It seemed so. Every family slaughtered, and every farm razed, served only to spread an insidious terror in the lands nearer the wall. And the seeping blight on the collective morale of Britannia, of Albion, was spreading southwards.

Zeki had brought similar news from Ceneu in Rheged. Pabo had been sent to the relative safety of Viroconium under the pretext of wooing Pasha. Vortigern didn't suppose he would be well received. The girl was headstrong and hadn't been the same since the pestilence had nearly claimed her. And who knew how much longer Viroconium would be safe? Cunedda had apparently driven the Dalriadans into focussing their raids further north. Perhaps they would trouble the Kaldi for a while instead. Similarly, in Dumnonia, the Hibernians had been driven back. But they too had channelled their aggression elsewhere. No word could be elicited from Triffyn or his people. Rumour abounded that Dyfed had fallen to the Hibernians, and that Cunedda had split his men into two, half to keep watch on the northern reaches of Powys and the rest to ride to Dyfed's rescue. Viroconium was suddenly vulnerable on two sides. And who knew whether the Kaldi would venture that far south and west?

'They must be happy eating frozen nuts,' Vortigern grunted, and Selwyn's dour visage offered little in the way of contradiction. 'We must hope for a mild season and an early spring.'

'We could move the men north at least to Eboracum?' Selwyn offered, glancing at Osric. The Jute had been quiet. Since he had triumphantly delivered his news that the Angles would stand with them, he had been met with a deluge of Vortigern's dark thoughts.

Vortigern turned to him. 'You trust these men?'

'They are not so different from me,' Osric replied. 'They want to fight, and they are good at it.'

'But they aren't enough, are they?' Vortigern sighed. Forty more fighting men and women were hardly going to send the Kaldi running back over the wall.

'They might raise the morale of the rest of the men,' Selwyn suggested. 'They might.'

There was something to be said for moving northwards, even with the onset of snow. It would be a hard march. Food was an issue. Game was scarce. But then the supplies at Verulamium weren't going to sustain them through the cold months ahead, anyway. And if the Kaldi didn't venture that far south until the spring, they would have time to rebuild. Perhaps.

'Appius would be happy to see us,' Selwyn smiled slightly. 'He must be shitting himself.'

'If the Angles don't finish him first.' Osric chuckled.

'I thought you said you trusted them?'

'No,' the Jute shook his head. 'I said they want to fight. And they do. If we give them a worthy opponent, they will fight loyally. If we don't, they might take the fight elsewhere.'

Vortigern reached for his wine. His head hurt. He missed Sevira. He missed her counsel as much as her touch. She never supposed to advise him what he should do, but she listened. In the quiet privacy of their bed, she listened to the worries that assailed him. She held him quietly as he railed against those who opposed him and, when he fell quiet, a look from her dark eyes would reveal to him what he should do. He missed those eyes. And her touch. He felt an overwhelming urge to return to her, to make sure Viroconium would remain safe. He needed to know she would be safe.

'Neither the Dalriadans nor the Hibernians are likely to venture much inland, even if they gain footholds.'

'You know that for certain, do you, Selwyn?' Vortigern angered at Selwyn's insight. Were his fears that transparent?

'The Kaldi are the immediate threat.'

Vortigern nodded slowly. Selwyn was right. They must take the fight to the northern barbarians first. If they prevailed, then they could secure the western shores and keep Viroconium safe. If they failed, then it wouldn't matter. Albion would be lost. He looked at Osric. The Jute grinned at him. He was hungry for a scrap, even with one ear.

'Vortigern!' The shrill voice of Sextus, unannounced, reached the high king's ears.

'Come.'

Sextus swept into the room, his face puffed with indignation. 'I have word from Appius.'

'He sent word to you, but not to me?' Vortigern didn't even stand to meet him. The anger in his voice would have to be intimidating enough.

'Well, yes,' Sextus spluttered.

'Why?'

'Why not?'

'I am high king.'

Sextus looked at the other men and shuffled uncomfortably. Selwyn and Osric offered him nothing more than stern faces set in clear support for their leader. 'And I, well, I don't know. Perhaps he thought you had enough to worry about.'

'And yet here you are, intent no doubt in worrying me.'

'The Angles are rising.'

Vortigern glanced at Osric, who gave only half a shrug in response. It's what they do.

'Is this your flare for the dramatic or do I have Appius to thank for it?'

Sextus glared at him. 'They have laid waste to several villas. They are savages. Dogs! At least the Romans kept a firm hand on their leash. What do we do? We give them land.'

Osric coughed quietly. Vortigern saw Selwyn hide a smile.

'There is more than enough land to go around, and I'd be surprised if they have more than a stretch of scrub.'

'That's probably why they are rising!' Sextus squealed. 'They want more.'

Vortigern sighed.

Sextus composed himself and summoned the courage to look directly at Vortigern. 'There is discontent among some of the council. I don't suppose that comes as a great surprise.'

Vortigern returned the stony stare, waiting until Sextus' shoulders slumped a little, until he took half a step back and threw his chin upwards in defiance. His confidence was bluster, posture. He had no means to challenge Vortigern, and everyone in that room knew it. Not alone, at any rate.

'Your Albion is falling apart. We should look to our own.'

'We are Albion.' Vortigern stressed each word carefully. 'I'll tell you this one more time, Sextus.' He stood up, leaning heavily on the table as he glowered over the smaller man. 'The fucking Romans are done here. They aren't coming back. And if the extent of your ambition, and Titus' ambition, and Appius' ambition, is to sit in your plush Roman chairs in your crumbling Roman villas, drinking Roman wine and fucking little Roman boys while the rest of the island goes to shit around you, then you pose a bigger fucking threat to the rest of us than the Kaldi, the Dalriadans and the Hibernians put together.'

'And the Angles,' Osric chimed sarcastically, sniggering. Vortigern snapped his head round, angry at being interrupted, but then grinned.

'And the fucking Angles,' he echoed. 'So, leave me your Saxons and you can keep all your lily-faced merchants who don't know one end of a sword from the other. I only want men beside me who can fight, who want to fight, who believe in the fight, who believe in Albion.'

Sextus' chin wavered. He was trembling and barely hiding it.

'Now fuck off and let the real men talk.' Vortigern turned his back on Sextus and exhaled deeply before lifting his cup to his lips and draining it. When he turned back, Sextus was gone.

'I think that put him in his place,' Selwyn smirked.

Vortigern slumped back into his chair.

'I hope not. We need every man we can get.'

'But—'

'I just hope he's as proud as I think he is. Or we're fucked.'

* * *

Zeki woke just before dawn. He turned his head to the lightening sky, waiting for the first hint of colour. It had been a clear night, a frosty night. He had fallen asleep under the winking gaze of countless stars, wrapped tightly in two blankets by the dying embers of a fire. It felt good to be among fighting men again. Even in the cruel embrace of winter, it felt right to be part of something. He didn't know exactly what the fight meant or why it mattered. Tutoring the boy, Catigern, had not been an unpleasant task. He had enjoyed the comforts of the villa, eaten and drank well, slept in a soft bed. He had been intrigued by Pabo with his wandering eye, all filled with the promise of pleasure. But that could wait. Zeki was among his brethren now, his warrior kind, and he preferred a bigger purpose. He preferred to be led. And he liked Selwyn. He was a kind man. Dour of late, but kind. It had been good to see him again.

As promised, the sun spread orange over the horizon, pushing the cold light away. The frost on the ground glistened as Zeki stirred the fire back into life again. Around him, swaddled in their own blankets and furs, warriors slumbered. Dozens of great wooden props leant up against the cool stone of the town walls, with skins stretched between them, and beneath them slept the men who would fight the Kaldi.

As the sun crept up into the pale sky, a quiet upheaval began. It was more than a band of men rising to stoke the flames and cook some breakfast. There was a subdued clatter of armour and swords mustering. The men who gathered up their few weapons and fewer possessions were Britons, as far as Zeki could tell, men he had heard hailed from Ceint or Londinium. Some fires, only glowing embers but still with life in them, were stamped out. The nervous whinnies of several horses filled the air, the hot breath of the animals clouding upwards as their riders mounted them. Where were they going, these men?

Zeki gathered a thick fur cape around him. He hadn't expected to decamp just yet, but perhaps, even in this chill, there was a battle that needed to be fought. So he set off in search of Selwyn. He would know.

Teeth

Emrys looked like he'd grown. Rozena stole sidelong glances at him as they trudged wearily through the heavy snow that carpeted the higher ground. His face had changed, too. It appeared to be set harder. There was a resolute curve to his jaw, a clenched determination. His amber eyes burned still, but the flame, such that it was, had darkened. The line on his cheek where the bear claw had opened the skin had faded and thinned into a hard white scar, befitting a warrior. He was fast becoming a man. Rozena wasn't sure she had ever thought him so handsome as he looked then.

'It's getting cold.' She exaggerated a shiver, desperately wanting to stop and make a fire. It had been two long days and nights since they had fled the carnage at Viction's villa and climbed up into the dark snowy hills. They had exchanged few words, and all had been practical, concerned with the immediate plight they faced. She had mentioned what she had heard about a high king in Viroconium, and Emrys insisted he knew in which direction the place lay, so off they had set. If she had known that the journey was going to involve an ascent to almost above the treeline, being exposed to the biting wind and stinging snow, she might have suggested an alternative. Not that Emrys would have listened. As handsome as he looked, he surely hated her.

'We'll stop soon,' he muttered. 'We need to find somewhere sheltered from the wind, or we'll freeze to death.'

As short on comfort as the sentiment was, Rozena was glad he hadn't completely ignored her. Perhaps the worst of this freezing trek was over.

They were at least over the peaks and descending towards the relative warmth of trees.

'Emrys,' she whispered, stopping in her tracks. He looked back at her, his brow furrowed. She lowered her eyes in shame. 'I'm sorry.'

'Don't be.'

'Emrys, please, we used to talk about everything.'

'Now is not the time.' He turned and started walking away.

'I know you loved her.'

He stopped.

'I mean, you became close, didn't you?'

A forced sigh. Emrys' shoulders slumped. He turned back to her briskly, his face torn between rage and anguish. 'Is that all you think about? Is that all it means to you? And here I thought you felt guilty, but really, you are just jealous.'

His words were flecked with bitterness, and cold as the wind that lashed her face. 'I love you, Emrys. I always have. You know that. I'm not jealous.' She bit down onto her cold cracked bottom lip, feeling the skin break and a hot bead of blood bubble up.

'I don't just mourn Carina.' Emrys looked away, staring up at the flurries of snow. They settled on his face without a hint of melting, sticking to his eyebrows and his hair. 'I mourn all of them. I loved them all. I loved Viction. I loved Krestell. They were family to me.'

'To us,' Rozena whispered.

Emrys nodded. She took a step towards him, feeling his pain.

'And I love you too.' He looked at her suddenly, hot tears melting the snow from around his eyes.

He needed her. He loved her. She took another step forward, wanting to throw her arms around him and kiss his cheeks. It was just the two of them. Again. It always came back to that.

'But I can't work out if it was all your fault or not.'

She stopped in her tracks. He might as well have slid a pugio between her ribs. 'I didn't know,' she stammered.

'Didn't know what?'

She felt her own tears swelling around her eyes. 'Viction killed their kin.'

'Viction was searching for you. He didn't tell me, but I knew he was. Whatever he did, he did for you.'

'Emrys,' she pleaded.

'Because you upped and ran away.' Emrys threw his arms wide in angry incomprehension.

But surely he knew that she couldn't have stayed. She couldn't bear seeing him becoming closer to Carina. He was right. She was jealous. And why shouldn't she be? She had always loved him, as he had her. Why couldn't he see the pain that had caused her? 'What was I supposed to do?' she lashed out at him, choosing anger over shame. There was nothing to be ashamed of.

'You left us.'

She'd never heard Emrys shout before. 'You left me no choice,' she shouted back. For all she knew, he had wanted to make her jealous, and this was all as much his fault as hers. 'Why didn't you just let me go? If you and Viction hadn't come looking for me, if Viction hadn't picked a fight with the Angles, you'd all be warm and cosy in the villa right now.'

Emrys glared at her, his eyes stormy and wild. Then he turned his head and looked away. 'You left me,' he muttered.

Beyond him, shadows emerged from the trees. Three of them, at least. 'Wolves,' she hissed in sudden terror.

Emrys snapped his head around. 'Run,' he said, as he drew his spatha.

'Run where?' Rozena retrieved her father's sword from its swaddle on her back. The blade felt impossibly heavy in her tired hands. 'They're all around us.'

They were. A quick glance behind and to their sides revealed that the pack had formed a ring around them. A ring that was gradually closing in. The beasts' heads were low over the ground, all eyes trained on their prey. The flash of steel had done little to instil caution in them. Emrys and Rozena were still an easy meal.

'We need to run,' Emrys breathed. 'I can't fight this many. We can't fight this many.' He was clearly exhausted as well. They would be lucky to even

286

injure a couple of them before being overwhelmed.

'If we run for the trees, we only need to survive that far. We can climb out of reach.' The nearest trees were twenty yards away. It wasn't far, but there were three wolves in the way, and a dozen more that would chase them down the moment they ran. But if they didn't run, the pack would be on them soon enough, anyway.

'You run. I'll hold them off as long as I can.' Emrys looked at her earnestly.

As much as she might have appreciated the heroism, Rozena knew it wasn't the best plan. She had no desire to rush three wolves on her own, clear in the knowledge that he would surely be killed. 'That's a shit idea,' she snapped. 'We go together.'

Emrys nodded. 'Ready?'

'No.'

He raised his spatha in front of him and screamed as he began ploughing through the snow down the hill towards the trees. Rozena followed his lead. The three wolves in front of them snarled and kicked up spumes of fresh snow as they began to run up the hill. The other beasts were doubtless already hot on their heels. This was madness, and surely suicide.

For a moment, she thought they might just make it. The wolves in front of them peeled off to either side of them. Emrys flailed his sword at two of them, swinging with such fervour that Rozena imagined he could cleave these animals in two if he had the chance. The wolves backed off, watching closely, just out of reach of the flashing blade.

'Go!' Emrys took a bold step closer to the now snarling wolves. Perhaps if he took first blood, the pack would think better of eating them and might slink off into the dark woods in search of a less aggressive meal. Rozena quickened her pace, heading for a low branch that would be a good start in getting out of reach of the hungry jaws. She glanced over at Emrys again and felt herself pale when she saw that another pair of wolves were heading for him at speed. They had flanked him. She called to him in alarm and, when he looked back at her, the expression on his face was one of sudden horror. Seeing it, she quickly came to the horrible realisation that she must have been flanked. And they were already upon her.

The jaws fastened around her left forearm, and the wolf's weight threw her into the snow. The pain was instant and excruciating. She screamed. The wolf's body landed heavily beside her, its teeth still deep in her flesh, and she knew it was only a matter of time before another set would find her neck and finish her off. Her sword was still in her right hand. She swung it clumsily down across her body, knowing she was as likely to hit herself as the wolf. The blade found fur and flesh and the animal yelped in pain and let go of her arm.

As the blood pounded in her ears, and the growls and howls of the wolves filled the brittle night air, she caught a fleeting glimpse of Emrys. He was still on his feet, with a wolf lying motionless nearby. But another had latched itself onto his side and more were surrounding him, waiting for the best moment to attack.

Rozena tried to get up. Her arm was burning with pain, but she wasn't done yet. She pulled herself to her knees and had just got one foot on the snow when the second wolf hit her. It barrelled into her, its paws slamming into her back between her shoulder blades, and threw her face down into the freezing ground, pinning her there with all the weight of its body. The sound of snapping jaws told her it would all be over soon.

Paws pushed her head into the powdery snow. She thought she heard a dull thud, maybe a cry. Emrys, perhaps. Had he fallen too? And then the weight pushing down on her increased, and everything went dark and quiet.

* * *

She woke up on her side. Yellowed teeth, red with blood, likely hers, leered back at her. She screamed.

The wolf was dead. It was as dead as she should have been. Its open maw gaped in front of her, and the falling snow already freckled its grey fur.

She was alive.

Hands pulled her to her feet. Emrys?

Not Emrys.

She teetered, but the hands caught her. Her vision swam back. Before her stood several dark-haired men, their bodies clad in black leather jerkins. A face leered towards her.

'Must be your lucky night,' it said.

'Emrys,' Rozena gasped. The pain in her arm had dissipated for a while, but was burning again.

'He'll live.'

Rozena glanced around. There were three dead wolves bleeding in the snow nearby. A man pulled a spear from one. The other two were pinned with several arrows. Beyond them, Emrys. He staggered towards her, a smile of relief on his face. He clutched his side, and she saw blood on his hands.

'You're alive,' he said simply as he stumbled into her and pressed his cold cheek against hers. 'We're saved.'

'This one's mine, I think.' A voice boomed out, impossibly deep. Rozena turned towards it. There was the largest man she had ever seen. He was at least two heads taller than Viction, tall as a stallion, and broad, his black leather armour stretched tightly over a muscular frame. A dark beard fell from his chin, but his head was hairless. He leant over and picked up a dead wolf as if it were no more than a puppy and threw it over his shoulders.

'Thank you,' Rozena said quietly, awestruck by the giant.

'You're very welcome.' The giant beamed back at her, then turned and issued instruction to his men. 'Bind them both.'

VI

MEMENTO MORI

'If a man knows that he will die inside of thirty minutes, he will not do anything trifling or foolish in these last thirty minutes, surely not anything evil. But is the half century or so that separates you from death essentially different from a half hour?'

(Leo Tolstoy)

Black and Blue

Derelei ran her finger along the flat of the blade of her uncle's sword. She frowned. That day in the fort could well have been her best chance to kill him. She had failed. Her need for vengeance had only deepened with Wroid's death, surely decreed by Drust. Modwen had paid for that with her life, but it wasn't enough.

Tugen had made a fire before he'd vanished into the misty morning in search of food, and the flames were a welcome comfort in the chill of the day. Derelei hadn't been sure they should linger anywhere for long; she could practically smell the hordes of Kaldi in the air. As far as she and Tugen and Zala had come from the wall, Drust and the rest of the seven kingdoms wouldn't be far behind. The villages they'd passed through reeked of fear. Word had spread. Death was stalking the land, and there was little or nothing anyone could do about it. Except flee.

Her shoulder hurt. Zala had bound it and rubbed it in some foul smelling paste she had ground out from some hurriedly foraged leaves. Whatever it was, it had helped; the pain was duller than it had been, but it ached. Her arm felt stiff, and she could barely raise it to the horizontal. At least it wasn't her sword arm. As hindered as she was by the injury, she could still fight if need be. Somewhat.

Zala fed the fire, tossing a couple of stout branches into the flames.

'We shouldn't let it get too big,' Derelei muttered. 'We don't want to attract attention.'

Zala looked at her, her eyes gleaming. 'And we don't want to let the cold do your kin's work for them, do we?' Her mouth opened into a broad

293

grin, and her dark features glowed in the firelight. 'Besides, surely even your kind would rather sit by a fire of their own in this weather than kill innocents for fun.'

'Perhaps.' Derelei was not so sure. The Kaldi were well adapted to the bite of winter, and likely more than happy to use it to their advantage, but there was no sense in scaring the girl any more than necessary.

'I was glad when Tugen didn't kill you,' Zala said simply, her eyes locked on the dark centre of the flames. 'When you were tied up. It would have been so easy.'

Derelei shivered despite the fire. Zala's tone was level and cold. She had lost her entire family, just as Tugen had, at the hands of the Kaldi. 'And now?'

'Now,' echoed Zala thoughtfully.

'You find mercy less appealing, now that you have suffered and lost as he has?'

'I understand the desire for revenge.'

'As do I.'

Zala looked at Derelei, tears brimming in her green eyes. Eventually, she nodded. 'We are all wronged. All three of us.'

'And we will share our vengeance,' Derelei said firmly. Drust had so much to answer for, and more as each day passed. His terrible assault on the Britons would leave a wake of orphans and widows wailing among the piles of the dead.

'I am not a warrior.' Zala wiped her tears away.

'I'm not sure Tugen is, either.' Derelei's brief smile faded away under Zala's sudden scowl. 'Yet, at any rate.'

'I think he feels more duty to me than he does to revenge.'

Derelei sheathed Drust's sword. 'That is no bad thing, to look to the future rather than the past. I wish I could do the same.'

'You, of all of us, need to.'

Derelei didn't question the girl, choosing instead to think about what she had said. Perhaps she was right. Derelei had not lost her family as Zala and Tugen had; the only family she had known for her adult life, Drust, still lived. No, Derelei's circumstances were different. Her people had cast her aside. She was kinless. She was a stranger in a new land, a land that feared the woad-stained barbarians that hailed from north of the wall. As much as Zala might stand out more than she, especially now that she was no longer cloistered amongst several other Ethiopes, she would not be as sourly greeted as Derelei. Moreover, as feared and despised as the Kaldi were already, by the time Drust had finished cutting a swathe into the heart of Britannia, they would be utterly reviled.

'I am who I am,' Derelei muttered obstinately. Even in the ragged company of Zala and Tugen, she knew she was alone.

'Look what I found,' a voice sounded damply from a shape lurching out of the mist. Tugen had returned. He had with him two horses.

'How did you get these?' Zala jumped up, tempering her joy with a cautious tone as she stroked the first mare's nose. 'Did you steal them?'

'I wouldn't say that, exactly,' Tugen grinned.

'I don't ride,' Derelei stated. She had never been on the back of a horse, and the idea of it filled her with an unfamiliar anxiety.

'You'd better ride with me, then.'

Zala's face fell slightly. She clearly wanted to ride pillion with Tugen, and have her arms wrapped tightly around him as they travelled south into relative safety.

'No,' Derelei sighed. 'I will learn. Quickly.'

* * *

Though Tugen wasn't entirely sure that Derelei would agree, the horses made travelling infinitely more bearable. They had walked for three days on end and had been exhausted. Zala cried for most of the first, and Derelei was clearly in pain and remained stoically quiet. That first night, as Tugen had gone in search of what game he could find to roast on the fire, Zala had treated Derelei's wound. That simple act, born from a desire to ease the suffering of another, had calmed her raging grief a little. She had slept later, curled into him, sharing a blanket. Derelei had kept watch, despite her injury, and still trudged onwards through the whole of the next day. She had let Tugen keep watch for most of the second night, relieving him a bit before first light.

He didn't see any reason to tell the other two how he had come by the horses. It was better, albeit a slight on his excellent character, to let them think he had stolen them. He would never have done that, though. Not there. Not then. Not while the Kaldi were on a southward march. The villages they had passed were all the same. Word had spread fast. They were met by frightened faces, people strapping possessions to whatever animals they had in readiness for a southerly flight.

And rightly so. When Tugen had ventured into the misty morning in search of any kind of food to sustain the three of them, he had come across a remote homestead. Thinking he could trouble whoever lived there for some bread, he had crossed the threshold and called out. No reply had come. Nor would it ever. Sprawled across the cold floor of the dwelling, a farmer and his wife lay in dark pools of blood. Slaughtered. The Kaldi had already been there.

He had found the two horses, oddly untouched, in a paddock behind the dwelling. At the time he hadn't realised how averse the Kaldi were to horses. There had been evidence of pigs too, but they were gone. He had taken the horses and hurried back to the others.

Derelei had overcome that aversion mercifully quickly. Tugen didn't want Zala to know how close the marauding Kaldi were, but they had needed to make haste on their southward journey. They had made better progress the next day, and a wave of relief had swept over Tugen when he recognised what could only be Dere Street. The Roman road, he knew, had once continued north of the wall and into the lands of the Kaldi. But there it had suffered centuries of neglect and plunder. Derelei's eyes widened when she saw the cobbles, the dark vein that stretched out towards the horizon.

'We'll be able to move faster now,' Tugen smiled.

'Good.' Derelei looked around her, scanning the landscape.

'What's wrong?'

'We're being followed.'

Tugen felt Zala stiffen behind him on the horse and hoped Derelei would have the sense to spare her any frightening insight. 'Well, we must look peculiar. Bound to raise some curiosity.'

Derelei shook her head. 'Kaldi,' she said through gritted teeth.

'A war band?' asked Zala, a quiver in her voice.

Tugen glared at Derelei.

'Doubtful,' Derelei held his gaze for a second, understanding flashing across her eyes. 'Probably just a scout or two.'

Zala's grip on Tugen remained tight. He felt her press the side of her face against his back and squeeze him. 'Let's push on anyway,' he said with some authority.

* * *

Scouts or otherwise, the Kaldi came. Six of them emerged from the trees and fanned out as they confidently approached, weapons readied. With their faces and bodies blued in woad, they moved like spiders as they stalked brazenly towards them. Derelei hurriedly leapt down from her mount and drew her sword. She was untrained as a rider, and the thought of fighting on horseback wouldn't ever have occurred to her. Even Tugen felt vulnerable, rather than empowered, on the back of his own animal. He hurried Zala to the ground and followed her, pulling at his sword.

'Keep the horses safe,' he whispered to her. Her terrified eyes shone wetly back at him. 'We'll be alright. Derelei is formidable.' He barely believed himself. Two against six was poor odds, even if Derelei was at full strength. Watching her flex her wounded shoulder, he realised she was still far from that.

With a frightful screech, the Kaldi broke into a run. Derelei moved forwards to meet them as Tugen nervously weighed his sword in his hand, determined only to keep Zala safe. He would let them come to him. Three of the Kaldi converged on Derelei, who was suddenly lighter on her feet, her old self, hopefully. She swirled and danced, her great blade flashing and crashing against the smaller swords of the other Kaldi. Two of them fell almost immediately. Her blade was met by a solid parry from the third, but he was thrown off balance and Derelei flung her foot between his legs. As he bent in pain, she flipped her sword and drove it down into his back.

Tugen planted his feet firmly and raised his sword to meet the Kaldi blade that bore down on him. It was a solid block, though the brash metallic clatter was louder than anything he had heard in his training. The Kaldi blade slid down the length of his sword, and Tugen pushed it away, forcing the warrior to step back. The second blue face wasn't far behind, so Tugen pressed his advantage, stepping forward and swinging his weapon. It found flesh and Tugen felt the hot spray of blood across his face. He had cut deep into the painted side of the Kaldi, a wound that would be unlikely to heal, but his foe was still on his feet. And still armed. Blood thundered in Tugen's ears as he went for the kill. His first kill.

He lunged forward, using the point of his sword, sensing his opponent was too pained to parry it effectively. He was right. The blade sank into the Kaldi's abdomen. Tugen could feel it grating against ribs, hard flesh and bone resisting the thrust. So, he pushed harder, leaning into it, falling with it onto the dying man. Not even the desperate fist of the man, weakly striking at his ear, could deter him from his purpose.

He rolled off the half-naked warrior and stumbled to his feet. His head was swimming. He glimpsed Zala, wide eyed, holding the horses, then turned to see Derelei in close combat with another Kaldi. Then he saw the last one. He was almost upon him, javelin in hand. Tugen felt his heart pounding as he scrambled for his sword and tried to pull it from the dead man at his feet. It slid and scraped from the man's rib cage, but too late. Tugen glanced up just in time to see the last Kaldi's javelin arm slingshot forwards, releasing its deadly missile at him.

He must have blinked. The next thing he saw was Zala's face in front of his. Her eyes, already soft with tears, flared open when the javelin struck her in the back. Her mouth opened, reddening with blood, as if she wanted to say something to him. But no words came. He wrapped his arms around her and held her to him, catching her as her legs buckled.

Feeling his own tears suddenly hot on his cheeks, he lowered her as gently as he could towards the ground, resigning himself to die beside her. As her eyes fluttered, struggling to stay open, a slight smile played across her blooded lips.

And then she was gone.

He buried his head in her shoulder, sobbing, and waited for the sword to come.

But it was a hand, not a blade, that he felt on his back. 'Tugen.' Derelei's voice sounded far away. 'Tugen.'

He couldn't lift his head. He couldn't bear to separate his cheek from Zala's.

Not yet.

Tarquinius

Her arm felt like it was on fire.

The bald giant and his darkly dressed men had carried her and Emrys, bound in rough hemp, down from the icy slopes on their horses. They were the biggest she had ever seen. Their hot breath had fogged the thin air even after they had descended below the line of snow. They had climbed again, a little, up a gentle slope. A great palisade of roughly hewn and cruelly sharpened stakes had reared up ahead of them, taller than the mounted men that had then spurred their horses through the similarly fashioned gate. Beyond the stake wall was a half derelict villa surrounded by some thatched huts, Roman architecture oddly juxtaposed with the more primitive Briton styled defences and abodes.

They had been pulled roughly from the horses and bundled into a secure and spartan room in the villa. A single small window let in a tiny amount of light, revealing cracked plaster walls and a filthy floor. A woman, her face creased and wrinkled more deeply than anyone Rozena had ever met, had smeared a foul-smelling salve onto her tattered arm and wrapped it tightly in strips of cloth. She had done the same with Emrys' side, though that had at least stopped bleeding. And then she had gone. Without a word. Without a smile.

Rozena didn't know if it was the wound itself, or the old woman's unguent, but a hot pain shot up and down her useless arm. She rubbed as hard as she dared at the rough cloth that shrouded it.

'You'll be lucky to keep that arm.' In the dark corner of the room where they had been imprisoned sat a man. His clothes spoke of wealth, though they were dirty and torn. Rozena started at the sight of the matted, greying beard sprouted out unkempt from his face when he leant forward into what little light entered the room.

Emrys bristled. 'Who are you?' he demanded.

The old man leant back into the shadows and sighed. 'Who was I? You mean?'

'Fine,' Emrys winced as sat up, his side clearly still causing him considerable pain. 'Who were you?'

'Ambrosius. Of Viroconium.'

'That's where we were heading.' They must be near, at least, thought Rozena.

'Well, you're here now. You'll have to make do with Mamucium, or what's left of it,' came the grim response. Ambrosius' tone suggested a horrible finality. 'What happened to you two?'

'Wolves.' Emrys said curtly.

'These men saved our lives,' Rozena admitted. 'Though they don't seem all that friendly.'

Ambrosius snorted. 'That they aren't, and you may well come to wish the wolves had finished you off.'

'We're prisoners,' Emrys said glumly. 'Why are you here?'

'Me? Believe it or not, I am a man of some means. Tarquinius feels I might represent some leverage.'

'Tarquinius?' Emrys asked.

'Leverage?' said Rozena.

'Tarquinius is the big bald bastard that lords it over this rabble. He's an entitled ogre of a man.' Ambrosius spat loudly. 'And yes, leverage. I don't know what he wants, but it seems he thought they could exchange me for it.'

'How long have you been here?'

'Since late summer.'

Emrys went quiet. The burning pain in Rozena's arm was making her head swim. She closed her eyes, willing the fire to be quiet. An involuntary sob burst from her lips, and she felt Emrys' arm snake around her gently.

She slumped against him, sliding down the dirty floor to rest her head on his lap as she gingerly held her withered limb to her chest.

'You'll keep your arm,' he whispered. 'I promise.'

And she let sleep fall over her like a much-needed blanket.

* * *

Low voices mumbled their way into her slumber as she resurfaced. She had been dreaming of home, of her father. And of Emrys, younger and unscarred.

'Slaves, then.' Emrys was almost whispering. 'Not prisoners.'

A grunt came from the other side of the room. Ambrosius. 'Well, it doesn't seem you have any other obvious value to Tarquinius. Wounded orphans, far from a home that no longer exists. Yes, you are slaves now.'

Rozena didn't move. She was comfortable, for the time being. Her arm still throbbed, but the pain had abated slightly. Perhaps the ointment was working some magic after all. Still, she didn't dare to move unless it returned in all its fury.

'I can chop wood, make fires,' Emrys said quietly, 'and I don't mind waiting a while until there's a decent opportunity to escape.'

'Good luck with that,' sneered Ambrosius bitterly.

'And what of Rozena? She will cook and clean?'

Ambrosius sighed, a great sad outflow of breath. 'And the rest.'

'The rest?'

'She's a pretty girl. Young. Strong, despite her ruined arm. Did you see many other women here?'

'Just the old crone.'

Ambrosius laughed bitterly. 'That old crone, believe it or not, is mother to Tarquinius. She is as bad as him. Twisted. She didn't tend to your wounds out of compassion.'

Emrys took a deep breath. Rozena felt his chest puff up above her. The gentle weight of his hand on her shoulder, much as it caused a slight discomfort in her aching arm, was like an embrace. When he lifted it momentarily, she felt vulnerable. He breathed out, and his hand settled once again on her.

'I won't let them hurt her.'

Ambrosius harrumphed and said no more.

* * *

Emrys awoke. He had fallen asleep sitting up, with Rozena's head nestled in his lap, but when he opened his eyes, she was sitting in front of him. Watching him. In the gloom across the room, Ambrosius was snoring. His rasping breath sounded like a blade being dragged over a stone floor.

'How is your wound?' Rozena asked him.

Emrys shifted his weight, feeling a twinge of pain in his side. He touched a hand to the dressing and felt it was dry. 'I will live.' He grimaced at her. 'How is your arm?'

'It burns still, but I can take it.'

Emrys nodded at her, feeling her eyes boring into him. 'What?' he asked.

'You have to kill me.'

Emrys almost laughed. He looked at her incredulously, searching for a hint of humour. They were in a desperate situation, but surely, they would find a way to escape at some point.

'I'm serious, Emrys.' Rozena leant closer, her eyes already filled with tears. 'I don't want to be their plaything.'

'What?'

'I heard you talking, you and Ambrosius, and we all know what I'm good for round here.'

'Rozena, no,' Emrys began. 'I won't let them touch you.'

'Don't be ridiculous. That beast will just squash your head with one hand if you try anything.'

'Then let him.' Emrys puffed up his chest.

Rozena looked at him sadly, as if wishing he were man enough to take on the giant Tarquinius and defend her honour. But there was no point even imagining he could.

'Please. I'm sure you could snap my neck, or strangle me, or even dash my head against the floor.'

'Stop!' Emrys felt a wave of nausea flood his stomach. The thought of such a thing horrified him, filled him with panic. 'Please stop.'

'No,' Rozena hissed. 'What do you think they will do to me? Do you think they will be gentle?'

'I'm not killing you!' Emrys felt his own tears begin to well. 'I couldn't.'

'Even if it meant saving me from them?'

He turned his head away, unable to look at her imploring eyes. His mind whirred with hideous images. Perhaps she was right. Perhaps she should be spared that fate. But then, perhaps such a fate could be avoided. They should at least try to escape first.

'Emrys.' He felt her good hand on his leg, squeezing him. 'Emrys, look at me,' sobbed Rozena.

He turned his wet eyes to hers and let out a sob of his own. 'I'm sorry.'

She shuffled forwards until she was close to him, close enough for him to fold his arms around her. For a moment, he forgot her wound and clasped her too tightly. She let out a weak cry of pain and he loosened his grip a little, but did not let go.

'Emrys,' she whispered. 'I love you.'

He felt a heavy tear roll down his cheek and into her hair. 'I love you,' he echoed.

'I want it to be you.'

'What?'

Rozena pulled her head back a little from his chest and looked up at him. 'I don't want them to take my maidenhood away from me. They don't deserve it. But you do.'

The nausea bubbled up again in Emrys. That it had come to this. He shook his head, fresh tears blooming at the corner of his eyes.

Rozena wiped them away and smiled at him. 'If I am to be ruined by these brutes, I want one chance at enjoying it, one chance at looking into your eyes. Those little suns. Give me that at least.'

'Here?'

'They deny us any other choice.'

'I don't think I can.'

Rozena's face hardened. 'I begged you to kill me, Emrys. Don't make me beg you to fuck me.' She began fumbling with her clothing as best she could with one good hand, then stopped and reached out to touch him. Her hand darted between his legs and gripped him.

'Wait.' Emrys grasped her gently by the wrist.

'I always meant it to be you,' Rozena breathed. 'Don't take that away from me.'

Emrys looked at her. His tears blurred her, and he reached out and felt for her face, bringing it closer to him, feeling her breath on his. He kissed her and released her wrist so that she could free him from his clothes.

'Did you do this with Carina?' she asked, pausing suddenly.

He shook his head. 'No, you will be my first, too.'

'It's going to hurt.'

Emrys nodded apologetically. Rozena shuffled forwards and Emrys felt her heat on him. She squirmed and mewed for a moment, struggling to position herself perfectly. And then, as Ambrosius snored in the darkness, Emrys gasped loudly as Rozena lowered herself onto him. And when she lifted her eyes to his and stared into them, he saw everything. Pain, joy, fear, love. Her mouth twitched between smiles and grimaces. Her body consumed him. And he gave himself to her.

She fell forward onto him—her face nestling into his shoulder—and sobbed. Her good arm snaked around his neck and threatened never to let him go. Softening slowly inside her, Emrys thought he felt different. Fear, something he had tried to ignore until then, bubbled up from deep inside and then dissipated through his limbs. Fear was not his enemy. He acknowledged it. And it mattered less. He could use it. His arms around Rozena felt different. They felt bigger, stronger. He would fight for her. He could fight for her.

Rozena slid from on top of him and curled up beside him on the floor. He took off his tunic and rolled it up beneath her head, then stroked her face until she fell asleep. Perhaps she felt as he now did. Stronger.

His thoughts were disturbed when the door to the room flew open. Two men stood there, silhouetted. Emrys leapt to his feet, ignoring the shooting pain in his side, and stood over Rozena.

'We're not here for you, boy.' A gruff voice came from the shadows, and the men advanced into the room.

Emrys braced himself, standing in their way.

One man shoved him hard, the flat of his hand hitting Emrys in his chest. Emrys staggered back a step or two, but stayed on his feet.

'Fuck off, boy,' came a second voice, as the man bent over to pick Rozena up.

Emrys lashed out with his foot, aiming for the man's face but connecting with his neck. It was enough to send him back a few steps, gasping for lost breath.

'Leave her alone.' Emrys challenged the men.

'Emrys.' Rozena stirred from her sleep and cried his name. There was the sound of a blade being drawn.

'You little shit,' the man he'd kicked said with an audible wheeze.

Emrys turned, ready to face the other man, but was met with the hard pommel of a sword. It struck him on the side of the head, and he immediately dropped to his knees. A foot followed, kicking him hard in the chest and knocking the wind out of him. He crumpled to the floor, incapacitated. His peripheral vision clouded and darkened, but he was just able to make out the men lifting Rozena from the floor as she cried out and kicked.

'Feisty bitch,' one man remarked. 'I look forward to having a go after Tarquinius.'

'If there's anything left of her,' chuckled the other as they shuffled out of the room.

'No.' His voice was a croak. Emrys tried to get up, but the darkness washed over him.

Easy Pickings

They had lost remarkably few men. To be fair, Drust hadn't expected to lose many, not since the fort. They hadn't needed to attack the fort; they could have easily slipped past it, crossed the crumbling wall any number of miles to either side. As many as they were, they could have gone unnoticed in the depths of winter. But Drust wanted his sword back, and he had guessed rightly that his niece would most likely have sought refuge in one of the few forts that held onto something resembling a garrison.

It didn't take a chieftain of all his years to work out that Wroid had taken his sword, and even a child could have guessed the traitor's purpose. His head still thumping from copious amounts of mead, Drust had gone to the drowning pit the morning after Wroid's deception and called out to Derelei, even though the sides of the hole showed obvious signs of scrabbling fingers and a deep rut in the mud where a rope had rested, heavy under the burden of an escapee. Wroid had freed her. And Drust had waited patiently until he could pay for that mistake with his life in front of the woman he loved.

But she still had his sword. Naturally, he was sentimental about the weapon. He'd carried it in every unbeaten battle he'd fought since he'd been old enough to wield a blade. And the best chance he'd had to retrieve it had potentially passed him by. If it wasn't insulting enough that she had carried his pride and joy into battle against him, and against her own people, she now had the blood of Modwen on her hands as well. And for that, if for nothing else, Drust wanted little more than to see the life ebb from her eyes.

'You wanted to see me?'

Drust tore his gaze from the fire he was staring into. 'Cailtram.' He nodded. 'Sit.'

The druid lowered himself to the ground and stared through the flickering flames at him.

'Tell me some good news.'

Cailtram looked at him carefully. 'It is all good. The war bands have all returned, our ranks are swelled, and there is little but corpse and carnage at our heels and opportunity before us.'

'But no sign of a worthy enemy?'

'Not yet. As you know, Gododdin was deserted and is plundered. Dunvallo's pathetic resistance was crushed. Bernaccia is ours. So is Rheged.'

'And Brude?'

'He has taken to the coast again and prepares to sail south.'

Drust grunted, nodding.

'How far south do you want to go?'

'I want a proper fight, Cailtram.' Drust looked beyond the druid, at the countless fires that peppered the surrounding landscape. Most of the seven tribes were there, more men and women than he had ever seen in one place, united in a common, bloody purpose. Brude had the rest, happily plundering the coast. Their time had been a long time coming, but here it was. Drust knew he should be jubilant, thrilled by the undeniable ascendancy he and his people were enjoying. But something gnawed at him. Surely it wasn't the loss of Modwen, no matter how much he had revelled in her company. Surely it wasn't the widening schism between him and his niece. Or his missing bloody sword.

'The gods smile upon us, Drust. We will prevail.'

Even Cailtram's words sounded hollow. Did the Britons not have their gods too? Had the Romans not had theirs? Why should the gods that Cailtram claimed to know have more sway than any other over the affairs of men?

'We will,' Drust quietly agreed. He was done with talking. 'Tomorrow, we continue south.'

Cailtram nodded. 'We will right every wrong.'

'Have Darlagh come and see me,' Drust said flatly, not even bothering to meet the Druid's eyes.

He could feel Cailtram looking at him through the flames for a while, silent. Doubtless, mired in sudden fury. Let him look, Drust thought. Let him rage. Cailtram was supposed to be above human attachment. He walked with the gods. He didn't need to be possessive. He was more than a man, supposedly. So, he could share his woman.

Eventually, when Drust looked up, the druid nodded solemnly, his dark eyes a mystery on the other side of the fire. If he was angry, he didn't show it. Drust wanted him to be angry. He wanted to test his loyalty. He wanted to challenge the gods. Everything else came too easily. Victory. Bloodshed. Why not strike at the heart of the gods that supposedly smiled upon him? Besides, if anything could spur him forward and cast off any irritating doubts about his purpose, it was the warmth that lay between a woman's legs. And that woman might as well be Darlagh.

Cailtram rose silently and drifted away into the shadows, probably muttering terrible curses as he went.

And when Darlagh came, moments later, she seemed to do so willingly. She proffered herself to her chieftain happily. It was an honour, after all. More than a duty. She was a fine-looking woman, as athletic as Modwen, and as eager to please. If she held any resentment towards him, she did not dare show it. In fact, he thought later, to anyone who might have witnessed it, she was the more enthusiastic party in their brief and violent coupling.

But when she presumably thought him asleep, she crept away. He opened one eye and watched her go, watched her skulk back to Cailtram. Let them plot, he mused. The machine of war was in full flow and he, Drust of a hundred battles, still undefeated, was on the cusp of the greatest series of victories his people had ever known. He would take back the lands they had once enjoyed, and more. He would destroy his enemy before him, take their lands and their lives, and not because of a druid or because of the gods or any other magic.

It was his time. It was his doing. And nothing was going to stand in his way.

Howl

Londinium, overall, was a pitiful sight. It had been pretty dilapidated the last time Osric had been there, many years before, but it was all but abandoned now. The empty streets were flanked by roofless buildings, many of which had given way to trees. Spring foliage sprouted verdantly through every crack and crevice they could find in their search for sunlight. The walls had fallen into the streets, and great piles of broken plaster and stone had become overgrown with sprawling weeds. Tendrils of ivy snaked across the mud-filled gutters in search of purchase on the dirty cobbles and beyond.

One quarter of the once great city still supported life. In the south-eastern quadrant, a few villas remained relatively unscathed. They were close to the port, now all but derelict but still apparently in receipt of the few traders that still bothered to travel to Britannia. In the villas lived a few families, families that had once been called wealthy. Not that the word meant anything now. It was a ghostly existence, a desperate clawing insistence that the old ways, the Roman ways, were still alive and well.

Even Osric, who didn't consider himself the most erudite of men by any means, knew that the life these people lived was a lie. He shivered in the damp morning, exchanging a grimace with Shabaka and Tsekani who waited with him and a dozen other of Vortigern's men outside the largest of the villas. The high king was in there, no doubt hurling more insults at the little runt, Sextus, to garner more support for his campaign. Osric, still acknowledging to himself his intellectual shortcomings, did not for one minute suppose that anything good would come of the meeting.

'I thought it was supposed to be getting warmer,' Shabaka grinned at him, as if sensing his unrest.

'Can't you feel summer in the air?' Osric shot back at him sarcastically. 'I might even take a swim in the Tamesis.'

Shabaka looked at the dark waters of the great river that skirted the southern side of the city on its languorous way to the sea. His face creased in disapproval. 'After you, my friend.'

'At least there are no dragons in there.'

'Crocodiles,' Shabaka corrected him. 'No. Too cold for them. And for any sensible man.'

Osric nodded. He wasn't sure Shabaka had realised he was joking. To be fair, he thought, it was sometimes hard to tell. Maybe he just had one of those faces. Prompted by the thought, he reached up and felt where his ear had once been. He definitely had one of those faces.

Tsekani rose to his feet, his eyes fixed downriver, and pointed. Osric followed his finger and squinted, trying to make out what the Nobatian had seen. A low mist swirled over the surface of the water; a stubborn haze that showed no sign of succumbing to what little sun shone over them.

'What is it?'

Shabaka was up and peering into the fog as well. 'I see it. There,' he pointed.

Osric stood up and leaned forwards, scrunching up his unfunny face. And then he saw it. A single sail.

'Traders?' Shabaka asked, his hand already hovering over his quiver. Tsekani already had an arrow nocked.

'I don't know,' Osric admitted, and drew his sword. They couldn't afford to be surprised. It was one small boat, by the looks of it, but who knew how many more sails might yet emerge from the gloom? 'To the bank. And be ready.'

The Nobatians and the Britons leapt into action and formed up on the side of the river in readiness.

As the boat neared, a voice floated over the still waters. 'Osric? Is that you? What luck.'

Osric did not recognise the voice. Nor could he make out the features of the man that stood in the prow of the boat, hailing him like some old friend. But he knew the accent. It was not dissimilar to his own.

'It is Wulfric. I have returned.'

So, it was Egbin's whelp, the boy who had promised to bring back ships full of warriors to fight alongside Vortigern. Osric peered beyond the boat, into the murk, but no more hulls emerged. As the boat drew close to the landing, Osric held up his hand to the men with him. 'Let him ashore,' he uttered gruffly.

Wulfric leapt the last couple of feet and landed squarely on the bank, beaming at Osric. 'I am a man of my word, Osric, Wolf of Britannia.'

Osric winced at the glib reference to his banishment so many years before. 'Just Osric,' he snarled, 'and I see no more than a handful of men. You are as full of shit as Egbin.'

Wulfric's smile wavered for a moment, but he persisted. 'I see you have lost an ear now. I hope your eyes are still sharp. Let us have words. If your hearing is up to it.'

The young Jute was undeniably cockier than he had been the last time they had met. His swagger was irritating, yet oddly comforting; he might well have been a younger version of Osric. Osric glanced at Shabaka, who still gripped his bow. The Nobatian shrugged.

'Fine,' Osric grumbled. 'I've nothing better to do.'

* * *

Sextus lay on his side, propped up on one arm, as a slender youth, maybe fourteen, poured wine deferentially into his waiting goblet.

'Thracian,' Sextus mumbled before greedily lifting the chalice to his lips. 'His grandfather was a gladiator. Dead now. So is his father. He died at sea. Still, he has good breeding.'

Vortigern sat as patiently as he could, trying to hide his contempt for the man opposite him. Sextus was fervently doing everything he could to hold on to as many Roman ideals as he could, even as far as keeping boys enslaved. 'Does he have a name?'

'Naturally,' Sextus laughed, 'but he responds just the same to whatever I feel like calling him. That will do, boy.' He waved the Thracian away.

'I must urge you to reconsider your position,' Vortigern began.

'Your men have already gone North, have they not?'

Vortigern took a breath, trying to remain calm. 'They have, Sextus. I have remained to bolster our forces.'

'How many are you?'

'Maybe five hundred.'

Sextus guffawed. 'My, how times have changed. That's not even a tenth of a legion. It's barely a cohort.'

'No,' Vortigern admitted, 'but the legions are gone.'

'How do you expect to command this island with a tenth of a legion? How do you expect to conquer the Picts, when even Rome thought it best to wall them in? I assume you know your history?' Sextus sat up, regarding Vortigern keenly. 'You know of the Ninth Legion?'

'I have heard the story.' Vortigern bristled, wanting nothing more than to cuff Sextus across his smug little face. If he didn't need more men, he would have done just that, and more.

'An entire legion lost beyond the wall. Slaughtered by your Pictish friends. A Roman legion, soldiers trained in war. An army. And what do you have? A rabble. Farmers.'

'We are an army.' It was the first time Vortigern had used the word. He hadn't thought of his men as such. They weren't all soldiers. Few were trained. But they had horses, and they had swords and spears. They were an army. 'And the Kaldi, perhaps more in number, are the rabble we will crush. The Ninth fell in hostile territory, doubtless picked off in handfuls in the dark, in the dead of winter, in a cruel landscape that favoured its own. The Kaldi are overreaching. They are not equipped to meet on a field of battle.'

'And yet here you are, desperate to secure more men. And why? Because you are afraid. There is fear in your eyes, fear that you will not prevail. You don't have enough men. And what few bucellarii I have at my disposal, expert as they may be, they won't make an iota of difference to the bloody outcome of your greed and ambition. Let the North fall, Vortigern. The Kaldi won't trouble us here.'

Vortigern glared at Sextus. The bastard might even be right, he thought. It was unlikely the Kaldi would surge as far south as Londinium. And he did not know how they would fare on the battlefield. He had never faced the blue-faced savages.

'Boy,' Sextus shouted. 'More wine. And bring some for the high king.'

The Thracian rushed in, clutching an amphora, and scuttled towards his master.

'Serve the high king first, you dolt.' Sextus threw a provocative grin at Vortigern.

'Thank you,' Vortigern muttered to the boy when he had filled his cup. The lad nodded, his hands shaking, then attended Sextus before shuffling away again.

'You could borrow him this evening, if you like,' Sextus smirked. He was clearly trying to get a rise out of Vortigern.

'So, you will not join us in our fight, Sextus? You are resolute?' Vortigern wasn't sure he had ever showed this much restraint, but he was determined to not lose his temper, even if it meant biting his lip until it bled.

'I will not. And nor will Titus. I'll save you the time and effort of petitioning him. I'm sure you have more pressing matters to attend to.'

Vortigern stood up slowly and lifted his cup to his lip. He slowly emptied it, using the time to calm his rising fury, then nodded at Sextus. 'So be it.'

'Oh,' Sextus sat up. 'I rather thought you might move on to begging me.'

'Like it or not, Sextus, I am the high king. I do not beg. Your decision to not support me is—'

'Are you going to threaten me now?'

'I was going to say that your decision is your own to make.' Vortigern straightened his tunic. 'Do you feel threatened?'

Sextus looked uneasy. 'I might, if I thought any of you were going to come back from fighting the bloody Picts.' He added a derisory snort, though his smirk had gone.

Vortigern turned his back and strode from the villa, his temper rising with each step. He had spent weeks trying to find more men and had come up empty-handed. It was time he put his, and Albion's, fate in the hands of the gods. He had already sent Zeki back to Viroconium to summon Ossian to Eboracum. They would need the druid. If for nothing else but morale.

He found Osric and the others, and his horse, on the banks of the Tamesis where he had left them. 'We ride for Eboracum,' he announced curtly as he approached, heading straight for his mount.

'A moment, my king,' Osric strode towards him.

'What?' Behind Osric stood a young man Vortigern did not know.

'This is Wulfric, of the Jutes.'

Vortigern looked at the man. 'I might have guessed his heritage, Osric. He looks a little like you did when we first met.'

Osric grimaced, his hand intuitively reaching for his missing ear. 'He claims to have friends with him.'

'Oh?' Vortigern dropped the reins he had taken from one of his men. 'And where are they?'

'Moored in the mouth of the Tamesis,' Osric murmured. 'Three brigantines. Maybe a hundred and twenty men. Fighting men. The best of my kin.'

Vortigern heard the bitterness in Osric's voice. He was acutely aware of the Jute's lack of compassion towards his countrymen. Whatever had caused him to leave them, years earlier, still scarred him as obviously as his other battle wounds. There was trepidation in the Osric's voice as well, however. If all Jutes were as formidable in battle as he was, then these boats might not bode well for any of them.

'Their purpose?' Vortigern asked quietly. It wasn't a huge number of warriors, but it would be more than enough to lay waste to Londinium in no time if that was their intent.

'He says they wish to fight with us.'

'They do? Why?'

Osric paused. 'Wulfric was among Egbin's men when we parlayed with him. He sailed home and, well, this is what he came back with.'

'And what do they want?'

'Their leaders are two brothers, Hengest and Hors. They claim to be descended from Woden himself.'

'Woden?'

'The chief of our gods. Most powerful.' Osric looked nervous.

Vortigern rolled his eyes. 'Of course they are. Why wouldn't they be? Again, what do they want?'

'To talk to you.'

There was every chance this was a trap. The idea that six score men would brave such a sea voyage and just appear off the coast of Britannia ready to pledge allegiance to him was far-fetched.

'You don't think it likely that they merely wish to discuss the terms of our surrender?'

Osric squirmed. 'It is possible. More than possible. It is likely that Wulfric merely told them we are few and spread thin. We are ripe for plunder, especially if the few men we do have are up north.'

Vortigern felt a knot tighten in his stomach. 'Perhaps we will end up being glad of Sextus' cowardice, after all. We might need his bucellarii.'

Osric nodded grimly. 'They might delay the inevitable.'

'Well, we'd better see what they want.'

Spring

There was warmth in the sun that spilled into the bedchamber. Spring had come to Dumnonia, and with it the promise of new life. Lamorna sat, her hands cradling her sumptuous belly, looking at her husband. He looked more scared than she was. He paced up and down, glancing at her with a furrowed brow.

'It won't be long now,' Lamorna told him quietly, through gritted teeth. The contractions were more frequent, until she barely felt she could recover from one before the next one was upon her. It had been an hour since her waters had broken. She was determined to remain strong. Joceline had told her she would come to realise that she had never felt pain until she had birthed a child. That grim prophecy was already beginning to come to fruition. But Vortimer didn't need to see that pain.

'I should summon someone. Someone needs to deliver our child.'

Lamorna smiled through her discomfort. It pleased her to hear him refer to the baby as theirs. 'Our son,' she spoke, the words separated by a sharp pain that took her breath away.

Vortimer took a couple of quick steps closer to her, his hands reaching out to comfort her. His impotence in the situation pained her. There was little he could do, except wait to be a father. Another sharp pain lanced through her abdomen.

'Joceline,' she hissed. 'Have Joceline come to me.'

Vortimer blanched, hesitating.

'Just do it. I don't care about you and her. I care about our son.' Lamorna gave him the most earnest look she could muster in the circumstances, needing to convince him of her sincerity. She really didn't care about his misadventures. She loved him. And always would. She smiled thinly. 'I care about us.'

Vortimer nodded and called out, his voice cracking. Lamorna heard a couple of other voices in relay and the rapid patter of feet as someone ran to fetch Joceline. Vortimer rushed back to her side and took her hand in his. His palms were hot and wet with sweat.

'I'm fine,' she lied. She felt anything but fine, but supposed that was exactly how she was meant to feel. 'It's fine.'

Another invisible spear thrust downwards inside her, hot pain shivering around her and causing her to cry out. She felt sweat mounting on her forehead and her breath quicken.

Joceline appeared barely a moment later, breathing hard. She had wasted no time getting there. 'Out,' she barked at Vortimer, who looked at her blankly. 'This is no place for a man. Get out.'

Vortimer glanced at Lamorna, who nodded at him. He took a deep breath and nodded in reply before turning away and leaving.

'Oh, Joceline, it really hurts.'

'Well, I did warn you.' Joceline smiled at her, a genuine kindness in her eyes. 'Let's try to get you comfortable, shall we? I found it easiest on my hands and knees, but you can squat if you prefer. Some women stand, I gather, but I'm not sure I'd recommend it.'

Lamorna tucked her legs behind her and crawled forwards onto her knees. Her belly hung heavy beneath her. Joceline piled up some furs under her, and she fell slowly forwards onto them as another pang ripped through her abdomen.

She felt Joceline's hands on her, felt horribly exposed.

'You need to push,' came Joceline's calm advice. 'On the next contraction, push.'

So she did.

And she screamed.

It felt like something was trying to turn her inside out. Jagged pain darted out to all corners of her body.

'Push.' Joceline's encouragement was louder, so Lamorna pushed again. Her head swam. She could hear the rush of her blood, the desperate hammering of her heart. As she pushed, she felt the corners of her vision darken. Joceline's voice drifted away, becoming fainter, even though she was clearly speaking at volume. In a haze, Lamorna thought she heard Joceline say something about 'feet'. She pushed again and felt a rush of hot wetness spill down her thighs. Surely that was a good thing. Her vision clouded still further. She felt as if she was drowning in tar, the heat stifling. Overwhelming. Gasping for breath, and in search of anything but the blackness, she strove to lift her head from the furs, her mouth agape.

For a fleeting and euphoric moment, finding the narrow shaft of sunlight that fell like a golden gleaming javelin from the window, she felt the wonder of creation all around her. The pain flowed out of her, liberating her. She was free. She was alive.

And in that moment, in that respite, as the painless darkness poured relentlessly in once again from her periphery, she felt it all slip away.

* * *

The mid-afternoon sun beamed down on Vortimer as he stood on the ramparts looking out over Dumnonia. On any other day, he thought bitterly, it would have been easy to describe the view as beautiful, almost paradisal. The heat of the sun was gentle, and a slight breeze ruffled his hair. Shadows of clouds moved languidly over the rugged ebb and flow of the moorland, animating its otherwise placid and stoic facade. The faraway bleating of newly born lambs drifted to him on the taunting wind. The winter, cruel enough even this far south, had receded. Everywhere life was blooming.

Almost everywhere.

When Lamorna's cries had stopped, he had waited, barely able to breathe, expecting a different kind of cry to herald the arrival of his son. Or daughter. Truth be told, he hadn't cared which it might have been. Might. Vortimer angrily wiped a tear from his eye. The gods were punishing him now, of that he had to be certain. What other explanation was there?

He had rushed into the quiet bed chamber after a few moments, still clinging to the hope that his newborn offspring had been too eager to clamp himself, or herself, to Lamorna's breast to bother uttering that first shout. That slight hope had been quickly dashed. He had seen Lamorna first, face down on the furs, motionless. Then he had seen Joceline, her hands scarlet with blood, her face drained of colour, staring at him. Her steel eyes had glistened with emotion, holding his own for the briefest of moments before dropping sorrowfully to the carnage before her.

His son, for it had been a son, had been born still. When he had passed, Joceline could not say or did not say, but the act of birthing him had been too much for Lamorna. Both son and wife had left this life and now walked with the gods. The very gods that had surely proclaimed some horrible justice on Vortimer for his crimes against them. For what, though? Yes, he had lain with Joceline. Yes, he had profited, if profit it was, from his own father murdering Custennin and placing him in command of Dumnonia. But what else had he done? It was surely disproportionate that he should be punished so, and unduly cruel to poor Lamorna. The girl had suffered enough in her brief life, at the hands of her monstrous father. Having it snuffed out so prematurely was an outrage.

Vortimer considered how close he had come to becoming a father. And he thought of his own father, ravenous for power and celebrity. If anyone should suffer, it should be his father, not him. And yet, in that moment of hating the man who had raised him, of bitterly resenting him for putting this whole sequence of events into motion with his wilful ambition and murderous disregard for humanity, his father was the one man whose company he instinctively and inexplicably craved.

'Vortimer!' The cry was an angry one. Anything less, and he would probably have feigned not hearing the voice that called him to attention. He would have happily ignored any plaintive cry. Nobody hurt more than him at that moment. He could have no pity for any other. Not that day. But anger. Even though he could not entertain anyone else being as angry as him either, he could not pretend to avoid the challenge.

It was Jac. Below him, beneath the ramparts, the captain of his guard was red-faced and puffy-cheeked, a sword gripped tightly in his right hand. Even from this distance, Vortimer could tell Jac had been crying. His voice was tremulous, and his eyes were red.

'Vortimer!' the boy shouted again. 'I want justice.'

He wanted justice. For what? Everyone knew he had been besotted with Lamorna. She had even joked about it. There had even been rumours whispered around the fort that Jac was plotting some kind of murderous coup. For what? Because he felt Vortimer had wronged Lamorna? Well, so he had. Grievously. And he would never forgive himself for any of it. But this little shit had no right to wave a sword at him in the hour of his loss, he thought, feeling his anger focus on the youth.

'Vortimer,' Jac hollered. 'Fight me. I demand it.'

Vortimer snapped. His confused grief and guilt twisted inside him into a violent rage that he instinctively knew could only be abated, probably momentarily, by authoring this brat's imminent death. Unarmed and wearing only his cloth tunic for protection, he roared and descended at pace from the wall, caring little whether he lived or died. Let Jac's blade pierce his broken heart if it could, else he would wrap his hands around the youth's neck and squeeze every ounce of life out of him.

Jac charged towards him, sword clumsily raised, all skill tainted by emotion. Vortimer barely got his feet onto solid ground before the blade arced viciously over his ducking head. Jac's momentum carried him forward and his shoulder cannoned into Vortimer and sent him crashing into the wooden staves of the wall. A cry of horror sprung up from the dozen other guards that had been standing, wide eyed, as the challenge had unfolded. Several of them sprang into action and rapidly placed shields around Vortimer.

'Back,' Vortimer cried, pushing at the men that blocked his view of Jac. 'Let him come at me.' One man looked back at him, horrified. Even this guard, who Vortimer barely recognised and certainly could not name, seemed replete with a sense of grief and loss that hung heavy in the air. 'Sword, now,' Vortimer barked, and the guard obeyed.

'If you must fight him, Lord Vortimer, please take my shield as well,' the guard stuttered.

'Out of my way.' Vortimer had only blood on his mind. Jac had on his stiff leather armour, festooned with hard iron rings, and greaves on his legs, but he carried no shield. This was to be sword on sword, and the best man would win. The loser would die.

'You might as well have killed her,' Jac spat at Vortimer once the line of sight between them was cleared. He stood, legs slightly bent at the knee, ready to fight. As skilled as Vortimer was, he also knew that Jac had a worryingly natural affinity for combat. Not until now did Vortimer realise how glad he had been that Jac had always fought for him, not against him. For a moment, in the depths of the anger that coursed through his body, he regretted not insisting on donning his own armour and settling this as a matter of honour.

He dismissed the idea. This was not about honour. This was about his need to crush Jac. He needed to kill. His son and his wife had been taken from him without him even being able to raise a sword to defend them. He had been powerless to intervene, to prevent their deaths. He needed to take back power over his life. And if that meant ending Jac's, then so be it.

Jac came at him. He came with the fury of the aggrieved, his blade flashing in the high sun. Vortimer was equal to it, his experience and skill tempering his own anger enough to fend off the flurry of attacks. The two swords clattered together, their shrill clash sending a handful of rooks skyward in surprise.

Vortimer's vision narrowed. He had eyes only for Jac. He watched his reddened eyes, searching in them for a clue where the blade would land next. He watched his feet, alert to any loss of balance. This is what Vortimer lived for. He was in his element. For a moment, everything else was forgotten. There was only the ringing in his ears of sword on sword. He looked to Jac's eyes again and saw a flicker of panic, of more than anger. Jac doubted himself, if only for an instant. That much was clear. Vortimer seized on that weakness and feigned a thrust, only to slash across and catch Jac across his calf. The sword clattered partly against the boy's greave but also found flesh.

It was a slight wound, only enough to slow Jac for the blink of an eye, but it also threw him off balance. Vortimer stepped forward, inside Jac's sword arm, and punched him hard in the face, sending him staggering backwards.

For a few rapid beats of his heart, Vortimer stepped back too, catching his breath. Jac would be on him again before he knew it, so he steeled himself and set his feet firm. Behind Jac, Vortimer spotted Erbin, hands to his face, watching the duel with bated breath, his eyes dancing with excitement. There was little doubt who he supported, Vortimer thought bitterly. Then he saw Joceline.

She stood behind a few other men, cleansed now of Lamorna's blood, but still pale. Her eyes, pale too, were fixed sadly on Vortimer. He looked back at them for the fleetest of heartbeats and felt a pang of remorse.

Jac charged, fuelled by the humiliation of first blood as much as by the indignation he clearly felt at Lamorna's betrayal and death. Vortimer was more measured now, his own anger dissipating. But any fury his counterattacks lacked was made up for by a cold precision. He offered Jac nothing. No openings. No weakness. And as the young captain tired, and as Vortimer knocked his blade nonchalantly aside time after time, it must have been clear to everyone how this fight was going to end.

Jac overreached. Vortimer saw his balance shift awkwardly, and that was all the invitation he needed. He parried hard, sending Jac's blade rattling from his grip, then threw his body forward and planted his shoulder into Jac's chest. The younger man toppled backwards and fell. Vortimer swiftly and deftly levelled the point of his sword at Jac's exposed neck.

'Go on then,' Jac spat bitterly. 'It's all you're good for, after all.'

Vortimer looked up, his blade unmoving, and found Joceline's eyes in the crowd. They offered him nothing. She stared emptily back at him.

'Finish it,' a voice cried out. The tone suggested mercy more than impatience. Nobody cheered or clamoured.

Erbin was staring at Vortimer, his face contorted with anticipation.

Vortimer pulled his sword away from Jac and took a step backwards.

'I yield,' he called out. 'I yield Dumnonia to its rightful son. Erbin.'

Erbin straightened when he heard Vortimer's words, his eyes lighting up. Vortimer looked at him. Into him.

'You can have it, boy. It's yours. You can have Jac too. Maybe he'll keep you safe from the Hibernians. Maybe he won't. But I'm done here.'

He threw the borrowed sword into the dirt, then turned and walked away.

* * *

The sea looked impossibly distant. She could barely hear it. She knew it was down there, at the bottom of the cliffs, but she fixed her eyes on the horizon instead of the raging foam beneath her. The flat block of greyness beneath the blue of the sky was oddly peaceful.

Vortimer was gone. He had gone from his scuffle with Jac and donned his best armour and cloak and strapped his sword to his side. He had gone wordlessly, without seeking her out, and had returned from his chamber to find only his horse. And when Erbin, needlessly sycophantic, had asked him if he wanted a handful of men, of his own men, to accompany him on his journey to Viroconium, he had declined.

'You need them more than I,' he had said with a wry smile. Then, more seriously, 'I wish to travel alone.'

And then he had looked at her.

She didn't know if she would have gone with him had he asked. She already felt broken. But then again, perhaps it might have been the only thing that could have prevented this.

'Enjoy Dumnonia,' he had said finally to Erbin, and he had looked at her again before spurring his mount out of the gate and onto the moors. Perhaps he had wanted to ask her. Perhaps she should have stepped forwards. But he looked at her as if she, too, were a corpse. Like his poor wife. Like his stillborn son. And perhaps she was just that.

Perhaps she should be just that.

And, with her eyes fixed on that perfect line where the sea met the sky, she allowed herself to fall.

Blooded

Nothing could have prepared Rozena for the vile attentions of Tarquinius. His private room was hung with dark drapes and lit only by a roaring fire. Slowly lifting herself from the floor where she had been flung by his men, she saw him. The man himself, if man he was, the man who had saved her and Emrys from the ravages of the wolves for his own twisted purpose, now towered over the fire with his back to her. He was stripped to the waist, his broad back marked with scars. A roll of fat curled around the back of his great bald head.

'You have a name?' Even speaking lowly, his voice was deep and resonant.

Rozena offered nothing. She wasn't sure she could speak if she tried. Tarquinius turned slowly, his chin dipped to allow him to look down at her.

'It matters little.'

Rozena closed her eyes, willing the pain in her withered arm to intensify so that she could feel nothing else. She squeezed the dressings with her other hand. Then she felt his hand on her, his huge fingers finding their way under her good arm and lifting her by her shoulder. Her feet lost purchase on the floor and she cried out as he ripped her dress from her. She screwed her eyes closed, then gasped as he flung her across the room. The brief sensation of flight was abruptly cut short by the pile of furs that awaited her. She landed on her wounded arm and cried out at the pain. Good, she thought. Let it come.

And then he was on her, flipping her onto her front and pulling her middle up to meet him. She pushed her face into the furs. They reeked of smoke mixed with a stale manly odour and the bitter tang of old blood. As she felt Tarquinius' huge hands grip her hips, she almost retched. Whether it was because of the overpowering smell of the furs and the man, or the grim knowledge of what was coming, she did not know.

As she readied herself for more pain, she forced her mind elsewhere. Anywhere but there. And in the dull glow of moonlight that pierced a gap in the wall, her eyes fell on a glint of metal, half concealed by the expanse of stinking furs.

* * *

Emrys paced. He couldn't sleep. Not since he'd come to, his head throbbing from the blow he had received. He fretted, wrung his hands, and muttered to himself. Ambrosius awoke after a while, doubtless disturbed by the soft padding of feet, and looked at Emrys sympathetically.

'I wish I could offer words of consolation, my boy,' he muttered. 'Sometimes the best we can do is hope for a swift end. For those we love, and even for ourselves.'

Emrys turned on him, angry tears sticking to his cheeks. 'She asked me to kill her before this happened. What would you have had me do?'

'It might have been a kindness,' Ambrosius said softly after a moment's thought. 'But I don't blame you for not doing it.'

'I've never killed anyone.' Emrys stopped and leant with the flats of his hands against the cracked plaster of the wall, and his eyes intent on the floor. 'I intend to, though.'

'That's the spirit.'

The door burst open a little later. An insipid light spilled in from the night sky, and Rozena tumbled into the room. The door was promptly closed again. Rozena lay for a moment in a quivering huddle, barely covered, her exposed flesh still glowing in the moonlight. She gripped her tattered dress in her arms, folded across her front, and drew herself into a tight ball.

Emrys went to her, clueless as to what he could do or say. As he neared her, his hand tentatively outstretched, not knowing whether she would flinch and recoil from his touch or fold herself into his arms, her head snapped up. Her eyes, red-rimmed and wet, gleamed. She unfurled her ruined dress, oblivious to her own exposure, and showed him what she had stolen from Tarquinius. A gleaming dagger. A weapon.

She gave Emrys the slightest of nods, as if he was supposed to know what to do with this blade. As if he was now in charge of their salvation. As if he should force his way out of this captivity and slay the dozen heavily armed men that noisily caroused nearby. He flashed an encouraging smile at her and instead removed his jerkin and placed it around her cool shoulders.

'I don't want to talk about it,' she hissed. 'Before you ask.'

He felt relief. No matter how horrendous his imaginings could be of what she had endured, he suspected the retelling of them would be worse.

'I found it in Tarquinius' room.'

For whatever reason, this meant that they had not yet passed her around among the other men of the fort. They had spared her that extra torment. For now, at least.

'He could have killed you.'

'I should have killed him,' she said bitterly. 'I wanted to. I could have. Maybe. Well, I'd have probably just injured him, then he'd have killed me and then you. At least this way, we might both escape. And him too, if he likes.' She motioned to Ambrosius with her head.

'But how?'

'Listen to them. They're drinking enough to put a horse to sleep. They'll be groggy and sore in the morning when they next open this door.'

'What if they don't?'

'Don't what?'

'Open this door.' Emrys looked down. Rozena's bare knees were tracked with two dark lines of drying blood, lines that disappeared upwards. 'And we're too weak. We're hurt.'

Rozena looked at Emrys, an eyebrow raised. 'I don't think I'll be allowed the luxury of time to recover from tonight. We'll only weaken more as more time passes. It must be now.'

Emrys nodded thoughtfully, pained, then reached for the dagger. Rozena threw the fabric over it in a hurry. 'What are you doing?'

'The knife.'

'Yes. It is my knife.' She frowned at him. 'And I intend to use it. What? You think I can't wield a little dagger just as well as you?'

'No, but–'

'But nothing. Besides, they won't expect an attack from me.'

She was right in that, Emrys supposed. He rubbed the raised welt on the side of his head, his hair sticky with his own dry blood.

'Are you alright?' Rozena asked. Emrys looked at her, his eyes searching hers. How could she ask him that? The wolf's bite on his side still wept, but her arm hung in limp tatters at her side. He had a mere bump on his head, while she had been brutalised by a cruel giant of a man.

'I am.' He nodded. 'And you will be too,' he added awkwardly.

Her face twitched, as if she wanted to agree with the sentiment at the same time as being fully aware that her life had, in the last day or two, changed forever. 'You are cold,' she smiled, as if to tell him not to worry about her. 'Come closer. There is enough of this rag to warm us both.'

'Are you sure?'

Her scowl was answer enough, and he was glad to shimmy up beside her. He snaked his arm around her shoulders and pulled her gently to him.

'Are you sure you don't think it better I take the knife?'

She punched his leg.

* * *

Little light fell into the room, but Emrys stayed awake and watched as the soft white of the moon slowly gave way to a warmer hue. The sun found its way over the horizon and threw its golden rays horizontally through the high window.

The dull thud of footfalls reached his ears, accompanied by a low grumbling mutter. Their captors were approaching. Rozena stirred from what had been a fitful but much needed sleep. She heard them too and was on her feet in a heartbeat, teetering for a moment. She was weak. She was hurt. This would never work.

'Give me the knife,' Emrys pleaded with her once again, this time deadly serious, but her eyes flashed with a well-earned anger.

Rozena squatted down close to the door and motioned Emrys to do the same on the other side. Across the room, Ambrosius stirred and opened his eyes. Emrys mouthed at him to remain quiet, and the old man nodded and pretended to return to his slumber.

The door creaked open, and two men shuffled inside. There were no pleasantries. A hunk of bread landed on the dirty floor and a flagon of water was dumped clumsily beside it. That was all the invitation Rozena needed.

She aimed the blade well. A stab to the body could easily have backfired, and she had the element of surprise on her side. Quick as a flash, she scuttled across the few feet of floor and jabbed the knife through the man's neck before slicing it out through his throat. He reared up with a strangled roar, clutching at the fountaining wound. Blood sprayed across the room, spattering Ambrosius, who snapped from his false sleep with a start.

Emrys wasted no time. He leapt from his squatting position and relieved the fast-dying man of his sword. As the weapon slid with a whine from its scabbard, Emrys knew the other man had to be right behind him. His beleaguered cry for help, subdued by the night's revelry, was raspy and ineffectual, and Emrys was glad that both men were, as Rozena had promised, somewhat groggy. The man had barely freed his own sword by the time Emrys had turned and thrust. He was still crouched, his feet wide and well balanced, and he pushed up with all his might, standing into the thrust.

He had always imagined it would be a straightforward thing to push a sharp sword into a man, especially one unencumbered by armour. He didn't anticipate how much resistance flesh possessed. For the briefest of moments, he feared that his thrust had not been strong enough. The point of his sword pushed into the man's stomach without penetrating. Then, as the man's own momentum carried him forward, there was a sickening wet sound as the skin broke. The man, his face contorted in surprise, fell forwards onto Emrys, and his body swallowed the cold steel right up to the hilt.

Pinned as he was for a moment, Emrys was morbidly captivated by the dying man's eyes. To his right, the other man lay still, blood still bubbling from his open neck. Emrys tried to push the weight from him, but found it difficult. And then Rozena was there, pulling the man's head up by his matted, long hair and slicing her knife across his throat before rolling him away.

'Do you think anyone heard?' she hissed, her face specked scarlet and a wild look in her eyes. Emrys could do nothing but stare back at her, feeling his own face drenched in blood.

'Nobody's coming,' Ambrosius' whispered. He had made his way to the open door and was looking out. 'Not sure how we get through the gate without being seen, though.'

Emrys' head spun. He needed to concentrate, to focus. He had killed a man. His first. But there wasn't time to think about that. Not yet. If they didn't put distance between themselves and this foul place, then they would not live to see another night. He clambered to his feet and pulled hard at the sword that he had left in the guard's belly. It slid free easier than it went in, and Emrys nearly overbalanced. He staggered back a pace or two, then looked to Rozena.

'There's a gap in the stake wall over there,' she motioned in the opposite direction of the gate. 'I noticed it when they took me to Tarquinius.'

'A postern,' nodded Ambrosius. 'I've seen it too. It leads to a rather perilous path down to the river, I believe. It won't be easy going.'

'Good,' Rozena grinned. 'Then they won't be able to come after us on horses.'

'No, they won't,' Ambrosius agreed, 'but by the time we reach the river, if our absence has been noted, they can easily have ridden the long way down and be waiting for us there.'

Emrys looked at Rozena. There was no stopping her now. She had, one-armed, killed a man. Two, effectively. She wore the blood well and seemed a little too eager to shed more, given half a chance. Only once in his life had Emrys seen a woman hold her own in combat like that. Then, like now, his life had been in the balance. The Kaldi woman had slain a bear in front of him and saved his life, but Rozena's feat was equally impressive. Emrys would never again hold fast to the traditional belief that a woman had no place in battle.

'We go now then,' Rozena stated simply. 'And we make sure our head-start is enough to ensure that nobody waits for us at the river.'

Ambrosius reached for the second sword that lay near the outstretched arm of the man Emrys had mostly killed, then looked at Rozena. 'Did you want it, dear?' he asked politely.

Rozena shook her head, content with the smaller blade, so Ambrosius lifted it, turning it delicately in his hand.

And the three of them, each now blooded, crept fast and low towards the postern gate and away from Tarquinius' fort.

Sea Wolves

He always got the shit jobs. Osric, despite the supposed seafaring blood that coursed through his veins, was not one for boats.

'You will like Hengest and Hors,' Wulfric grinned at him, all teeth and newfound bravado. The youth had come a long way since leaving Egbin's pathetic colony.

'Not as much as I will like the ground beneath my feet,' Osric replied dourly.

'This is nothing,' Wulfric continued. 'A river, meek and mild. Can you even imagine what the sea is like?'

Osric desired nothing less than discovering what the sea was like. It was wholly unnatural to him to rock and sway on the waves. The idea that anything more than waist deep water was beneath him was terrifying. How anyone entrusted their lives to some damp timber and set out beyond sight of dry land was beyond him.

'Don't worry. This boat isn't remotely seaworthy.'

Osric had wondered. Clearly Wulfric had borrowed or stolen this small boat just to navigate the Tamesis. The Jutes would not have risked one of their galleys in uncertain waters. Osric gripped the side, his knuckles white, and busied himself with remembrance.

He had been on the cusp of manhood when he had been exiled, a slender youth of fifteen summers, born and raised in the swamps given to the Jutes after the Romans had left. Had he been a year or two younger, he may well have remained in that bog. He may well have been treated with a measure of mercy or compassion. But no, he had been deemed man enough to be dealt the harshest of punishments. Banishment. He had been stripped of any entitlement or claim to his heritage, sentenced to roam the lands beyond in perpetual dread of a righteous execution. His crime had been murder.

He would have argued, and still would, that his actions were in the interest of the greater good. A cruel, older Jute, named Guthred, had been tormenting the younger members of the community for some time. Guthred had derived a sick pleasure in beating children who were too young to be remonstrated with the back of a hand, children who could not defend themselves. He claimed his actions were disciplinary, necessary, the way of their ancestors, designed to toughen up the young and ready them for the trials ahead. But every child that Osric saw was afraid of Guthred. They hated him but could do nothing.

One morning, Osric had seen Guthred holding a child, barely five years old, over a barrel of rainwater. He had dunked the frightened boy's head under the freezing water until there was every chance he might drown. And Osric had snapped. He had pulled a short blade from his tunic and slit the bastard's throat.

And he'd do it again. Guthred had been a bully, a manipulative abuser who could sway any adult into believing him over the treacherous words of a rebellious child. And Osric had seen and heard enough. He had ended Guthred's miserable life without a hint of regret before something hideous had befallen one of the children.

For that, he had been banished, branded a wolf, forbidden from entering Jutish society ever again. He could be killed on sight without fear of reprisal. His life was forfeited. He was nothing.

And the boy who had narrowly escaped a drowning, Osric realised, was Wulfric.

'Ship ahead,' Wulfric called.

Ahead in the estuary, three galleys appeared out of the mist. Over a hundred Jutes sat on board, and any of them could rightfully slide a seax between Osric's ribs. If they were so inclined.

* * *

Hengest was perhaps half a dozen years younger than Vortigern, and as many older than Osric. He was a tall man, broad in the shoulders, with a plaited beard, and was unmistakably a ruler. Standing with his feet firmly askance in the prow of the lead galley, he barely swayed with the river's swell as Osric clambered awkwardly aboard.

'This is Osric,' Wulfric announced him. 'He is one of the high king's most trusted advisors, and as noble a man as I have met on this island.' Wulfric was clearly enjoying his role as intermediary.

Hengest held out his hand, stony faced. Osric offered his own, and the Jutish leader clamped his firm grip around his forearm.

'Well met, Osric. I have heard a great deal about you.'

Osric grimaced. 'And I have heard little about you, but I am honoured to be in the presence of the gods.' Flattery seemed appropriate.

Hengest laughed. It was a deep, throaty laugh, confident and haughty. 'This is my brother, Hors.'

Hors was closer in age to Osric, broader than his older brother, but not as tall. He thrust his arm out for Osric to take and nodded.

'He talks better with a blade in hand,' Hengest smiled.

'As do I,' Osric blurted out, almost apologetically. 'I am no ambassador. I am indeed close to the high king, but I am not known for my diplomacy.'

'Worry not, wolf,' Hengest said quietly. 'We are not here for diplomacy.'

Hengest knew. Wulfric must have told him. Osric instinctively looked around him, assessing his options. There were none. He was on a boat on water and could not swim. And he certainly could not fight his way out of this.

'I said not to worry, Osric of the Britons. We are your friends. We are your kin. Your allies. And we wish to fight with, not against, your king.'

'But why?' It was all the words Osric could muster.

'That, friend, is for the ears of the high king. You will take us to him?'

Osric paused, gathering himself, and held Hengest's haughty stare. 'I will,' he uttered. 'There are some conditions to your audience with him.'

Hengest stared back at Osric. There was something in that look, something so calculated that Osric was convinced there and then that he really was in the presence of greatness. He didn't trust the Jutish leader. He wasn't even sure he could like him. But the power there was undeniable.

'I would expect nothing else,' said Hengest with a wry smile.

* * *

Verulamium was far enough from the Tamesis that the Jutes would be tired from a day in the saddle. Tired, but hopefully not angered. Vortigern knew from Osric that theirs was a people not keen on riding. They were grounded, earthy folk who liked to keep their bodies as close to the ground as possible. Except, apparently, when they took to the sea.

He had tasked Shabaka and Tsekani with securing horses, going so far as to suggest purloining them from Sextus' stables. He would have liked to have seen the Jutish leaders' faces when they beheld the two Nobatians awaiting them with several horses. If they were serious about joining forces, as was purported, then they would be grateful of the hospitality Vortigern had arranged for them. If, on the other hand, they were here to discuss terms of surrender, they would be unlikely to acquiesce to the conditions set out. Only the bravest and most confident of leaders would ride the best part of a day to parlay with a king they wished to unseat, with only four kinsmen to keep them safe.

The more he thought on it, the more he became convinced that the Jutes were indeed here to help. And if that were the case, numbering well over a hundred, all potentially as formidable on the battlefield as Osric, then the Kaldi had better prepare themselves for a fight. Why the Jutes were prepared to shed their own blood in the defence of Britannia, of Albion, was the burning question. Closely followed by the matter of cost.

The descendants of Woden arrived approximately when Vortigern had estimated they would. Through a narrow window, he watched them dismount. He watched them rubbing their saddle-sore rumps and straighten their backs, glad to have their feet back on the ground. He saw them straighten their armour and their weapons and tighten the straps that held their small round shields to their backs. They joked and smiled, and Osric was party to the humour.

Their men, along with Shabaka and Tsekani, remained outside. Only Osric and Wulfric, both capable of interpreting duties, accompanied them inside the villa. Vortigern, careful to wear his own armour and shroud his shoulders with the finest furs he owned, remained on his feet to greet them.

Hengest was several inches taller than Vortigern, but was quick to bow his head in greeting.

'High King,' he announced clearly, 'I am Hengest, and this is my brother, Hors. We are honoured to be in your presence.'

Osric translated the guttural tongue.

'As am I to be in yours,' Vortigern crooned, motioning them to sit. 'I believe I am in the presence of divine blood.'

Wulfric whispered in Hengest's ear, and the big Jute beamed. 'We are proud of our heritage, and it is indeed a potent one, but we are not kings.'

'Why do you come to be here?' Vortigern saw no point in not getting to the point as quickly as possible. His directness was rewarded with a grin from the Jute.

'Let me answer in the simplest of terms,' Hengest began. 'We have no other home.'

Vortigern stared at him. It was not the answer he had expected. 'Are you sure that's what he said?' He asked Osric.

Osric nodded.

'Our lands are poor, and we are too many,' Hengest continued. 'It is our custom, when this is the case, to seek out causes befitting our strength in battle, to lend aid to those in need. The men in the boats moored in your great river are the finest warriors we have, brave enough to cross the sea in search of better fortune.'

'As you must be brave to lead them,' Vortigern said deliberately. 'But I am curious,' he frowned. 'Why would two brothers such as yourselves, descendants of Woden himself, I am told, be required to lead these exiles?

Surely your place is ruling over your people at home?'

'Exile is too strong a word, my king,' whispered Osric.

'It is the word I choose to use.'

Osric nodded obediently and translated. Hengest flinched but remained calm.

'It is precisely because of our heritage that we must lead these men. It is an honour in the eyes of the gods.' Hengest paused, pulling at his plaited beard. 'Like you, great king, we lead from the fore. You will not see any of our men steeped in blood in the heat of battle unless you first see us, more so than the best of them. I am certain you will lead the charge of your cavalry when called upon to fight. Am I right?'

There was more to this hulking Jute than met the eye, Vortigern realised. He had assumed he would be dealing with a man more accustomed to using brawn than brain. He could see that was not the case. Cavalry, Hengest had said. Vortigern had never dared to call his mounted warriors such, just as he had not, until recently, considered the men that fought for him to be an army of soldiers. These were Roman ideals. Yet there was a majesty to them that pleased him.

'You speak the truth.' Vortigern waved his hands with as warm a smile as he could manage. 'I would have it no other way.'

'Then we shall fight side by side,' Hengest offered.

'For honour?'

'Honour, yes, and a tract of land that we may call our own. Land of your choosing. Somewhere we can lick our wounds in peace before being called upon again to fight.'

The Romans before him had employed mercenaries from Saxony and its neighbouring regions before. They had bolstered their trained field army with scores of savages, thrown them into pitch battle ahead of their own men. They had been happy to rely on them, to sacrifice them, to reward them. They had paid in gold and silver and anything else that had been of value. The best currency now appeared to be land and, by the gods, there was a lot of that lying empty and untended. Whole towns were deserted, Roman forts run derelict where once hundreds of men would have barracked. There was surely room somewhere for a few more than a hundred of these Jutes, or however many might survive a clash with the Kaldi.

'Osric is a most valiant and formidable warrior. If you and your kin are of his ilk, then I would be glad to reward your service with a fine area of land. You have my word.'

Vortigern took several steps towards Hengest, his arm outstretched, and the Jute took it.

'And you have mine.' Hengest pulled Vortigern towards him, their hands clasped together, and knocked him firmly on the back with his other hand. 'We shall fight together. And we shall win.'

When Hengest released him, Vortigern stepped back, a flutter of excitement in his belly and a wilful grin on his face. 'So, Hengest, and you Hors—for you are welcome too—tell me, what have you heard about the Kaldi?'

Home

P asha knew she was dreaming. And while she had no control over the grotesque parade of visions she was being subjected to, she could at least move freely. Or so she thought.

She was in a cave, crouching her way down a winding passageway, the dank sweat of the rock under her palms. She could smell the damp, and with it the pungent and clawing sweetness of something rotting. A bright, reverberating dripping sound punctuated every faltering footfall, and a low chorus of moans echoed around her, sometimes far away and sometimes so close that she had to spin around to make sure nobody was behind her.

But she could see nothing. The darkness was inky and thick, and only her other senses alerted her to the narrowness of the passage she was traversing. She could touch both walls and had to duck when the ceiling dipped overhead. Occasionally, she almost lost her footing, her apparently bare feet slipping on the chilly, moist floor.

Eventually, a dim yellow glow beckoned to her. At first it was a pin of light that threw the faintest of shadows onto the stone, revealing the furry softness of pale lichens and moss. An occasional scuttling sound hinted at life. She wondered what many-legged crawling beasts might flourish in this environment. Beetles. Spiders maybe, feasting on beetles. Blind pale serpents that might feed on the spiders. Or spirits. Perhaps the sickly light that called to her was a spirit, lost and confused, caught between worlds. Surely this was a passage to the next world.

Pasha could have woken herself if she'd wanted, but she was not afraid. She had been close enough to death before, and this kind of vision was not alien to her. She wanted—needed even—to see what lay in the depths of this infernal place. So, she crept on towards the light, sensing it growing slowly closer.

The passage widened. She found she could stand up without fear of banging her head. The little light that bled onto the surrounding rocks gave her more confidence in her footing, and she moved faster, keen to reach the source of the light.

And then the floor fell away. She found herself on the edge of a precipice, stopping just in time. The light fell from above her, showing the edge of the ravine, but not quite reaching into its impenetrable depths. She leaned over as far as she dared, squinting into the dark well, certain that the light from above was there to illuminate something of import.

Then she was falling. The rock she had been standing on was loose and had crumbled beneath her inquisitive gaze. She closed her eyes and willed the fall to slow. She was in control here. This was her dream. She opened her eyes once the rush of wind in her face had abated; once her fall had halted. She was floating in the dark shaft with neither hand nor foot having any purchase on solid ground. And still there was darkness beneath her.

She willed the light to reach a little further and watched as it intensified. It was as if she were in a chimney, and the sun had reached its zenith above her. The pit was flooded with light, an angry orange light that threw a shadow of her onto the horror beneath. There, impaled on stakes as tall as a man that grew from the floor of the chasm, lay her mother. She was quite lifeless, a spike as thick as a tree jutting from her splayed abdomen. Her eyes were open in death, wide with shock, dark pools of abject horror.

Pasha willed herself upwards, recoiling from the sight. She sped up past the point from which she had fallen and up into the chimney, towards the fiery light, and out into the open air. She alighted near the peak of a mountain as the orange light above dwindled into a more scarlet hue, darker and more foreboding. It glowered through the bare limbs of a huge dead tree that was utterly out of place. The landscape, as much as she could see, was craggy and mountainous. Pyramids rose into sharp peaks in the distance, presumably the same as the one she stood on, except only this one had a tree growing from its slopes.

As she approached the tree, she could see what appeared to be a root at its base, arching out of the ground and silhouetted against the scarlet glow of the sky. As she rounded the trunk, she could see that it was not a root at all, but a leg. A man lay slumped against the tree, head bowed, and legs splayed. His arms hung limp to the side of his lifeless body, and the thick shaft of a spear protruded from his chest. Crouching, Pasha gently lifted the man's head to see his face better. It was Catigern. He was older than she knew him to be, but he was Catigern just the same. Her poor, sweet brother. His dead eyes looked back at her. His mouth lay open in mute protestation.

A strange cry tore her away from looking at Catigern. It was a rasping, coarse shout, not unlike a crow or a raven even, but oddly human. She spun around and saw, down the slope, the lithe nudeness of a man. He bounded fearlessly in a random, haphazard fashion, darting diagonally here and there. His hair was long and matted, falling across his bearded face so that she could tell nothing of how he looked. But he was utterly naked. His impossibly long and slender limbs flailed around him as he ran and cawed like a carrion bird.

'Wait.' She cried out, but the man either didn't hear her or he chose to ignore her. She set off down the slope towards him, the ground beneath her feet oddly soft and perilously uneven. Something gripped her ankle, and she fell forwards. She might have tumbled further down the hill were it not for her leg being caught. Angrily, she tried to pull her foot free, and reached down to see what had hold of her.

To find that it was a human hand.

She screamed, and set about prising the icy fingers from her, suddenly realising that the ground on which she now lay was not ground at all. It was bodies. Thousands of bodies. Some were whole. Some were just parts of the whole, arms and legs and heads. Men with gaping wounds and deathly grins leered at her in the gloom, masked in sticky, dark blood. The stench hit her nostrils again, and the soft rumble of moans rose around her. She kicked her leg free and clambered downwards, face first, trying to get to her feet. But the bodies were everywhere. The mountain was made of them, a huge stinking pile of corpses, of slaughtered men. Of death.

Caw. Caw. The naked man leapt amongst the bodies. And he laughed.

'Wait,' Pasha called out. She still knew she was dreaming. This wasn't real.

'Pasha.' The voice stopped her. She froze. It was her father.

Looming out of what was now, again, an inky darkness, her father's face formed amongst the clouds. It was shrouded in orange and red and yellow, aflame. His hair was burning brightly, his features melting.

'Find a way,' he implored her. 'Find a way.'

And the fire consumed his face.

And she woke, drenched in a cold sweat in the soft light of the morning.

And she went straight to her brother. To Catigern. She had passed her mother on the way, deep in conversation with Ossian. Sevira had flapped her hands as Pasha passed, as if she wanted to say something important. If it wasn't about her disappointment at Pasha's rejection of Pabo, then she no doubt wanted to know why Pasha had stopped her lessons with the druid. And the old man would have been unlikely to shed any light on that matter. Pasha imagined her mother chastising her, telling her how she had been so adamant that it was what she wanted, that she had shown so much promise, that she still had so much to learn. Well, she did. But not from him. He would wake some night, months or years later, she vowed to herself, stirred by an out-of-place sound, bathed in a cold sweat and fearing for his life. And he would face the cold steel of justice. But not now.

'Catigern.' She threw her arms around her surprised younger brother.

'What?' Catigern dutifully returned the embrace, his bemusement obvious in the way his hands flayed around behind her back. 'Pasha?'

She had barely spoken to him in months. In truth, they'd never been that close. But she had noticed his spectacular improvements in combat on the occasions she had seen him training with the Ethiope. She knew well that a heartfelt hug was the last thing he expected from her.

'Catigern, I need to go away.' She waved a hand in front of his face to soften his interruption. 'I need to go away, and I need you to promise me something.'

'Anything. What? Where are you going?'

He was a young man now, handsome and muscled. He had always been a bright boy, but now she could see he was more than that. His well-earned skills in combat had been accelerated in their acquisition by his brilliant mind. He was no brute, no hulking axeman or impenetrable colossus. He was lithe and lean and fair in the face. She knew enough of him to know that his heart, his brain, and his strength were in consummate union. He would make a great warrior, a better leader, and—if anything untoward were to happen to Vortimer—a more than worthy heir to the realm that their father claimed to rule. But he was still young. And she had dreamed him dead.

'I am going to continue my studies, away from all this. And you—you need to not fall into line beneath our father.' She held both of his hands in hers and looked him in his eyes.

'I am trained to fight. I should do as the other young men do.' Catigern looked at her, quizzical. 'What would you have me do instead?'

'Anything, brother. Anything at all. War does not care if you are the son of the high king, or the bravest or strongest man in the battle.'

Catigern looked at her, his arms relaxing. He smiled gently. 'Death,' he mumbled. 'Death does not care.'

She nodded. 'Please. Please.'

Catigern drew her to him, wrapping his arms around her properly this time. He squeezed her and pushed his head against hers.

'Don't go away for long,' he whispered in her ear.

She pulled away, eyes misting, and nodded breathlessly at him. 'I don't have the heart to tell Mother.'

'I'll tell her.' He nodded.

And she went. She left Viroconium without a backward glance, and every step diluted the terror she felt at her dream and calmed the rage that still burned in her against Ossian. There must be others who knew the old ways, who could teach her their secrets, who could help her understand her visions, who could unlock her potential.

* * *

Ambrosius knew there was something about Emrys, something unquenchable, something that burned in his amber eyes. The boy was more than a mere orphan, more than a refugee from the Kaldi ravaged lands in the north. The girl he sought to protect was made of similar flesh, too. Ambrosius had wasted no time in insisting that the pair of them remain with him in his villa in Viroconium. That they had been more than instrumental in his emancipation from the clutches of that ogre, Tarquinius, was reason enough for him to bestow upon them all his generosity.

'My wife and son were taken by the plague,' he explained to Emrys while Rozena slept—for once in comfort. He had bathed—his villa was one of the few to still have a working Roman bath—and had his matted hair shorn and his face shaved. He wore his purple tunic, indicative of an office no doubt a mystery to the lad. They sat on a low wall, the landscape beyond glowing in the orangey dusk.

'Our families were murdered,' Emrys finally volunteered, taking in the man before him. 'Death is death.'

'Well, there can be no vengeance on disease,' Ambrosius offered with a wry smile.

'I'm not sure I believe in vengeance.'

The boy's golden eyes gleamed. He had been cleaned up as well and given fresh clothes to wear. He had declined a haircut, but his face at least was clear of muck. The scar that framed his eye made him look older than he was.

'Vengeance is not a god to be believed in, Emrys. It is a base emotion, one which most men would fail to ignore in circumstances such as yours.'

'You are trying to provoke me.' Emrys was quick. 'And yes, I am angry. I wish death upon those that killed my family, on Tarquinius for what he did

346

to Rozena, on the Angles for murdering Viction and Krestell and Carina.'

Ambrosius sickened at the already long list of tragedies endured by this boy and marvelled at his calmness.

'But I do not wish to devote my life to hatred and bloodletting. I want to understand.' Emrys paused. 'I want to make things different.'

'Better?'

'Yes, better.'

'Well,' Ambrosius beamed at him, 'perhaps you shall, though it does seem to me that many things tend to become significantly worse before they can improve.'

Emrys stood up, straightening the tunic he wore. The tunic had belonged to Ambrosius' son. Whether Emrys knew that or not, he was clearly not comfortable.

'I still want to fight,' Emrys admitted. 'I do understand that change is a violent beast.'

Ambrosius nodded. 'And Rozena?'

Emrys laughed. 'She'll want to fight, too. And I'm not sure her views on vengeance are the same as mine.'

'You know that she cannot?'

'She cares little for tradition.'

'I mean, because of her arm.'

Emrys sighed, then smiled bitterly. 'I don't think that will stop her.'

'Well, it will for now.' Ambrosius stood. 'Come, let us eat. I have sent word to the high king's wife that we require the attentions of her druid. Perhaps he can do something for Rozena's arm so that she might stand beside you in the coming battles.'

'Thank you.' Emrys said quietly. 'Thank you for everything.'

'No. Thank you.'

Ambrosius ushered the yellow-eyed boy inside, feeling a long absent pang in his heart.

* * *

Saddle sore and weary, Zeki had been overjoyed when the summit of The Wrekin had loomed into view. He had spurred his tired horse forward, past the hill bearing the familiar fort and towards the gates of Viroconium. There he had reported to Sevira and Ossian, respectfully conveying Vortigern's wishes that the druid, and any battle-ready men fit enough to accompany him, make haste towards Eboracum. Then he had made his way to the river, intent on washing the grime of his travels from his aching body.

He would be glad to put an end to the weeks on horseback and emissary duties he had fallen into. But, for now, he was happy to be refreshed and cleaned by the cool waters. He stripped naked and waded into the slow-flowing stream, then slid forward noiselessly under the surface.

'May I join you?' Pabo was standing on the bank when Zeki emerged.

Zeki, caught drawing a deep breath after his submersion, could only nod. The noble successor to Ceneu, lord of Northern Britannia, was not wearing his bronze breastplate, nor any finery, as he was wont to do. His crimson tunic was tied loosely at the waist, his feet in sandals. Zeki chose not to avert his eyes, but watched intently as Pabo stepped out of his footwear and dropped his tunic to the ground. Naked, his eyes remained fixed on Zeki's for the whole disrobing. And then, with a slight smile, he stepped hesitantly into the clear water, in no hurry to conceal his nakedness. There was no need for further words.

Zeki rose to meet him, his own dusky nakedness in stark contrast to the pallor of the Briton's as they came together. Pabo held his arms open, inviting the contact, and Zeki wasted no time in responding to the signal. He pulled Pabo close, feeling the warmth of his body on his own, and kissed him.

A short time later, they lay naked together on the short grass of the bank. Pabo, despite his higher birth, was the more passive of the two, and rolled onto his front, inviting Zeki to lie on top of him. To have him. Zeki obliged, and when the passion eventually subsided into tenderness, they stretched out in the sun, legs intertwined, the black and the white of their skins knotted together in accord.

'I must go to Eboracum,' Zeki murmured. He wasn't sad that Vortigern required his blade, or that he must fight. He yearned for battle. But in that tender moment, the first Zeki had known for several years, there was an aching wistfulness to the sentiment. 'I would rather lie here all summer with you.'

'I shall go with you.'

Zeki looked at Pabo in surprise. He lifted himself up on one arm and searched the other man's face. Pabo was no warrior. His moulded armour was ceremonial at best.

'I can fight,' Pabo insisted, his fingers trailing over Zeki's chest. 'I can fight as well as any man.'

'But—'

'You don't believe me?' Pabo had a twinkle in his eye, a provocative air about him.

'I had no idea,' Zeki said playfully.

'Few do.'

Zeki wasn't sure he believed Pabo. The man was slender, soft. His hands, when they had caressed Zeki, had been smooth, not calloused. The muscles in his arms and legs were wiry, not weak, but not like those of a man who had raised a sword and shield.

'You need not risk your life. Your people will need you.' Zeki preferred the idea that Pabo would be here waiting for him when he returned, rather than bloodied beside him on the battlefield.

'My people need me to fight.'

'Your people need you to live.'

'I intend to.' Pabo reached down between Zeki's legs, instantly stirring the passion once again. 'I rather enjoy it.'

The soft whinny of a horse was enough to separate the two men. Zeki looked around, spying the rider an arm's throw down the river. He sprung to his feet, but there was no time to conceal his nakedness. There was barely enough time to pull his sword free from its scabbard. Pabo stood up behind him, unarmed.

'Zeki?' the rider called out.

349

Zeki lowered his sword and tried to ascertain who the man was.

A wry chuckle came from the man on horseback. 'Are we at peace?'

And, as the rider neared them, Zeki finally recognised him.

'Vortimer.' He bowed his head in respect. 'Welcome home.'

Zeki had always liked the high king's first-born son and had been disappointed when he had been sequestered in Dumnonia. While it had elevated him in terms of power, and no doubt served Vortigern's purposes, it had still seemed more of a punishment than a reward.

Vortimer grinned as he pulled his horse up alongside the two naked men. 'I do hope I didn't spoil a moment.' He shamelessly glanced down at Zeki's retreating cock. 'As for home, I have a feeling I won't be here long. Word has it my father gathers forces in Eboracum?'

Zeki nodded. 'We are to join him presently. This is Pabo, son of Ceneu of Rheged.'

'Ah! Well met, Pabo, son of Ceneu.' Vortimer smirked. 'I will greet you more formally when you are attired, if you don't mind. And when you're quite done with each other, perhaps we can all travel together?'

VII

CARPE DIEM

'The earth has guilt, the earth has care,
Unquiet are its graves;
But peaceful sleep is ever there,
Beneath the dark blue waves.'

(Nathaniel Hawthorne)

To Arms

Rozena was furious. Not even Emrys had come to her defence. Not even he, who knew her better than anyone, had spoken up on her behalf. He had quietly—no, quite vocally, actually—agreed with Ambrosius and the smelly old druid man who had dressed her wound yet again. They had all come to the decision, as if it were theirs to make, that she could not possibly journey to Eborakon, or Eboracum as Ambrosius insisted on calling it, to join the fight against the Kaldi. Her arm was simply too much of a handicap, apparently.

After the druid had muttered his excuses and gone, Rozena reminded Emrys and Ambrosius how she had fought perfectly well with one hand to instigate their escape from Tarquinius.

'There were two men, and you had the element of surprise,' Ambrosius told her gently. 'I concede I was mightily impressed with your passion and your vigour with a small blade, but—'

'But we're talking about a battle,' Emrys stated simply. 'Hundreds of men. Maybe more.'

She turned on him. 'And you? Are you battle ready? Really? Just because one of those brutes was clumsy enough to fall on your sword, you think you are suddenly this great warrior?'

It was unkind, and she knew well that Emrys had trained long and hard and impressed Viction with his natural ability. But still, being well trained and adept in single combat did not make him any more ready for pitch battle than she was. And they were right. Her left arm, savaged by the wolf, was still nothing short of useless. Only by some miracle had it

353

escaped infection. Ossian, the druid, had come at Ambrosius' behest, and had smeared another foul-smelling unguent on her scarred flesh. It was healing, he had told her, but would never be as it was. She didn't take to the druid at all. He was cold and arrogant and seemed resentful at having to tend to her.

'I don't want to lose you.' Emrys put his hand on her good shoulder, and she could see in his eyes that he wanted to hold her, maybe even kiss her. 'I need you here when I return.'

She nodded, a frown still wrinkling her forehead, anger still rippling through her. Anger chiefly directed at Tarquinius. Her father's death was far from forgotten, but a more recent and more disgusting offence had supplanted it.

'I want Edoma to pay for what she did.' There was also the small matter of the Angle's betrayal. Emrys' face fell when she mentioned her. He perhaps had even more to avenge.

'Our fight is not with the Angles,' he said, his face stiffening when he saw her brow furrow further. 'But if I see her—'

'You must kill her. She murdered Krestell. And Carina.' Rozena felt a pang of guilt, knowing the names were like blades to Emrys. He winced when she said them.

'You just stay alive,' Ambrosius interrupted, beaming at Emrys. 'You are my son now, as Rozena is my daughter. I do not wish to lose either of you.'

The old man had indeed staked a parental claim on them both. Destitute after the loss of his own family to the pestilence, and indebted to them for his freedom, he had brought them before him the day before and expressed his desire to welcome them formally into his family. What that meant, she was not sure, but there was no denying the comfort that Ambrosius' villa provided.

'I would sooner you remained as well,' Ambrosius said to Emrys. 'I cannot say that I am an admirer of our high king, or a believer in the sincerity of his ambitions.'

'As far as I've heard, he wishes to unite the land,' Emrys replied. 'Surely that is what we all want?'

'Do you?' Ambrosius raised an eyebrow.

'I do.' came the firm response.

Ambrosius frowned slightly, shaking his head in bemusement. 'It is a noble cause, and one that I am surprised to see favoured by one so young. Perhaps you would do better than Vortigern, for I am sure your heart is purer than his.'

'What did he do to you that you doubt him so?'

The question surprised Ambrosius. 'Nothing, really. I mean, his dear wife and our druid friend saw no reason to help liberate me from my most recent predicament. For that, I have you both to thank. But your youth perhaps prohibits you from seeing the darker sides of people.'

'I think we have seen plenty of darkness,' Rozena interjected angrily. 'More than enough already.'

'Yes, yes, I know you have suffered,' Ambrosius blustered a little. 'Just believe me when I say that sometimes the worst men present the best intentions.'

'So, who are we to trust? You?' Rozena blurted.

'Ambrosius has little ill to gain from being kind to us,' Emrys said quietly.

'Not if we are as young and stupid as he says we are!'

'He's not the high king. He's taken us in, as Viction did.'

'As Edoma did to me.'

'Rozena!' Emrys gasped. 'It's not the same.'

Ambrosius held up his hands. 'It matters not,' he said emphatically. 'I do not ask you to fight for me or die for me. I do not crave power or recognition.'

Emrys sat quietly, pondering. 'I will still fight,' he said after a while. 'Whatever Vortigern desires for himself, I believe in the cause. I want to see peace and unity for our people. I want a land where we do not live in fear that strangers will come and burn our villages, murder parents and children, rape women—'

'Well, that's not going to happen,' Rozena spat bitterly, thinking of Tarquinius. 'You can't vanquish fear.'

Emrys nodded sadly. 'I can try,' he whispered.

* * *

He felt a wholly different man from the one that had left Viroconium beside his father three years previously. Then he had been ambitious. He had been in awe of his father. He had been loyal.

Vortimer glanced back over his shoulder at the rabble that followed him along the Roman road north, towards Deva and beyond. He was glad Zeki was there. His new companion, Pabo, rode beside him. Pabo was bedecked in his outmoded imperial finery, his bronze breastplate, and his crimson cloak. He managed to make it not look ridiculous, as if he were the only person in the land that could dress like that and get away with it. Zeki repaid Vortimer's look with a smile and a nod. There was no doubt the Ethiope, like Vortimer, was looking forward to an honest fight. Vortimer had lost any taste he might have had for ruling. Power was one thing, might in battle, victory over a worthy opponent. But three years of taking charge in Dumnonia had beaten any princely ambitions out of him. Let the likes of Erbin have that, he thought. Let the weak, the mousy, the scheming and manipulative ones do that business.

His apprenticeship in Dumnonia had changed him. He no longer revered his father, or even the idea of him. The notion that he had begun his campaign to assert himself as high king by murdering Custennin left Vortimer with a vile and bilious taste in his mouth. That Vortimer, a mere puppet in place of a first-born son, had been forced to endure the deaths of his wife and unborn son, all in the name of his father and of Albion, filled him with resentment. He hated his father. He felt used, a mere piece in a game, and he wanted no part of it.

And yet he was on his horse, armed and armoured, riding to join the swelling ranks of Britons who were loyal to this treacherous, self-appointed, high king. Vortimer allowed himself a wry smile, glancing to his left where the druid, Ossian, rode beside him. The old man was as bad as his father, a snake in the grass. He had transferred his loyalty when it suited and would no doubt do so again.

Ossian's face was stony. He stared forwards, gently swaying with the movement of his mount. Vortimer thought that the old man, despite the fact his eyes were open and fixed on the horizon, was fast asleep. Perhaps he was in some meditative trance, seeking wisdom from some higher power ahead of the coming hostilities. Or maybe he was just an old fool, too tired to focus on what his horse was doing, vulnerable to anyone that doubted his station enough to attack him. One thing was for certain, Sevira had not been sad to see the back of the man.

Vortimer, by the time he had reached Viroconium after his long ride from Dumnonia, had realised the prospect of seeing his mother again was a far brighter one than that of renewing his jaded acquaintance with his estranged father. In that he had been, again, disappointed. She had made the right noises, said the right things, maybe even been happy to see him. She had embraced him, squeezing him so tightly that he imagined she knew, or could feel, everything that had befallen him in his time away. A tear had rolled down her pale cheek, left unchecked while she looked into his eyes and seemed to read his innermost thoughts.

Then she had pulled away, perhaps seeing something in him that he had barely even recognised himself. She was as lost to him as his father. Her partnership with the man he now resented so deeply coloured her with the same disdain. Worse; he felt nothing for her.

'Where's Pasha?' he had asked, far more interested in his sister.

'Gone,' she had replied, curtly. Wounded. Whether she was wounded by his tacit rejection of her affection, or the unexplained absence of her only daughter, he hadn't been sure.

And he had gone from her to prepare for yet another lengthy ride, a journey to his father's side. But he wasn't going because he believed in his father, or to support him in any way other than with a sword in his hand—for the fight was at least the only thing that made sense.

He wanted to be there when his father fell.

'Brother!'

A flurry of hooves. To Vortimer's right, Catigern appeared. He had insisted on coming too, and Zeki had nodded sagely when questioned about his abilities in a fight. Vortimer's little brother had grown up. Behind

357

him rode another youngster, one with which Catigern was already friendly, a quiet lad with striking golden eyes. Emrys. He made Vortimer uneasy. There was something about him.

'Vortimer,' Catigern hailed him again. 'We have a long ride ahead of us. I would love to hear some stories from your adventures in Dumnonia.'

'I bet you would, brother,' Vortimer smiled. Catigern was the one person, apart from Pasha, who he felt love for. 'What kind of story would you like?'

Catigern tugged at his reins and pulled his horse in step with Vortimer's. 'Battle. How was it facing the Hibernians? And women. I'd love to hear about the women.'

Vortimer grimaced. 'There are no happy endings with the latter, no stories I would tell, but we did have a few scraps on the beach. The Hibernians are a tough bunch.'

* * *

Emrys was becoming increasingly uneasy. Their meagre column of a few warriors, an old man, and some barely blooded teenagers was closing in on Mamucium. It seemed inevitable that they must pass by it to travel on towards Eborakon. And even with the presence of Vortimer, clearly accomplished in battle, and the formidable-looking Ethiope, Emrys did not believe that they could prevail against Tarquinius if the monstrous man confronted them.

'Having spoken to Ambrosius, who was also at the ogre's mercy, Tarquinius sounds like quite the beast,' Ossian muttered in affirmation of Emrys' plea to Vortimer. They had stopped for food and to let the horses rest, and Emrys had found himself unable to remain quiet. He had first confided in Catigern. Then, on his new friend's invitation, had presented his case to Vortimer himself.

'He is a head and shoulders taller than even you,' Emrys told Vortimer. 'And he is twice as broad.'

'Have you seen him fight, though?' Vortimer asked.

'Not as such.'

'I doubt a man who preys on weary travellers and old men has the courage, or skill, to stand in battle with someone who is likely to fight back. The man is clearly a coward, and I don't imagine he'll dare trouble us.' Ossian folded his arms across his chest smugly. 'He wouldn't dare attack Vortimer, son of Vortigern.'

Vortimer looked embarrassed. He waved aside the druid's platitudes. 'I think, more to the point,' he said slowly, 'this Tarquinius ought to be rounded up and forced to face the justice he has too long eluded. How many men had he?'

Emrys looked back at Vortimer. There was something in the man's eyes, something worn out and saddened. 'He didn't need many. We killed two. Maybe another four or five. And his mother.'

Vortimer forced a smile. 'Well, sometimes the mothers are the worst of all.' He placed a hand on Emrys' shoulder. 'But we'll spare her life at least.'

Under the Woad

Tugen had barely spoken in days. They had glumly and quietly made a decent pace southward along Dere Street. A road. Derelei took little time to marvel in its construction. Even way past its best, it was still something she had never seen before, an arrow-straight dark line across the landscape imbued with little more than an overbearing sense of destination.

'We must be near Eborakon now,' Tugen muttered, half to himself.

Derelei nodded. There was such little delight in journeys bound to a rocky path, a journey measured only by how much closer you were to where you were going.

'The Romans, and some Britons, call it Eboracum,' Tugen continued in a grim monotone. 'I'm sure your people, or whoever decides to ravage this land next, will call it something else in time.'

Zala's blood still stained Tugen. He wore it like a bitter memory, dried and darkly crusted across his clothing and his face. They had stopped to drink at a stream, and he had taken care to not wash away the crimson. But there was no evidence of bitterness towards Derelei. She had considered several times how remarkable it was that he didn't hold her responsible, purely because of her erstwhile kinship with Zala's killers. She wasn't sure she would have been so forgiving.

That was the only lightness in her heart as they continued down the road. She thought, as she had every day on this strange thoroughfare, that it was horribly uncomfortable to walk on those stones. She steered her pony along the edge of it where possible, letting its feet sink gently into softer ground. It was quieter and no doubt easier underfoot, even for a horse.

'My father told me that once these cobbles rang out with the feet of hundreds, thousands even, of Roman infantry.'

'Do you wish they were still here?'

Tugen shrugged. 'I don't care. I never knew them. I don't think my father did either. But maybe they'd be useful.'

'In stopping my people?'

'They kept your people away for centuries.'

'But they couldn't conquer them.' Derelei felt a pang of guilt, even though Tugen's tone wasn't remotely inflammatory. Instead, he was desperately stoic. Flat. Zala's death, and perhaps those of others before, had stripped him of the last vestiges of his humanity.

'They didn't need to,' he mumbled.

'Well, it might have been better if they had. For your people.' Derelei couldn't imagine there being enough men among the villages they had passed, in this empty countryside, to stop Drust and his army.

'My people are your people now.' Tugen's mouth curled up ever so slightly, the faintest hint of warmth. It was clearly the best he could muster, and Derelei was glad of it. She smiled back at him.

'Is that Eborakon?'

Columns of smoke dotted the horizon ahead. Small swirling skeins that, were they closer, would have spurred their appetites even more than the mere sight of them did. They were campfires, nothing sinister, and they spoke of a great many men gathered for one unquestionable purpose.

'I don't think so,' Tugen said as he leaned forward on his saddle, sniffing the air. 'But it will do.'

'It surely will. I'm starving.' Derelei kicked her beast into a trot.

'It's likely an army of Britons,' Tugen cautioned, matching her pace.

'Aye. And?'

'And you think you can just ride in there and ask for a leg of mutton?'

The thought of it alone had Derelei salivating. 'I do.'

'They might not be as understanding as Kiros.'

'Well, if this lot decide to tie me to a post,' Derelei grinned at Tugen, 'the least you can do this time is to cut me free, rather than waving a knife in my face.'

Suddenly more confident in her riding abilities, she spurred her mount on faster still.

* * *

The smells reached them first; warming aromas of hearty stews bubbling on dozens of campfires, the comforting tang in the air of rabbit flesh crisping slowly over flames. Sounds came next. Tugen heard the chatter of men, the scrape of metal, the excited whinnying of horses.

When they crested the shallow hill that afforded them a view of the assembled army, Tugen gasped. There were so many. He felt his mouth hang open and his pulse quicken with hope. The Kaldi might yet be stopped.

'There's not enough,' Derelei said plainly as she rode beside him towards the throng.

Tugen closed his mouth. It was true, the sight of the Kaldi approaching the fort had been an impossible sight. They were more than were here. And he knew well the ferocity the Kaldi brought to battle. He knew Derelei could match three men with ease. And, if the same could be said of all her kin, she was right. There weren't enough.

They approached and were greeted by half a dozen mounted men who rode out to meet them.

'Who commands here?' Derelei asked, sitting tall and unafraid on her horse.

The men laughed. Apparently, she and Tugen posed less of a threat than the men had previously thought.

'Who wants to know? A woman and a boy?' The lead rider guffawed. 'Fuck off and leave the men to their business. If you know what's good for you.'

Derelei was not intimidated. 'I want to know. I am Derelei of the Kaldi,

362

a Pict, a painted one, from north of the wall. And I would like to talk to whoever commands this rabble.'

Tugen looked down. It was a provocative thing to call the biggest army of Britons he imagined had been seen for centuries.

However, the Briton, who had until moments ago been grinning from ear to ruddy ear, fell quiet. Tugen peered up from under his lowered brow and saw that the men's faces were serious. They squinted at Derelei with renewed suspicion and could doubtless make out the traces of woad that patterned her face and arms.

'I have more on the rest of my body if any of you need to see.'

A couple of the men leered at the suggestion, toothless grins opening on their faces, but the man in charge held up his hand to stop any rumblings.

'We'll be sure to examine your corpse for further evidence. Are you sure you wish to claim this heritage?' His hand gripped the hilt of his sword at his side, and the other men followed suit.

Derelei laughed.

'She's niece to Drust of the Kaldi,' Tugen blurted out. 'Her uncle leads the attack.'

'What? Boy?' The Briton turned on Tugen. 'I'd be quiet if I were you, or you'll go the same way.'

'She has fought against her people already. And killed more of them than any of you have, I'd wager. She knows their ways. She is an asset.'

The man looked from Tugen to Derelei and stared, slack jawed, for a moment. Tugen allowed himself half a smile, certain that his powers of persuasion had triumphed.

'And I'm Julius fucking Caesar,' the man spat contemptuously. 'You're a spy, most like.'

'If she's a spy, what am I?' Tugen asked hurriedly.

'Fucked if I care, boy.' The man glanced sideways at his companions. 'Shall we have some sport, boys? She's a fine-looking woman, Pict or not.'

Tugen heard the scrape of Derelei's sword being pulled free. She was still on her horse, which didn't bode well. Even Tugen knew the value of combat on horseback was most felt at full tilt, at a bone crushing gallop

363

where hooves could kill as readily as blades. He pulled back on his reins and encouraged his horse backwards.

Derelei went the other way. She rode towards the men. There was no time to raise a canter, let alone a gallop. But she urged her beast towards the men, sword held at arm's length to her side, a fierce look in her eye.

'How many of you need to die before I get to see your commander?' She flashed her dark eyes from man to man and was answered with half a dozen blades being drawn. 'Surely not all of you? So be it.'

With a deftness that surprised Tugen, Derelei was more capable and confident on her horse than any of the men were on theirs. Accustomed, as they would have been, to riding at full pace into a fray, their horses fretted. Their hooves tore at the soft earth while their riders were intent on finding balance and knowing where best to hold their swords. Derelei, a novice rider, stalked towards them with unerring clarity. It was then that Tugen realised that all the time on the road southwards when he had assumed she was slumped in her saddle, muttering to herself, Derelei had been talking to her horse. She had been bonding. She was a natural.

The leader of the men swung his blade clumsily in Derelei's direction as she walked her horse towards him. It was as if time had slowed down. She fended off one errant swing of his blade with her own, ducked a second, then deftly cut the straps from under his horse. He slid quickly towards the ground, in grave danger of being trampled by his own mount.

A second man had cajoled his horse into sword range from Derelei, but found himself with his off-hand closer to her than his sword-hand. Derelei leaned towards him and simply pushed him, with the back of her sword hand, sprawling onto the ground near his comrade. The other four, believing they might fare better on foot, quickly dismounted, and formed an arc around Derelei and her horse.

With a skill Tugen could barely believe, Derelei caused her animal to rear up, hooves flying in the faces of the advancing men. One was unfortunate enough to get his head in the way of a hoof and collapsed to the ground with blood pouring from his temple. The other three, increasingly uncertain of themselves, watched Derelei perform a tight pirouette on her horse.

One of them, quick enough at least to raise his sword in defence, had his blade shattered as she swung the Kaldi chief's prized sword in a vicious downward arc. Another nearly lost an arm as her blade bit into his shoulder. The third dropped his weapon and scuttled backwards out of range.

'Who commands here?' Derelei asked again.

'I'll present you,' said the first of the men, the leader, now on his feet again and with his hands outstretched in submission. 'We're all friends here.'

Derelei, who still had her sword primed, levelled at his chest, nodded with a grin. 'What do you call this place?' she asked.

'Isurium Brigantum,' the man mumbled.

* * *

In Selwyn's assessment, it was as good a place as any for Vortigern's army to assemble in the face of the oncoming Picts. Isurium, at the convergence of Dere Street and Watling Street, had been quite the fortress in its time. It was facing dereliction, but was still mercifully intact in parts. The northern facing wall was high and solid, with a deep bank and further tricky ditches at its feet. Several stone bastions, though crumbling in places, would still provide archers a superb vantage point over any assailing force. The villas of the town were in decent shape, sporting crude but still impressive mosaics of the foundation of Rome. The one set aside for Vortigern, when he arrived, had presentable representations of Romulus and Remus themselves, interacting with the famous she-wolf.

The infamous Ninth legion had barracked in Isurium before their fateful march north of the wall, and the irony that one of Rome's most reputed units had called this place home before supposedly falling foul to the Picts in the north was not lost on Selwyn. This is where the Picts would come to them. This was his chance to do better than the Ninth. Either that or they'd be destroyed and all everyone would still talk about for centuries to come would be the legion that was lost beyond the wall.

For the time being, cruel destiny aside, there was still talk of the heroic

365

Ninth. Some talked gamely, desperate to emulate some of the military greatness of Rome, keen to remind the Picts that their place was far to the north. Even those least sympathetic to Roman heritage still wanted to believe that this band of men could do what the legions could not. Prevail against the painted people.

Selwyn, commanding from an adjoining building to the villa reserved for Vortigern, was happy for his men to find morale wherever they could. He had never been in command of so many men in all his years, but was determined not to let anyone see how nervous that made him feel. It wasn't a matter of numbers. Men who shared a mission, a goal, were the same if they were ten or a hundred. The difficulty he recognised with this assembly of tribes was that there wasn't necessarily a perfect uniformity to the mission. There was enmity amongst the ranks already, and it felt like violence could break out at any minute without a single Pict in sight.

And then they brought her to him.

A Pictish woman. A Kaldi warrior. Her beauty struck him before he even noticed the faded outline of the woad on her face. Her dark eyes, mounted on sharp, pale, cheek bones, fixed on him with a haughty confidence that took his breath away.

'Who are you?' he asked simply, not knowing what else to say. He had already heard how she had taken on half a dozen of his men and, oddly, left them all alive. It was clear she could have slain them all in a heartbeat. Drust was her uncle, or so someone had whispered in his ear. But all he wanted to know was who she was.

'I am Derelei of the Kaldi, and my sword is yours to command.' She lowered her eyes respectfully. 'For now, at least.'

'For now?'

'I wish to aid your cause to destroy the Kaldi.'

'Destroy?' The sheer presence of the woman made it impossible for Selwyn to string more than a couple of words together. She was beautiful and terrifying at the same time. Purely from the way she held herself, he could tell that she was as strong as any man that fought for him, and likely as skilled with her sword as any man he'd known. He marvelled that his patrol had been foolish enough to engage her in combat, presumably with some sordid intent in mind. He smiled to himself at that folly, happy that she had humiliated them rather than slaughter them, and wished he could have seen her in action.

'I want only to end the life of my uncle, who it just so happens is leading the seven kingdoms here with every intention of killing every last Briton he sees.' She paused, frowning at Selwyn. 'Do I amuse you?' she asked provocatively.

'I mean no disrespect.' Selwyn held his hand up submissively, half expecting her to fight him bare-fisted. She had at least surrendered her weapons before being admitted to him. 'It's just I don't mind saying I have never seen a woman so impressive.'

Derelei relaxed slightly. Her shoulders dropped, but still she did not smile. 'Your women do not fight,' she stated.

'No, they do not.' Selwyn held his smile, more nervous than before.

'Your men would do well not to smile at a woman who can fight. Many of them will be cut down by the blades of Kaldi women in the coming battle. Dying with a smile on your face is still dying.'

Selwyn nodded gravely; his smile vanished. 'Well said, Derelei. I would welcome your counsel on how to avoid those numbers being sufficient to lose us the battle. Are all your kind as accomplished as you?'

It was Derelei's turn to smile. 'Not that you know of my accomplishments beyond chastening a handful of your dogs, but no, they are not all as experienced in combat as me.'

'Well, that's something.' Selwyn sighed, happy to have provoked amusement in Derelei.

'But even the least skilled of them is still worth two of yours.'

Selwyn looked at Derelei, searching her dark, unwavering eyes. He felt her staring back into him and, for a whimsical moment, hoped that she liked what she saw as much as he did. 'That's some fearsome propaganda. Let us hope it's not entirely true.'

Derelei kept looking at him. She held his eyes for so long that he had to look away.

'And where would you fight? It hardly needs saying that many here would feel uneasy with you by their side.'

'I will fight beside you, my lord,' Derelei said quietly, 'as I imagine you lead from the front. And that is where I want to be.'

Selwyn felt a flush of excitement that surprised him, a strange bloodlust mixed with desire that could only be described as sexual. He didn't know what to say. He didn't know what he wanted more; to fight beside this woman or lie with her. Perhaps only both would be enough. And there was something in her eyes that suggested she felt the same intangible quandary. He checked himself. There was no reason for her to feel that way. She was a savage from beyond the wall, an interloper, a refugee, a woman driven by vengeance, a potent warrior who was also strikingly beautiful.

The urgent entrance of a messenger interrupted Selwyn's inner torment. 'My lord, High King Vortigern approaches.'

In the Open

The fort at Mamucium sat on a sandstone ridge that fell away quickly towards the river beneath. Roots of the trees appeared as clawed hands desperately clinging to the reddish soil of the steep bluff. The river itself, along with its precipitous bank, formed a perfect defence to the west. Vortimer led his small band of men in from the south, along the Roman road, where the incline was gentler. What had once been turf and timber ramparts, bolstered with stone from the moors to the east, were now little more than earthwork slopes. Some of the original stones were visible, but the rest had surrendered to the gradual egress of soil and the growth of long grass and wildflowers. It was less than imposing.

There was no obvious sign of habitation. Vortimer glanced back at Emrys, whose countenance was pale.

'Once again, Vortimer,' began Ossian sternly, 'my best counsel is to ride around and past this place. Why look for fights where there is no need?'

'But there is a need, Ossian.' Vortimer looked at the druid grimly. 'This Tarquinius is clearly a monster that needs to be dealt with, for the good of all.'

'Well, it doesn't look like he's even here,' Ossian muttered, probably hopefully.

Vortimer had little respect for the old man. If indeed he was possessed of arcane powers, as druids were supposed to be, it was less than obvious. It was more likely that he had lived for as long as he had by transferring his loyalty to whoever wielded the biggest stick, that his greatest wisdom lay in his ability to jump from a sinking ship, and in his years of abject sycophancy veiled by a carefully constructed mystique.

Anyway, Vortimer craved a fight. If his desire for violence could serve some honourable purpose, such as delivering justice to Rozena, then that was justification enough for this incursion. He had seen the pain on Emrys' face when he talked about her and what had happened here. Vortimer couldn't help but think of Lamorna and Joceline. He had loved both women, both in different ways. Sharp memories of each clawed at him from the inside. He felt shame. He felt guilt. He felt the need to counter his previous failures with a magnanimous deed that might better the life of an innocent girl, or at least bring her some little peace in the aftermath of her trauma. And he felt the overwhelming desire to punish a crime; if it could not be his own, then Tarquinius would pay the price for now.

They paused outside the gate and dismounted. Vortimer kept Zeki close to him, instructing Pabo to bring up the rear in case of a surprise attack. Ossian fell back to stand beside the tall man in his bronze breastplate, clearly anxious.

'Catigern and Emrys, you remain in the rear-guard as well.'

Catigern's face fell. He was seventeen, but untested in combat. Vortimer wanted him to remain safe.

'I need my best two men to make sure Ossian is unharmed. My father would not thank me if anything happened to his druid.'

That placated his younger brother. Vortimer nodded to Zeki, and they led the way through the gates. Three other youngsters recruited from Viroconium followed. Carian and Derfel, maybe eighteen years old, dark and swarthy Powys men, had practically begged for a chance to serve with the high king. Jodoc, quieter, a handsome young man with a fairer colouring, drew his sword with an air of nervous excitement.

Inside the wall the ground was flat, littered with the odd stone, and overgrown. A huddle of huts, bearing little resemblance to anything Roman, occupied a corner of what was close to a large square of land. Other more derelict buildings, fashioned from the same stone that had adorned the turf ramparts, lined the far wall. The perimeter was at its loftiest on the western side, where the ground fell away towards the river.

On open ground, Zeki instinctively flanked Vortimer, moving to his left. Derfel and Jodoc fanned out to his right while Carian followed behind him. The others formed a vague arc around the old man to the rear.

'There's nobody here,' Ossian hissed. And maybe the druid was correct. There was no immediate evidence of recent fires, no smell or sound of human occupation. The ground was untroubled even by horses' hooves. Vortimer wondered if the boy might have imagined the whole sorry story.

'Emrys.' Vortimer turned to face the boy, who looked nervously around him over his drawn sword. 'Are you certain this is the right place?'

Emrys nodded gravely, with no hint of guile. If the boy's story was a fabrication, then he believed it. The rest of the men fanned out, and Vortimer watched Ossian bend over and examine something on the ground.

'What is it?'

Ossian stood. 'Part of a relief, a carving. I think we should leave now.'

Vortimer growled in disapproval. They were in an abandoned fort with no obvious threat. Why should a stone carving spook the druid? He marched over towards Ossian and looked at the ground. A slab lay in the long grass, a crude rendition of a man slaying a bull carved into its surface.

'Why does this concern you, druid?'

'You look but you don't see.' Ossian sighed impatiently. 'Don't you see how the grass and the weeds have been cut around the edge of this? It has been tended.'

Vortimer looked again. Ossian was right.

'Be alert, everyone,' he whispered, his hand gripping the hilt of his sword more firmly.

'That's not all,' Ossian murmured, standing tall and peering around, looking for something. 'Ah, here!' He scuttled off through a stone archway into a roofless building. 'It is as I thought.'

Vortimer followed the druid through the arch and found him standing at the top of some steps that lead down into the ground. 'A wine cellar?'

'Fool!' Ossian exclaimed bitterly. 'It is a temple. To Mithras.'

'And what? Why would a temple to a long-forgotten god concern us?'

Vortimer sneered. The followers of Mithras, a fearsome warrior born from rock, were as legendary now as the man himself. Vortimer had not even heard the name since he was a small boy. He didn't remember the particulars of their belief system, but he knew that members of this secretive cult had been greatly feared on the battlefield and beyond.

'You think they all went with the Romans?' Ossian asked. 'Why would they? The Romans followed their one God, the Christian God. Why would those that sought to revere Mithras not want to remain here and worship in peace, unchallenged by the Roman authorities? Yet again, Vortimer, my best counsel is that we leave this place at once.'

Vortimer scratched his chin, pondering the stairs. They descended into an oily darkness. If there was anyone here at Mamucium, this is where they would be hiding.

'Light me a brand,' he instructed Zeki. 'Let's take a look inside.'

Ossian made some blustering noises of disapproval, but Vortimer was resolute.

Zeki made short thrift of producing a flame, and Vortimer was soon holding aloft a burning torch, its orange tongues fretted with black smoke from the oil. He led the way down into the retreating darkness.

It was only once he had found himself hidden from the daylight that he realised he hadn't specified anyone remain above ground to keep watch. He glanced at Zeki beside him. The Ethiope's dark face had taken on a glowing ochre hue in the torchlight. The flames danced in his gleaming eyes and, with a nod of the head, he let Vortimer know that he understood the oversight.

'You stay here, Zeki.' Pabo's soft voice rippled through the darkness a moment later. 'The stairs are narrow and slippery, and I'm not one for dark places. I will keep watch.'

Zeki returned to Vortimer's side, and the party descended further.

The stairs opened into a chamber that appeared to be carved from the stone itself. Vortimer passed the brand from his left to his right, looking around. The already reddish umber of the rock shone like wet blood where the light touched. The room they found themselves in was long, longer than the reach of the torch. Its ceiling was vaulted, with low benches lining the base of the longer sides. Strange markings had been etched into the stone walls.

'It's primitive, but it is most definitely a shrine to Mithras. Look at this carving.' Ossian breathed heavily as he scrabbled towards the wall, his hands tracing an image of two men eating. 'Mithras and the Sun god devour the flesh of the slain, now sacrificial, bull.'

Vortimer snorted contemptuously. 'And is that what they do down here? Do they aspire to be gods? Do they drink blood?'

Besides their hunger for self-righteous bloodshed, Vortimer knew nothing about the practices of devotees of Mithras. It had no place in Britannia any more than the Romans did, despite what Ossian claimed.

'The mysteries of Mithras are known only to his followers,' Ossian explained unhelpfully. 'I have gleaned what little I know from barely heard whispers on the wind.'

'If Tarquinius is such a man, and his men as well, then we should exercise caution.' Zeki spoke up. He spoke only when necessary, and Vortimer was cautious enough to listen to him.

'Well, there's nobody down here, anyway. And if there is, they can stay here. Let's go.'

* * *

Emrys, along with Catigern, emerged into daylight. The other younger men had exited the cave first and were standing around, curiously luxuriating in the sunshine. Emrys paused, immediately on edge, but moved forward to allow Ossian to bumble up into the light beside him.

'Where's Pabo?' Emrys asked to anyone who would listen.

Vortimer and Zeki appeared from the stairs. 'Pabo?' echoed the Ethiope.

Emrys noticed the wet red of fresh blood on the grass near where he was standing and quickly pointed it out to Vortimer, whose reaction was immediate.

'Defence!'

For a moment, as already drawn swords were raised, a shadow blotted out the sun. The more experienced men braced, their legs quickly finding firm purchase on the earth. Emrys noticed Derfel looking skyward, following the trajectory of whatever missile was incoming as it hurtled into their midst.

Zeki's cry of horror rang around the crumbling walls. Emrys, whose eyes were spotted from looking towards the sun, forced himself to focus on the spherical object that had landed damply on the ground nearby.

Pabo was no more. His dead eyes leered up at them all. Where the rest of him was, they could not yet tell. And there was no time to think about it.

The first spear struck Derfel, whose mouth was still agape in wonder, square in the back, and erupted from his chest. He teetered and fell, quite dead, and the rest of them spun around to face their attackers. Jodoc was the next to fall, another javelin piercing him through the neck as he turned. It had been hurled with such force that its trajectory was flat. Its fierce momentum carried it through Jodoc's neck such that almost half of the shaft emerged from the other side. Jodoc toppled over sideways, gravity seeing to it that he slid some way back down the length of the spear before he crumpled to the ground. A couple more spears flew wide of their marks.

Four men stood in a wide line with Tarquinius. All wore the same dark leather armour. All now had swords in hand. The four men, big and broad as they were, stood at least a head or two shorter and a good deal slighter than the bald-headed Tarquinius.

Zeki unleashed an anguished war cry and, for a moment, Emrys was sure he would charge right at the giant, but Vortimer intervened.

'Hold! Zeki, hold,' he barked. 'Catigern, see Ossian to safety. Now.'

'The postern.' Emrys waved his arms toward the corner behind them. 'It leads to the river.'

Catigern nodded, his training sufficient to quell any desire he had to stand and fight rather than be on protective duty. He ushered Ossian away from the fray.

And a fray it was.

The four black-leather clad men advanced ahead of Tarquinius, who was beaming with a perverse enjoyment of the unfolding drama. Zeki and Vortimer walked in unison towards them, legs moving in step and swords twitching with readiness. Carian hesitantly fell in to Zeki's left and Emrys hastened to join to the right of Vortimer.

He was suddenly quite afraid, calmed only by his own training. Viction had prepared him for this, warned him of how he must use his fear. He breathed as deeply as he could, sucking in the warm summer air and feeling it invigorate his brain at the same time as calming his nerves.

Zeki broke first, impatient, and apparently desperate to avenge Pabo as if he were his own brother. His blade flashed and whirled as he lay into the first of Tarquinius' men. The fury of his attack was such that he drew first blood quickly, before anyone else had even clashed blades. A second of the villains was upon him, and he parried two sets of well-aimed blows. As Carian joined him to help, Zeki had already run one of the enemy through. He pulled his blade free with a scream that sounded more anguish than victory.

Vortimer ran to attack a heartbeat after Zeki charged. And his swordsmanship was obvious immediately. Emrys watched in awe as the high king's first-born confidently took on the other two foes. His skill was apparently not unnoticed by his opponents, since one peeled off and made a beeline instead for Emrys.

As Vortimer's sword found the throat of the man he fought, and as he then squared up against the now advancing Tarquinius, Emrys crabbed around to give himself a better vantage point from which to begin his first authentic experience of battle. The ambush he and Rozena had exacted as part of their escape from this fort, terrifying as it had been, was not the same as this.

Somewhere in the back of his head, he heard the words he had told Rozena, words that Viction had drummed into him repeatedly so that, when the time came, he wouldn't need to hear them; he would just act. *Don't watch your opponent's blade. Don't watch his feet either. Watch his eyes. Maybe you'll see something in them that will tell you what he is going to do.*

Before he does it.

The sword came at him from above, a vicious downward scythe that was intended to throw Emrys off balance. Or split his skull in two, if he was too slow to parry it.

Emrys held his own blade horizontal above his head, stopping the attack. The crash of the two blades was deafening, far louder than he had ever heard in the ludus. His opponent was clearly stronger than him, so Emrys would have to be faster. He rolled out of the block, letting the other man's sword slide down the length of his rather than take all the impact. The man, stinking of fish and stale mead, was a foot taller than Emrys. Emrys' deliberate soft parry clearly took him aback, and he inadvertently followed his sword down towards the ground, momentarily losing balance.

Emrys darted to his side, trying to draw his blade across the fish-eater's stomach. The stiff leather armour did its job, though. The sword glanced off it, failing to penetrate the hide. And the man spun and found his balance again.

Worse still, Emrys had shifted his position. Where previously he had made sure the sun was behind him, hoping it would make things difficult for his opponent, now he had the glare in his eyes, and his opponent was little better than a silhouette. A silhouette that grew quickly larger as it neared again.

Next came a neck-high slash. Emrys ducked. Pure intuition, and perhaps a distant ingrained memory of training, led him to thrust forwards. His centre of balance was low, strengthening his position, and his blade held its course. It slid into the man's midriff, beneath his leather breastplate, finding soft flesh as the man moved forwards onto it.

The roar of pain brought with it even more malodour, which Emrys ignored as he spun out of reach of the angry riposte. Glancing down at the wound he had caused, Emrys saw he had not been as accurate as he forethought. He had wounded the man, sure, but his blade had merely cut deep into his side rather than pierced his gut. It was a serious enough wound, and it would slow the man down a bit, but it would not precipitate an end to the fight just yet.

The sound of ringing metal was everywhere. Emrys conscientiously focussed on the man and the sword in front of him, but in the briefest moment of respite, he noticed Vortimer backing away from a terrible onslaught from Tarquinius. The giant looked unbeatable. Surely not even Vortimer could repel that attack.

Emrys rounded again on the man trying to kill him. Blood now poured from the man's middle, and his actions were slower. Again, the sun was in Emrys' eyes and the man came at him, lurching out of the light. Emrys held up his sword in front of his face and caught the rays of the sun. The silhouette changed at that moment. As the reflected sun hit the man's face, illuminating his blood-spattered beard, Emrys could make out his eyes. They, like any good swordsman's, were not fixed on Emrys' blade, but on his open right flank. The man spun, unleashing a mighty cleave with all the strength probably left available to him; enough to cut Emrys in half at the waist.

Emrys couldn't duck the blow. He couldn't jump it. He surely didn't have time to bring his sword across in defence against it. But he knew where it was aimed. So, he fell backwards. He threw himself back and down and out of the lethal path of the heavy sword. It whispered above his falling head by the merest of inches, but that was all Emrys needed.

Such a blow is pure attack. There can be no quick recovery if it fails. Sure enough, the black-armoured fish-eater was suddenly well off balance. Emrys had only to brace himself against the ground and thrust upward.

This time, his aim was true. His sword ripped through the leather into the man's rib cage and burst out of his back. Emrys rolled away—keen not to be underneath the man when he fell—and tugged his sword free.

He had fought. He had won. Exhilarated, Emrys clambered to his feet and looked around. Vortimer was desperately fending off a flurry of attacks from Tarquinius. He staggered backwards, unable to maintain his footing, and fell. The gigantic man pressed his advantage and raised his blade with a horrible sense of finality.

Zeki, who was in the process of pulling his own sword free from the last of the henchmen, leapt to Vortimer's defence, forcing Tarquinius to turn on him rather than finish off Vortimer. He did so with a frightening power, his weapon clattering against Zeki's and sending the Ethiope sprawling to the ground as well. Tarquinius, clearly happy to have swatted Zeki aside, turned back to Vortimer.

'Tarquinius! Look here.'

The shout was loud enough to stop Tarquinius in his tracks. Something in the tone of voice, Carian's voice, forced him to pause. Carian had found the crone, the giant's mother, and had her in his grasp. One of his hands pinned her arms behind her back, while his other held a short blade to her wrinkled neck.

Emrys couldn't see the expression on Tarquinius' face. There was no way of knowing how effective this scurrilous gesture would be. Given the brief respite, both Vortimer and Zeki began scrabbling to their feet as Tarquinius took a cautious step towards his mother and Carian.

Carian's knife pressed tighter against the woman's neck. The dusky youth had a jittery look in his eyes, like an untamed stallion. Dread was thick in Emrys' throat as Carian, with a grim smile on his face, wrenched his knife arm suddenly sideways. The crone's neck opened, and she fell forward onto the earth, twitching her last.

That brutal act proved too much for Tarquinius, who ran with a yell at Carian. The lad didn't stand a chance. His feeble parry could never be enough. Tarquinius' sword smashed through the smaller blade and cleaved downwards into Carian's skull.

Vortimer, recovered from the battering he had received, pulled the javelin free from Derfel, who lay dead nearby, and hurled it at Tarquinius. It caught him in his neck as he turned, eyes blazing, to wreak more havoc on those still alive. Zeki and Vortimer, like wolves closing in for the kill, rushed towards him. It surprised Emrys to see Tarquinius still had a good few swings of his sword left in him. He fought to the end, blood streaming from his neck, on his knees. Even knelt on the ground, he was nearly as tall as his assailants. But, flanked by the two experienced warriors, even he stood no chance. Despite nearly wounding Vortimer, Tarquinius finally fell to a well-aimed blow from Zeki.

His head, like Pabo's had been, was severed neatly from his body.

* * *

Catigern had missed the fight. Only when the last echoes of clashing steel had faded did he look back through the postern gate, with Ossian peering over his shoulder. The druid had been protected, and the fight was won. His brother was still standing.

But he was angry.

'What are we?' Vortimer roared. 'What are we that we slaughter women now?'

Catigern saw the corpse of the old woman, her neck open and still bleeding. Beside her, Carian lay in a sprawled mess, his head split open.

'Carian has already answered for his actions,' Zeki muttered.

'Never mind all that!' Ossian ignored Zeki and stormed confidently past Catigern. 'We have just lost three good young men. And you are bleeding.'

Vortimer was. His arm was cut. He shrugged. 'I'll live.'

'But Jodoc doesn't. Derfel doesn't. Carian—'

'Carian paid the price for saving my life in the worst possible way. I despise what he did,' Vortimer interrupted the druid, 'but, thankfully, the brute is dead.'

The great hulk of Tarquinius' body lay in the reddened grass. His head lay beside him.

'Your father would not have risked his men to avenge the mistreatment of a girl,' Ossian continued.

Vortimer glared at the druid. 'No, of that I have no doubt. And I am happy to say I am not my father. And it has not been a waste. Emrys has proved himself an able warrior. What do you think, boy, has justice been done?'

Emrys, who had been standing a little further away, walked into the circle of men that now stood around the giant corpse. Catigern, noting that his new friend was mired with blood but apparently unhurt, felt a twinge of jealousy. He wished he had been given the chance to fight.

'Rozena would have rather dealt the killing blow herself,' Emrys said quietly, 'but I think she would be happy to see this monster prevented from causing harm to anyone else.'

Vortimer nodded gravely and pushed his way past Ossian. 'I need to wash my wound. Then we shall be on our way again.'

'I would like to bury Pabo,' Zeki said quietly.

The Wild

P asha had no idea where she was going. She had headed west from
Viroconium, on the old Roman road. It was the smallest of the
roads that emitted from her home-town and the least travelled.
The hills that rose on the horizon were the most obvious starting point for
her search. What she was searching for was also something of a mystery.
However, she was confident that, whatever it was, she'd know it when she
found it.

The weather had been kind to her. The nights had been warm and
the days dry. Ossian had at least taught her the best plants to forage
for sustenance. She had taken some provisions from Viroconium, but
they were already dwindling fast. The forest on the lower slopes of the
hills provided her with a full sack of berries, nuts and tubers that would
hopefully sustain her as she ascended. She had with her a small pot to
cook in, a flint to light a fire, and a decent knife that would cut most things
that needed cutting. She was otherwise unarmed, a fact that caused her
consternation as the way became steadily more rugged.

There was no great reason the terrain should make her any more
vulnerable to wild animals, or bandits, or anything or anyone else that
would wish her harm. None except that the further west and uphill she
went, the further she was from what she knew as civilisation. Not even the
Romans had bothered much with these parts, as far as she knew, so there
was every chance that bears, wolves, and even desperate men roamed the
hills.

Undeterred, she pressed on, finding the higher slopes even tougher going.

She came across bubbling streams, some too big to jump over. She stepped through them gingerly, marvelling at the shocking coldness of the water, wondering if she might learn to catch fish from them. She scrambled up slopes of scree, letting loose shards of shale and slate clatter and crack their way down the hill behind her. The noises of the breaking stone rattled their strange rhythms around the valley in percussive echoes.

Nearing what she had thought was a peak, she stopped for breath and a handful of berries. She took out her skin that she had filled with the cool water of one of the many streams she had traversed and gulped the liquid down.

There was something ominously familiar about the view, though she was sure she had never in her life been there before. She was above the trees now; her plan being to traverse the peaks of these hills and see what lay on the other side. Several bald summits surrounded her. She knew this landscape. Perhaps she had been here before. Perhaps her father had brought her here once on his horse when she was little. But no, she was certain she would have remembered that.

Frowning to herself, she looked southward, and her mouth fell open. There, on the top of the next hill, grew a solitary tree. She was far too far away to even try to identify what kind of tree it was, but she could tell that it grew at an odd angle, as if permanently bent by the winds that must often rage over this exposed ground.

She was certain she had seen that tree before.

In a dream.

She set off hurtling down the hill without even really thinking about why she was in such a hurry, nearly falling twice. Once she nearly got her foot caught in a rabbit hole, tripping over a concealed stone and tumbling forwards. She got up and dusted herself off, pausing briefly to notice the burrow and realised how much more painful the fall could have been. More watchful, but barely any less hurriedly, she continued her way and was soon climbing again, her eyes fixed on the twisted tree on the slope above her.

By the time she reached it, she was so filled with remembrance of her dream she half expected to see Catigern sitting at its base, pale and lifeless, impaled. But her brother was not there. Nobody was. It was just a crooked dead tree, its twisted branches dark against the white of the overcast sky. She slumped to the ground, breathless.

It was then that she noticed, among the unearthed roots, an opening. The tree clung to the rocky hillside against all odds. Its desperate limbs, starved of a decent depth of soil, had found a grip on the grey stone. She imagined the roots like fingers of a clenched fist, grasping at the skin of the mountain. And there, beneath and amongst those roots, framed with the dour roughness of the granite, was a portal. A doorway to another world, perhaps.

The more cautious part of her brain acknowledged that it was merely a cave, likely enough a den to some animal that she would be better off avoiding. A bear might live in such a hole, she thought. Or a mean solitary wolf, shunned by its pack and hungry in its isolation.

She entered the cave.

The entrance, big enough to admit a man bigger than her—so feasibly a bear—led to a passageway in which she could easily stand. The rock jagged at her on both sides, and she felt her way in the growing darkness, curious to see how far the light from without would reach. After several steps, however, the roof sloped downwards, and it forced her to crouch. Suspecting that she had reached the limits of the cave, she readied herself to return to the daylight. But as the sun ceased to assist her view of the interior, she noticed a pale yellow glow in the gloom.

Fumbling, she felt her way forwards more, and saw that a narrower shaft led deeper into the mountain, and the dull light she could see came from within.

She pressed on.

She had to crawl. Vaguely aware that crawling backwards might prove harder, she contemplated just how far she should proceed. She was just about to stop and commence a slow feet-first wriggle when the tunnel opened suddenly into a chamber. She bustled her way forward and could soon stand. And see. The rock walls glowed with a strange insipid light, illuminating the room.

For a room, it was. Notwithstanding the shallow pool of water along one wall that reflected the points of strange light, there was evidence not of beast but of man. Dry straw lay spread out in the unmistakable shape of a bed. The air was dank, heavy in her lungs. The light was enough to make out the bedding, and a cup, and an animal skin. She strained her eyes to see what else would yield a clue as to who lived there.

But she did not need to decipher the mystery. The mystery revealed itself.

A scuttling sound made her start, and she spun on her feet. The dampness of the smooth stone was enough to cause her to slip and fall painfully onto her back.

No animal rushed to attack. No spiders or beetles or rats scurried over her prone figure. Instead, a face appeared above hers. A man, leaning over her. Filthy, matted hair fell to either side of his bearded face. His eyes, bright and wide, looked as if they belonged in a younger face than the one leering at her.

'Pasha.' He called her by name.

She backed away from him as best she could, pushing herself with her feet along the cave floor and up against the clammy wall.

He stood over her. Unabashedly as naked as the day he was born.

'Who are you?'

'I was wondering when you would come.' He ignored her question and pulled at his dirty beard while he looked at her. 'You should go home. There's nothing good here for you.'

It wasn't a threat. He said it so matter-of-factly.

'Why?'

'The bear is coming,' he answered idly, scratching a buttock.

She looked around wildly, wondering if this was indeed a bear's den, wondering why he would be here if it were.

'Not a bear,' he tutted. 'The bear. Never mind. You dreamed about me, yes?'

Yes. He had been on the mountainside, leaping from corpse to corpse, laughing.

'You made noises like a raven.'

'How lovely. Yes, that was probably me.' The man squatted in front of her, looking her in the face with an intensity that made Pasha shrink back against the dank embrace of the stone behind her.

'How do you know about my dreams?'

'How do I know you've had them? Well, you're here, child. Isn't it obvious? Why else would you be here? Exactly here?'

'I—I don't know.'

'Well, think about it,' he snapped impatiently.

'And how do you know my name?'

The man, who she realised wasn't as old as he had first looked—in fact he perhaps wasn't that much older than she, under all the hair and the dirt—gave a chiming and quite musical laugh.

'Because I am naked, possibly mad, in a cave in the hills. You give me no credit for knowing what is afoot in this land. You don't imagine I couldn't know that your father is the self-proclaimed high king? Not the bear, mind you. Not by a long shot. You imagine I couldn't know that you have been wronged, that you want to understand who you are, that you are meant for better things than the wastrel who pretends to rebuild Albion?'

Pasha stared at the man, open-mouthed.

'You think I have always been up here, dirty, and alone? You don't imagine for a moment that I might have been driven to this. What could I possibly know of the Laigin, of Lorcan, of Loegaire, son of Niall of the Nine Hostages and king of Tara? I'll tell you what I know of them. They have sacked the place I call home, overrun it. Moridunum to you. Caerfyrddin to me, the most ancient settlement in Dyfed. Triffyn is dead and his son, Aergol, missing. I suppose that doesn't really answer your question, but it does pose a few more, doesn't it?'

Pasha nodded, dumbfounded.

'How could I possibly know all these things? More importantly, am I what you came looking for?'

Pasha continued nodding, certain of it. 'What is your name?' she asked.

The man smiled. 'I am Myrddin Willt. Just Myrddin really, but some folks added the Willt at some point not long ago. Shall we go out into the clear air and make a fire, Pasha? I promise to put some clothes on.'

And with that, he turned and scurried into the tunnel that led to daylight.

Sacred

Vortigern was in high spirits. It was good to be with his men again. With all the men. He had made haste to Isurium after meeting with Hengest and Hors, riding swiftly northwards with the two Nobatians. Selwyn had done well holding the fort and making the villa habitable. Isurium had seen better days, but it had the makings of an excellent defensive capability. Not that Vortigern had any intention of relying on it. His scouts had returned with news that the Kaldi masses, a fearsome multitude, were perilously nearby. Vortigern had already issued orders for the men to mobilise.

'I want to meet the Kaldi in open battle,' he announced to the gathered chieftains. Einion nodded enthusiastically. Elaf and Nudd, flanking the big man, smiled with approval. 'I have no interest in defending Isurium. I want to drive the savages back where they came from.'

'When can we expect the Jutes?' asked Appius nervously. He was a slight man, with a permanent nervous sneer plastered over his face. Vortigern sighed.

'Yes, when will they be here?' echoed Einion enthusiastically. 'I wish to share a drink with your man, Osric, before we fight.'

'Soon, I hope.' Vortigern had sent a wary Osric with the three galleys and the army of Jutes with the expectation that they would sail up the eastern coast and then make their way inland. In the absence of Sextus and Titus and their men, the Jutes would need to prove decisive in the imminent battle.

Selwyn, respectfully quiet beside Vortigern, spoke up. 'I have sent word to Leofric of the Angles to join us. I'm sure he will be here soon.'

'How are they integrating with our men?' Vortigern asked, avoiding Appius' rolling eyes.

'Quite well, actually. Surprisingly, perhaps.'

'In truth?'

Selwyn smiled slightly. 'In truth, the sooner we have a common enemy to fight, the better.'

Vortigern nodded. It was to be expected. Such a gathering of fighting men, from different parts of the country and beyond, was bound to be a fragile peace. Emotions were high. The lust for combat could only be tempered for so long.

'You have devised a defensive plan if we need one?'

'I have,' said Selwyn proudly. 'The bastions and the northern wall are solid and can be lined with archers and spearmen. I have had the men deepen the ditch and added sharpened stakes.'

'Fine. But we won't need all that, will we?' Vortigern rubbed his hands together confidently.

'Better to have and not need—'

'Than need and not have. Quite. We cannot fail.' Vortigern beamed at the men seated around him. 'This is where we lay the foundations for our new Albion.'

It was at that moment that Vortimer and Ossian appeared.

'Father,' Vortimer called out. And Vortigern leapt to his feet, a broad smile spreading across his face.

'My son,' he exclaimed, rushing forwards to clasp the outstretched hand. 'How is it that you are here? And with Ossian too.' Then he waved his own words aside. 'It matters not. My heart swells and I am grateful.'

'As does mine,' Vortimer said with a forced smile. 'It has been quite an adventure already.'

'And you will tell me all about it tonight. About everything. I am grateful that you have torn yourself away from your wife to be by my side for this great battle.'

He turned to Ossian.

'Well met, old friend. We have need of you here.'

'Indeed.' Ossian bowed his head solemnly. 'It is the eve of a new dawn—'

'Catigern is outside,' Vortimer interrupted.

'Catigern? Here?'

Vortigern's heart quickened. His youngest boy was here, Catigern, barely a man. The thought of losing him in battle scared Vortigern, but the prospect of seeing him filled him with joy.

'Bring him in. Fetch him here.'

* * *

The ride from Mamucium to Isurium had been a considerably easier journey than the last time Emrys had travelled that way, albeit in the reverse direction. They followed the road that he and Rozena had not known about, avoiding the upper reaches of the spine of hills that separated the two places. The weather was fairer too, which helped. And Emrys carried with him a sense of satisfaction at his handling of the combat they had endured against Tarquinius and his men. He felt relief that justice, rather than vengeance, had been done—though if asked what the difference between the two was, he might have failed to offer a convincing answer.

By the time they had found the vast encampment within and without the walls of Isurium, Emrys was certain he was in the right place. It was time to stand with his king, to protect his people, to repel the invading Kaldi. It was time, perhaps, to mete out some of that same justice on the people that had—so long ago—uprooted him from his happy family life in Bernaccia.

Catigern stood beside him, stroking the nose of his horse.

'Why did you not go in with your brother?' Emrys asked him. Zeki, too, had remained outside, but had gone in search of a place to empty his bowels after the long ride.

Catigern shrugged. 'I'm the youngest. It isn't my place.'

'But he's your father.'

'I know.'

Catigern didn't appear troubled, so Emrys shrugged too.

'Do you miss her?' Catigern asked. 'This girl you so passionately fought for.'

'Rozena.' Emrys never tired of saying her name out loud. 'I do. Always.'

'She must be quite special.'

Emrys nodded, opening his mouth in readiness to talk about her at some length. His words stopped in his throat, as he saw the Angles approaching.

It was Edoma. That's what Rozena had said her name was. He could never have forgotten that face. And beside her was her brother, Wine. Emrys felt his heart race, heard the dull roar of his own blood in his ears. His peripheral vision darkened as he glared at them. Because of them, Viction, Krestell and Carina were dead. Slaughtered. Because of them, he and Rozena had fled into the mountains where they had been savaged by wolves and, worse, abused by the now dead Tarquinius. Seeing them brought visions of Rozena to mind. He saw her shredded arm, saw the blood that ran down her leg after Tarquinius had used her, heard the pain in her voice when she tried not to cry. Edoma and Wine. They had taken too much from him.

'What is it?' Catigern hissed next to him, his voice barely penetrating the pounding in his head.

'The Angles.'

'The Angles?'

'Yes.'

He had told Catigern the story, and Catigern had been disgusted. Appalled.

'Justice or vengeance?'

'What?' Emrys couldn't think straight. These people were not friends, not allies. They were murderers. 'Justice,' he muttered.

'Quite.' Catigern drew his blade demonstrably and took several steps forward towards the approaching Angles. There was a third with them, an older man that Emrys did not recognise, a small distance behind.

'Cat!'

'Draw your sword, Emrys. I can't fight them alone.'

Emrys had no choice. He drew his sword, and this time the Angles took note. Edoma saw them first, recognising the challenge, and drew her own blade. Wine followed suit.

'The boy from the ludus,' Edoma exclaimed. 'So now you want to fight?'

Emrys found his tongue. 'I should have fought you before. Had I known the depths of your murderous depravity, I would have.'

'You found the girl, then?'

Carina. Gutted by the Angle bitch. Sweet Carina. He could have loved her. He did love her. He almost lost Rozena because of her. She had not deserved the fate she was dealt.

Catigern was tossing his blade from hand to hand, eager to show off the skills he had learned. He threw a toothy grin in Emrys' direction, encouraging him.

'Where's Rozena?' Edoma asked, walking towards them threateningly.

'You don't get to mention her name,' Emrys answered, walking to meet her, standing shoulder to shoulder with Catigern.

And then they were on them. Edoma came at Emrys with a snarl. He fended off her first attack easily. Wine, slower than his sister, made an ineffectual advance on Catigern, who immediately parried and drew blood with a quick thrust. Wine squealed in pain, blood wetting the upper arm of his tunic.

'Hold! Hold!' A deep voice erupted from behind Edoma and Wine, who had raised his guard again. The third Angle hurried towards them, bellowing. 'Lower your swords. Edoma! Wine!'

Edoma and her brother exchanged glances and backed away a couple of steps, swords still raised. Catigern cared little for their clear retreat and pressed for advantage. He slashed at Wine again, knocking the blade from his hand.

'Catigern!'

Vortimer had emerged from the villa and seen the fight. Zeki appeared from around a corner, hurriedly dressing himself and fumbling for his weapon.

'Catigern, these are our allies,' Vortimer called out, his hand resting uncertainly on the hilt of his own sword. It wasn't clear that he believed the words he spoke.

Catigern stepped back too, and for a moment everyone gathered their breaths. The older Angle, his face scarlet with fury above an impressive blonde beard, fearlessly strode amongst the half-lowered swords. He batted Edoma's down and glared at her, then turned on Emrys and Catigern.

'Is this how your people repay us?'

Emrys frowned. As far as he knew, he owed nothing to this man.

'This woman,' he blurted out, pointing at Edoma, 'killed my friend, his wife, and his young daughter. In cold blood.'

Ossian appeared in the courtyard, immediately shrinking into the colonnade to watch from afar. Behind him, a large man, an older version of Vortimer, appeared. He looked angry.

'What is this? Leofric? What say you?'

'What say I, High King? Your brats attacked my people, unprovoked. And this woman, as this boy disrespectfully calls her, is Edoma, who I have recently taken as my wife. An attack on her is an attack on me.'

Emrys eyed the high king. This was Vortigern. This was the man they were all here to follow. This was the man that wanted to unite the land and bring peace to all.

'Well, one of these brats, as you call them, is my son,' Vortigern said levelly. 'And I heard this other young man accuse your wife of murder.'

'I've never seen this boy before,' Edoma blurted out.

'You lie!' Emrys turned towards her, shouting out indignantly. 'You murdered a child, a beautiful child, and her mother.'

'You are mistaken, boy,' Edoma spat at him.

'Silence.'

Leofric, leader of the Angles, stood tall, arms raised above his head, his face still burning with rage.

'I do not bow—we do not bow—to the laws of your people, Vortigern. It is not for some whippet, even one of your own blood, to draw a blade on my people with an unfounded accusation of crimes we do not even recognise. We offered our might to your cause out of friendship—'

'You trade your might, as you call it, for land, Leofric,' Vortigern interrupted. 'Nothing more.'

Leofric glared at Vortigern, his eyes popping.

'So let us put this aside and concentrate on the battle ahead.' Vortigern waved his hand indolently. 'If it pleases you, Leofric.'

'Father!' Vortimer still had his hand on his hilt. 'If this woman, wife of a chieftain or not, has wronged one of our people, we should hear more of it.'

Emrys held his breath, expectant.

'No, we should not, Vortimer,' the high king sighed. 'Catigern, come here to my side.'

Catigern scowled, looking first at Emrys, then at Vortimer, and finally at his father. His face fell. He backed away from the Angles with reluctant submission.

Emrys, crestfallen, exhaled noisily, then glared at Edoma. She would have to wait.

'You may count yourself lucky if we turn up for this battle of yours,' Leofric blustered. 'You have your conversations. We will have ours. Maybe we will fight. Maybe we won't. Maybe we will just come and mop up your blood after the painted people have defeated you.'

With that, the Angles turned around and walked away.

And Emrys turned to face his king.

* * *

It was a short enough walk from the walls of Isurium to the stones, but far enough that the clamour of Vortigern's combined forces was little more than a muted buzz on the wind.

Ossian was seeing them for the first time in over a decade, but little about or around them had changed. Five towering menhirs, the tallest at least four times the height of a man, formed an almost perfect line across the countryside. The smallest had a slight lean, but the angle hadn't increased since Ossian had last seen it, so perhaps that was how it was supposed to be.

Legends told of a giant buried beneath the earth here, the tips of his stone-turned fingers all that remained visible above the grass and the soil. The detail of what might have caused his petrifaction escaped the stories Ossian had heard, but he gave such myth little credence. Other wild campfire tales decreed the obelisks to be shafts of great stone darts or spears. Many men, foolish and uneducated as they were, believed not just in one giant, but that this land had once been widely populated by such beings. So, if these were not fossilised digits of one such monstrosity, they were apparently relics of gigantic weapons; missiles hurled perhaps, or even arrows shot from enormous bows.

Ossian knew otherwise.

The stones were sacred, erected in a time long before the Romans, by druids. By his people. The stones, like him, had survived the Empire's grip and occupation; more than could be said for the rest of his people. Ossian, as far as he knew and was concerned, was the last of his kind. The last druid. The Romans had seen fit to slaughter the other wise men of this island. They could not tolerate a faith older and truer than their own, preferring instead to stir into the minds of people inflammatory propaganda, lies that spoke of human sacrifice, cannibalism, and devil worship. But devils were their faith's creation, their bugbear. At some point, the Romans had stopped believing in the old gods, their versions of them, and had spread the word of a single, solitary deity. In opposition to their creator and his angelic host were apparently legions of demons, devils, and horrid chthonic monsters whose only real purpose was to be to scare people into piety.

It was nonsensical. There was no reason, Ossian thought, why gods would behave like that. Like men. There seemed no reason to squabble and carp and vie for mortal spirits. The old gods were distinct, easy to understand.

Ossian walked swiftly between the stones, pausing to lay both hands on each of them. They hummed with ancient energy and power. In the face of the apparent growing dissent in the ranks of Vortigern's so-called army, it felt more important that Ossian do what he could to channel that energy and call upon the assistance of the old gods in the coming fight. He muttered prayers to Rudiobos, Smertrius and Belatucadros, gods of war, and to Belenus, the god of healing. They would need each one, especially if the hot headed Leofric made good on his threat to boycott the conflict.

The line of stones led to the banks of a river. Ossian knew that once this had been the site of blood sacrifice. Not human, as the Romans would have had people believe, but of sheep or goats, mostly. The river's murky slow depths told little of the animals that had bled here for sacred purpose. And the fields to the north, mused Ossian, fields which would soon be stained with the blood of Kaldi and of Britons, of Angles and Jutes, Nobatians, Saxons, and whoever else might fight and fall in this battle that might decide the future of Vortigern's Albion, would also devour the dead and drink their blood. And in time, nothing would scar the landscape and tell future generations of what occurred here. Nature would revive herself.

Only the stories of those that survive keep alive the memories of those that fall.

Ossian's part in all this was especially important. As a druid, only he could invoke the support of the gods. Only he could bless the men that would charge screaming towards the Kaldi. Only he might lend some healing to those that were injured. Only he could steer Vortigern towards his dream.

Towards Albion.

The Waves

Osric was no mariner. Despite his Jutish blood, he had been born in Britannia, and had avoided setting foot on any sea-going vessel. There was nothing sensible about floating on a changing expanse of freezing water with who-knew-what lurking underneath its surface. It was madness to don armour—even the simplest leather jerkin would hasten a man's descent in water—and carry heavy metal weapons on some wobbling boat. Especially in the absence of any ability to swim.

Osric wondered how many of these Jutes, his countrymen, could wriggle free of their fur and leather and iron rings if their ship listed too far. How many of them, like him, would have no clue how to stay afloat or swim to safety? Yet not one of them was remotely perturbed. They rowed with a garrulous vigour. The sail was up too, though they had not hoisted it for some time. Apparently, they had been too close to land. Only when the danger of hidden rocks became an issue had they ventured further from the coast and raised the flapping fabric. Yet still the Jutes rowed, adding what speed they could to the help provided by nature herself.

Hengest and Hors sat in the prow of the lead boat and grinned at Osric's unhappy face. Hengest had seemed mildly offended at Vortigern's suggestion that Osric accompany them on the boats. It wasn't a matter of not trusting the Jutish brothers and their galleys filled with fearsome warriors. Vortigern needed Osric to make sure they got to the battle. Osric knew the lie of the land. Yet as much sense as Vortigern's plan made, Osric could barely hide his disappointment.

'You'll be fine, Osric,' Vortigern had told him with a firm slap on the back. 'Besides, you'll get to know your own people better. That might prove useful to me later.'

The constant rocking and listing amounted to perhaps the most unpleasant sensation Osric had ever felt. His stomach rolled with it, a tiny sea barrelling around inside him, threatening to surge forth at any moment. He barely resisted the constant urge to throw up.

'You should drink some mead, wolf.' Hors grinned, offering him a horn.

Osric held up his hand in refusal, feeling himself blanch even more. It was a terrible suggestion.

'More fool you. It helps.' Hors tipped most of the contents of the horn into his own mouth. As the boat lurched to the port side, a portion of it spattered down his knotted beard. Hors laughed and wiped at his chin with the back of his hand.

Hengest grinned and stood up to watch the waves being swallowed up by his ship. There was a fine drizzle in the air, and a swirling mist had dropped a veil over the barely visible land.

'If the sun doesn't come out soon, we won't have any idea where to land,' Hengest announced, unconcerned. Perhaps he was happy to put trust in some higher power.

Whatever faith the Jutish leader had in his gods was ill-placed. He had barely uttered those words when a wind picked up, lashing Osric's face with freezing spittle from the sea. His already frizzy beard quickly became wetter and colder. The drizzle thickened into heavy drops of rain that caught in the strengthening wind and stung his eyes. The sky up ahead grew dark. Black. The sea took on its colour, becoming a foreboding and churning darkness of fast-growing waves that surely threatened to overturn even the sturdiest of ships.

'Down sail,' Hengest shouted, and the oarsmen shelled their blades and hustled to lower the sheet. Osric, his knuckles white against the tar-black timber of the ship's side, looked back at the other two galleys. Their sails were rapidly lowered as well. Osric imagined the reluctant Egbin and his settlers enjoying this about as much as him, though Wulfric was doubtless in his element.

'What now?' Osric asked, not even trying to conceal the fear in his voice.

'Now we rely on the skill of our boat-makers,' Hengest grinned at him. Still unworried.

In the depths of the black clouds, a sharp prong of lightning flashed silently.

'Shouldn't we head towards land?' Osric shouted to the brothers.

Hors shook his head. 'We are safer here. We cannot risk being dashed against rocks.'

'This is madness!'

A sharp peal of thunder punctuated Osric's words. It was the loudest noise he thought he had ever heard. The resonant rumble rolled around them with the promise of nothing good.

'Curse you, Vortigern,' he muttered to himself.

War Cry

Some fleet-footed messenger had brought news to Drust. Good news. Brude had beached his boats before a storm had ravaged the coast, and his entire clan were hastening to join the fray. They were fed, watered, and more than ready to fight. Drust was in a fine mood.

Darlagh enjoyed his good humour as she reclined on the furs that they had just used as a bed. There was a degree of privacy, even if she cared little who saw her. Some helpful underlings had stretched some skins across a few hastily, but securely, erected poles, forming at least half a shelter. It was a screen behind which she had happily pleasured Drust. Both were daubed in woad, physically and mentally primed for combat. He sat beside her, his patterned chest heaving after his exertions, a broad grin on his face.

'Nothing like some vigorous fucking to get you in the mood,' he laughed, reaching for his cup.

'I am glad I please you,' Darlagh purred. She made no effort to cover herself. She was already painted from the waist up, anyway. Concentric circles of woad ringed her hardened nipples, and a whole panoply of blue beasts chased each other around her stomach and ribs, interspersed with spirals and other intricate shapes. Her face, like his, was also carefully adorned.

Drust emptied his cup and stood up with a satisfied grunt. 'You please me as well as any other woman.'

Darlagh wasn't certain he had meant that as a compliment, but she took it. She knew well how much passion he had shown for Modwen. The two of them had been friends, after a fashion, though Darlagh had always been jealous of Modwen. She had wanted to catch Drust's eye. She had wanted to be his first mistress. Aife, his wife, was crippled and old and useless and could surely not last many more winters. Drust had long needed the young blood, and Modwen had leapt at the chance.

But Modwen was dead now. And Darlagh, who had previously attached herself to Cailtram purely to remain in the frequent presence of their leader, had taken her friend's place. Cailtram, as sullen as ever, had not been best pleased. But he had said little, as was his way. And besides, he had no claim on her. They were not man and wife, and nor could they ever be. He was a druid. And druids did not take wives.

Darlagh stretched and held out her hand to take a cup of ale from Drust. He lowered himself beside her and watched her as she drank, then poured a little of the contents of his own cup over her breasts. The woad was set hard now and was untroubled by the liquid. Even the roughness of his tongue as he lapped at her cool, blued flesh would not disturb her battle canvas.

If Aife did die soon, Darlagh pondered, *Drust would look for a new wife. And if she could bear his child—*

'What are you plotting?' he asked her, his eyes wolfish in the firelight.

'I was imagining that maybe your seed has already taken hold in me.'

Drust laughed. It was a joyous laugh, as if the idea appealed to him. As it should. He had no children. One boy, she heard, had died young. A second had fallen in battle, barely a man. The line of succession came from Drust's mother, who had birthed two boys as well. In the absence of other females to continue the line, Drust had taken power. And, as Darlagh had heard it told, he had exiled his own brother across the sea for some unspoken crime. The banished brother was father to the now equally banished Derelei. Derelei. Darlagh didn't think the simple bitch had even realised that she, after her disgraced father, was next in line to succeed. Not that it mattered now. She was gone, likely dead.

'You'd love that.' Drust's eyes pierced her.

'I would.'

It wasn't customary for a Kaldi man to have an heir, but with nobody else—as far as Darlagh was aware—to continue the line from Drust and his mother, Darlagh thought it quite reasonable that she might be the person to establish a new line.

'And who would I fuck when you are fat with child?' Drust teased her.

'You think I could not please you with an enormous belly? You'll find me just as accommodating with my udders dragging on the ground.'

Drust licked his lips. She had him. His eyes were ablaze with lust, and she readied herself for him to launch himself at her again.

* * *

Cailtram found the stones with ease. The moon had colluded with him and stayed out just long enough for him to make out their towering shapes in the darkness, then slipped behind a dense bank of clouds to conceal his dangerous pilgrimage. He knew of the stones and had even visited them once before. The wall never really contained druids. He had always come and gone as he wished, not advertising his Kaldi heritage when abroad in the south. Knowing the Kaldi warriors were encamped not far from the ancient monoliths had thrilled him. It had been portentous, though he understood the Britons, camped even closer, would feel the same.

The shallow waters of the river flowed quietly between him and them. With the moon in retreat for now, the surface was dark and unwelcoming, but Cailtram was not deterred. He looked around him, checking again for any sign of patrols from the Britons, but saw nothing to cause alarm. Beyond the stones, the sky was stained a dirty orange from their fires and thick with smoke that carried with it the aromas of cooked meat. From what he had seen of their army, such that it was, the Britons were already outnumbered. With Brude's arrival from the east, victory was all but guaranteed.

Slipping into the cold water, Cailtram whispered his entreaties to Bridei, the mother goddess, ruler of rivers and wells. He cupped his hands as he waded waist deep through the gentle current, and cleansed his hair and his face, feeling Bridei's blessings upon him and his people. In the morning, before the battle, he would smear his long hair with the excrement of animals and expose his nakedness to the enemy. The gods of war would like that, but it was Bridei who would see them to victory. Of that, he was certain.

The stones, as he already knew, were great in stature, and impressively arranged in a line that climbed out of the river. But they were plain, untouched by chisels, just primitive bare rock. The stones the Kaldi had erected over the centuries, far to the north, were always intricately decorated, respectfully adorned with carvings, images that told stories of his people. How uncultured and basic these Britons were, he mused. How could they possibly hope to prevail? They had fallen to the Romans, and now they would fall to the Kaldi. Their women would become mothers to Kaldi warriors and poets and druids. Their youths would tend the land and the livestock the Kaldi way. Their men, their unimaginative simpleton men, would perish.

As Cailtram ran his hands over the surface of the largest stone, the moon threatened to break free from its nebulous constraints. A soft light fell over the rocks and over Cailtram's upturned face. It was time he returned to his people and readied himself for the next day.

The water was colder on his return crossing, and Cailtram quickened his pace back towards the Kaldi encampment, eager to warm himself beside a fire. He made straight for where he knew Drust was, to report on what he had seen of the enemy's inferior numbers.

Darlagh was there. She reclined on furs, unashamedly naked, unashamedly subjected to Drust's carnal whims. It was what she had always wanted, Cailtram realised, but he felt the sting of her treachery keenly.

'How many battles now, without defeat?' Cailtram asked Drust, trying to ignore Darlagh.

'Who's counting?' Drust grinned, offering the druid a draught of ale. 'Even before Brude's lot turn up, we will have them on the run.'

'Then we shall crush them once and for all.' Drust needed no boost to his confidence. He was clearly expecting nothing short of outright victory. 'It will be a great day for our people, Cailtram.'

'It will.' Cailtram glanced at Darlagh, who looked back at him with a smile. She didn't even seem remotely aware of her betrayal.

'You have my deepest thanks.' Drust put his hand on Cailtram's shoulder and looked earnestly into his eyes.

'I am merely a conduit,' Cailtram said quietly. 'The gods clearly already favour you. My closeness to them is a mere formality now.'

Drust nodded. Cailtram wasn't sure the ageing warrior even bothered believing in the gods. He practically thought himself one of them.

'Drink, druid. Empty your cup, for tomorrow we shall sip from the skull of a high king.' Drust bellowed with laughter at his ridiculous proposition, though Cailtram considered that if anyone would do such a thing, it would be Drust.

The ale slipped warmly into his belly, but its taste did not please Cailtram. Nothing would, while Darlagh lay there, flaunting herself.

'Does it bother you, me having her here?' Drust asked with rare concern. Cailtram shook his head. 'No,' he said. 'You have every entitlement.'

Drust's brow furrowed, reading the obvious lie. 'Darlagh, go and fetch some food for Cailtram. He is hungry.'

Darlagh nodded, with the faintest hint of resentment, and got to her feet.

'There is no need,' Cailtram objected dutifully.

'There is every need.' Drust waved Darlagh away. 'You are skin and bones, man. We have an arduous day ahead of us.'

Drust filled their cups again and slurped back the warm liquid. Cailtram held his ale between two hands, looking into its depths, aware that Drust was still watching him.

'You're a druid,' he began, 'but you can still be a man.'

Cailtram nodded, feeling his anger bubbling inside him. He wasn't angry at Drust. Not really. Drust had every right to do whatever he wished. He couldn't be challenged. Cailtram was untouchable, invaluable in his position as a druid. It was what it was.

He raised his cup to his lips and downed the ale in one long gulp, happily barely tasting its bitterness, then handed it back to Drust.

'I must go and ready myself for the morning, and for victory.'

Drust nodded quietly, and Cailtram slipped away from the furs and the fire and into the inky darkness of the night.

He found Darlagh easily. She was obediently carrying a smouldering rabbit carcass up the hill towards where Drust waited. She stopped when she saw him, surprise flashing briefly across her face.

'Thank you, Darlagh,' Cailtram said as he moved forward to relieve her of her the rabbit.

But he already had his short dagger in the palm of his hand.

The blade slid easily into her exposed stomach. It was a simple knife, without a hilt, and Cailtram thrust forward with such venom that it he thought his entire hand might follow the blade into her abdomen. Blood gushed over his wrist and Darlagh slumped forward into his arms. Her weight was a surprise, and he sank to his knees, lowering her with him.

'You will not be missed,' he told her bitterly.

Her dark eyes, wide in shock, were filled with tears. Her mouth moved, but no words escaped it.

'Not by Drust, and not by me.'

That was a lie. Cailtram felt, beneath his fading anger, the unmistakable pang of regret. He would miss her. He had loved her. But he had lost her. Drust had as good as blessed this brutal justice, so Cailtram feared no reprise. The battle would go ahead the next day, and Drust would emerge as the victor, champion of his people. Cailtram would remain at his side, his trusted druid.

'You would have made no difference to tomorrow's fight,' he told her as he watched the life ebb from her. 'You made no difference to Drust's life, or to mine, or to anyone's. You are nothing.'

She lifted a hand weakly, touching her palm to Cailtram's cheek, but he pulled away and stood up. She tried to crawl up the hill, as if she believed she still needed to return to Drust, and Cailtram's anger bubbled up again.

He stood over her and lifted her head by her hair, then drew his knife across her throat.

The blood sacrifice was complete.

At Sea

The bonfires stretched for as far as the eye could see. The sky was thick with smoke and song. Laughter born of apprehension carried through the night air to Emrys as he walked among the camp with Catigern. As impressive as the gathered throng of warriors was, he couldn't help but feel anxious about what the next morning would bring. If the enemy numbered as many as they, or more, the battle would be the bloodiest event he or anyone had witnessed.

Viction had prepared him for this.

'Single combat is what I can train you in,' the old warrior had said. 'Do not forget that even the biggest battle is just lots of single combats. You do your bit and trust your comrades to do theirs.'

But Viction had not faced the Kaldi. Every whisper about the painted people was hissed in awe and fear of their savage ferocity. When they swarmed towards them, how would Emrys pick out an opponent? And how would they fight?

'I just wish he wouldn't look down his nose at me.' Catigern was complaining about his father. After the narrowly avoided fight with Edoma and Wine, Vortigern had taken Emrys and Catigern aside and bombarded them with angry words.

'I don't expect mere boys to comprehend the delicate nature of diplomacy,' he had said pompously, glaring at them with controlled ire. 'I don't expect you to understand how difficult a task it is, has been, to unite this many diverse people in a common cause. But your petty squabble has potentially undermined everything I have done. You may well have

406

jeopardised the future of Albion. And for what?'

It had been a rhetorical question. Emrys had known that. But that didn't stop him trying to explain to his king how the Angles had murdered Carina and Krestell in cold blood.

Vortigern had waved his hand dismissively at that point. 'I've done plenty of bad things myself. We all have. It's who we are. Whatever that woman did, she will answer for it. But not now, and not by your hand.'

Catigern had objected briefly then, but Vortigern had silenced him with a withering look of disappointment. 'I hear you fight well, son,' he snapped, 'but there is still so much you need to learn about life.'

'What bad things have you done, Father?' Catigern had asked with a disrespectful tone.

'Nothing I care to reveal to you. But everything I do is designed to further the dream of peace and unity.'

'Like putting shit on a flower to help it grow.'

That had silenced Vortigern for a moment. He had looked at his son, then at Emrys. Then he waved them aside with an angry harrumph.

'I'm not sure he looks down his nose at you,' Emrys replied to his friend as they passed a group of men engaged in some kind of drinking game. 'I think you frighten him.'

Catigern laughed. 'I think it's you he is wary of.'

'I don't see why.'

'I do.' Catigern offered little more on the subject and left Emrys clueless as to what he meant.

More than anything, however, Emrys felt the weight of disappointment in his heart. His personal audience with the high king should have been one of awe and wonder. This Vortigern was determined, apparently, to unite the people and make Britannia—or Albion, as he kept calling it—powerful, safe, civilised, and free from marauding savages. Yet there was nothing genuinely noble about him. He was driven by something not too different from what had made a monster out of Tarquinius. Was he just ambitious, hungry for power, desperate for recognition and applause? Perhaps Emrys' ideas of what made an outstanding leader were just naïve and childish.

'Do you like your father?'

Catigern stopped walking and looked at him. 'He's never really bothered with me,' he said quietly. 'Vortimer is the oldest, and Father expects a lot from him. Pasha, our sister, is the favourite, but he's screwed that up.'

'How so?'

'She left. I think she wants to be a druid.'

'Like Ossian?'

'Let's hope not.' Catigern smiled.

'But he loves you,' Emrys pressed Catigern. 'I saw it in his eyes.'

'I suppose. You can't be disappointed in someone unless you love them.'

'I am disappointed in your father,' Emrys confessed, 'and I certainly don't love him.'

'But you love the idea of him.'

Emrys could see that Catigern shared his disappointment. He could also see that Catigern was saddened. He was about to offer some words of comfort when someone barrelled into his side and sent him sprawling to the ground.

Emrys twisted his body the instant he felt the impact, making sure that he fell on his side and could offer some resistance to his attacker. But, as he raised his clenched fists, both to guard against assault and to press an attack if he could, he caught sight of his assailant's face.

'Tugen?'

Tugen laughed. Dear Tugen.

'Sorry about that,' Tugen beamed. And then he was on his feet, hauling Emrys upright again and folding his arms around him in an embrace. Emrys had a flashing recollection of them playing with practice swords in the woods, of the bear that had so nearly killed them both.

'You always used to see me coming. What's wrong with you?'

'I wasn't expecting to see you,' Emrys said, laughing, as he stepped back from his old friend and looked him up and down. 'You've changed.'

'So have you. Still ugly though.' Tugen pointed at the scar on Emrys' cheek. 'Who's this?'

'Catigern, son of Vortigern.'

'The king?'

'The same.'

Tugen gave a low whistle. 'You've found yourself in fine company. Well met, Catigern.'

Catigern nodded at Tugen, still bemused at the manner of his appearance.

'And Rozena?'

'She lives. A great deal has happened.'

'Has it now?' Tugen grinned suggestively.

Emrys blushed. 'And that, yes.'

'We have a lot to talk about,' Tugen said, more seriously. 'But first, there's someone you need to meet.'

He didn't recognise her at first. As she walked towards them, tall and lithe, there was something familiar about her gait. She prowled like a cat. It was only when she was close by that he could see on her face the faded stains of woad that marked her as a Kaldi. As the only Kaldi he had ever seen that close before. Her. The woman who had saved his life. The woman whose people had slaughtered his family, Tugen's family, Rozena's family.

'I am Derelei,' she said quietly, her unwavering gaze fixed on Emrys' eyes. Then she lowered her chin, an unexpected gesture of respect, of submission. And Emrys realised she wished for his forgiveness.

* * *

The morning light came with a veil. A thin mist clung to the camp and across the landscape. Vortigern stood atop the walls, looking northward. He had been up for some time already. It had been a short night. He had spent much of it persuading Leofric to stand and fight beside him. The damage caused by the yellow-eyed lad had at least been mitigated.

The soft yellow glow of the sun through the mist brought back memories of those eyes. There was something about the boy that troubled Vortigern greatly. It was as if he possessed some quiet power, one perhaps unknown even to himself. Vortigern shivered, the hair on his arms standing. But this was no time for superstition. Ossian, standing to his left, provided enough of that.

Selwyn, as instructed, had reported to him before first light, bringing with him the Kaldi woman who wanted to stand with them against her kin. He had marvelled at her when he had set eyes on her. She was tall, as tall as he, and her limbs were long and strong. She held herself with confidence and a clear readiness. Standing quietly behind Selwyn, her dark eyes studying him intently.

'We are ready,' Selwyn offered curtly. 'To a man.'

'Good,' Vortigern stated as he peered into the shifting whiteness. 'Have Catigern fight close to Einion. It'll be the safest place for him. Vortimer will ride with me. When the Jutes attack from the east, we will ride in from the west and flank the Kaldi.'

'And if the Jutes do not show up?' Ossian interrupted, annoying Vortigern.

'They will.'

'Their ships may have been lost at sea. Anything is possible. Surely, we should hold the walls until we have word of them?'

Vortigern held up a hand to silence the druid. 'We have our cavalry. If the Jutes fail to appear in the east, we will just drive the Kaldi into the sea under our hooves. I suggest you ready yourself to bless the men, Ossian.'

The druid, his face shadowed, nodded, and made his way down from the parapet.

'Your name is Derelei?' Vortigern turned to the woman.

She nodded. 'Yes,' she offered quietly, 'and Drust is close kin to me.'

'I've heard. You vouch for this woman, Selwyn?'

Selwyn glanced at Derelei. 'I do. She bested one of my patrols without killing a single man.'

'We'd best hope that her skills are exemplary among her people then.'

'You should not underestimate them,' Derelei spoke up. 'Drust has never lost a battle.'

'I have heard this too. Will you help me?'

Derelei stepped forward. 'I will. I will find Drust, and I will kill him myself.'

'Wonderful,' Vortigern beamed. A wronged woman could be a powerful ally. 'I would have other help from you too. I need you to translate for me.'

There were certain formalities to a battle of this size. Druids on both sides would normally do their thing, cursing and blessing in alternate directions, imbuing the proceedings with a sense of supernatural foreboding. And the commanders, of which Vortigern as high king was one, would exchange a barrage of insults and threats. The idea was supposed to be that a significant level of intimidation might obviate the battle altogether. But that rarely happened.

'I hear you ride well,' Vortigern continued. 'Surprising for a Kaldi.'

'I am new to it, but I find I have ability.'

'Will you ride with us into battle?'

Derelei threw a sideways glance at Selwyn, who seemed to like the idea as well, and nodded enthusiastically.

'Excellent. That's settled then. Shall we mount up?'

* * *

It didn't take the sun long to burn off the fog. The swirling white vapour spiralled up into the clear sky, leaving the earth moist and ripe for a fight. Derelei rode behind Vortigern and Ossian, with Selwyn mounted beside her.

The line of Kaldi on the horizon was like nothing she had ever seen. It was a thin dark stain, a diseased vein that promised nothing but destruction. The Britons were surely outnumbered. By as much as half again. And Derelei knew well that, man to man—or woman—the Kaldi would be more fierce, more deadly, and more merciless than any of these unpainted Britons.

The four of them stopped their horses, more than a spear's throw from the quiet ranks of Kaldi. A naked man, more blue than white, bound forwards from the masses. Derelei knew it was Cailtram, though he was barely recognisable. He danced forwards, his muscular arms outstretched and his long legs kicking widely out to his sides. His long hair, no doubt fetid and slick with shit, spiked out from his head like a grotesque star. He jabbered curses at them and grabbed his cock and waved it at them, then turned and bent over and brandished his bare buttocks at them.

Derelei smirked. She wondered if the Britons, who did not know Cailtram, found his behaviour at all intimidating. She looked over at Ossian, wondering if the old man was preparing himself to shimmy out of his long robe and try to scare the Kaldi with his shrivelled nakedness. Of the four of them, only Ossian looked uneasy.

'Your turn, Ossian,' Vortigern said drily.

'This man is not a real druid,' Ossian muttered. 'I am the last of my kind.'

'Tell that to the Kaldi,' Vortigern replied.

'It is mere mummery.'

'It is spectacle, Ossian, and the Kaldi believe in it. So, we shall give them one. Fortunately, we have their chieftain's niece with us. That should be enough to rile them up.' Vortigern smiled over at Derelei, who replied with a solemn nod. She was ready.

Vortigern straightened up, getting as much height as he could on the back of the horse, and addressed the Kaldi.

'I am Vortigern, High King of the Britons, ruler of all Albion.' he began. 'You are not welcome here.'

Derelei translated.

'I invite you to crawl like the putrid vermin you are back beyond the great wall and hide in your little shit-daubed hovels. You are not welcome here.'

Derelei stood high on her horse, bellowing the king's words in the Kaldi tongue.

'And pray to whatever cow-fucking gods you bend to that I do not ride north to dig you out of your stinking holes and rip you all to pieces. You are not welcome here. This is my land. This is our land.' Vortigern held his arms out wide, his face turned up to the sky.

'You are not welcome here. And know this. Your chieftain's own niece is here beside me. She tells me that Drust is a stinking pile of pig shit who hasn't even managed to sire children. Is this who you would follow to your miserable deaths?'

Derelei delivered the insults with suitable aggression, thrilled at how her voice rang out in the still morning air. Drust would be listening, of that she was certain.

'Hear me now, Drust.' She added to Vortigern's words with her own. 'Today is the day I kill you. With your own sword. Vortigern may want you to flee, but I want you to fight. I shall look in your dying eyes before the sun goes down.'

She nodded at Vortigern, who looked pleased with himself.

'To the east, look,' said Selwyn, who had uttered nothing since they had ridden out.

The four of them looked eastward. The sun, still low in the sky, beamed warmly back at them. But there, against the glare, a host of men approached.

Vortigern snorted with laughter. 'See Drust, even the Jutes have come in search of your head.'

Derelei translated.

A deep laugh rang out from the Kaldi line.

'Look more closely, High King of the Britons, ruler of all Albion.'

It was Drust's voice.

'I see no Jutes,' Drust continued. 'Only my cousin, Brude, and scores more thirsty blades besides.'

His laughter was joined by that of several others, and soon it sounded like half the Kaldi were laughing at them. Vortigern's face fell. He looked, panicked, towards Selwyn, whose face was ashen. Derelei peered against the sunlight and realised that Drust was indeed correct.

'The Jutes must have perished already,' Ossian said with a quiver in his voice.

The Kaldi's raucous amusement subsided gradually, and Drust's voice floated across the field towards them once more.

'Ride back to your men and prepare to die. I have no interest in your surrender.'

VIII

VAE VICTIS

'Time is a sort of river of passing events, and strong is its current; no sooner is a thing brought to sight than it is swept by and another takes its place, and this, too, will be swept away.'

(*Marcus Aurelius*)

Blue

The Kaldi charge was a deluge of blue. Of thrashing limbs and naked torsos. Of screaming, murderous rage and flashing blades. Of imminent death.

Vortigern, still mounted, watched them come, watched them surge up the gentle slope towards his people. They didn't even wait for Brude and his warriors to reach the battle. They had barely left Vortigern and the others time to return to their lines. And why would they? Why should they? They were savages.

Only they weren't. The long-limbed woman straddling the stallion to his left was testament to that certainty, no matter how intent she was on her own personal vendetta. Like her, behind the blue paint and the screaming, the monsters that were careening towards the Britons were no less civilised than the Angles or the Jutes. Perhaps even than the Britons. They could no more live on battle than any other race of people. They farmed and built houses and boats. They played and loved and procreated and told each other stories and sang and drank and shit like everyone else in the world.

But they were not Britons. They belonged north of the wall, where the Romans had left them. They would never pledge allegiance to him, nor recognise his vision for a united land. For Albion. They needed to be driven back. At any cost.

Vortigern looked back at the walls of Isurium, wondering briefly if they might have been better making use of the defences. He could make out Ossian's head above the wooden staves, surveying the battlefield. Safe for now. No, they needed to win this on the offensive. They needed to wholly repel the invaders, not just defend a meaningless fortress.

Beside him, he could sense Derelei was itching to ride hard at the enemy. Her horse sensed it, too. Its hooves kneaded the earth anxiously and its head twitched from side to side. She shifted on its back, her eyes wide with anticipation.

'In time,' he told her. 'Our horses will flank them. We need them to engage first.'

She nodded impatiently.

Vortimer sat to his other side, motionless, his eyes narrow as he watched the flood of blue. He shouldn't even be here, thought Vortigern. He should be in Dumnonia. Only his wife and child, Vortigern's first grandchild, were dead. He had abandoned his post and his responsibilities, disobeyed his father's orders. And yet Vortigern was glad he was there. Dumnonia might be in the hands of Custennin's idiot son, but so what? Vortigern was already high king. He didn't need their support any more. The war for Albion was already here.

The Angles were forming a huge shield wall on the western end of the line, nearest to the horses. Leofric had blustered and postured for half the night about whether he would fight, but Vortigern had been certain that it was all show. The Angle was no fool. He knew Vortigern needed him and his kin, so he manipulated the situation to hustle for more land. Well, he could have it, for all the worth it had.

Beyond the Angles were the rest of the Britons on foot. Einion commanded there, and there was no better totemic figurehead to have in a battle than the enormous 'Onion'. He towered over the men that surrounded him, visible down the entire length of the line. Vortigern had made sure his youngest, Catigern, would fight close by the giant. Zeki was there too. He had trained the boy. He would stay at his side. It would be the safest place for him.

But how safe? The tide of woad was upon them. The Kaldi hurled themselves into the overlapping circles of the Angle shield wall, trying to clamber up and over them. They dropped like flies there, skewered on the spears that jutted out from behind the wall. But there were so many of them. How long could the shield wall last against such an onslaught?

Vortigern could see Einion, head and shoulders above the fray, swinging his sword back and forth. He couldn't make out Zeki or Catigern or the boy with yellow eyes that no doubt fought there as well. The Kaldi were thickest there, in the middle of the line, as if they intended on splitting the ranks of Britons in two. They fought with a fearless ferocity Vortigern had never witnessed before.

'We should ride sooner rather than later,' Vortimer muttered bleakly.

'If we go too soon, we will be flanked.'

'And if we go too late, we'll be even more outnumbered.'

Vortigern scowled. Vortimer had a point, but he couldn't risk his horses yet. They needed to wait for the advantage.

'Selwyn.' He turned to his loyal captain. 'Are the Nobatians ready?'

'Always.'

'Do it.'

Selwyn signalled to Shabaka and Tsekani. The two men already had arrows nocked to their bowstrings, their thighs straining against their horses' flanks. More skilled on horseback than anyone else there, they could ride unhindered amongst the Kaldi and loose their deadly missiles. They would kill several and hopefully instil fear in the enemy.

Shabaka and his brother, Tsekani, spurred their mounts forward and tore free from the line of stationary cavalry. Both men had their bows half drawn by the time they were up to speed. Shabaka loosed his first arrow. It thudded into the bare chest of a large Kaldi warrior, who dropped to his knees and fell face forwards to the ground before disappearing under a hundred feet.

Tsekani was no less deadly. There were so many targets it was almost impossible not to hit something. Shabaka had already pulled a second arrow from the quiver on his back and let it fly. Tsekani did the same. The speed with which the two men could nock and loose their arrows was awe-inspiring. They both manoeuvred their mounts with a frightening expertise, the tiniest of pressures from their knees steering the animals left and right, goading them into gallops or reining them back to shy upwards on hind legs. Vortigern watched as Shabaka sent his horse's front hooves crashing down on a Kaldi skull while sending an arrow through another warrior's heart.

The painted ones gave way to the two riders, quickly realising the danger they represented, and the Nobatians charged through them untouched, leaving a score of men and women dead in their wake.

Vortigern turned to Derelei. Her jaw was set, her face stony. Nothing in her expression gave any clue about her feelings. Only her eyes moved now, darting across the throng of people. She was searching for the one person that mattered to her.

'Drust,' she announced simply, and Vortigern looked where she was looking.

There he was, at the head of a tight-knit cohort of warriors, his mouth wide with a bloodthirsty war cry. Where some of his kin had scattered in front of the volley of arrows from Shabaka and Tsekani, he turned to face the approaching horses.

Derelei stood tall on her horse beside him and shouted her uncle's name. Vortigern knew he couldn't contain her much longer.

'Hold,' Vortigern growled. 'Hold the line.'

He watched as Shabaka loosed an arrow that felled the man next to Drust. The Nobatian wheeled away, nocking another. Tsekani raised his bow arm and took aim. But Drust was ready for him. He pulled his arm back and hurled a javelin with all his might at the approaching rider.

Whether he was aiming for Tsekani, or the horse, Vortigern would never know. He didn't see the javelin hit, but it surely did. Tsekani's horse crumpled beneath him, tumbling forwards in a mess of limbs and throwing the young Nobatian from its back.

The Kaldi were upon him in no time. He never stood a chance. He died next to his horse, pierced by half a dozen swords, as Drust roared in Vortigern's direction.

'We must ride,' Derelei said coldly, her teeth gritted. 'Now.'

* * *

'What do they wait for?'

The shield wall was still holding. Just. Edoma leant into it, looking westward to where the Briton king sat, unmoving, on his horse. The Kaldi hurled themselves against the wall. Through the gaps, she could make out their eyes, bright against the painted patterns on their faces. They were wide, filled with fury, drunk on battle, and unafraid.

One of them must have leapt from the back of one of his fallen kin, as a spiralled face appeared atop the shields. Leofric, beside her, thrust his spear into the Pict's open mouth with a quick jab, then pulled it out again. Blood showered down on them both and the dead man slid back down the front of the tight mesh of shields.

'Just hold the wall,' Leofric rasped. 'He'll have to charge soon.'

They were waiting for the charge. It was a signal for them to break the wall and make an attacking arrowhead formation that could penetrate those left disoriented after the onslaught from the cavalry. Cavalry, that's what they called it. Edoma thought that a little too grand, a little too Romanesque. She had never seen Roman cavalry, but her father had told her about his experience of facing it in their homelands. She doubted this motley rabble of Britons, however well they could fight on horseback, possessed the discipline of a Roman unit. But then, maybe they didn't need it against this enemy. The Kaldi were as averse to horseback fighting as the Angles.

As if to validate her distrust of mounted battle—surely it was a foolhardy endeavour to rely on a beast to keep you safe—she watched as one of the dark-skinned Nobatians was cut down from his steed and slaughtered without mercy.

They might have to hold the wall a while longer.

She was happy to be beside Leofric. She was happy he had noticed her. Not that he shouldn't have. She knew full well she could best any of the other women amongst them, and most of the men as well. Who else could he have chosen? He was older than her, but he had more than proved his virility on their wedding night. Fuelled by hours of mead consumption and revelry, they had consummated the marriage noisily, without caring who heard. And in the quiet aftermath, wrapped together in furs and firelight, he had told her how they were not going to be serving the high king of the Britons; they were going to fight for a prize that he would be compelled to bestow upon them. Land. Better land. Fertile land, and not the sodden bog that had been forced upon them by other Britons.

Fertile land. That is what she would be as well. She would bear Leofric a son. And as the colony grew, as more of their kin came from across the sea, her son would one day rule. Perhaps, in the language of the Britons, he might one day be a king in these lands.

'Push.'

Leofric was on the offensive now. He urged the other Angles forwards, their shields still locked together. The advance was slow, but certain. Edoma stepped over fallen Pictish warriors, their bare blue bodies blooded and grimed in mud.

'We've got them on the run now,' Wine shouted gleefully to her left. Her brother was not really deserving of such a prominent position in the formation. He was young, and not as experienced in battle as some others. But he was her brother, and she had asked Leofric that he be able to fight beside her.

'Boar's head,' came Leofric's shout on her right. And in unison the shields separated and Leofric strode forward, hurling his javelin at the mass of Picts that still pressed towards them.

The Angles formed up alongside and behind their chieftain, in a wedge formation. Edoma had pride of place on his left shoulder. She hurled her spear as well, watching another Pict fall next to the man her husband had killed, then drew her seax. And then the Picts were upon them.

As she parried and hacked, blows raining down on her shield, she saw the Briton cavalry thundering towards the rear of the Pictish lines, as planned. She ran through a wide-eyed, blue-faced woman, briefly musing about why even the Pictish women chose to fight without any kind of armour or clothing. She pushed the lifeless body away from her, freeing her seax to continue fighting. A large Pictish man ran past her with a blood-curdling scream, a great blade scything downwards.

Wine.

She slammed the hefty wooden boss of her shield into the face of another Pict as she turned to look over her shoulder for her brother.

And she barely recognised him. He was still teetering on his knees. He had taken a blade to the head, a clean downward slash that had bitten deep into his skull and driven his head apart to the nose. His killer had already fallen to several other seax thrusts. But there was nothing to be done for Wine.

He shouldn't have been this forward in the formation. That was her fault.

But there was no time to grieve or feel guilt.

Promise

Reunited with Tugen, Emrys had been determined that they should stand together in the coming battle. They had both come such a long way from the days of sparring with wooden swords in the woods. Such a long way from that day, the day the Kaldi woman had saved them from the bear. The day their families had been murdered.

They had spent the night deep in conversation. Tugen relayed his time with the Ethiopes in the fort by the wall, his face darkening when he told how Zala had been slain by Kaldi scouts. Emrys knew his pain. He told him about losing Carina. He beamed when he talked about Viction and Krestell, about the training he had received, about the time he had spent with Rozena.

Rozena. Talk of her led to the conversation dwindling. Emrys had become reflective, wishing to see her face again, sad that he had left her behind again. He didn't tell Tugen everything about how he, and especially Rozena, had suffered at the hands of Tarquinius. He wasn't sparing his friend. It was just too painful to talk about.

'We have much to avenge,' Tugen had said solemnly, and Emrys had reluctantly agreed. He would sooner see the killing stop, but he knew the Kaldi needed to be stopped first.

Neither of them slept much that night. Once the thrill of meeting each other again had receded into the simple pleasure of each other's company, the sky was already lightening. And Emrys' pulse quickened again in apprehension of the coming battle.

When he saw the line of Kaldi on the horizon, he felt sick. The odds were not favourable. Far from it. Even if they prevailed, he realised, the losses would surely still be heavy. They would be lucky to see out the day.

They joined Catigern next to Einion, a giant that would have towered over even the brutish Tarquinius.

'Big bastard. They call him The Onion,' Tugen whispered in his ear.

'What's that got to do with his size?' Emrys hissed back.

'Fuck knows, and I'm still not going to call him that to his face.'

Zeki, standing shoulder to shoulder with his young protégé, Catigern, grinned.

Moments later, the Kaldi charged.

* * *

The Onion was agile for a man his size. He swept aside the first wave of Kaldi that swarmed towards him like ants. His giant blade, weighing more than most men could even lift, sliced limbs and heads from bodies with an effortless brutality. It was all Emrys could do not to just watch the man in action.

But as potent as Einion was, there were more Kaldi than he could ever fend off alone for more than a moment. Emrys quickly found his ears ringing, the shrill metallic clash of blades punctuating the constant cacophony of screams and grunts and war cries. Like everyone else there, he swung his blade as hard and fast as he could. Like everyone else there, he imagined, he fought more to stay alive than to kill. All the bravado and masculine talk he had overheard in the day and night leading up to this clash faded into distant memory, their essence distilled into a heady mix of noise, sweat, blood, and a communal and desperate bid to live.

Whether the Kaldi felt the same, he did not know. But they were men— and women—just the same. The women! That was a difference he found difficult to comprehend. The Briton men might have wives and families wherever they called home. They might live to see them again, but the odds were just as likely that they would not. Their wives would grow old alone. Their children would no longer know the love of their fathers.

But the Kaldi ranks were formed of both men and women. A cursory glance suggested that there were probably more men, but there was likely a woman to every three men.

And it was a tall Kaldi woman that came at him next. Nothing in the way she moved could separate her from her male counterparts. Her hair was matted and scraped back from her stained face. Angry zigzags of woad made her face—her frenzied, mouth-agape face—appear like an arrowhead hurtling towards him. Only her breasts betrayed her sex. Emrys was not distracted by them, but they threw his mind into disarray, into a second of self-doubt. He had sparred once with Rozena. He'd even postured aggressively towards Edoma. But he'd never really considered earnestly trying to kill a woman.

He brought up his blade too slowly in defence. The arrow-faced woman had seen his hesitancy and had brought her sword down towards his head. It was a dangerous attack in most circumstances, and one that could be relied upon only if you were utterly confident in your superiority. Even a mediocre swordsman, given enough time to react, should be able to sidestep such a blow and offer a deadly retaliation against which there could be little defence. Emrys was more than mediocre, but his tardy reaction cost him. The force of her blow knocked his hurried parry downwards and her blade found his outstretched leg.

Emrys staggered backwards, trying to focus his mind. Hesitation was death. That's what Viction had taught him. And yet he could not help but reach for the wound in his leg. Feeling the hot wetness of blood on his hand, he glanced downwards, taking his eyes off his attacker. As much as it hurt, and as much as it bled, he knew it would not be the death of him. Not, at least, if he could take his mind off it and continue fighting.

The Kaldi woman had recovered from what could easily have been her killing blow. She was already coming at him again when he looked up. It wasn't the full-blooded charge that it had been, but he still barely had time to get his sword up in time. She slashed at him, trying to sever his head from his body, but this time he braced himself against the attack. Her sword clattered into his and stopped dead. He pushed back against it, rounding his shoulders to throw her balance, then let his sword continue its natural arc downwards and into her exposed shin. Such was the momentum of his sword that it cleaved clean through one leg just above her ankle. She crumpled to the ground; her face contorted in horror and pain. Emrys turned his sword in his hands and plunged it into her exposed chest.

For a moment, Emrys breathed. He knew he should pull his sword free in the same motion, always to be ready for the next attack, but he paused, waiting for her body to stop twitching, for her eyes to cloud and close. In that instant, the sounds of the battlefield receded to a dull roar, like far-off waves. There was only him, his sword, and the dead woman. He had killed her as quickly as he could, as mercifully as he could. She could never have crawled from the battlefield with a foot missing and live.

The pain in his leg brought him back. Sound rushed in on him again. The shrill clatter of swords was underscored with a whining metallic hum. Catigern was there, looking over at him as he pulled his own sword from the chest of another Kaldi. His face was grim, set, grimed in enemy blood. He nodded briefly at Emrys before spinning lightly on his feet to fend off the next attack.

'Emrys!'

Was that Tugen calling him?

Another Kaldi came at him, a slight man with flailing hair. Emrys was ready this time. He swatted the attack away and let the man career into his waiting shoulder. It was enough to wind his opponent and, as the Kaldi warrior crabbed a little to his side trying to recover, Emrys lunged forwards. Use the point of the sword, Viction had told him. That's why it's sharp!

The blade disappeared into the man's neck, ending his life quickly. Emrys pulled his sword free and reeled around, searching for the next opponent. In the seconds it took him to survey the battlefield, he saw Einion still mowing his way through the Kaldi, bleeding but not slowed. Catigern was holding his own too, dancing his way between swords and taking on more than one opponent at a time. He was a natural.

That was as good as it got. Everywhere else, Emrys could see only bleeding Britons. They were losing. The ground was red with blood, and the Kaldi had not lost the larger part of it. The Kaldi that had made it through the line in their first charge—and there were many—had run out of Britons to fight and were turning back towards him and the few of his kin that still stood. Another wave was still streaming towards them from the north.

'Tugen?' he shouted in desperation. His friend was nowhere to be seen. 'Tugen!'

* * *

He could hear his name being called.

Just let me stay here a while, Tugen thought.

Tugen was stuck. Trapped under the bulky corpse of a large Kaldi warrior. The man had practically impaled himself on Tugen's sword and then fallen onto him. And as ignominious as that was, the searing pain in Tugen's wrist suggested that the impact had broken it, rendering his sword hand utterly useless. The only plan he could muster in his pain-addled brain was to lie there, practically concealed under the dead man, until the battle had finished raging and the crows were picking clean the bones of the fallen. Then, whichever side triumphed, he could crawl free under cover of darkness and live to see another day as far away from there as he could get.

Someone was calling his name. Emrys. There was an urgency to it, an urgency that Tugen wanted to curse. He twisted his head, trying to see his friend. He saw Einion first. The man-mountain was unmistakable. Unstoppable. And there, just beyond, hemmed in by two of the enemy, Emrys was barely holding his own. He wasn't shouting for Tugen anymore, but he clearly needed assistance.

Tugen grunted with effort and pain and pushed his way free of the weight that lay on top of him. The big warrior rolled over onto his back. Tugen's blade still jutted from his gored belly. But there was little he could do with it. He tried to grasp the hilt with his right hand, but the fingers were incapable of gripping. The pain throbbed in his hand and up his arm. Instead, Tugen bent over quickly and snatched up the lighter Kaldi javelin with his left hand. It would have to do.

He could not let Emrys fall, not while he had breath in his body. The bodies of dead Britons littered the ground, and he stepped through them as nimbly as he could, hastening towards his friend. The spear felt heavy in his weaker hand, but he could at least hold it properly. Eyeing one of the Kaldi, he tucked the shaft under his arm and quickened his pace. He knew he was standing on men, both dead and dying, but his best chance of success depended on pace.

Emrys swayed dramatically out of the path of a scything sword and overbalanced. Something must have caught his foot too, because he was suddenly down on one knee. Vulnerable. He had probably done well not to fall flat on the ground, but he could not get to his feet in time to stop the next blow.

Tugen sprinted across the bloodied ground, spear tip levelled at the Kaldi who would surely end Emrys' life. He watched as the man raised his sword arm high and realised he could do nothing except scream. So he did. He opened his mouth as he ran and bellowed the most fearsome and blood curdling war cry he could muster. It was anger and anguish combined. Fury at this enemy that had taken so much from him. Grief at even the thought that Emrys would be added to the number of lives lost.

And it worked. They all looked to him. Emrys, still on one knee, saw him and smiled. The Kaldi turned on his heels mid-swing and brought his sword around in a futile defence. Tugen leapt the remaining distance with no thought other than to destroy his foe. He saw fear in the whites of the Kaldi eyes, a look he had not expected to see, and a horrible recognition of the inevitable. The sharp tip of the javelin struck the man inside his shoulder and slid through his body with barely any resistance. Tugen followed, barrelling into him and hurling him backwards into the mud.

Beside him, Emrys was up again, holding out a hand. Tugen offered him his left hand and was soon standing. The Kaldi lay motionless at his feet.

'Does that count?' He grinned at Emrys.

'Count?'

'As saving your life.'

'Most definitely. Where's your sword?' Emrys asked with urgency.

Tugen shrugged, happy in the moment to have helped his oldest friend. And then, seeing movement over Emrys' shoulders, his eyes opened wide with amazement.

'The cavalry! Look!'

The high king and his mounted warriors were ploughing through the Kaldi ranks. He made out Derelei riding close to the king, a grim look of determination on her face, her sword cutting swathes through her painted kin.

As Emrys turned back from that glorious sight, perhaps the turning of the tide, his smile of relief melted into an open-mouthed expression of horror and, in his golden eyes, Tugen saw his own imminent death.

It felt like he had been punched in the back. Right between the shoulder blades. The blow knocked the wind out of him. And yet he did not fall forwards onto Emrys. He still stood. Emrys' look of horror contorted into an angry snarl. Emrys' blade lifted skyward. And when Tugen looked down, he saw another blade, slick with blood he knew to be his own. Its cruel point extended at least a hand's length from his chest.

And then it disappeared, pulled free, and Tugen felt his knees buckle beneath him. He was just about aware of the ground rising to meet him as he collapsed, his vision already darkening. As Emrys stepped from view with a silent scream, Tugen realised that his wrist didn't hurt anymore.

Nothing did.

Fools

Despite being the veteran of a number of what he would probably now call mere skirmishes, Selwyn had not seen the likes of this battle. As he followed Vortigern and Vortimer in a charge upon the scattering masses of painted people, he couldn't help but feel exhilarated. His horse was as big as the high king's and as well trained. The thunder of hooves was rhythmic, percussive, the sound alone enough to inspire awe.

Like Vortigern, Selwyn carried a spatha. The Roman cavalry had made good use of the weapon long before it had become standard-issue for their infantry, replacing the gladius. And it was plain to see why. It was a long blade, but still easy to swing with one hand while the other held the reins. Vortigern and Vortimer carried theirs low to their right, ready to slice through any Kaldi that avoided falling beneath the horses' hooves. Selwyn did the same, glancing across protectively to Derelei, who rode beside him.

Her sword was different—a little shorter, but significantly broader. She had told him it was Drust's sword. Drust had good taste. It was an enviable weapon, even if its lack of length made it less effective from horseback. Derelei didn't return his look. She focussed on the masses of her people in front of them, resolute. He knew she was looking for Drust.

They had seen Drust briefly, when Tsekani had fallen, but he had melded back into the melee again, surrounded by his people and falling Britons. Shabaka, who would have time to grieve his brother later, was riding wide of the main force, finding any opportunity to loose his deadly arrows into the backs of the Kaldi.

Selwyn thought they should have charged earlier. He had felt sick at the sight of his comrades falling under the relentless wave of blue. But Vortigern was determined that they needed to do more than just flank the Kaldi. They couldn't anyway, not without the Jutes arriving from the east. Selwyn had cursed the decision to rely on outlanders in such a pivotal role in their battle plans, but what was done was done. Now they needed to surround the Kaldi and provide respite for their men on foot, forcing the Kaldi to confront the horsemen.

To begin with, the Kaldi barely even acknowledged the onslaught of cavalry. Horses and riders careened into them, crushing them with heavy hooves and slashing those left standing with their swords. Soon they began to scatter. They didn't run, but nor did they continue the assault toward the walls of Isurium. Instead, they split into pockets of warriors, spears turned against the galloping beasts.

It didn't take them long to work out that a well-aimed and well-grounded spear could stop a horse in its tracks and violently unseat its rider. Rather than waste missiles by hurling them, they dug the bottom of the weapons' shafts into the earth and angled them up at the surging horse breasts. Selwyn saw several of his comrades catapulted from the backs of their mounts and land amongst a flurry of thirsty blades. They died faster even than their horses, the beasts often wheeling grotesquely tail-over-head before thudding to the ground.

The sting was taken out of the charge, and they were reduced to relying on horsemanship, digging one leg and then the other into the animals' sides to turn on the spot and maintain the advantage of height over their stationary enemies.

Selwyn hacked down at several Kaldi who surrounded him. Vortigern and Vortimer were in the same predicament. Like him, they were deft at controlling their animals. The Kaldi continued to fall beneath his steel. He spurred his horse to rear up on its hind legs, its hooves smashing the skull of a Kaldi that had strayed out of reach of his blade.

Another horse shot past him at a pace. It was Derelei. She had all but withdrawn her blade from the action and was riding further into the thick of the Kaldi, risking herself and her horse. She was bent low over the animal's neck, as if she were talking into its ear and coaxing it onwards.

'Derelei!' Selwyn called in vain. She would neither hear nor heed him. 'Stand your ground.'

Nobody else noticed her ride away from the rest of them. Nor should they have. There were enough Kaldi to keep them all busy. Selwyn lashed out angrily with his sword. He shattered an enemy's sword and then cleaved downwards into his skull. Selwyn kicked the already dead man in the face, sending him to the ground in a mist of red.

Curse Derelei. She would get herself killed. That was always the risk, and Selwyn knew well enough that as commander of the men he could not break rank and pursue her. She would have to fend for herself. He felt the desperate fury bubbling up inside him and slashed at a couple more Kaldi, severing the first's arm at the elbow and beheading the next.

He did not want her to die. Not her.

Not since Pasha had any woman moved him. He did not expect her to look at him as he did her. He was just another man, another warrior. But she—she was a revelation, oblivious to her own beauty, which made her even more alluring. She was innately asexual, which made him lust for her even more. She was like the surface of a lake on a cloudy, still day, dark and motionless and full of promise. There had to be something more beneath her dour exterior. He couldn't bear the notion that he would never get to find that out.

* * *

Derelei swung herself down from her horse. It had served her well.

She had found Drust.

Once she had spotted him—half a head at least taller than most—amongst the throng, she had ridden hard towards him, caring for nothing else, shouting his name at the top of her lungs. Until that point, she had only struck those who had stood in her way—admittedly a fair few—while she searched for him. And he, as soon as he had seen her, had bellowed his own challenge.

As much as she had taken to being atop a horse, she was eminently more comfortable, and confident, with her two feet planted firmly on the earth. She brandished Drust's sword provocatively in front of him, making sure he could recognise the ornate pommel and guard.

'You want it back, Uncle?' she taunted him.

He grinned lasciviously back at her, disgustingly vulpine, and began walking towards her with a slow and considered malice. How could she have ever cared for this man? He was kin no more.

'Oh, I will have it back,' he called out to her as he waved aside anyone else that wanted to attack her. He wanted her to himself, as she did him. 'And I will see you gutted like the slippery fish you are.'

'Not today, Drust. Today, it is you that will see your insides slither like snakes in the mud at your feet. You are the traitor, not I.'

He squared off against her, his sword raised casually. She knew he was poised. She knew that, despite his age, he still had faster hands than most men half his age. He would be ready for whatever attack she chose. She hung back as well.

'How do you work that out?' Drust licked his lips, clearly savouring the exchange, as if it was some kind of foreplay to the main event.

'You betrayed your own family.' Derelei spat on the ground between them, her hands beginning to tremble in anticipation.

Drust laughed. 'I did that long before you were of age, woman. I banished my own brother, your father, for a far lesser crime than yours. Why should I be any kinder to you?'

'Because you were like a father to me.' Derelei regretted saying that the instant it came out of her mouth. It made her sound weak, sentimental, emotional.

Yet Drust looked at her, and for a moment in his eyes she thought she saw a little of the softness she remembered from times past, north of the wall. And then the look was gone. His sword lashed out at her, striking like a snake at her head. She reacted with the same speed, parrying the blow with ease.

'You're a fool, Derelei.' Drust raised his weapon again, his eyes steely once more. 'All that I have could have been yours, as your father's daughter.'

She had never really considered that. He hadn't once groomed her for succession, so the idea hadn't ever taken root in her mind.

'You had the best claim,' Drust continued. 'And you fucked it all up.'

Behind his blade there wasn't a hint of regret in her uncle's eyes, but there was still something in his tone that suggested he might have preferred events to have turned out differently to this.

'I want only one thing,' she snarled at him.

'I know,' he sighed. 'My head. Come on then, have at it.'

She knew he was waiting for her to attack, and had tried to resist the temptation, but she could no longer hold back. She flicked her wrists deftly, landing a heavy blow on Drust's blade and following up with a lightning-fast thrust. Drust, equal to it—expecting nothing less—stepped nimbly to one side to avoid it and brought his sword crashing back against hers.

They danced around each other, evenly matched, swords clashing. Neither pressed for advantage. She was certain that he would tire first, make a mistake, overbalance. Yet, all the time, he smirked at her. She knew why. She was surrounded. The only reason she had not been cut down by half a dozen other Kaldi swords was because Drust had made it clear he wanted to fight her alone. If—when—she delivered the fatal blow, she would live to enjoy it for only the briefest of moments.

Drust was older than her, significantly, but he was nearly as quick. And probably stronger. He rained blows down on her sword, clearly hoping to rattle her into making an error. She was more fleet of foot. She tried to evade as much as parry, to make sure his strikes were wasted on thin air more than on her blade. Her feet shuffled and skipped. Her sword flashed with controlled thrusts and feints. She would find his weakness.

The terrain offered little help. It was relatively flat. However, she noticed that the ankle-deep grass concealed occasional rocky outcrops. She spotted a jagged specimen a little behind Drust's right leg, so danced a little to her right to try to wheel them around in line with it. Drust followed her, pivoting where he stood and continuing his measured assault, his feet firmly on the ground. She would have to press him if she wanted to uproot his stance.

She evaded a slightly clumsier swing than usual from Drust and saw her chance. She squatted and swung her blade low to the earth. It worked. Drust could not parry the blow in time, so had to take a step backwards. He lost no balance, however, and brought his sword down on Derelei's vulnerable back. She twisted in time to ensure the blow was not fatal, but the keen edge of his blade bit into the back of her shoulder as it glanced off her.

Drust laughed, as if he sensed victory. First blood was his, and he doubtless knew it was because she had overreached. But he did not know why she had done so, nor why she continued with her strategy.

Again, despite the rush of pain and blood, she ducked low, thrusting this time, aiming for his shins. He knocked her blade away but took a defensive step backwards as well. She was ready for his counterattack this time, parrying a fearsome blow above her head and using it to push him back further still. His back foot landed awkwardly on the ridge of the half-hidden stone, sliding several inches to the ground beyond. It was enough to upset his balance.

And it was enough for her to stride forwards, arcing her sword at arm's length towards the gap that had opened in Drust's defence. Her blade found his thigh, cutting deep into it and sending him yet further off kilter. He stumbled back, his leg wobbling beneath him. It was a serious wound, and Derelei sensed victory. She had seconds to finish him, else the rest of the Kaldi would swarm upon her before he died.

A spear flew at her from the Kaldi ranks, missing her head by inches. They were already coming to Drust's aid.

'Derelei!'

She ignored the voice that called her name and took a couple of long strides towards the injured chieftain. In his retreat, his leg gave way, and he fell backwards, landing heavily on the ground.

Another spear hurtled past her. She had to lean out of its path and watch it go by.

'Derelei,' the voice came again, more urgently.

It was Selwyn. Beside him, his horse was sinking to its knees, a spear jutting from its chest. Selwyn had slid from its back already and had his sword in hand and a grim look on his face.

Derelei was barely concerned with why Selwyn should be there, frowning at her. She turned back towards her target and was confronted with a line of Kaldi. Drust was already concealed. Through the bare blue limbs, she could make him out limping away from the fight, leaning on Cailtram.

'Drust,' she called out in frustration, muttering curses against the young druid who was helping her uncle to safety.

There was little else to be done. Half a dozen swords were advancing on her. Any of them might have been hesitant to face her in single combat, but together they were supremely confident. They would all be happy to carry the news of her death back to Drust when the battle was over.

She braced herself. There was no sense in retreat.

'You're a fool,' grunted Selwyn as he planted his feet next to hers.

'You're the bigger fool.' She grimaced back at him. 'Why did you follow me?'

Selwyn glanced at her, a pained look in his eyes, then shrugged with as much nonchalance as he could muster. Knowing very well why he had followed her, she gave him a rare smile and lifted her sword in readiness, dimly aware that behind Drust's people, Brude and his clan had joined the melee.

Routed

Vortimer glanced at his father. The older man fought with confidence. Too much, perhaps. No, not too much. He could wield a sword and control a horse; of that, there was no question. He hacked down into the Kaldi that surrounded him with something approaching glee, a self-righteous determination that his cause was the most just, that these were vermin who needed to be exterminated or driven back to the holes from which they had undoubtedly crawled. There was no anger in Vortigern's combat. He was too skilled for that. He was precise and measured.

But were his tactics sound? Did he command the hearts of the men that had joined him in this battle? Certainly, the talk of Albion roused the spirits. Anyone caught up in the grand ambition to establish some kind of unity amongst the people soon believed in it with a zealous fervour. The naysayers, the Roman types, the men who craved for the safety of imperial rule wanted much the same thing, anyway. They just hadn't believed that Vortigern could deliver it.

Yet, despite the high king's display of weapon skill, the battle was not going well. Vortimer knew his horse was tiring and slowing and becoming increasingly vulnerable. Soon it would not respond fast enough to his commands. Soon it would take a spear in its flank or its breast. And soon he would be on foot, fighting for his life like everybody else.

They had waited too long to charge. Surely. Vortimer had watched helplessly as the Kaldi had penetrated deep into the ranks of their foot soldiers. He feared for his younger brother. Even the mountainous Einion could scarcely prevail against that onslaught for much longer.

'Father,' Vortimer bellowed, smashing aside a probing Kaldi spear. 'Father!'

The walls of Isurium were still some ways behind them, but Vortimer could already see some of the Britons fleeing towards them. The Kaldi weren't bothering to pursue them. Not yet. Instead, they turned against the cavalry, all but powerless now. Their charge had ended, and horses and riders were mired in close quarter combat. Beasts were being slashed and stabbed relentlessly, and riders pulled from their mounts.

And they were all but surrounded. The fresh wave of Kaldi from the east was upon them.

'We must retreat!'

Vortigern threw a look over his shoulder. Blood darkened his visage.

'We can hold them from the walls,' Vortimer shouted at him. 'We're losing too many.'

Vortigern nodded and raised his sword arm, the blooded blade pointing high into the sky.

'Break,' he shouted. 'Break and reform.'

Vortimer followed his father's example, spurring his horse into action and finding a way through the swords and the spears. Other riders followed and formed up on them, wheeling to the north in a tight circle. Vortimer goaded his horse forwards, knowing it was already labouring, and drew up beside his father.

'What are you doing?' he shouted across over the thunder of hooves.

'We strike again,' came the response. His father's face was a grotesque mask of blood, broken by a manic grin. 'We hit them hard.'

'The horses are exhausted. We don't have the numbers,' Vortimer vociferated in frustration. 'We need to fall back to the walls.'

Vortigern shook his head and drove his mount forward. Vortimer growled to himself, infuriated. Perhaps his father had not seen the Kaldi flanking manoeuvre. Perhaps he had not noticed an entire clan of the bastards hemming them in from the east. And if he had, he was mad. There was no way they could penetrate this number of Kaldi with their remaining horse.

Vortigern was leading them all to their destruction.

* * *

As he turned his horse back to face the battle, Vortigern's heart sank a little. He had known they were losing but had not fully appreciated the number of Kaldi that still fought on. Scores of Britons lay dead and mortally wounded in the mud, and many who were unharmed were busy fleeing for the safety of the walls.

He knew his son was looking at him and turned to face him.

'We charge again,' he said flatly, and waved aside Vortimer's objection before he voiced it. 'If we retreat, we will lose even more men.'

Those that fled on foot would become the primary targets if the cavalry did not attack. Vortigern knew his son just didn't see the bigger picture; he lacked experience in command. He could not yet appreciate how difficult some decisions were. They would lose men and horses, but they would allow others to reach safety. Only then could they fall back to the relative safety of Isurium and try their best to repel the Kaldi onslaught. It was not ideal. It was not the crushing victory he had hoped for. But that would forever evade him if he did not act immediately.

A solitary horse broke free from the ranks of blue, two men on its back. Vortigern peered over the neck of his own horse, irritated at having to delay the charge. As the horse came nearer, he realised the riders were not two men, but a man and a woman. The Kaldi woman, Derelei, was at the reins, and behind her was Selwyn.

'Selwyn,' Vortigern barked when the pair were within earshot. 'You broke ranks. Why?'

Both Selwyn and Derelei were bleeding from several small wounds.

'Drust is mortally wounded,' Selwyn said without hesitation.

'You got to him?'

'Derelei did.' Selwyn clearly wanted to smile.

Vortigern glared at Selwyn, wanting to reprimand him for his ill-discipline. But this was positive news.

'But he lives?'

Derelei lowered her eyes. Vortigern could sense her disappointment.

'For now. Not for long, I'd say.' Selwyn gave Derelei a reassuring nod.

'Yet again, Selwyn, your choice in female companion is nothing if not inappropriate.' Vortigern had long been aware of rumours that his daughter, Pasha, had been involved with Selwyn. He had never said anything to the man, or to his daughter. It could never have lasted, anyway.

Derelei looked up at his comment, her eyes bright and proud.

'Selwyn saved my life,' she said simply. 'And Drust would not be so wounded if it weren't for his support.'

'Excellent,' Vortigern grunted. 'But I don't see the Kaldi fleeing behind their fallen leader. It would seem removing the snake's head does not, in fact, kill the beast.'

There was still the small matter of leading his remaining men back into the deadly fray.

'Do we have another horse?' he asked loudly, and a riderless beast was ushered to the front of the line. 'I assume you are both ready to continue the fight?'

Derelei nodded without hesitation. Selwyn's reaction was slower, but still reluctantly affirmative.

'This time you keep to formation.'

The pair nodded; Selwyn was visibly more chastened than Derelei.

'Look to the east,' a voice cried out. Shabaka was standing high on his horse, peering across the battlefield. 'Men to the east.'

'What men?' Vortigern strained to see. A band of warriors was indeed approaching on foot, at pace. 'More of the bastards?'

That would surely spell an end to the defence of Albion.

'Jutes,' came Shabaka's fevered response. 'They carry the stallion banner of Hengest and Hors.'

A wave of excitement swept through Vortigern at the news. The Jutes had not perished. They were here. Osric had made it. Hengest and Hors, his new allies, had made it. The sea had not claimed them, as Ossian had pessimistically surmised. The fight was still alive.

He could make them out now. Several arrow-like formations of men bore down on the Kaldi's left flank. Hengest would be at the head of one, and Hors another. The round Jutish shields were raised, and their glinting spear heads prickled forwards as they ran. The roar of their battle cries reached Vortigern's ears. It was the Kaldi's turn to be hemmed in.

Again, raising his blade to the sky, Vortigern dug his heels into his horse's flanks.

'Charge!'

Land

The victory was decisive.

Hengest and Hors led their warriors right into the thick of the enemy, spilling Kaldi blood with merciless abandon. Spear, sword, axe and seax. All became mired in blood. The Jutes even utilised their shields as weapons, smashing skulls and snapping limbs as they pressed through the Kaldi ranks.

Vortigern led his tired cavalry in one last vicious onslaught, pinning the surrounded Kaldi against his Jutish allies. Wherever Drust had got to, he was not seen again that day. The remnants of his army were forced to fall back, and before long fled northwards to escape with their lives.

Osric leant on his shield, his face and forearms caked with blood. He was breathing heavily, bent at the knees, but smiling. Around him, Jutes laughed and chattered garrulously, revelling in the aftermath of the battle. They had lost only a handful of warriors, men who were now being welcomed with honours into the glorious halls of the next life.

'You fight like an animal.' Wulfric sauntered over to him. 'Not bad for a one-eared man,' the young Jute grinned.

'Like a wolf?' Osric leered back at him provocatively.

Wulfric might have blanched a little under the filth on his face.

'I meant no disrespect in telling Hengest.' His voice faltered in reply.

Osric waved away Wulfric's apparent penitence. 'It does not matter. You fought well too. For a pup.'

'You remember me now, then?'

'I do.'

Osric tried to straighten his legs, to stand up, but they felt unbearably stiff. He stumbled and leant more heavily on his shield. Wulfric extended an arm to help him upright.

'Cramp.' Osric grinned at the concerned face. 'Must be getting old.'

Wulfric looked fondly at Osric. 'I still owe you much,' he admitted.

'You owe me nothing, boy.'

Osric stretched his legs, feeling the cramp ease slowly, and gazed northwards. The last of the Kaldi were disappearing over the horizon.

'You think they'll be back?' Wulfric asked him.

'I have little doubt of it.'

Hengest strode towards them through the other Jutes, Hors by his side.

'That was a fine scrap, wolf.' The grizzled warrior beamed at Osric. He had stripped off his jerkin and furs and was bare chested. A thick mesh of hair, matted with blood, covered his broad chest. 'I'm off for a wash in the river before seeing Vortigern. Will you come with me?'

Vortigern. Osric had spent the last week or so in the company of Jutes, an experience that had awakened in him a feeling of who he could have been. They were a different breed to the Britons. They were sturdy men, happy to laugh and sing and fight and swear, filled with a simplicity of purpose that he found reassuring. But he had not enjoyed his time at sea and marvelled at how their boats had weathered the storm. For a time, he had been certain they would be overturned, and he would drown, or be smashed bloodily against some jagged dark rock, never to be seen again. But they had ridden the waves like seals, soaked to the skin but intact. Planting his feet on dry land after that had felt like being reborn. He had clambered gratefully up the beach and the headland. Not even the host of Kaldi blades that awaited them could dowse his burning sense of relief.

He had fought joyously, like he'd never fought before, untouchable and filled with mead and commonality with his fellow Jutes. They all fought like him, great growling masses of sinew and muscle and a macabre enjoyment of the death they dealt.

'I will,' he told Hengest. He wanted to see Vortigern. He wanted to stand next to Hengest and Hors when he did so and be at one with them.

'So be it then.' Hengest clasped his hand. 'You must be glad to be home.'

'I am,' Osric answered without thinking.

'As are we all. I think we've earned ourselves a place here.'

Leaving Wulfric, Osric walked beside Hengest and Hors down towards the river, treading between fallen Britons and Kaldi.

'Will you stay with us, Osric? With me?'

The thought had occurred to him. Osric had wondered what he would answer to such an offer.

'I don't know,' he answered honestly. This was his home. It always had been. It wasn't a new home, as it was going to be to Hengest and his kin. Osric felt keenly his years of loyalty to Vortigern, to Selwyn, and to all the men he had known for so long. As much as he was still reeling from the thrill of fighting amidst the shield wall, shoulder to shoulder with other Jutes, he was also keen to discover who among Vortigern's men had survived this battle.

'It is no matter,' the big Jute told him. 'You are one of us. You always were, and you always will be. Perhaps for now it will suffice that you act as intermediary between myself and Vortigern.'

Osric nodded thoughtfully.

'You are no longer wolf. Your crime, if crime it was, is pardoned.'

His exile had never been an actual concern. The Jutish community had, until now, been tiny and far away. Only Wulfric remembered him, and fondly, and for good reason. Osric had never feared for his life. Hengest did not need to offer him this sanctuary, but the gesture did not go unappreciated.

'I am honoured, Hengest,' he said humbly. 'Thank you.'

No matter what standing Hengest had or had not in their homeland, he was reported to be the direct descendant of Woden. His pardon was second only to an endorsement by the Allfather himself.

* * *

He wasn't sure he had ever really seen Ossian smile. Not in a genuine, unimpeded, joyous manner. Vortigern felt his own mouth turn up as well. There was much to rejoice, despite the casualties they had suffered.

Elaf and Nudd had both fallen beside Einion, who was wounded but would recover. Appius had come out of the carnage unscathed, though Vortigern doubted he could claim much personal victory. Both Appius and Einion had already been to see him, in the villa of Isurium, in the immediate aftermath of the battle. Einion limped and grinned, his body still seeping blood in half a dozen places.

'Scratches.' He had laughed his injuries off.

Appius, who had found time to take off his armour, was less jovial. He was, however, verging on obsequious. He pledged his undying allegiance to Vortigern and vowed that he would steer Sextus and Titus to the same position. Vortigern had accomplished what none of the three of them had believed possible.

Albion.

He had, for the time being at least, realised his ambition to unite the land of the Britons and expel the invaders. The Kaldi had always been the biggest threat, more than the Hibernians, the Dalriadans or even the Scotti, and they had run for the hills with their tails between their legs. Not that the victory hadn't been hard fought. Vortigern was in no way oblivious that the tide could as easily have gone the other way. Their losses had been heavy, and they would need to find and train more men. They would need more weapons. The Kaldi were hurt, but they would likely be back. Cunedda had the Dalriadans under control and would, with some help, hopefully drive the Hibernians back into the water. And the Scotti were more intent on incursions north of the wall. But, for now, Albion was a reality.

Mercifully, his sons had survived too. Vortimer had fought beside him and fought well. Even if he had spoken out of place, it had been in the heat of battle and could be easily forgiven. Catigern was safe and had apparently carried himself well. He would make a better, cleverer warrior than his older brother. And perhaps, one day, even his father.

Albion.

Ossian nodded at him, as if reading his thoughts. The druid had allied himself with Vortigern for this exact outcome. He had known, in his other worldly ways, that Vortigern would be the man to achieve this feat. And, by the gods, he had been right. Vortigern's supremacy now as high king would surely go unchallenged.

He watched through the window of the villa as Leofric walked away from his 'audience'. The Angle chieftain had been humble before him, his manner quite different from how it had been in their previous exchange. And Leofric had beamed from ear to ear when Vortigern had bestowed upon him and his people the former kingdom of Lindsey, including the ruined Roman town of Lindum. Appius had fought alongside Vortigern, so he was wary of giving the Angles land too close to Eboracum. The marshy fens of Lindsey, prone to flooding in the wetter months, would contain the Angles for a time at least.

Outside in the courtyard, Leofric stopped to greet someone. Vortigern leaned forward to see more closely. It was the Jutes, Hengest and Hors, and with them, Osric. Vortigern smiled to see his old Jutish champion, relieved to see he had survived, despite never doubting that he would.

'A victory for the bards to sing about,' crowed Hengest bombastically after bowing low to Vortigern. 'You are indeed a worthy high king of all Albion.'

Vortigern, waiting patiently as Osric interpreted, took the Jutish chieftain at face value, and replied honestly. 'We might have struggled without your assistance, mighty Hengest.'

'We enjoyed the fight.' Hengest waved his hand dismissively. 'It was your strategy that won the day.'

'Not without heavy losses,' Vortigern sighed.

Hengest clapped him on the shoulder, a less ingratiating gesture than his exaggerated bow.

'Our brothers will be feasting in the hall of the gods while they wait for us to join them.'

'Quite.' Vortigern relaxed his shoulder, letting the Jute's hand slide away. He glanced at Ossian, who no doubt shared his incredulity that the Jutes imagined the next world to be a never-ending, mead fuelled orgiastic feast. Their kin, the Britons who had fallen, would wander like shadows in Annwn, the Otherworld.

Nonetheless, and despite Hengest's forced modesty, Vortigern knew well that the day was won more than a large part because of the Jutes' fearless and timely intervention. They were fully justified in expecting their reward.

'Does Zeki live still?' Osric spoke up on his own account, stepping forward from the brothers.

'He does, Osric. It is good to see you, old friend.'

Osric beamed. 'It is good to be here, my king.'

'Will you live with your kin in their new lands?' Vortigern asked him. Hengest straightened at the mention of land. He clearly knew a little of the Briton tongue. And it was no secret that all he really wanted was a haven for his people.

'I would serve my king,' Osric answered hesitantly. 'As long as you will still have me?'

'Always,' smiled Vortigern, then turned back to Hengest.

'I have set aside a tract of land for your people in Ceint.'

Ossian had cautioned Vortigern against his proposed course of action. Titus ruled Ceint, and would be furious at the slight. Sextus, in Londinium, would be equally mortified at the proximity of a Jutish population. Vortigern had waved aside Ossian's advice. Infuriating the trumped up little Romanites was only part of his intention. He wanted to vex them. He wanted them to pay for withdrawing their support. Had it not been for the Jutes, Albion might well have begun its final descent into oblivion that day. It was perfectly justifiable that they be suitably rewarded, and at the expense of those who could so easily have contributed to failure.

That aside, Vortigern did not want the Jutes any closer to him than they needed to be. They were a volatile people, and worryingly adept in battle. He could not yet decide how far he could trust Hengest. By giving them an isolated corner of Ceint, with the expectation that they would join his army if required, he would be keeping them at arm's length. Any insurrection or ambitious expansion would have to go first through the rest of Ceint and Londinium before stretching further into Albion.

Hengest was smiling broadly. The gift of land pleased him.

'Our blades remain at your service whenever those blue bastards decide to return,' he pledged. 'I would ask only one small thing of you, Vortigern, High King of Albion.'

'Ask away.' Vortigern opened his arms in a display of generosity.

'I have my most loyal warriors here with me,' Hengest began. 'I would ask permission that more of our kin be allowed to join us in Ceint. We will need more hands to farm the land. Some of the men have wives and growing children.'

Vortigern nodded, suddenly missing Sevira and Pasha.

'There is room for your families as well. You have my blessing.'

Hengest nodded solemnly.

'And you have our gratitude.'

Behind the Wall

Drust was barely aware of most of the ignominious trek northwards. The wound in his leg, though bound and stuck with some noxious muck Cailtram had cooked up, seeped through its dressing. Fever took him, and he was confined to a roughly hewn fan of ferns and branches that two of his warriors had to drag over the rocky ground.

In the evenings, Cailtram tended to him and when the druid was otherwise occupied, a young woman he did not recognise bent over his face and wiped the sweat from his brow. He slipped in and out of sleep, sometimes seeing the fading blue of her pretty face looming over him in rare moments of clarity. Perhaps she could replace Modwen as his mistress. But hadn't someone already done that?

Derelei. He remembered fighting her. He remembered the sharp pain of her blade—his blade, stolen by her—as it sliced into his leg. He remembered falling back into the arms of his warriors and being carried to safety. And he remembered Cailtram's face looking down at him, curiously unemotional, telling him that the day was lost. Brude had returned to his ships, and they were all heading home. And then little else that made any sense.

For a moment, as they skirted around the great craggy rocks above Eidyn, he felt a pang of fear. An unfamiliar feeling. He must be finally getting old. When he was conscious, he looked skyward. He tried to ignore the jolt and bump of the slopes. The cliffs of the Gododdin stronghold threatened to black out the harsh light of the sky, and panic rose in his helpless body.

Cunedda and his men would see to the rest of them. They had overreached. He had overreached.

But Cunedda never came. He was elsewhere still. Eidyn's peaks drifted from view and Drust slumbered more, plagued by dreams of impossible battles, visited by the faces of those who already roamed the next world. Modwen and Darlagh—that was her name, he remembered—fought like cats, claw handed, threatening to rip each other's eyes out. Wroid stood behind them, laughing cruelly. Behind him, another familiar shaped figure lingered on the edge of the shadows. He strained to see who it was, but the closer he looked, the more the shade slipped back into darkness.

'Who are you? Speak.'

And then the sun poured in, rouging his vision, and driving all the spirits away into some unseen darkness. He wondered if he had called aloud. He opened his eyes, squinting against the glare. They must have passed the wall. Some time ago. He was home.

The loch shimmered like a great silver fish; its surface gently rippled by a cool breeze. The hills that rose around its shores were already showing signs of autumn, and what heat there was in the day would soon be gone. Winter was long this far north, and harsh. But it was home.

'How do you feel?'

Cailtram appeared.

'Better,' Drust muttered. 'Clearer. I wish to walk from here.'

Cailtram stopped the men that pulled his travois and held his hand out. Drust clasped it, feeling Cailtram's strength. Gods, he was weak. No matter, he would recover in time. He let the druid take his weight and rock him up onto his feet. He winced as a sharp pain lanced through his wounded leg.

'Can you stand?'

Drust flapped his arms at the druid. 'Stand back. Let me try.'

The fever had passed. Drust looked down at the dressing on his thigh. It was dry, no longer oozing.

'You will live.' Cailtram smiled at him kindly. 'I'm not sure you'll be doing a lot of fighting, but you will live.'

Drust was aware of his history. Drust of a hundred battles, they had called him. But now he had lost his first battle, and nearly his life. He wanted to chastise the druid and assert his conviction that he would indeed return to fight again—and win—but he paused, looking along the shore of the loch towards the cluster of huts that was home, towards the crannog that sat on its stilts out on the calm water. War could wait. He wanted a home cooked meal and a warm fur to lie on. He wanted to see his wife. Aife. But something else troubled him still.

'Who was the woman that tended to me?'

'The woman?' Cailtram asked.

'Yes, druid. Young, pretty. She wiped my face while I was in the grip of fever.'

Cailtram scowled. 'There was no woman, Drust. I—'

'You what?'

Had he dreamed her? Why? No matter. And then he recalled the other shadows of his dreams, the one with the hidden face. Perhaps that had been her. Perhaps she was just someone he had known; someone he had cruelly forgotten.

Drust hobbled as best he could along the bank of the loch, his eyes fixed on the columns of smoke that rose from the houses. Finally, he saw his own house, and tried to quicken his pace. Cailtram bustled along beside him, arms outstretched and ready to catch or support him if he stumbled.

But he did not falter.

He stopped short of the house, his eyes darting to its roof. No smoke spiralled up through the hole there. He cocked his head, frowning, feeling Cailtram's hand hovering by his shoulder. Closing his eyes, he pictured the face of the woman who had pervaded his fevered dreams. He remembered her now. And he remembered himself as a younger man, flush with the thrill of first love.

A tear squeezed itself reluctantly from the corner of his eye. He felt his legs go weak beneath him. It was as if a hole had opened in the ground on which he stood, filled with sticky, clawing mud. He felt himself being sucked into the pit, held up only by the druid's hands. He closed his eyes still more tightly, remembering the shadow, willing it to show itself, certain now that he knew who it was.

And as the face passed from darkness into light in his mind's eye, he felt his chest contract with such violence that he could have sworn a dozen arrows had pierced his lungs at once. He let out a single mighty sob and pulled himself free from the hands that held him up.

He knew she was gone. Aife was dead.

High King

The ride back to Viroconium was long. Too long. Vortigern longed to share his victory with Sevira. Ossian, who rode quietly beside him, was not the most uplifting company he could have imagined in the wake of glorious success. The old man was dry and matter of fact, smiling only occasionally. Often, he dozed, rocked by the gentle motion of the horse beneath him.

Selwyn rode behind them, next to Derelei. They had perhaps bonded in more than just combat. But Vortigern could not sit in judgment. The defection of the Kaldi woman could have been almost as instrumental in the eventual routing of Drust and his people as the Jutes' timely intervention. Besides, he hadn't seen Selwyn smile in years, and anything was better than his secret pining for Pasha.

Einion had headed back with his Atrebates to Calleva, carrying the corpses of Elaf and Nudd with them. The fallen chieftains would be afforded a burial befitting their standings and their contributions to the fight. Appius had scuttled back to Eboracum. The Angles had set off into the heart of Lindsey. And Hengest and Hors and their fierce Jutish warriors had returned to their boats to sail south to Ceint.

Vortimer and Catigern rode together, deep in conversation. Vortigern had gleaned something of what had befallen Dumnonia under the supervision of his eldest son. It was less than positive news. Erbin, as far as he knew or remembered, was probably not the fittest of leaders. Doubtless too, he would have little love for Vortigern and might need to be pushed back into line. But Dumnonia was a long way even from Viroconium, and Erbin's people were nothing if not fiercely opposed to travel. It was a shame, however, that Vortimer's child had not survived the trauma of birth. Perhaps Lamorna had been too young. Or too ruined by her father, the tyrannical Custennin. Vortigern shouldered the responsibility for that. It had been a poor match for his son. The next would be better.

As the familiar sight of The Wrekin loomed into view, Vortigern smiled at the sound of Osric and Zeki laughing in the ranks behind him. He looked forward to sharing wine and stories with them. Vortigern had instructed the column of men to continue past the fort on The Wrekin. He wanted all those who had fought for Albion to be welcomed into Viroconium as heroes. There would be several long days and nights of feasting and celebration ahead of them, regardless of how stiff and aching their limbs were from the long journey.

He found Sevira waiting at the gates for him and slid gratefully from his mount to embrace her.

'Wife,' he murmured into her ear as he held her, feeling her arms tight around his back, 'it is done.'

'You are home,' she whispered simply in reply, reminding him of what was most important to her. 'Are our boys safe as well?'

'They are. Ride with me.' He mounted his horse again and pulled her up behind him. Vortimer and Catigern weren't far behind. He felt Sevira twist to look back at them.

The rider he had sent ahead to announce his arrival could only have beaten them by a day or so, but word had clearly spread through Viroconium like wildfire. People lined the cobbled Roman streets. As Vortigern led his men on towards the old forum, with Sevira holding on tighter than she needed to behind him, cheers filled the air.

'Where is Pasha?' he asked, leaning his head back beside hers.

'Catigern did not tell you?'

'Tell me what?'

'She has made her own way from here,' Sevira said sadly. 'I'm sure she is fine. We shall talk more on that later.'

Vortigern frowned slightly, worried for his daughter, but he trusted his wife. And Pasha was as strong as she was stubborn. Whatever choices she had made, he doubted he would have had the power to dissuade him had he been there. And that was another sticking point; at some juncture, in the days to come, he would have to break it to his wife that he would soon be travelling to Verulamium and on to Londinium and Ceint, to make sure that Titus and Sextus were being suitably accommodating to his Jutish allies. Sevira would not take kindly to another period of absence from her husband.

But telling her could wait. The cries of the jubilant crowd rang raucous in his ears as he clutched Sevira's hand in his. He held power now, and with that power came responsibility. It was everything he and Sevira had dreamed of; she would have to understand his duties.

'Vortigern,' the people of Viroconium chanted as one. 'Vortigern. Vortigern.'

'High King of Albion,' Sevira whispered proudly into his ear, and Vortigern beamed.

Golden

Rozena cried for several hours after Emrys told her about Tugen. He held her, grateful at first, happy to feel her in his arms again. Then he too began to weep, remembering the friend he had thought he might never see again, the friend he had ushered to safety up a tree when a bear had attacked them, the friend who had stood with the Ethiopes on the wall, the friend who had then reappeared and saved his life in the heat of battle.

Emrys had begun by telling Rozena of the death of Tarquinius, and even that had elicited a single tear from her. She had smiled thinly, bitterly even, then asked to hear about the great battle against the Kaldi. She didn't ask about the Angles, and he decided that there would be plenty of time later to tell her of his confrontation with Edoma, now wife to Leofric. The loss of Tugen was more than enough sadness.

The din of the revellers beyond the walls of even Ambrosius' villa, which lay on the outskirts of the town, made it impossible to ignore for long the simple fact that the day was one for celebration and remembrance. The old man himself, in his finest purple, sashayed into the chamber where Emrys sat holding Rozena, his stride imbued with the energy of a man years younger. He carried with him a small amphora.

'Come on, you two,' Ambrosius said kindly. 'There is feasting to be done. Perhaps I underestimated our king after all. Let us have a drink before we join the party. I have unearthed some very old and very fine wine.'

Emrys released Rozena, who wiped her eyes with the hand of her good arm. Her other still hung limp by her side, much improved but still weak.

She looked at him and nodded.

'Tugen would be the first to join in the celebrations,' she smiled sweetly. 'Of that I am certain.'

'I'd say you're right,' Emrys agreed, taking her hand loosely in his.

'I am sorry about your friend,' Ambrosius said solemnly, resting a hand on Emrys' shoulder. 'You must tell me more about him and honour his memory properly by sparing no detail of his excellent character. But first, let us drink to your own safe return.'

Ambrosius poured three cups of wine and set the amphora down.

'You know, Emrys, your name and mine are the same.'

'What do you mean?' Emrys smelled the wine. It had an earthier scent than the sweetened wine he had tried before, a muskiness that tickled his nose.

'Ambrosius comes from the word ambrosia, the food of the Roman gods. It means "immortal". Emrys means the same thing in the Briton tongue.'

Rozena grinned and sipped her wine. 'You're a god, Emrys.'

Emrys gave her a friendly shove, and a little wine spilled out onto the stone floor.

'Mind the wine.' Ambrosius chuckled. 'No, you're not a god, Emrys, but I am certain you have quite a future ahead of you.'

'I'm just happy to be here now,' Emrys said quietly.

'As are we all,' agreed Ambrosius. He took a long sip of the wine and sighed quietly after swallowing it.

Rozena snuggled closer to Emrys.

'Speaking of names, son,' Ambrosius said, 'I wonder if you would consider taking on a name that has been important in my family for some generations.'

'I—I'd be honoured,' Emrys stammered.

'It's rather fitting, given the extraordinary colour of your eyes.'

'Oh?'

'Aurelius. The golden one. It usually refers to yellow hair, but that's a little commonplace, shall we say, when compared to eyes of that colour.'

'The golden one,' echoed Rozena, wide eyed. 'It suits you.'

Emrys smiled into his wine as he took a sip. At first it possessed the familiar sweetness of similar draughts, but then he felt his throat being coated with an almost dank woodiness and an oddly pleasant warmth. He closed his eyes for a moment and enjoyed the flavour, briefly imagining what it must have been like to live in a Roman society, then opened them and nodded at Ambrosius.

'Aurelius,' he enunciated, letting the roundness of the name's syllables roll languidly around his wine-stained tongue. 'I like it.'

Epilogue

Wulfric counted at least sixteen sails. The boats had rounded the headland in the fading orange of the late autumn sunset and found their way through a wispy mist that clung to the waves, into the safety of the shallows. Hundreds of Jutes leapt into the slow swirling foam and waded ashore, chattering. There were, as Hengest had promised, farmers and women among them. But they were mostly warriors, men weighed down with spears and shields, seaxes hanging from their belts, knotted beards on their faces and hungry looks in their eyes.

'I'm not sure this is what High King Vortigern had in mind,' pondered Wulfric aloud. He couldn't hide the nervousness in his voice. This looked like anything but an influx of mere settlers.

'I expect you're right,' said Hengest next to him, a proud smile stretched across his face.

Wulfric had pledged allegiance to Hengest before the battle against the Kaldi, and his performance in that battle had earned him a place among the Jutish chieftain's hearth warriors. It was an honour Wulfric did not take lightly. He had never enjoyed any kind of recognition until that point in his life. Egbin, his previous chieftain, had barely noticed him.

'Egbin was a colonist, not a chieftain. He was fat and lazy and thought only of himself,' Hengest had told him earlier. Egbin, who had reluctantly joined Hengest's men in the fight against the Kaldi, was no more.

'You, Wulfric—you brought us here,' Hengest had continued. 'So, you deserve to stand here beside me.'

And Wulfric had blushed at the compliment.

Hengest put his arm around Wulfric's shoulder as they watched the scores of armed men trudge across the wet sand towards them.

'Do you not think the Angles will do the same? And the Saxons? The Britons are fools. They were abandoned by Rome and can't even defend themselves. This fertile land is more than they need, and we have bought a slice of it with a fight and a pretend allegiance.'

Hors looked over, a slight smile on his face. 'And if we want more of it, what's stopping us from taking it?'

Wulfric nodded. They were right.

And then, among the burly warriors, emerging from the array of shields and spears, appeared the most beautiful woman Wulfric had ever seen. She walked in long, lean strides, untroubled by the shifting surface of the sand beneath her bare feet. Her hair fell all copper and blonde around her shoulders, catching on the sea breeze from time to time to resemble a nest of writhing yellow and red snakes. She walked with her chin high, her eyes scouring what was to her a new world, full of wonder and potential.

'You don't touch her, Wulfric,' Hengest's voice broke the spell. 'Not even in your most private dreams. She is not meant for you.'

The great Jute grinned at Wulfric, but he clearly meant every word he had just said.

'Who is she?' Wulfric asked. There was no sense in pretending he had not noticed her.

'She is my daughter,' Hengest stated proudly. 'Her name is Hrothwyn.'

Glossary

Aetius - Roman General

Albion - Ancient name for Britain

Angles - Germanic tribe, who would later give their name to England.

Annwn - To the Britons, the underworld

Atrebates - Tribe of Britons from what is now Sussex, Berkshire and Hampshire

Belgae - Tribe of Britons from what is now Hampshire

Bernaccia -Region in the north-east Britannia

Boar's Head - A battle formation adopted by Germanic tribes.

Britannia - Roman name given to Albion, now Britain

Briton - Native of Britannia

Caerfyrddin - Celtic name for Carmarthen in Wales

Calleva - Roman name for a settlement, now Silchester, in Hampshire

Cantii - Tribe from Ceint, now Kent

Ceint - What is now Kent

Cornovia - Region of what is now the West Midlands

Crannog - Ancient house built on an artificial island on water

Currach - small boat used by Hibernian/Irish

Dalriada - Celtic kingdom in north-eastern Ireland and western Scotland

Decurion - Roman council official

Dere Street - Roman road running from York and into Scotland

Deva - Roman name for Chester

Doctore - Trainer of gladiators

Dumnonia - Region in west of Britannia, now Devon.

Dyfed - Welsh kingdom

Eborakon - Briton name for York

Eboracum - Roman name for York

Eidyn - Briton name for Edinburgh

Fascina - a weapon, three-pronged trident

Fosse Way, The - Roman road between what is now Exeter and Lincoln

Gladius - Short Roman sword

Gododdin - Tribe of Britannia, from what is now Northumberland

Hibernia - Ireland

Iaculum - weapon, a weighted net used by gladiators

Isurium Brigantum - Roman town, now Aldborough in North Yorkshire

Jutland - Land of the Jutes, now Denmark and North Germany

Jute - native of Jutland

Kaldi - called Picts by the Romans, the painted people from North of the wall

Lactodorum - Roman town, now Towcester in Northamptonshire

Lancea - Roman lance

Lindum - Roman town, now Lincoln

Londinium - Roman town, now London

Ludus - training facility for gladiators

Mamucium - Roman town, now Manchester

Moridunum - Roman town, now Carmarthen

Nobatian - Nubian kingdom near what is now Egypt

Picts, The - name given by Romans to the Kaldi

Pilum - Roman spear

Pugio - Roman dagger

Rheged - Region of Britannia, now similar to Cumbria

Regni - Tribe of Britons from what is now Sussex

Saxon - Germanic tribe

Scotti, The - Irish tribe who, through conquering, gave Scotland its name

Seax - short sword carried by Germanic warriors

Sica - curved sword used by gladiators

Spatha - Roman long sword

Tamesis - The River Thames

Verulamium - Roman town, now St. Albans

Viroconium - Roman town, now Wroxeter

Votadini - predecessors of the Gododdin

Watling Street - Roman road, linking Dover and London to Wroxeter

Wrekin, The - Tall hill near Viroconium, home to a hill fort

About the Author

A sometime professional musician, then writer and director of a handful of feature films, Drew has always loved the written word. He was the somewhat opaque ghostwriter for Royd Tolkien's bestselling memoir, *There's a Hole in my Bucket: A Journey of Two Brothers*, and *Albion* is his first published work of fiction.

He has lived in Ireland, Italy and America but now lives not all that far from Buckingham with his wife, Victoria, and their daughter, Indiana.

You can connect with me on:
- https://drewcullingham.com
- https://twitter.com/CullinghamDrew
- https://instagram.com/drewcullingham

Printed in Dunstable, United Kingdom